ACCLAIM FOR THE BELLE MEADE PLANTATION NOVELS

"For lovers of historical romance, *To Wager Her Heart* offers the very best of both history and romance. Tamera Alexander's well-told story details the early years of Fisk University as a school for freedmen after the Civil War. I was fascinated from beginning to end. This thoroughly enjoyable novel proves why Tamera Alexander is one of the genre's most beloved authors—and one of my favorites."

—Lynn Austin, bestselling author of
Waves of Mercy and *Until We Reach Home*

"A steadfast heroine, a redemption-seeking hero, and a complex Southern society in post-Civil War America seamlessly combine in Tamera Alexander's *To Wager Her Heart*. Fans of Alexander's Belle Meade Plantation novels will fall in love with this new installment— but the real stars are the depth of research and the masterful attention to setting the perfect historical scene. Honor. Faith. And love . . . this novel's a journey in them all!"

—Kristy Cambron, bestselling author of
The Illusionist's Apprentice and the Hidden Masterpiece series

"Having read all of Tamera Alexander's books, it came as no surprise that *To Wager Her Heart* is another masterpiece of storytelling. This is a book for everyone—and I highly recommend it!"

—Veronica Brayboy, avid reader from New Jersey

"Tamera Alexander has created a story that blends true historical events with unforgettable characters. Her vivid depiction of the struggles of the newly freed slaves, the expansion of the railway, and the journey of the Jubilee Singers brings post-Civil War Nashville roaring to life. *To Wager Her Heart* interweaves heroic life challenges with rich spirituality and a sigh-worthy romance."

—Susan Anne Mason, award-winning author of
Irish Meadows and the Courage to Dream series

"No one writes southern fiction better than Tamera Alexander."

—Patti Jo Moore, avid reader from Georgia, on *To Wager Her Heart*

"From the very beginning of [*To Wager Her Heart*], Tamera Alexander invites readers on a remarkable journey, traveling alongside resilient characters determined to do what's right even when family and peers choose prejudice and contempt. Well done, Tamera! This was a journey that I didn't want to end."

—Melanie Dobson, award-winning author of
Catching the Wind and *Beneath a Golden Veil*

"Tamera Alexander is one of my favorite authors, so I expect a lot from her novels. *To Win Her Favor* is captivating beyond expectation! This novel has everything readers are looking for—rich characterization, page-turning intrigue, a heartwarming romance charged with tension, and more!"

—Cindy Woodsmall, *New York Times* and CBA
bestselling author of Amish fiction

"Tamera Alexander has done it again. Her imagination and skillful pen intertwined with history takes the reader on a beautiful journey. *To Win Her Favor* is sure to stir the heart and open the mind."

—Jenny Lamb, director of Interpretation and
Education, Belle Meade Plantation

"Already a *USA Today* bestseller, [*To Whisper Her Name*] draws a fresh thread in this author's historical fiction tapestry. Tamera Alexander's painstaking research into the people, places, and times of which she writes is evident on every page, and she depicts the famous residents of post-bellum Nashville with great detail and even greater affection."

—USAtoday.com, Serena Chase

"Alexander writes a beautiful story of love, friendship, and finding purpose."

—*RT Book Reviews*, four stars (for *To Whisper Her Name*)

TO WAGER
HER HEART

Also by Tamera Alexander

Belle Meade Plantation novels
To Whisper Her Name
To Win Her Favor
To Wager Her Heart
To Mend a Dream (novella)

Women of Faith Fiction
The Inheritance

Belmont Mansion novels
A Lasting Impression
A Beauty So Rare
A Note Yet Unsung

Timber Ridge Reflections
From a Distance
Beyond This Moment
Within My Heart

Fountain Creek Chronicles
Rekindled
Revealed
Remembered

A BELLE MEADE PLANTATION NOVEL

TAMERA ALEXANDER

TO WAGER HER HEART

ZONDERVAN

To Wager Her Heart

Copyright © 2017 by Tamera Alexander

This title is also available as a Zondervan e-book.

Requests for information should be addressed to:

Zondervan, *3900 Sparks Dr. SE, Grand Rapids, Michigan 49546*

Library of Congress Cataloging-in-Publication Data

Names: Alexander, Tamera, author.
Title: To wager her heart / Tamera Alexander.
Description: Grand Rapids, Michigan: Zondervan, [2017] ⏐ Series: Belle Meade
    Plantation novel; 3
Identifiers: LCCN 2017006670 ⏐ ISBN 9780310291084 (paperback)
Subjects: LCSH: Horse racing--Fiction. ⏐ Belle Meade Plantation
    (Tenn.)--History--Fiction. ⏐ Tennessee--History--19th century--Fiction. ⏐
    GSAFD: Historical fiction. ⏐ Love stories. ⏐ Christian fiction.
Classification: LCC PS3601.L3563 T65 2017 ⏐ DDC 813/.6--dc23 LC record
    available at https://lccn.loc.gov/2017006670

Printed in the United States of America

---

17 18 19 20 21 / LSC / 20 19 18 17 16 15 14 13 12 11 10 9 8 7 6 5 4 3 2 1

*In honor of the original Jubilee Singers
of Fisk University, Nashville, Tennessee.
Your courage and faith inspire us still.*

We now have this light shining in our hearts, but we ourselves are like fragile clay jars containing this great treasure. This makes it clear that our great power is from God, not from ourselves.

2 Corinthians 4:7 NLT

Preface

M uch of the novel you're about to read is fictional, though there are plenty of real people and real history woven throughout. For instance, the Fisk University Jubilee Singers and their immensely important and courageous strides in the nineteenth century are true and are woven through the fictional threads of this novel. And there really is a Belle Meade Plantation in Nashville—the Queen of Southern Plantations, as it's still known. Built in 1820, the mansion still stands today and warmly welcomes visitors.

The first time I stepped foot onto the grounds of Belle Meade Plantation and learned of Uncle Bob Green, Susanna Carter, and so many other former slaves who lived and worked at Belle Meade, I knew I wanted to write stories that included them, the magnificent estate they helped to create, and this crucial time in our struggling nation's history.

Tennessee in the 1870s represented a striking dichotomy. The state boasted some of the largest plantations in the South, along with their former slaveholders, as well as a talented and articulate group of educated African American men and women who turned the world upside down and changed the culture of that era. Their contributions and gifts still resonate today.

Tennessee dominated the thoroughbred racing industry in the United States at this time, with Belle Meade Plantation serving as the preeminent stud farm in the nation. Does the name

Secretariat sound familiar? What about Sunday Silence and American Pharaoh? Those champion thoroughbreds, and countless others, trace their lineage to Belle Meade Plantation.

While this novel is peopled with characters who lived during that time, their overarching personalities and actions as depicted in this story are mostly of my own imagination and should be construed as such.

Thank you for entrusting your time to me. It's a weighty investment—one I treasure and never take for granted. I invite you to join me as we open the door to history and step into another time and place.

Welcome (once again) to Belle Meade,

Tamera

Chapter ONE

Nashville, Tennessee
August 9, 1871

*A*lexandra Jamison had always wanted a sister. Instead, she had three brothers. All older. Two were the spitting image and temperament of their father. Jacob, the third and her favorite, was not. And as though the world could not abide the anomaly, war had met him on the battlefield—and won. For that alone, if not for a thousand other reasons, she would never forgive that war.

As for the other two brothers, they'd escaped home and the shadow of their father as soon as possible. If only she could do the same.

If the carriage parked in front of her house on Sycamore Lane—the lushly treed thoroughfare home to some of Nashville's finest residences—was any indication, her father's plans for her were hardly "escape." More along the lines of "out of the frying pan, into the fire." A man nearly thrice her age waited in the study. She imagined his marble-knobbed cane propped just so against the bookcase beside his chair. To be fair, she'd never actually seen Horace Buford walking with a cane, but she felt certain there must be one looming in his very near future. A future she was determined not to share, no matter her father's opinion.

Which her mother would quietly support, never giving voice to her own thoughts on the matter. If she even had thoughts of her own. Which was another frustration.

Alexandra loved her mother; she simply didn't understand her. At times she felt as if she scarcely knew her.

And all of this, Alexandra thought, as she climbed the steps to the front porch, was what a sister was for. To share all the secrets, the heartaches and fears. The frustrations that came with seeking to honor the two people who had given her life. But how did she do that when her parents' hopes and plans for her life differed so vastly from her own?

At twenty-five, she'd expected to be beyond all this. But life hadn't turned out at all as she'd expected.

The daisies in the pots by the top step looked freshly watered, yet still showed signs of fatigue beneath the blazing August sun. She could commiserate. She felt more than a little worn herself. She'd wanted to forgo the midweek Nashville Women's League meeting that morning, but her mother had insisted she attend—while claiming she herself was too burdened by the heat to accompany her.

"The Jamison name must be represented, Alexandra," she'd said. "After all, we're one of Nashville's founding families, and we must stay abreast of all the latest goings-on. And the gossip there is always so rich."

All that talk of who was marrying whom, of what was best served at high tea, of *Godey's* latest fashions . . . Though the league did routinely undertake a number of worthy pursuits to help the needy, the trappings and topics of high society simply weren't Alexandra's cup of tea anymore.

Not after David. Not after Dutchman's Curve.

She reached for the front doorknob, aware of her defenses rising. This house had long ceased being a safe haven. Especially when she knew her father was home. Did all daughters feel this way about their fathers?

Yet another question for the sister she didn't have.

He hadn't approved of her choice in David. David was a teacher. And a gifted one. But that wasn't prestigious enough for Father.

The handsome brass placard by the front door bearing her father's name shone with a deeper luster than usual. He must have had Melba polish it that morning, which only meant one thing.

A prospective client. Alexandra glanced back at the carriage, heartened that perhaps it wasn't old Mr. Horace Buford waiting inside after all.

She opened the door as the blast of a train whistle split the morning air. Its shrill sound brought her up short and prodded memories best left undisturbed. Images of splintered railway cars and broken bodies. Screaming wheels and grinding steel that was heard over two miles away. She squeezed her eyes tight as the familiar sense of loss flooded back through her.

Tomorrow it would be one year. How could so much time have passed? Especially when a part of her still felt stranded back there on that horrific morning on Dutchman's Curve . . .

"As long as your loved one lives on in your memory, he'll never really be gone," people said. But that was a lie. David *was* gone. And he was never coming back.

The whistle blasted again, sounding closer this time, and she could smell the acrid scent of smoke and cinders in her memory, could feel the unearthly jolt of the train as the car she'd been riding jumped the rails. And she could still see David's broken, partially burned body that had been laid out in the cornfield alongside the others.

She hurried inside and slammed the door behind her, working to shut out the haunting sights and sounds.

"Miss Alexandra . . . you all right?"

Heart racing, Alexandra looked up. "Melba," she whispered, and saw concern swiftly gathering in the older woman's eyes.

"What's wrong, child? You comin' down with somethin'?"

Alexandra shook her head. "I'm fine. Just a little overheated, that's all." Did anyone else remember what tomorrow was? Surely Melba hadn't forgotten.

"It's hot as blazes out there today, ma'am. You shoulda taken that little parasol with you."

Seeing the hint of a smile on Melba's face, Alexandra attempted to return it. "You know how I *love* parasols, Melba."

The older woman laughed, the melodic sound like home itself. "Even as a child you didn't like them things. But your mama, she sure did. Made you carry one everywhere."

"Don't I remember . . ."

Alexandra set her reticule on a side table and watched as Melba arranged a bouquet of fresh-cut flowers from the garden in the antique vase on the center table. The former slave was as much a part of her life as anyone in this house. More so, in some ways. Because Melba saw things Alexandra knew her parents didn't. Even as a little girl, Alexandra had never been able to fool her.

Much like another slave she'd known as a child. A slave she'd loved with all her heart, but who apparently hadn't loved her in equal part.

She heard voices coming from her father's study. "A prospective client?" she asked softly.

Melba nodded. "Man new to town, your papa said."

Her father had moved his office into their home four months ago. He said it was because the building where he rented space in the center of town was not being properly maintained, but Alexandra secretly suspected it was due to finances. Six years since the war had ended, and business in Nashville appeared to be improving. But the number of attorneys still seemed inordinate to the need.

The door to the study opened and her father peered out. "Alexandra, you're home. Good. Would you join us, please? I could use your assistance."

"Of course."

He pushed the door closed again.

Knowing better than to keep him waiting, she quickly brushed the street dust from the front of her dress.

"Let me help you with that, ma'am." Melba came up from behind and gave her backside a good hand brushing. "Seein' what tomorrow is, Miss Alexandra, maybe we could get your blue dress back out. Or that teal one with the white lace collar that looks so pretty with your blond hair. If you're ready."

Alexandra turned. "I knew you'd remember."

Melba sighed. "That's a day this old woman will never be forgettin'."

Alexandra hugged her, appreciating the way Melba's arms came around her shoulders, strong and protective. And the way the woman smelled. Like fresh coffee and bread warm from the oven.

A quick glance in the mirror over the table, and Alexandra entered the office—and confirmed that the carriage out front most definitely did not belong to Horace Buford.

The stranger who rose from his seat rivaled even her father's height, which was saying something. His impeccably tailored black duster hit him slightly above the knee, and with trousers tucked into dark leather boots, he looked more like an outlaw or a gunslinger than a gentleman from Nashville, Tennessee. The shadow of a day's growth along his jawline and the Stetson on his head—inside the house, no less, did the man have no manners?—only added to that persona.

Something about him held challenge too. His stance, perhaps. Confident. Almost aloof. The opposite of her David, who could make any person feel at ease. A characteristic that had only enhanced his giftedness at teaching. Open, honest, compassionate—all attributes that had made her fall in love with him from the start.

And reasons that—oddly, tragically—had contributed to his untimely death.

"Mr. Rutledge, allow me to introduce my daughter, Miss

Jamison. Likewise"—her father looked her way—"this is Mr. Sylas Rutledge, owner of the Northeast Line Railroad and recently come East from Colorado."

Colorado. Well, that part fit. A wild, untamed territory for a wild, untamed sort of man. "Good day to you, Mr. Rutledge."

He nodded. "Ma'am."

Ma'am? What kind of proper greeting was that?

It was then she noticed the dog sitting at his feet. A dog! In her father's study. Which told her the man must be wealthy. Because Barrett Broderick Jamison never allowed animals in his home, much less in his office.

The dog, a full-grown foxhound by the look of him, stared up at her, his big brown eyes exuding a warmth his master's lacked. It was a beautiful animal—brown and tan with white markings on his face and white socked feet. With tail wagging, he moved toward her. Alexandra reached out to pet him, but at a quick snap of Mr. Rutledge's fingers, the dog dropped to a sitting position.

Alexandra pulled her hand back. "I'm sorry, sir. I was simply going to pet him."

Without speaking, Mr. Rutledge looked down at the dog and nodded once, and the dog began inching toward her. Alexandra gave the hound a good rub behind the ears, feeling sorrier for the animal by the minute.

"I need a standard property deed for Mr. Rutledge," her father said, busy sorting through papers on his desk. "Mr. Rutledge, you can take that with you and review it. Or if you prefer, I can have my daughter fill it out for you right now, and then I can file it for a small fee. That will get the process started nicely."

"I'll take it with me."

Alexandra did as her father asked, sensing that his prospective client wasn't so much a prospect as he was a prospector. She'd assisted in enough of these meetings through the years to get a swift sense of whether a person was ready to sign. Mr. Rutledge from Colorado had no intention of signing anything today.

Granted, she had just walked into the meeting, but her guess was that the man was on a fact-finding mission and not ready to commit.

She took a step closer to him and held the form between them. "Mr. Rutledge, allow me to briefly review the legalities involved in a Tennessee property deed. This document transfers ownership of real estate, of course, and contains the names of the old and new owners as well as a legal description of the property—which will need to be verified at the county courthouse. Depending on the nature of your land purchase—"

His eyes were fixed on her as she spoke, and the close attention made her a little self-conscious.

"—we may also need to consider drawing up a warranty deed, a grant deed, and perhaps a quitclaim deed. A quitclaim deed releases—or *quits*—any ownership claims a person may have in a piece of property. Mineral or oil deposits, for instance."

She paused, but he said nothing.

"Does all that make sense, Mr. Rutledge?"

"Completely."

Guessing they were done, she handed him the form. He folded it and slipped it into the pocket of his duster without so much as a thank-you or even a nod. The man had a lot to learn about Southern gentility and working with the businessmen of this city.

His coat shifted and Alexandra saw that he was wearing a pistol on his hip. Like one of those outlaws described in the dime novels. She could hardly believe it. Did the man not realize he was in civilization now? This was Nashville, Tennessee, not one of those lawless cities out West.

He tugged the brim of his hat. "Mr. Jamison." He glanced back at Alexandra without the slightest hint of a smile, yet she detected a gleam in his eyes. As though he knew a secret she didn't. "Ma'am," he said softly, then strode from the room, the dog following loyally at his heels.

Her father followed him out, but Alexandra stayed in the office and watched from behind the curtain at the window. Owner of the Northeast Line Railroad. She surmised he was here to bid on the contract for the Belle Meade Station project that Mary Harding had told her about. Per Mary, her father, General William Giles Harding, had called for bids from railroad men around the country.

Alexandra smiled, taking pleasure in the fact that Mr. Sylas Rutledge stood little to no chance of winning said bid. Because she knew General Harding, and the man did not take kindly to outsiders. She turned from the window as Mr. Rutledge's carriage pulled away.

Her father came back into the office. "Good. You're still here, Alexandra." He began straightening the papers on his desk, his manner brusque, which communicated his displeasure. "We have a dinner guest coming tonight, so please take extra care in your appearance and do your best to make him feel welcome."

Alexandra stilled. "A dinner guest?"

Her father looked up. "I believe that's what I just stated. Now let me be. I have another appointment."

She opened her mouth to inquire further, but his dark look dissuaded her.

"So, Miss Jamison . . ." Horace Buford peered at her from across the dining table, studying her as he might a prized cow. "You are look-ing quite ravishing this evening. That color becomes you, my dear."

She'd chosen the plainest, highest-necked, most unflattering gown in her wardrobe. It being brown, her absolute worst color, was an added benefit.

Feeling her father's stare, she forced a smile. "Thank you, Mr. Buford. You're most . . . kind."

Mr. Buford downed the last of his wine, then snapped his fin-gers for more, and Alexandra caught the fleeting shadow crossing her mother's face even as she was reminded of Mr. Rutledge and his dog. Thinking of that man while looking at Mr. Buford served to frame Sylas Rutledge in a significantly better light than she'd viewed him earlier that day. Uncouth as the man may be, he was "a mite easier on the eyes" than what was currently in her line of sight. That's what Mary Harding would say, with that coy smile of hers, and it would be a great understatement.

Sylas Rutledge was darkly handsome. In a mysterious and not quite trustworthy sort of way. But she sensed he knew it, which always lessened such a man's overall appeal.

"Let me offer my congratulations, Horace, on the purchase of your new home." Her father shot Alexandra a look that said she'd best join in the conversation. "The Morrison estate is quite a handsome one."

"Yes, indeed it is. And I got it for a steal!" Mr. Buford laughed, revealing a mouthful of veal. "It's a pity, of course, that another of the once esteemed families of Nashville is no more. But if someone must benefit from the situation, why should it not be me?"

What little appetite Alexandra had quickly dissipated. How was it she was sitting here again in the same situation? Staring across the table at an older colleague of her father's, her mother furtively smiling from one end of the table, her father openly frowning at the other. The unspoken agenda of the evening was written plainly, painfully, between every line of forced conversation.

Dinner dragged, and it finally came time to retire to the central parlor. Alexandra was about to make her excuses not to join them when her father spoke up.

"Alexandra, if you'll escort Mr. Buford into the parlor, your mother and I will be there shortly."

She sensed something pass between them and stiffened. "Actually, I'm quite fatigued, Father. I believe that I'll—"

"That you'll accompany Mr. Buford into the parlor, as I suggested. Thank you, Alexandra. Your mother and I will be there shortly."

The air crackled with dissent.

Alexandra could feel Mr. Buford looking between them, and

though she held not a trace of special feeling for the man, she also didn't consider it fair that he be caught in the midst of this tug-of-war with her parents.

"Mr. Buford—" She gestured. "Won't you join me in the parlor?"

"Nothing would please me more, my dear."

He touched the small of her back as she preceded him into the parlor, and her skin crawled. She chose one of the two wing-back chairs, knowing her father wouldn't be pleased. It was a small victory, but she would take it.

Mr. Buford settled himself on the sofa. He glanced at the empty space beside him, then back at her. "Would you care to join me, Miss Jamison?"

"Actually, I'm fine right here. Thank you."

She looked anywhere but at him. From her peripheral vision she could see the pendulum of the grandfather clock swinging back and forth, back and forth, slicing off the seconds. But not fast enough.

"Miss Jamison, as I'm sure you are aware, I am a man of considerable wealth and well respected in this town. I am also of sound health and possess great vigor for my age. I'm not prone to anger, nor do I drink excessively."

Not wanting to meet his gaze, but unable to be outright rude, Alexandra slowly looked back. He smiled a smile she wished he hadn't.

"Some might say I have a great deal that would recommend me to one of the fairer sex, though I would never assume to say as much on my own behalf. Even if it were unabashedly true."

"Mr. Buford, allow me to interject. I sincerely do not wish to—"

He rose from the sofa with surprising agility and came and knelt before her. "I've spoken with your father, Miss Jamison, and he's of the mind that you and I would make an excellent match. I agree with him wholeheartedly. Hence, I'm here to—"

"Mr. Buford, I must stop you." Alexandra tried to stand, but he grabbed her hand.

"You are such a delightful creature. I find I'm growing more fond of you by the moment."

He brought her hand to his mouth to kiss it, his upper lip glistening with sweat.

Alexandra pulled away before he succeeded and rose to put distance between them. "Mr. Buford, my deepest apologies to you, but my father did not consult with me in this regard. Please forgive me, but I must speak plainly. More so than I usually would."

Using the arm of the chair for support, he stood. "There's no need to be shy, my dear. I realize that while your family no longer possesses the level of wealth it once did, your connections in society and your family name have much to recommend you. And you personally have in abundance assets any man would find desirable in a wife."

"Mr. Buford—" Trembling with anger at her father, at his inconsideration, Alexandra forced out the words. "While I am . . . honored that you would consider me worthy of your affections, I cannot accept your proposal."

"But . . . your father assured me that you—"

The door to the parlor opened and her father entered. She spotted her mother standing in the foyer beyond him, wide-eyed and watchful.

"Mr. Buford, I mean you no ill will, but I'm feeling rather tired. I'll leave you and my parents to your conversation." As she left the room, her father grasped hold of her arm and pulled her aside in the foyer. She saw the sliver of patience he'd possessed evaporate from his expression.

"You ignored my wishes once in this," he whispered. "You will not do so again."

"You cannot force me to do this."

"Oh, but I can." His grip tightened. "I am your father. I have every right to make such decisions for you. You are well of age. This is for your own good and the good of our family."

Alexandra jerked free, and the surprise in her father's

expression gave her unexpected courage. "I'm sorry, Father. But this is my decision." She grabbed her reticule from the table where she'd left it that afternoon. Then heard her mother's voice behind her.

"Please, Alexandra," she whispered. "Listen to your father."

Alexandra turned to see tears running down her mother's cheeks. "Mother, you can't believe this is best."

"He's your father, Alexandra. He's the head of this home, and you must see the wisdom in—"

"No." Alexandra shook her head, her own tears threatening. "I can see it in your eyes. You don't agree with him. Why don't you say something? Why won't you stand up for me?"

Fresh tears rose in her mother's eyes. But hearing footsteps coming from the parlor, Alexandra raced out the front door and down the street.

Chapter *Two*

*H*er chest tight with emotion, Alexandra walked and walked until a stitch in her side finally caused her to slow her pace. The sun had long set, and though she had no destination in mind, she kept going. She only wanted to put distance between herself and her father. And the well-meaning but ill-guided Mr. Horace Buford.

The exchange in the parlor played again and again in her mind, and with each repetition she grew angrier. Yet a part of her knew her father was right. Not that she needed to marry Mr. Buford, but that the time had come for her to do something with her life.

Because here she was . . .

Nearly twenty-six years old and still living in her parents' home. Most friends her age had married years ago and had children now. If David hadn't died in that accident, they, too, would be married and she would be out from beneath the weight of her father's demands.

But even before then she should've found a way to leave after the war, as her older brothers had done—despite the hardships such a decision would have incurred. But those potential hardships were what had kept her in place. She'd been too afraid to venture out on her own.

Then David came along. He was everything she'd ever wanted.

He offered her love, safety, a nice—if modest—home, and she'd accepted his proposal without hesitation. Only to have the life they'd planned together wrenched from her grip without warning, because of a train engineer's careless mistake.

Harrison Kennedy. Would she ever forget that name, and all he'd taken from her?

The image of David's face rose clear in her memory, and she recalled their last exchange before they boarded the train that morning at the Memphis station. And after such an enjoyable two days of searching and finding a place to live that was located near the school's campus.

"The workers I was speaking with earlier can't read, Alexandra, so they don't even know what's in the contract they were given. Yet they're expected to sign it when they get back to Nashville, if they want to keep their jobs. Why don't you and Melba go ahead and ride in the ladies' car. They'll allow her to ride in there since she's with you. And I'll ride up front with those workers."

She smoothed the perpetually crumpled lapel of his suit, which somehow befitted his occupation as a university professor. "Do you think they'll allow it? For you to ride in a freedmen's car?"

"I doubt anyone will say anything. But if they put me out, I'll come find you and Melba before we pull out of the station."

She had nodded, so proud of the man he was. And thankful to Melba, who stood off to the side, the perfect chaperone—and her trusted confidante. "Must you always be the teacher, Mr. Thompson?" she'd teased.

He shrugged. "Any and all who would seek to learn should be allowed to pursue an education."

She smiled at his oft-quoted phrase. "West Tennessee State School is fortunate to have you joining their ranks."

"They're fortunate to have *us* joining their ranks, Alexandra. I couldn't be doing what I'm doing without you. I hope you know that."

She loved this man so much. His generosity and kindness,

his intellect, the way he never allowed social mores to deter his beliefs and purpose in teaching. Being raised in an abolitionist family had shaped his views early on, and he had gently coaxed her to the truth that had resided just under her skin for as long as she could remember.

"I'm so proud of you, David. You're an excellent teacher."

"I don't know about that last part, but at least I can review the contracts and explain what they're signing. But about that first point . . ." He glanced around them, then winked and kissed her quickly on the forehead. "I feel the same about you. I'll see you at home!"

I'll see you at home . . . I'll see you at home . . . The words echoed toward her from that day.

But she never saw him alive again.

Alexandra wiped the tears from her cheeks as the void inside yawned wide and vicious in the growing darkness around her. It was then that she heard it.

Singing. Somewhere in the distance.

She looked around, then spotted light coming from the windows of a building at the far end of the street. Walking closer, she came to a billboard out front that read *Wednesday, August 9, 7 o'clock, Masonic Hall presents Handel's* Cantata of Esther. Drawn by the familiar composer and his rendition of the biblical story, as well as the majestic voices, she opened the door and went inside.

The lobby was dimly lit.

Glad she'd brought her reticule along with her, she readied to pay an admission, but the lobby was empty. No one was minding the front table. Piano music swelled, as did a soprano voice so rich and full, so ethereal, goose bumps rose on Alexandra's arms despite the warmth of the building. A chorus of voices joined in then, and she closed her eyes, letting the beauty of the harmonies soothe the edges of her lingering hurt.

Compelled by the music, she continued down a hallway that opened into a small auditorium. To her surprise, the seats were only half filled with patrons. Difficult to believe, considering what she was hearing. But when she looked toward the performers on the stage, she stopped stock-still.

Every singer was Negro.

In addition, the audience consisted mostly of Negro men and women. Only a handful of white people were in attendance. And though the discovery didn't leave her discomforted in the least, she couldn't help but acknowledge she'd never been at a concert attended by black and white together.

David would have delighted in it.

A pang of longing hit her again, and she quickly claimed a seat toward the back, wondering if she would ever cease missing him. She knew from losing dear Jacob in the war that time helped heal the wounds of loss. But David had filled her life in ways no one ever had. He'd challenged her to demand more of herself, to see the world in ways she hadn't before. He'd made her a far better person than she'd been before he came along.

And she didn't want to go back to being that other woman ever again. She wanted her life to have meaning. Beyond an arranged marriage she in no way desired.

The tempo of the piano music changed, and the voice of the powerful soprano on stage soared into upper registers. Alexandra found her attention riveted once again, as was everyone else's, and she gave herself fully to the music, grateful for the distraction. Such perfection in a voice—and delivered with seeming ease. The cantata flowed from one piece to the next and finally into the duet Alexandra had been anticipating.

Her eyes watered as she drank in the familiar lyrics, first from Queen Esther as sung by the talented soprano, and then answered by a handsome young tenor in the persona of King Ahasuerus.

Who calls my parting soul from death . . . Awake, my soul, my life, my breath. Hear my suit, or else I die . . . Ask, my queen, can I deny?

Gradually the rest of the troupe joined in again, and far too soon the last note of the music faded and the audience rose to their feet in applause. Alexandra joined in, filled with gratitude and—

She squinted. What was Mr. Sylas Rutledge doing here?

He'd been seated two rows in front of her on the opposite end. But standing well over six feet tall—and dressed in that dark duster like the gunslinger he apparently considered himself to be—the man was easily distinguished in a crowd.

He certainly had not struck her as the classical-music-loving sort. But at least he'd had the decency to remove his hat this time, so perhaps there was hope for the man after all.

At that moment, one of the singers stepped to the front of the stage, and the patrons sat back down. Alexandra did likewise, turning slightly to the side to lessen the chance that Mr. Rutledge would see her. She was none too eager for a second meeting with the man and whatever business reconnoitering he was conducting. But she needn't have worried.

He didn't return to his seat, but slipped quietly down the side aisle and exited the auditorium.

"Thank you, kind ladies and gentlemen." The young man on stage spoke in a deep register, his voice resonating in the silence. "We appreciate your venturing out on this warm summer eve to hear us perform Handel's *Cantata of Esther*, a most moving oratorio. At least we believe it to be so."

He smiled, and Alexandra laughed along with everyone else. Only then did she notice the minimal scenery on stage and the lack of elaborate costumes. But it hadn't mattered. The voices were everything.

"As part of the student body at Fisk University," the speaker continued, "we appreciate your support and invite you to talk with one of us afterward if you're interested in hearing more about the school and its academic program. And now may I introduce the president of Fisk University . . . Mr. Adam Spence."

Applause rose again as a man made his way from the audience to the stage. "Good evening, friends. As Mr. Green has already stated, we appreciate your coming out to enjoy this fine concert and supporting Fisk University with your ticket purchases. Customarily, Mr. George White, Fisk's treasurer and this troupe's illustrious leader, would be speaking to you, but he is unable to be here this evening. In addition, our usual pianist finds herself unwell. So allow me to extend a special thank-you to Miss Anderson for her accompaniment tonight."

The audience clapped, showing their appreciation, and the young Negro woman seated at the piano stood and bowed. Alexandra took the opportunity to peer back at the door. Mr. Rutledge had not returned.

"Our students at Fisk are all freedmen," President Spence continued, "by which of course I am referring to both men and women. But Fisk University exists to offer an education to *any* person who would seek to learn, regardless of the color of their skin."

His statement prompted still more applause, and Alexandra joined in, feeling a stirring at the familiar echo of President Spence's statement. So much like what her David had said.

"As president of Fisk University, I can assure you that these fine students possess an extraordinary thirst for learning. We're very proud of their accomplishments and of our school. We're also in need of teachers, so if you're experienced in that regard, please seek me out and I can share with you more about those opportunities."

Following further comments, President Spence invited them to bow their heads as he closed the evening in prayer. Alexandra followed suit, but couldn't keep her eyes closed.

She kept peering up at the stage at the Fisk students, then back down at her hands, trying to account for the fluttering in her stomach and the inexplicable sense of closeness she felt to David in that moment. And to the dreams they'd shared for their life together.

✺

Later that night, Alexandra returned home to a mostly darkened house, save for a lamp burning low in the foyer. She half expected to find the front door locked, based on how abruptly she'd departed, but the knob turned easily in her hand. She locked the door behind her, turned down the lamp, and slipped quietly up the darkened stairway and into her room. As familiar with her childhood bedroom in the dark as she was in the light, she retrieved the matches and lit the lamp on her bedside table.

The flame cast a warm glow across the bed and onto David's photograph on her dressing table. She sat down on the bench, picked up the cherished likeness of him, and stared into his kind, open gaze, her thoughts still racing from her conversation with President Spence.

Had she found what she was supposed to do? Is that why she'd "happened" upon the concert tonight? A thrum of excitement skittered through her, followed swiftly by a flood of uncertainty.

She glanced at David's trunk—full of books and teaching materials—at the foot of her bed, and wished for the hundredth time that she'd made more progress in her studies with him. Despite his insistence that she always caught on quickly and that her mind was like a sponge. But time had seemed limitless back then. She'd thought she had a lifetime to learn from him, to soak up his knowledge.

She'd had a governess growing up, of course, who had seen to her primary education. Later, as a young woman, Alexandra had wanted to attend the Nashville Female Academy with a handful of her friends, but her father refused. Yet she'd done a good amount of tutoring children through the years, so what knowledge she'd acquired she put to good use.

"I wish you could tell me if this is what I'm supposed to do," she whispered, running a finger along the edge of the frame. "And oh, how I wish you were still here."

But in a sense he *had* been there with her tonight, hadn't he? She'd felt his presence. And then that song . . .

After the concert she'd heard the chorus members singing softly in a back hallway. It was a song she hadn't heard since childhood, and the lyrics and depth of feeling in their voices still haunted her.

In the morning when I rise, in the morning when I—

A knock sounded on the bedroom door.

She returned the frame to the dressing table and crossed the room, hoping it wasn't her father.

"Mother." Relieved, she stepped aside and allowed her entrance. Even in the low light she could tell by her mother's red-rimmed eyes that she'd spent the evening crying. Guilt pinched the measure of excitement she felt.

"Darling, I've been waiting up for you." Her mother reached back and closed the bedroom door. "I wanted to make certain you returned home all right. Where did you go?"

"I walked. And walked some more." Alexandra offered a smile. "I needed time to think. To . . . clear my head."

Her mother nodded, hands clasped at her waist, then sat down on the edge of the bed. Alexandra joined her.

"Alexandra . . . I know you still miss David very much, and I realize Mr. Buford is not the man you would have chosen. But he is a good match, a practical match. And he'll take care of you. You'll never want for anything."

"Anything except a man I desire to spend my life with. A man I can admire and respect. And who will respect me and my opinions in return."

A shadow pierced her mother's expression. "Alexandra, your father is—" She closed her lips tightly and glanced away. When she looked back, her features were resolute. "Your father has only your best interests at heart. You must believe that."

"I believe he thinks he knows what's best." Alexandra weighed the cost of what she was about to say. "But I simply don't agree. Furthermore, I think it's perfectly acceptable to have opinions that differ from his. And to express them."

Her mother stared, then reached over and covered Alexandra's hand on the bed. "As you know, your grandparents arranged your father's and my marriage. When I married him and pledged to love, honor, and obey him, I scarcely knew him. But that doesn't negate the promise I made in front of family and friends and God that day."

"But it also doesn't negate that you surrender what you think and who you are," Alexandra said softly. "At least, that's how it appears to me."

Her mother offered a weak smile. "The world is changing, my dear. I'm not blind. I see that. And you are changing along with it. And while I believe a time is coming when women will have vastly more opportunities open to them, we must all move within the confines of the world in which we currently reside. And you, my dearest, are caught in an . . . in-between time."

Alexandra searched her mother's expression and glimpsed a depth of understanding that both surprised and heartened her.

"Granted, you're not living in my world," her mother continued, "and yet the world you desire has not yet been fully birthed. I know you have dreams, that you and David had dreams. But the door on those dreams has closed, my dear. And heartbreaking as that is, you must accept it."

"I do accept it, Mother. Truly. I know that the dreams David and I shared are in the past. But that doesn't mean I can't have my own version of those dreams. Women are doing so much more these days than they once did. The war brought so many changes. Women are working in offices and factories now."

Her mother stared. "So you're thinking of going to work in an office? Or a factory? And being what? A seamstress in a mill? Alexandra, you're from one of the finest families in Nashville. As I said, we all must move within the confines of the world we're in. And that, my dearest, is not your world."

Alexandra started to object, then thought better of it.

"It is well past time, Alexandra, for you to marry, to establish your own home, to have children. And with the war having taken so many of our men"—her mother's chin trembled—"including our precious Jacob, your choices are greatly narrowed. Even you must agree with me on this . . . A woman can only choose among the options available to her. So consider your decision carefully, dearest. Because despite what happened this evening, Mr. Buford's designs toward you remain unchanged." She gave Alexandra's hand a tight squeeze. "And though I consider you the finest and loveliest daughter I could ever have requested from the Lord, none of us is guaranteed a second chance. You have been given one, my dear. Take it. While there's still time."

Her mother rose, pressed a kiss on the crown of Alexandra's head, and closed the bedroom door behind her as she left.

Long into the night, Alexandra lay awake weighing her mother's counsel against the urgings of her heart, all while asking for wisdom from above and listening for the slightest whisper in her heart from the Lord.

Or even . . . from David, if heaven allowed such things.

Sleeping little, she rose long before the sun with fresh conviction, knowing without question what she had to do. Gone were the years of acquiescence and blind obedience. The time had come for her to choose her own path. And she was going to do it.

No matter the cost.

Chapter
THREE

*D*ilapidated and rotting, the rows of former Union Army hospital barracks up ahead looked as though they might collapse with the slightest breeze. But Alexandra continued down the street, chin slightly tucked and eyes averted. Not ashamed of where she was going . . . and yet she knew how people could talk. Foot traffic was busy for a Thursday morning, and she didn't want to give anyone fodder for conversation that might find its way back to her parents.

With high hopes and taut nerves, she focused instead on the events of last night and on what—and *who*—had led her to this place, to this moment. She thought, too, about all that was happening behind those ramshackle, decaying walls ahead. New lives were being built, futures forged with fresh direction—and she intended to be part of it.

Though she'd left the house later than planned, she still managed to leave before her father had awakened. Yet another sign that God was on her side in this decision, because the man rarely overslept. Now if she could only hold to the unwavering courage she'd had upon first awakening, instead of listening to the questioning murmurs within.

The whistle blast of an approaching train jarred her thoughts, and she looked in the direction of the train tracks—some fifteen yards away—as the iron beast churned toward her, bound for the Nashville station.

Her pulse edged up a notch.

She regretted now that she'd told Mary Harding she would meet her at the train station later, despite her friend's kind invitation to attend General Harding's special unveiling. Alexandra knew Mary remembered the significance of this day and was attempting to lift her spirits. And since Mary Harding never took no for an answer . . .

As the train drew closer, Alexandra made out the name along the side—Northeast Line Railroad. Mr. Rutledge, yet again. For saying so little, the man certainly had a way of making his presence known. She wondered if he'd enjoyed the concert last night as much as she had, and if such a pastime was typical for him. It still seemed hard to believe, based on what little she knew of the man.

The line of passenger cars came into view, and even through the dirt-smudged windows, she could see the people within— talking, reading their newspapers, some of them likely dozing to the rhythmic rocking of the cars on the rails. Oblivious to what could happen in the space of a single, solitary breath.

The first few passenger cars thundered by, and she forced herself to watch even as, in a blink, the rush of the train pulled her back, and she was back in the ladies' railcar as it left the tracks that day on Dutchman's Curve. She relived that sickly feeling of being airborne, her stomach twisting as her body, weightless, hung in space for what had to have been only seconds—though it felt like an eternity—before the passenger car slammed onto its side in the cornfield.

Alexandra drew in a shaky breath. *You are not on that train. You are not on that train. You are* not *on that train . . .*

And she hadn't stepped foot on another train since.

She loathed the fear that still gripped her, this weakness in herself, yet she couldn't make herself climb on board. She'd tried. Mary had even enticed her with the gift of a trip to New York City. Alexandra had politely declined. Someday . . . In time. At least that's what she kept telling herself.

She continued down the street and didn't look back.

The relentless August sun sweltered in the cloudless blue overhead. Regardless that the watch pinned to her shirtwaist read half past nine, a trickle of perspiration inched its way down her back. And her feet, how they ached. Especially after all the walking last night.

The distance from home had proven farther than she'd calculated. A little over two miles, which customarily wasn't too far to walk. But in these boots and in this heat and humidity . . .

She'd decided against taking one of the family carriages, knowing that if he were asked, Dockery, their driver, would tell her father where she'd gone. And her father would most definitely ask. This was a decision she wanted to keep to herself until she was certain that what President Spence had said was correct.

And until she'd had time to lay the proper groundwork with her parents. Though precisely how to do that hadn't yet come to her.

She passed storefront after storefront, some businesses still solvent with doors open, but many long closed, their shingles left to hang at odd angles, the names of the abandoned shops barely legible. Broken panes of glass and cracked windows bore testament to better times. But one shingle in particular drew her eye, and she slowed her steps.

The last building on the opposite side of the street.

The sign's weathered wood was cracked and dried, but the painted-on letters, faded with time, were still readable. *Porter's Slave Pen*. Reading the name, even silently, felt like someone slipping a dagger between her ribs.

Her gaze trailed to the yard adjacent to the building, to the rotting auction stand leaning to one side, half caved in from time . . . and long-delayed justice. An image rose, vivid in her memory. An occurrence she'd witnessed only once, by mistake—if her mother's hand covering her eyes had been any indication—as the family carriage paused in the street traffic.

Yet it was an image she would never forget.

Alexandra squeezed her eyes tight, the mental picture a marker in her young life, one that had shaped her far more than her parents realized at the time. Far more than *she'd* realized.

Then, as if bookending that event, she'd read an article in the *Nashville Banner* shortly before the end of the war that announced the closing of this . . . establishment. And told how Porter, the owner, had buried piles of manacles and chains in the yard, as though he could simply cover up what he'd done and forget his part in the buying and selling of human life.

She averted her gaze and continued on, renewed purpose in her step and a vigor in her chest that all but dared to be challenged.

No grand signage marked the entrance. Only a dirt road leading to the rows of one-story framed buildings that once made up the Union Army compound of Fort Sill, but that now housed the nation's first school dedicated to the higher education of freed people.

A continuous front porch connected this particular row of barracks, and Alexandra realized after a moment what was missing. She'd expected to see students milling about, visiting between classes. But to her disappointment, the porch and surrounding common areas were empty.

She hurried up the steps leading to the barracks marked *Administration*, her grip tightening on her teaching satchel.

In her conversation with President Spence following the concert last night, he'd instructed her to ask for a Mr. George White, whose offices were located in this building. He'd assured her she didn't need an appointment.

Taking a deep breath, she opened the door and was met by the sharp tang of sweat and stale cigar smoke—and something else she couldn't place but somehow knew was distinctly male. She discreetly pressed a forefinger beneath her nose and then heard a feminine chuckle.

"It's pungent. I know," a woman's voice chided, the slightest

Northern accent detectable. "You can thank all the Union soldiers who convalesced here during the war. Thousands of them passed through this compound, we're told."

Alexandra's gaze quickly adjusted to the dimmer lighting, and she spotted a middle-aged Negro woman seated behind an old farm table now serving as a desk. The woman's gaze was as sharp and discerning as her smile was welcoming.

"The smell's always worse in the deep of summer," the woman continued. "Brings all that living out of the wood. And the dying too, I guess," she added softly.

Alexandra lowered her hand to her side and managed a smile. "I suppose one could say that we should be able to withstand the smell . . . considering what the soldiers withstood while they were here."

Understanding deepened in the woman's features. "Yes, ma'am. We often say much the same to each other when it's an especially potent day. Now please, how may I be of service?"

Briefly debating whether or not to use her real surname, Alexandra decided that being forthcoming was best. "I'm Miss Alexandra Jamison, and I'm here to see Mr. George White. About a teaching position," she added quickly. "I spoke with President Spence following the concert last evening. He said Mr. White was the gentleman with whom I needed to speak. I don't have an appointment, but President Spence said that wasn't required. And I'm able to wait. For a while, at least."

The woman rose, her gaze appraising. "I'm Mrs. Chastain, the administrative secretary. Allow me to see if Mr. White has time for an introduction. Have a seat over there if you'd like, Miss Jamison."

Mrs. Chastain disappeared down a hallway, and Alexandra noted the confident, cultured manner in which the woman conducted herself. She was tall and stately, and possessed what some might term "handsome" features for a female.

Alexandra shifted her weight, the soles of her feet beginning to throb, and she decided to accept Mrs. Chastain's invitation. But after sitting for a moment her nerves got the best of her, and she rose again.

"Miss Jamison?"

Alexandra looked up to see Mrs. Chastain standing in the hallway.

"Follow me, please, Miss Jamison." Then the woman paused. "By chance, ma'am, did President Spence give you any . . . advice for your meeting today with Mr. White?"

"Advice?" Alexandra studied her expression, unable to decide whether she saw warning in the woman's features—or amusement. "No, Mrs. Chastain, he didn't. Is . . . there something you think I should know?"

The secretary's eyes narrowed. "Have you ever known someone who speaks their mind without fully thinking it through? Or they might think it through, realize they shouldn't say anything, and then do it anyway? Someone who has no qualms whatsoever about stating the truth even when the truth might be better left unstated?"

A layer of her confidence evaporating, Alexandra nodded.

"Well, that's Mr. White." Mrs. Chastain smiled. "On a good day."

She continued down the hallway, and Alexandra knew she should follow. Yet she couldn't help but glance behind her at the door through which she'd entered moments earlier. Then she thought of David and the conviction she'd felt in the middle of the night and turned back.

She followed Mrs. Chastain down the narrow, shadowy corridor until the woman paused by an open door backlit with sunlight.

"Mr. White, Miss Alexandra Jamison to see you, sir."

Inside a cramped office stood a man, book in hand, beside an open window. He was a very tall man. Six foot three at least, his large, lanky frame appearing even more so when backlit by the sun.

"Come in, Miss Jamison." Intent on his book, Mr. George White did not look up. "I understand you're here on President Spence's recommendation to speak with me about a teaching position. However, he and I have not spoken in recent days, so I was unaware that we had an appointment. Which, of course, we do not actually have because you did not make one. So please come in and swiftly state your business. I have a class to teach shortly."

Though she'd been warned, Alexandra was still taken aback by the man's direct manner, which sounded even harsher in the clip of his crisp New York accent. She stared at his profile, waiting for him to look at her.

When he didn't, she glanced at Mrs. Chastain, hoping to take a cue from the woman after such a welcome. But the secretary only chuckled, her expression saying she found the man's behavior not the least surprising. Then wordlessly she retreated down the hall.

The overloud *ticktock* of a clock from somewhere inside the office seemed to echo Mr. White's command for swiftness, so Alexandra stepped inside. A straight-back chair waited not two strides from her, yet she dared not presume to sit without invitation.

Based upon President Spence's heartfelt plea for teachers, she'd expected a warm, even exuberant welcome, not this cool reception, and her nerves inched up another degree.

A framed wedding photograph on the wall—of a slightly younger Mr. White along with his wife, Alexandra presumed—gave a hint as to what the man looked like in more congenial moments. Something she wasn't certain she'd ever see.

She cleared her throat. "In speaking with President Spence, I learned about what you're doing here at Fisk University. I'd heard of the school before, of course, but I've never had any personal dealings with the institution." *Institution* seemed too fancy a word to describe a campus composed of old army barracks gone to rack and ruin, but she tended to exaggerate when she was nervous. "I understand you have nearly two thousand students enrolled here, Mr. White, with more seeking admittance. That's quite impressive."

His attention remained on his book, and the silence lengthened.

The clock's rhythmic *tick tick tick* sliced away at her confidence. "Something else the president and I discussed last night after the concert was—"

"You attended the concert?" Mr. White looked up at last, his dark bushy eyebrows framing piercing blue eyes. "What was your opinion?"

She hesitated.

"About the singers, Miss Jamison. What did you think?"

"I-I thought they were . . . exquisite. Tremendous."

"And your favorite part of the cantata?"

Her smile came easily. "By far, sir, it was the duet 'Who calls—'"

"'—my parting soul from death.' Yes, yes, that's a splendid piece. Handel outdid himself. And Miss Porter is a tremendous talent."

"The soprano? Yes, sir, she is indeed."

He clapped his book shut. "How did you hear about the concert? Did you receive a flyer? A personal invitation?"

"Actually, neither of those, Mr. White. I was out walking and happened upon it."

He eyed her, nodding. "Continue stating your business. Except"—he gestured—"please move ahead to your teaching experience."

The man was precisely as Mrs. Chastain had pegged him, which could actually be considered refreshing, if framed in the right perspective. At least Alexandra didn't have to guess what he was thinking.

"I'm an experienced tutor, Mr. White. I was schooled by my governess until the age of twelve, and from there I studied on my own—"

"Any advanced education? College, perhaps?"

She hesitated. "No, sir. But I am very well read and—"

"Why do you desire to teach at Fisk University, Miss Jamison?"

He crossed to his desk, his eyes never leaving hers, and eased his generous frame into the worn leather chair, the aging springs squeaking in protest.

"Well, sir . . . I . . ."

"It's a straightforward question, Miss Jamison. One we ask of every instructor who applies to teach here."

With thick black hair that joined a coarse, heavy beard and mustache, George White possessed commanding features that made an already tempestuous-looking brow appear more so. Even if she hadn't known who he was—the treasurer of Fisk University, and the school's music director—she would have guessed him to be a man who held a position of authority and influence.

She straightened, her damp chemise sticking to her back. "I'm here because I desire to help the freedmen in their new lives. I believe we have a responsibility to teach any and all who would like to learn. Up until recently, the freedmen have not been afforded that opportunity. And I would like to help change that."

His brow furrowed slightly. "Continue."

"As I told President Spence, I have an excellent command of a basic education, and even beyond in some subjects. I can teach spelling and reading. I can instruct students in sums and penmanship, in American and European history. And I'm well read in literary works and poetry. I have a fairly good command of French and German. And I know some Latin, though it's rusty from disuse, I'm sure. But I assure you, my utmost desire in wanting to teach here is to do whatever I can to ease what must still be a difficult transition for new students entering Fisk, and to share what knowledge I possess with them."

She punctuated her response with a smile, which went unreciprocated.

"Those are altruistic goals, Miss Jamison. Quite noble. But we must be careful when we adopt the view that we are humbling ourselves to help someone less fortunate."

She swallowed to moisten an overdry throat. "Sir, if I sound as though I'm having to humble myself, it's only because I'm—"

"Adjusting to this new world. Yes, I've heard that explanation before."

"But, sir, that's not what—"

He raised his hand in a manner worthy of the most venerated schoolmaster, and she knew better than to interrupt again.

"Regardless of what a great many people in this part of the country believe about the freedmen, Miss Jamison, they possess keen minds and a thirst for knowledge. They want to better themselves, no differently from you or me. And they are worthy of those pursuits, madam, not because you and I deem them so, but because God Almighty does."

"Yes, Mr. White. I'm attempting to—"

"Allow me to share a bit of wisdom with you, Miss Jamison. And in doing so, to clear up a common misconception among many Southerners, and Nashville society specifically." Gaze unrelenting, he continued with nary a breath. "Every scholar here at Fisk is educated in multiple branches of study—in languages, science, mathematics, literature, history. Our students, both the very young and older, excel in their educational pursuits, and advance far beyond a basic education. That is why, in fact, we usually do not hire teachers who do not possess some level of formal preparatory education. However, we do make exceptions. And though I commend you, Miss Jamison, for your willingness to teach at Fisk University, it is imperative that our instructors possess the proper motivation behind that desire. For instance, it would not be in Fisk's best interest to hire someone who feels as though they have a debt to repay. Or who pities the freedmen. Or, for that matter, has something to prove to society . . . or to their closest family members, perhaps."

His gaze deepened, and Alexandra wondered if he was privy to her personal situation. But . . . no, he couldn't be. Could he?

"Such ambition would be self-centered," he continued. "And in the long run would not serve our scholars or Fisk's reputation well. Would you agree?"

Feeling at once vindicated, yet also guilty as charged, she nodded. "I would wholeheartedly, sir."

He smiled then, and it was a most pleasant expression. "As I have had to tell others who have come with less than honorable intentions—not that I am questioning yours in this manner, mind you—our scholars here have no need of a white deliverer. And they already share a common faith in our Savior." He laughed softly. "And we are not him. All we desire are teachers who are willing to teach people who want to learn and who deserve no less than our very best."

Liking this man more than she would have thought possible awhile earlier, Alexandra smiled. "I appreciate your sharing that with me, Mr. White, and I can assure you—"

"You *cannot* go back there, sir! *Please! Sir!*"

Mrs. Chastain's authoritative voice carried down the hallway, as did the heavy pounding of footsteps.

Chapter FOUR

A man burst into the office, red-faced and seething.

Alexandra stepped swiftly to the side, uncertain whether to stay or go. Which soon proved a moot point, as the intruder blocked her exit.

"See here, Mr. White!" The man held a crumpled piece of paper in his grip. "I received your letter this morning and here's what I think of it!" He ripped the stationery into shreds and sent the pieces fluttering. "Nine months. *Nine!* That's how long it's been since my company has been paid by your school. Yet I've continued to deliver supplies from my mercantile. *Every* month you've begged and pleaded for more time to honor your bill, and I've given it. Well, I'm here to tell you that your time is up, sir! Fisk's account is due in full. With interest! And if you cannot assure me that—"

"Mr. Granger!" George White's deep voice thundered through the room as he unfolded himself to his full, imposing height. With a glance he dismissed Mrs. Chastain, then stepped from behind his desk, his expression severe. "Sir, I am in the midst of a—"

"I don't give an eyetooth what you're in the midst of!" Granger turned and, as if only now seeing Alexandra, gave her a brief yet scorching glare.

His gaze flickered, and Alexandra quickly bowed her head.

Granger. Of Granger Mercantile. She shopped there on

occasion. She didn't know the store owner personally, but she was certain her father did. While the possibility of Barrett Broderick Jamison knowing George White—or anyone else associated with Fisk University—was slim, her father knew *every* business owner in town.

If Mr. Granger happened to recognize her—or learn her name—news of her being here would get back to her father lickety-split. The possibility sent her heart plummeting.

"I've already contacted my lawyer," Granger continued, and Alexandra chanced a look up, relieved to see him focused again on the target of his wrath. "As have five other of Fisk's suppliers, Puckett's Dry Goods and Caldwell's Dairy among them. You'll be hearing from *all* of us very soon."

The sternness in Mr. White's features hardened into anger—and desperation, if Alexandra read the man correctly.

White stepped closer until he towered over the mercantile owner. But Granger—blessed considerably more in breadth of stature than in height—outweighed him by a good sixty pounds and didn't back down.

"Mr. Granger, you know our situation here." White's voice quieted to molten steel. "The majority of our scholars are dependent upon themselves. Some of them are as young as twelve or thirteen, and they must earn their own support while securing their education at Fisk University. So it's upon that truth and the importance of our mission that I entreat you again to—"

"I operate a business, White, not a missionary barrel. I've been more than patient." The man hesitated, his struggle mirrored in his expression. "Mine was the first business in this city to agree to supply this school, because I believe in what you're doing. But I simply cannot continue to carry your debt. I have my own creditors to pay." His features firmed. "The entirety of Fisk's obligation to my mercantile is due immediately. And if you cannot pay your note by the end of the month, then my attorney will take charge of the situation."

"Again, Mr. Granger, I would kindly appeal to your Christian nature in this matter. If you could only see your way to—"

"It is my Christian nature, sir, that has sustained my patience thus far. And it is that same nature that appeals to yours now. Good day, Mr. White."

Granger strode from the office, leaving George White to stare after him, unblinking. A moment passed, and Alexandra wondered if she should simply take her leave.

"Well," he finally said. "My sincerest apologies to you, Miss Jamison, that you were forced to witness such an exchange."

He turned and looked at her and, regardless of how he'd treated her initially, Alexandra found herself more than a little sympathetic. Especially considering what this could mean for the school—and her chances for employment.

"I was raised with three brothers, Mr. White. I am well acquainted with arguments. Or 'spirited discussions,' as my mother always termed them."

He managed a faint smile. "Are they older or younger than you? Your brothers."

"All older, sir."

"And do they still reside here in Nashville?"

He was an inquisitive man. "The eldest two reside out of state. They're both married and have families. The youngest brother, Jacob"—she briefly lowered her head—"now resides with Christ."

"The war," he said softly.

It wasn't a question, yet she nodded. "Still, my family considers ourselves blessed. We only lost one. Many lost all."

"As these very walls around us attest," he said softly. He crossed to the window, the lines of his face seeming to grow more pronounced.

She watched and waited, trying to remain hopeful.

From outside, murmurs of conversation and laughter drifted in. The students, she guessed, and she caught glimpses of them as they passed. A warm breeze brought with it the scent of sunshine and baked earth. In the distance a train whistle sounded. The Northeast Line Railroad, no doubt, if recent experience held true.

Sensing dismissal and finality in George White's lengthening silence, Alexandra let out her breath. "I appreciate your time, Mr. White. I sincerely wish you and your scholars all the—"

"Please have a seat, Miss Jamison."

She did as asked, cautiously heartened.

"Did you bring references with you today?" he asked, easing into his office chair.

She withdrew a letter from her satchel. "I have a recommendation letter from a Mr. Pruitt, written some time ago. I tutored all five of his children and have used the letter he penned as a reference in obtaining other tutoring positions. In all fairness, I've never taught in a classroom setting. But I believe I can. I'm not afraid to try."

He perused the letter, eyebrows lifting on occasion. "No," he said as he read. "I do not believe you are afraid, Miss Jamison."

Her gaze fell to a stack of papers on his desk, and without thinking, she began to read the page on the top. Despite the words being upside down, the neatness of the handwriting made reading them nearly effortless. A list of popular, lighthearted songs mixed with some classics: "Oh! Susannah," "Beautiful Dreamer," "How Can I Keep from Singing?" Perhaps it was a list for an upcoming concert.

Mr. White quietly placed a book atop the stack. "Mr. Pruitt praises your abilities most highly, Miss Jamison."

Realizing her impertinence, she started to apologize. But he held up her reference letter, no trace of judgment in his gaze.

"It would appear you're most certainly qualified for a teaching position. However, as you are now keenly aware, Fisk University is facing . . . severe financial challenges." He looked away. "The school's financial support has waned in recent months, and we're facing difficult decisions. So although we *do* have immediate need of your services, I fear the compensation would be minimal at best. Far below your expectations. All of our faculty are currently teaching at half salary until the situation changes. Which, for a starting teacher, would mean scarcely a dollar a week."

Alexandra took in the news. Even less than she would earn in a factory position. "I understand." She heard the disappointment in her voice.

"I'm sorry, Miss Jamison. I wish the circumstances were different. But perhaps you'll allow me to keep you in mind for future opportunities, should they arise. Although with your skill and tenacity," he added, subtle humor in his tone as he returned her recommendation letter to her, "I'm certain you'll secure another teaching position long before that time arrives."

He rose, but she remained seated, her thoughts spinning. The same sense of conviction that had led her here to his office, that had reminded her so much of David, pressed strong inside her again.

"I don't want to teach elsewhere, Mr. White. I want to teach here. At Fisk. If there's a place for me."

The man's face lit as he sat down again. "Well, that's an unexpected but most welcome announcement, Miss Jamison. Of course, the final approval of hiring does not lie solely with me. I must seek the board's approval as well."

"Do you think the board will look favorably upon me?"

"With both President Spence's recommendation and my own, I'm all but certain they will."

A sense of excitement skittered through her.

"However . . . they may still wish to speak with you themselves. You see, all of Fisk University employees are members of the American Missionary Association. Our goal here is not simply to educate our scholars in secular studies, but to educate them for eternity as well. Because without knowledge of the Creator and the wisdom imparted through his Son, his Spirit, and the written Word, our scholars would still be lacking the most important education of their lives. Of everyone's life."

"I hold the same convictions, Mr. White. In fact, the reason I'm here today is because I believe the Lord led me to that concert last night. Which in turn led me here. And again, I assure you I have no hidden motives. No need to right a wrong or to assuage guilt. I simply want to serve where I can make the greatest difference in people's lives. To be part of something that's important. Something that"—she hesitated, questioning the wisdom of being so transparent—"will live beyond me. And I believe that what you're doing here at Fisk University fits that objective. In every way."

Over steepled fingers, George White studied her. "Though some might argue that 'the bloom is off the rose' in your case, Miss Jamison, you are certainly not yet a spinster. Still, you speak of wanting to be involved in something that will live beyond you. I'm curious as to why."

Alexandra stared, dumbfounded. Did the man not realize how blatantly rude his statement was? How he'd insulted her? Grateful to Mrs. Chastain for warning her about his brusque nature, she searched his gaze. Seeing the honesty therein, combined with an undeniable—if at times hard to see—kindness, she swiftly decided he'd meant no offense. Perhaps his devotion to speaking the truth had blinded him to the correlating command to do so in love.

Setting aside her bruised pride, she managed a smile. "While it's true, sir, that twenty-five feels much older than I anticipated"—nearly twenty-six, but he didn't need to know that—"I do believe I have a *few* productive years ahead of me yet."

Surprisingly, the man's blue eyes twinkled.

"And as for contributing to a work that will live beyond me," she continued, "what person possessing breath and half a wit could have any other view? Especially having lived through the past decade. Death has an uncanny way of making people examine what they're doing with their lives. Would you not agree?"

He held her gaze, a smile forming. "Indeed I would, madam."

"I understand from President Spence that Fisk teachers live on the campus, as do students, and take their meals here. May I assume there would be room for me here as well?"

"That is correct, our teachers do live in barracks on the premises, but at the current time I believe all of the female faculty accommodations are occupied. May I assume you currently have a place to live, Miss Jamison?"

She hesitated. "I do. I live at home. With my parents."

He nodded. "I thought I recognized your family name. Your father is the esteemed Attorney Barrett Jamison, widely known in this city?"

She nodded. "He is, sir."

"Perhaps you would be able to continue living at home until the time comes when a space opens here?"

Alexandra weighed her response. If she told him that wasn't an option, he would ask why. Then she would have to tell him about what she anticipated would be her parents' complete lack of support for her decision. Which could jeopardize her opportunity to teach here. Yet she couldn't say yes. Because she knew better.

"I'm afraid, Mr. White, that my living at home will no longer be an option once I inform my parents that I've secured a position to teach here."

The room went very quiet.

"I see," he said softly. "You would not be the first woman who has sacrificed greatly in order to teach freedmen, Miss Jamison. However, you will definitely be the first of your number here in Nashville. Every teacher here at Fisk is from the North and is accustomed to a humble, meager life of servitude. And with one exception, all of the female teachers are older as well. Most have never been married, although there are two widows among their number." He held her gaze. "Are you certain you're ready for the challenges that will be demanded of you?"

"Oh, yes, sir. I've considered my decision thoroughly."

The slow nod of his head hinted at doubt, yet the warmth that started in his eyes then spread across his face filled her with fresh hope.

"Very well then, Miss Jamison. Once I learn the board's decision—which should be today since they meet here this afternoon—I'll do my best to get word to you no later than tomorrow. Assuming their response is favorable, and I have every reason to believe it will be, I'll speak with the female faculty and see if one of them has an idea for housing. I'm sure someone will."

He rose, and she did likewise, scarcely able to believe she'd gotten the job. Or had all but gotten it. He'd said the board's approval was more of a formality. Then she remembered something important.

"On the back of my reference letter, Mr. White, I listed an address where all correspondence is to be sent. It's important it be delivered to that address."

"Yes, yes, of course." He nodded as he came around the desk. "We'll do that. What a blessing you're going to be, Miss Jamison, to our new group of incoming students. And what a rewarding journey you have ahead of you. Yoking my efforts with those of the freedmen has represented one of the greatest blessings—and burdens—of my life. But those two things always seem to go hand in hand in ministry, do they not?"

Alexandra nodded instinctively, thinking about his earlier question about the challenges she would face. Namely, she thought about where she would live if there was no room here. She did have a little money set aside from tutoring in recent months. Not much, but enough to pay for room and board for a week or two.

"One last item, Miss Jamison . . . May I offer an apology for my nettled frame of mind when you first arrived? I was deep in thought and rarely react in a decent manner when pulled away from my work. It's a fault my dear wife continually encourages me to improve upon."

Alexandra found herself surprised yet again by his honesty. "Thank you, Mr. White. I assure you, no harm was done." She turned to go, then thought of a point he'd made earlier that she wished to add to. Though it was an addition she wouldn't have shared with just anyone.

"For the record, sir, I agree with what you said earlier about freedmen having no need of a *white* deliverer, and about how we share a common faith in Christ. Yet I do find it interesting that many historians agree on something about our beloved Savior. A fact that I'm certain the study of antiquity bears out." She worked to hold back a smile. "Although I'm not at all certain it's a fact my fellow Southerners will appreciate knowing."

He gave her a quizzical look. "What fact is that, Miss Jamison?"

She let her smile come then. "That Jesus wasn't white either."

She could still hear the man's laughter as she exited the barracks.

∽

Sylas Rutledge climbed down from the railcar, his sights set on General William Giles Harding, the man of the hour—and the man who was going to replenish the capital Sylas needed, following his recent purchase of the Northeast Line Railroad. Although Harding didn't yet know it.

Sy had never laid eyes on the man before, but one of the porters onboard had pointed him out. Upon first impression, General Harding was far older looking than what Sy had expected. The scraggly beard that almost reached the man's waist didn't help. Looked a bit like one of the old miners who shuffled from creek to creek back in Boulder.

"Got him ready for you, Boss!"

Sy turned and spotted Vinson striding toward him through the swell of spectators gathered for Harding's public unveiling. Sy always enjoyed watching people watch Vinson. The man was a lean two hundred and fifty pounds of solid muscle, his bald black head polished to a sheen. And at the moment, glistening with sweat. Vinson always made an impression.

Sy removed his hat and raked a hand through his hair. He'd been warned about the South's oppressive summers, but this was worse than he'd imagined. Give him the dry, cooler climes of the Colorado Rockies any day.

He wondered why the general had chosen today for this event . . . Surely he realized it was one year to the day since the accident happened. Sy could hardly believe that much time had passed.

As the train had approached Nashville earlier that morning, he'd looked west across the city in the direction of Dutchman's Curve and recalled the newspaper account of what had happened on that section of single track line. Where his father—or stepfather, in the eyes of the law—had breathed his last. While Sy wanted to see the place for himself, and hoped to make some peace with the ruin of it all, he also dreaded it.

His father, the engineer of the ill-fated No. 1, had been one day away from retiring from the Nashville, Chattanooga and St. Louis Railway. That run from Memphis to Nashville was to have been his last.

And as it turned out, it was.

Sy only hoped Harrison Kennedy had known what a difference he'd made in the lives of a mother and her little boy abandoned by an itinerant gambler, a man Sy had been too young to remember. Kennedy, a career railroad man with an insatiable appetite for learning, had taken them as his own. Sy still remembered what his mother had said after marrying Kennedy. *Sylas and I didn't know what happy was until you came into our lives.*

That was the truth.

Ironic then, that when her doctor in Colorado recommended a milder climate due to her weakened constitution from scarlet fever in earlier years, she and Kennedy had moved East in '62—where she succumbed to influenza during her first winter in Tennessee.

Sy still regretted not being able to attend her funeral. But that was part of living back in a mining camp. Come winter, it wasn't always possible to get out. His father had wired and encouraged him to wait until spring. Then spring came and the mine got busy and another year slipped by. Followed by another. And another.

Sy knew early on that the mining town life and its temptations weren't what his father would have chosen for him, yet Harrison Kennedy hadn't uttered one critical word. Not while in Colorado, and not in his letters after he'd moved to the South. He didn't have to. Sy knew the man well enough to know what he thought.

It was that knowledge—along with the jolting reminder of life's fleeting quality—that finally drove Sy to make a change.

Sy thought again of the concert he'd attended last night, and of how much his parents would have liked it. He'd happened upon the billboard outside the Masonic Hall while on his evening stroll. And though he was somewhat acquainted with Handel due to his father's influence, he'd never heard of the *Cantata of Esther,* but he'd enjoyed it. Especially the song a man and woman had sung together, about calling a parting soul from death. He'd contemplated the lyrics long into the night.

Reining in his thoughts, he slipped his hat back on and whistled for Duke. The foxhound bounded down from the platform, tail wagging. Sy reached down and scratched the dog between the ears. A snap of his fingers, and Duke fell into step beside him as Sy made his way back to the lead stock car, grateful for the progress he'd made since coming East three weeks ago.

He'd traveled from Charlotte, North Carolina, to Charleston, West Virginia, to complete a survey of his next potential railroad project. It involved purchasing four consecutive parcels of land between those two cities, and all from different land owners. The key was to purchase each piece of property from its owner without the others being any the wiser.

Because if word got out prematurely that the potential purchaser was the owner of the Northeast Line, the landholders would most assuredly join forces and hold out for a much higher price. Or other bidders could step up, which would lead to a bidding war. Which wouldn't benefit him at all. No, he needed to get this done quickly and quietly.

But first he needed a replenishment of capital, which is where General Harding came in. Then he needed investors for the land purchase. He hoped his connection with Harding would bridge that gap as well.

He met Vinson by the open door of the specially refitted stock car and climbed up inside. "He make the trip all right?"

"Like the champion he is, Boss." Vinson hoisted himself up beside him.

Sy cautiously approached the prize-winning stallion. Enquirer was easily one of the most magnificent animals he'd ever seen. A bay stallion standing over sixteen hands high with the longest shoulder, deepest heart-place, shortest saddle-place, and most powerful quarters recorded for a thoroughbred to date. According to what he'd read in the *Denver Post*, Harding had paid ten thousand dollars for him. "No telling how much this fella will bring for a stud fee."

The stallion tossed his head as though eager to share his own thoughts on the matter, and Vinson laughed.

"Look at him, Sy. Already getting himself worked up about being with those sweet fillies."

Sy smiled, then glanced out the door in Harding's direction, his mind on the meeting awaiting him. General Harding had referenced receiving other bids for the railroad project, yet Sy felt confident his bid would be the most competitive. Harding had also mentioned something in his letter about attending a dinner at Belle Meade, indicating that details would be provided later.

"Get the gangplank set, Vinson, but make sure this fella's kept out of sight until I give you the go-ahead. I want *you* leading him down the plank too. These stallions can be temperamental."

Vinson shot him a look. "As we both well know."

Sy nodded. "Harding said he wants a production. So we'll give the man a production."

"So he'll give *you* what you want."

"That's the plan. But from what little I've been able to learn about him, Harding drives a hard bargain. And I'm not the only one wanting this contract. There are sure to be a few more bidders. Plus I'm an outsider, Vinson, being from Colorado. That won't help me."

"You'll get it, Boss. You always get what you put your mind to."

"Maybe." Sy rubbed the back of his neck. "Be on the lookout for one of Harding's men. Robert Green is his name. He's to take charge of the thoroughbred once you get him off the train. And have Winslow check those brakes again. Something sounds off."

"Winslow checked all the brakes before we pulled out of the station this morning." Vinson met—and held—his gaze. "But I'll see to it he checks 'em again."

Sy nodded and turned.

"Oh, and . . . Sy?"

He looked back.

"Just so you know . . ." Vinson's voice went quiet. "I haven't forgotten what today is. You're not alone in missing him."

Unprepared for the knot forming at the base of his throat, Sy gave a quick nod.

"He was mighty proud of you for what you made of yourself in Colorado, and would be proud, too, of you buying this railroad. But especially for what you're doing . . . to clear his good name."

Sy tried to look anywhere but at his friend, the knot in his throat making it difficult to speak. "Just . . . see to things, Vinson. All right?"

A smile ghosted Vinson's face. "Yes, sir, Mr. Rutledge."

Sy made his way through the crowd, Duke at his heel, and it took several deep breaths to work the tightness from his chest. It wasn't within him to converse about such things, but it did feel good to know he wasn't alone in his memories.

The whistle blasts of an outbound train a few tracks over pierced the air with an almost mournful quality.

You want to work at developing your own way of tugging the pull cord, Sylas, his father had taught him before Sy was even tall enough to reach the rope unaided. *That way, you can put some feeling into the sound. You can make it happy or sad. Or quick sounding, like it's telling everybody to listen up! Each operator has his own style of blowing the whistle. Most times, I can tell you who the engineer is simply by the sound of the blast.*

Sy's steps slowed, the memories tangling round him. He wondered what the whistle blasts had sounded like on Dutchman's Curve. Or had there even been time to signal a warning?

It had taken well over a month for the news of his father's death to reach the mountains around Boulder. And by that time, Harrison Kennedy had already been hastily buried in a grave somewhere here in Nashville. Not beside Sy's mother in the Nashville City Cemetery where he should have been buried—and would be, once Sy uncovered the truth about what had happened on Dutchman's Curve and cleared his father's name. Which was the driving force behind why he'd wagered the majority of his wealth and bought the Northeast Line.

That, and the fact that gambling was in his blood.

Railroad tycoons were a loyal bunch. And ruthless. They'd think nothing of laying the blame at an innocent man's feet in order to protect their investment. Just so long as the railroad didn't have any culpability. If the truth of Dutchman's Curve had been buried, and Sy believed it had, it would stay buried. Unless someone from the railroad uncovered it. Still . . .

Considering what he stood to lose if he didn't win the bid on Harding's project and he failed to secure investors for the land purchase, this would prove to be his biggest gamble of all. With all his holdings invested, he stood to lose not only the Northeast Line but perhaps the railroad back in Colorado as well. Everything he had. But if it worked . . .

He'd make his entire investment back and a lot more.

Enough to buy that ranch on the outskirts of Boulder that he'd been eying for years now. Companies and investors from the East were acquiring enormous plats of Colorado land, and he needed to get his share while he could. And this was his chance. Perhaps his last one.

From the corner of his eye, Sy spotted General Harding making his way toward the station platform and went to intercept him.

"Pardon me, sir," a sultry voice said even as Sy felt someone pressing up against him in the crowd.

He looked down and met a woman's gaze, instantly knowing her for what she was. Never mind the expensive clothes, hairstyle, and other well-displayed assets. The boldness in her smile and purpose in the hand she laid against his chest left no doubt as to the nature of her intent.

She moved closer. "The moment I saw you get off that train, I pegged you for a man who would appreciate some . . . memorable companionship this afternoon."

Sy caught hold of her wrist before things could get more interesting. The mining towns back West were full of brothels. Once he'd even paid his money and started up the stairs to the room. Then something had stopped him. To this day, he didn't know what. He'd turned around and left, a dollar poorer than when he'd walked in. But he'd never regretted that decision. And though he often desired a woman's company, that particular brand of it held no appeal.

Mindful of the folks around them, and of Harding specifically, he kept his voice low. "While I don't doubt the skill of your companionship, ma'am, I must refuse."

"Come now . . ." Her calculated smile grew falsely intimate. "I'm certain a man like you would enjoy—"

Not wanting to lose track of General Harding in the crowd, Sy turned back in that direction but spotted another familiar face instead. Miss Jamison, the daughter of the attorney he'd visited yesterday, was making her way toward him on the platform.

From what he could tell, the young woman hadn't spotted him yet. And considering his current predicament, he aimed to keep it that way.

Chapter
FIVE

Moving away from the prostitute, Sy glanced in Miss Jamison's direction again, only to see she'd stopped a ways back to speak to another young woman in the crowd. They were deep in conversation, neither of them looking his way. He searched again for General Harding and finally spotted the man crossing the station platform and entering through a door of an adjacent building.

The letter from Harding said the meeting would be brief and held at a location behind the ticket office. For a limited number of people, judging from the way it was worded. Immediately following the meeting, Harding would present Enquirer to the ever-growing crowd.

Sy headed in that direction, Duke trotting loyally at his heel. He couldn't help glancing once more in Miss Jamison's direction. She certainly had a quality about her that drew a man's eye. And it wasn't just her face and curves either, or that mass of blond hair piled atop her head begging to be taken down, though those attributes were plenty appealing. It was more in the way she conducted herself. With quiet confidence and decorum. She was intelligent too. That much was clear.

The fact that she hadn't tried to draw his attention was probably part of it as well. The woman hadn't seemed interested in him in the least.

But why was he even thinking about all that? He hadn't come to Nashville looking for a wife. He was here to work a deal, find some answers, and return West with plenty of money in his pocket and a lucrative expansion to his railroad.

And anyway, from what he'd seen thus far, Southern women were far too soft and delicate for the untamed life of Colorado. Although . . .

He'd sensed an undercurrent between Miss Jamison and her father in the office yesterday. Like an invisible tug-of-war going on between them. And in his estimation, the daughter had been winning. With a single look, she could put a man in his place.

The father struck him as being a little desperate for business, and he talked a lot too. Which was good in one way, because Sy had left Jamison's office knowing a great deal more about local businesses than he had when he'd walked in.

But confidentiality in this next project was crucial. So though he thought Jamison could manage it, could he trust the man to be discreet?

As he left the station platform and walked toward the building where the meeting was to be held, he passed vendors with carts laden with food. The aromas of freshly baked bread, sausages, and popcorn gave the event a festive feel. And reminded Sy of breakfast long past.

Scarcely pausing, he plunked down coins for a sausage and ate it as he walked. When he reached the stairs, he tossed the remainder to Duke, who caught it midair. Sy signaled for him to stay, and the foxhound found a patch of shade beneath the platform and hunkered down, the thump of his tail saying plenty.

Sy deposited his trash in a rubbish bin, then opened the door he had seen the general enter a moment before. At first he thought he was in the wrong place. The room was packed. Standing room only. But there was General Harding at the front of the room.

All of these men were here about Harding's railroad venture? He took closer count. Nearly sixty men. And finely suited dandies, every last one of them. All of them twittering away like banty hens on a Sunday picnic. Sy rubbed a hand over his stubbled jaw and removed his hat, thinking he should've made acquaintance with a barber before coming here this afternoon.

While he hadn't taken Harding's written response to his bid to mean he had clinched the deal, he had thought—mistakenly, from the look of things—that it meant he was in the final running.

"Gentlemen, please . . ." General Harding raised a hand. "May I have your attention?"

A man seated toward the front turned, and when Sy saw who it was, his jaw tightened. Harold Gould. That was all he needed.

If this turned out like last time . . .

The man already controlled more than nine thousand miles of track, compared to Sy's twenty-five hundred. Gould probably hoped to take advantage of Harding's venture of bringing the railroad from Nashville to Belle Meade by then pushing the line on southward into Mississippi sometime in the future—if Harding was open to it. Which is exactly what Sy wanted to do.

Thing was, Gould probably already had the needed capital, after besting Sy out of the last deal in Colorado. Gould caught his eye—and smiled.

Sy did likewise and gave a confident nod, while his gut churned.

"Gentlemen!" Harding said again, and the crowd fell quiet. "Thank you for coming here today."

As Harding offered a welcome, Sy realized the man had a presence about him, scraggly beard notwithstanding, along with an unmistakable air of wealth. The general's war record was well known, as was the fact that he'd been imprisoned by the North for several months. Not that Sy or anyone else out West had spent much time thinking about that war.

He'd been too busy operating a mine and running cattle on the side while making a small fortune, then building his first railroad. All by the age of twenty-four. His father had been right, in that regard. Looking back, Sy could see that he'd been right about so many things.

"I appreciate your interest in my venture to bring the railroad to Belle Meade Plantation's front porch," Harding continued. "As most of you likely know, this is something I've desired to do for a long time. And with the annual yearling sales steadily growing in attendance, I want to do more than simply bring interested buyers to Nashville, the finest city in the South. I want them to arrive at Belle Meade in style!"

A round of applause and several hearty cries of "Hear! Hear!" rose from some of the men gathered. Sy wasn't one of them.

He grudgingly admitted to himself that Harding *did* have a commanding quality about him. Sy shifted his weight. Thing was, he tended to rub men like Harding the wrong way. And those men had the exact same effect on him.

"My plans also include laying a macadam road from the turnoff at Harding Pike all the way to the plantation. This will ease the transportation of those still seeking to travel by carriage or wagon. I desire that the Belle Meade depot be designed and constructed in a manner that complements the style of the house, of course. And it's my preference that eventually this railway be part of a route that would extend southward. After all, Belle Meade is the premiere stud farm in the country as well as a working estate, and we have much to offer railroad patrons. Now I'll entertain a few questions, then we must adjourn for a special presentation of another exciting addition to Belle Meade that arrived a short time ago."

"General Harding!" Gould rose from his seat near the front. "My name is Harold Gould, sir, and I want to tell you what an honor it is to meet you and to hear from you this morning. Indeed, it's a privilege, sir, to be in the same room with such an esteemed businessman and ally of the railroad men of America."

More applause rose, and Sy exhaled, glad he'd worn his boots.

"And now my question, General Harding," Gould continued.

"Have you narrowed down the top bids at this stage? And has any one bid in particular garnered your attention?"

Even though Gould didn't glance back at him, Sy knew the man was goading him. He also knew Harding would never answer such a question in public.

Understandably, Harding's smile was that of a man holding his cards close to his vest. "I've been in contact with several of you already. And while there are bids that have certainly gained my attention, if there is someone in this room who still desires to submit a bid, he may do so with my plantation manager." He gestured to a man standing off to the side.

"But you would be advised to do so quickly, because I'm hosting a dinner tomorrow night at Belle Meade for all *approved* prospective bidders so that they may gain a clearer understanding of my vision for the project. Pursuant to that evening, I'll make my decision and award the project the following week."

"And just how do we know who's on this approved list, General Harding?" Too late, Sy realized that his frustration over the number of bidders, and Gould's being among them, had colored his tone.

Squinting, General Harding peered over those gathered. "And your name, sir?"

"Sylas Rutledge. Owner of the Northeast Line Railroad."

Harding paused briefly as recognition—or was it irritation?—shaded his features. Sy hoped Harding would recall that it was the Northeast Line that had pulled into the station awhile ago with the man's newest blood horse on board. But he wouldn't bet on it.

"Well, Mr. Rutledge, as I was about to explain . . ." General Harding addressed his audience. "If those who have received a letter from me will visit the table set up in the breezeway outside after our meeting, my business manager will let them know if their bid has advanced to the next stage. Those approved will then receive an invitation to dinner. Does that answer your question satisfactorily . . . Mr. Rutledge?"

Cordial sarcasm of a distinctly Southern style tainted Harding's tone, and Sylas managed a nod. His first exchange with the man had not gone as planned. He could all but feel Gould's smirk, and made a point not to look in his direction.

Another man stood, stated his name, along with a string of banal compliments, then asked a question. Sy only half listened, fingering his hat in his hands. He already knew what he needed to know—that the odds of his winning the Belle Meade project were not as favorable as he'd thought. And that Harold Gould was going to do everything possible to shut him out.

After a few more questions and answers, Harding concluded the meeting.

Sy attempted to make his way toward the front to talk to Harding about Enquirer, maybe try to improve the man's opinion of him a mite. But the swell of men pressing for the general's attention prevented it.

Sy finally turned to wait by the door when he noticed a black man standing off to the side watching him. The man's pristine white apron and distinctive black bowler made him stand out in the crowd. He had a kindly look about him, something that said he belonged.

Sy offered his hand. "Sylas Rutledge."

The man's grip was firm. "The Mr. Rutledge who brought the general's new blood horse."

It wasn't a question. "One and the same."

"You the owner of the Northeast Line too. Ain't that what I heard you say?"

Sy nodded, getting the feeling an opinion was being formed. For better or worse, he couldn't say.

"I'm Robert Green, head hostler at Belle Meade Plantation. But everybody calls me Uncle Bob."

Sy nodded slowly. "Uncle Bob it is then." This was the man responsible for all of General Harding's thoroughbreds? Interesting . . .

"From what I hear, sir, you hire mostly black men for your railroad. Not just the porter jobs, but the other higher-ups too. That right?"

Sy raised a brow. "News travels fast in these parts."

Uncle Bob laughed.

"I hire the best men for the job, plain and simple. Nothing more, nothing less."

The man regarded him for a long moment, then smiled. "You ain't from close around here, are you, Mr. Rutledge?"

Sy laughed. "No, I'm not. I've spent my life out in Colorado. Up until about three weeks ago when I finally ventured East."

"Colorado, you say." Uncle Bob's dark gaze turned appraising. "Got me a friend out that way. Ridley Cooper. Good man. Owns a ranch near Denver. Got his start right here at Belle Meade."

Sy shook his head. "Can't say I've heard of him. But if he's a good man, I'll have to look him up when I get back. I've been to Denver many times, but have spent most of my life in or around the mining camps. Boulder, Breckenridge, and some others."

Uncle Bob frowned. "You a miner, sir?"

"Used to be. For a while."

"Any good come of it?"

Again Sy smiled. "You could say that. But the main good came from knowing when to stop mining and when to start managing a mine instead. And selling to the miners. I began raising cattle. Didn't know much about it at first, but you learn real quick when you have to."

Uncle Bob laughed. "That you do, sir. And them miners, they always gotta eat."

"That's the way I saw it. Or . . . came to see it, after a while."

"What'd you mine for?"

"Gold, mostly. But some silver too."

"And you found some?"

"A fair amount."

The older man shook his head, his laughter pleasant. "I once had me a dream of goin' out that way. Just to see it, mind you. Never had no plan to go and stay."

"You should see it, if you can. It's beautiful country. The Rocky Mountains . . ." Sy briefly closed his eyes, able to remember them better that way. "You'd swear the highest peaks reach straight up to heaven's doorstep. But once you climb one of them, and you catch your breath—"

Sy gave him a look, and Uncle Bob chuckled.

"—you stand there and look up . . . and you realize just how much more sky there is to go."

Sy could see the image so clearly in his mind. And as he had on those occasions when he'd scaled the mountains, he wished he'd had the ability to capture the image of those snowcapped peaks and the vivid blue of the sky. Their beauty couldn't be communicated with words.

"*Lawd* . . ." Uncle Bob sighed. "I bet standin' on one of them mountaintops makes a man feel all kinds of powerful!"

"That's what I expected to feel the first time I climbed up there." Sy exhaled. "But what I mainly felt was . . . small. By comparison."

Uncle Bob said nothing for a moment, only looked at him, then nodded slowly. "So where's the general's new thoroughbred, Mr. Rutledge? He done made the trip all right, I hope?"

"He made it fine." Sy gestured in the direction of the train. "Enquirer's in the first stock car. Man by the name of Vinson is seeing to him. Go on down and see the horse for yourself, if you like. You can't miss Vinson. He's about the size of a mountain and—"

"He that boulder of a man I seen movin' through down there awhile back?"

"That'd be him."

Uncle Bob nodded. "I'll find him."

"You'll find *who*, Uncle Bob?"

Sy turned to see General Harding walking up to them with Harold Gould in tow, smirk intact.

"I's just telling Mr. Rutledge here, sir, that I's gonna go check on Enquirer."

Determined not to make another misstep, Sy stuck out his hand. "General Harding, I appreciate the opportunity to bid on your project. And also your trust in allowing me to transport your thoroughbred today."

"Mr. Rutledge." Harding gave a succinct nod, much like his handshake. "I trust you delivered him in excellent condition?"

Sy matched his gaze. "I did, sir. He's one fine animal."

Without a blink, Harding turned to Uncle Bob. "I'll make my way to the podium while you go check on the horse. Make sure he's ready for the presentation."

"Yes, sir, General. We'll be ready."

Harding turned back. "Mr. Gould, would you care to join me as I walk?"

"Why, I'd be honored, General Harding." Gould shot Sy a look. "Mr. Rutledge, it's a pleasure to see you again."

Harding paused. "You two know each other?"

"Oh, yes, General." A glint sharpened Gould's eyes. "Mr. Rutledge and I met about a year ago when we were bidding for the same railroad out West. A line that runs from Denver to Colorado Springs. I came out on top in that bid, sir. But as I recall, that was Mr. Rutledge's first attempt to acquire a legitimate railroad operation. Up to then"—Gould smiled—"he had himself a little operation that ran between some mining towns in the Rockies."

"*Has* an operation," Sy corrected. "I still own the Silver Line."

"Oh, do you? Quite a feather in your cap there, Rutledge."

Harding's brow knit. "So, Mr. Rutledge . . . You've only owned the Northeast Line for a year?"

"Actually, only about nine months, sir." Sy slipped his hat back on. "The Northeast Line was all but bankrupt. I started turning a profit after seven weeks."

Gould laughed. "Yes, how *are* the rail markets in the smaller eastern towns these days? Booming, I take it."

Sy smiled. One quick jab, that's all he wanted. That's all it would take too. Gould was soft and spongy. The man hadn't spent the last few years carving out his fortune from the unrelenting Rocky Mountains.

"Kind of you to inquire, Gould. The markets are growing steady and strong. After you, General Harding."

Sy indicated for the general to precede him through the door, and Gould swiftly fell into step behind the man, tossing Sy a dismissive look as he did. Sy followed a few steps behind, all but certain there would be no envelope waiting for him at the table. Or if there was, it would likely soon be withdrawn. Along with his invitation to dinner.

He strode back to where he'd left Duke and whistled once. The dog hopped up and trotted toward him, tail wagging as though he hadn't seen his master in days. Sy gave him a good rub, then headed back to the breezeway.

When he turned the corner he saw Harding's business manager involved in a deep discussion with a man he'd glimpsed in the meeting room minutes earlier. He sighed to himself. Just what he needed. Yet another bidder on the project.

Then he spotted someone seated at the table to his right at the very moment she spotted him. An unmistakable spark of interest flitted across Miss Jamison's expression—though she quickly tucked that interest back beneath an attractive countenance of confidence and decorum.

Not that any of that mattered, Sy quickly reminded himself. He was here to clear his father's name, work a lucrative deal, then head back West with his pockets lined and that ranch outside of Boulder as good as his.

Chapter
Six

*F*ace-to-face with Sylas Rutledge again, Alexandra found herself annoyingly tongue-tied and blushing for no cause.

"Miss Jamison, nice to see you again, ma'am."

"Thank you, Mr. Rutledge," she managed, pleasantly surprised
at his show of etiquette. "You as well."

He peered down at her from beneath the brim of his Stetson.
"Don't tell me that in addition to being an assistant attorney, you're
a plantation foreman as well."

She couldn't help smiling. "No, sir. Mr. Walters, General Harding's
business manager, is presently occupied. So the general requested
that Miss Harding, his daughter, and I assist at the table."

Seated beside her, Mary was speaking with another of the bidders, so Alexandra searched the box for Mr. Rutledge's envelope,
trying not to think of how his voice sounded like the slow pour of
fine bourbon into a glass. Or the rich taste of chocolate melting on
her tongue. How had she not noticed that before? But then, he'd
scarcely said a handful of words in her father's office yesterday.

She handed him the envelope. "Congratulations on being one
of the final bidders on General Harding's project. Once you read
the letter, Mr. Rutledge, you'll find that the general has extended an
invitation for you to join his family for a *soirée* tomorrow evening
at their home. The address and directions are included within.
May I mark you as attending?"

"You may, Miss Jamison."

Alexandra made a mark by his name on the list, catching a glimpse of the man's faithful companion, who was watching her intently over the edge of the table. She smiled at the dog but didn't dare try to pet him again.

"The best of luck to you, Mr. Rutledge."

"Actually, I don't hold much stock in luck, Miss Jamison. I quit that claim some time ago." He eyed her. "You don't think I need one of those special deeds to make it official, do you?"

Alexandra laughed, surprising herself. How long had it been since she'd laughed so spontaneously? "No, sir. No quitclaim deed required in this instance."

He held her gaze a tad longer than necessary, and the thoroughness of his attention combined with that same indefinable quality she'd glimpsed yesterday summoned a heat inside her that traveled from her face down to her toes in the space of a heartbeat. And took her breath with it.

"Much obliged to you, ma'am, for your help."

She responded with a polite, parting nod, then made herself look past him to the next man in line. Yet she was aware of his every move as he and his foxhound made their way to the station platform.

She noticed Mary eying him too and knew her friend would question her at the earliest opportunity.

Perhaps the man wasn't so wild and untamed after all. But she knew enough to know that General Harding preferred to work with likeminded businessmen. Namely, Southern gentlemen like himself. So Mr. Rutledge was at a disadvantage from the start.

"And who exactly was that?" Mary whispered when the line at the table cleared momentarily. "And how do you know him?"

"His name is Mr. Rutledge. And actually, I don't know him. I've only met him once, when he came to see my father yesterday. I know he's from Colorado and that he's the owner of the Northeast Line Railroad." And that he appreciates music, she thought, and adores his dog. Though she kept those two observations to herself.

Mary slipped her hand into the crook of Alexandra's arm. "He's a bit rough around the edges, I'd say," she whispered, turning to watch him. "But from where I sit . . . he'd be well worth taming!"

"Mary Elizabeth Harding!" Alexandra glanced at her friend in mock alarm.

"Well, look at him, Alex. Tall, dark . . . and a little dangerous."

Alexandra nudged her. "While two of those qualities can be considered desirable, the last is decidedly not. Besides, you already have your perfect Mr. Jackson."

Mary sighed. "Howell *is* rather perfect, is he not?"

Alexandra loved seeing the light in her friend's eyes. "How are the wedding plans progressing?"

"Beautifully. My dress should be finished soon." A shadow eclipsed her smile.

"What is it?"

Mary shook her head. "All this wedding planning makes me miss Mother."

Alexandra hugged her. "I'm so sorry, Mary. She would have loved to have experienced all this with you. Your mother had such wonderful style too."

Mary looked at her hands in her lap. "It's hard to believe it's almost four years since she passed." As soon as she said it, empathy moved into her features. "And I know you're missing David today, Alex. He was such a fine man. As perfect for you as you say Howell Jackson is for me."

Alexandra steeled herself against the emotions simmering just beneath the surface. "Yes, he was," she whispered. "Even if he didn't have five children to usher me into instant motherhood."

Mary's grin found its place again. "I realize some people are talking, wondering how could I possibly want all those children. Even my aunt said she thought I had too much sense to take on that responsibility." Mary shook her head. "But I'm twenty-four years old, Alex. I'm long past ready to be a mother and to have my own home."

"You've been ready since you were five. You're going to be the most wonderful mother to those children." Alexandra smiled, thinking again about what her own mother had said to her last night. "And your husband-to-be, esteemed attorney that he is, is bound for marvelous things too, Mary. I couldn't be happier for you both."

Mary grasped her hand and squeezed. "I see you're out of mourning garb, and I'm glad. You honored him properly, Alex, but I'm glad to see you in color again. Although I think we can do better than dark blue."

Alexandra shushed her with a look.

"Is there someone . . . anyone who's caught your eye of late? After all," Mary continued hurriedly, as though anticipating a rebuttal, "it's been a year. A lot of people aren't even waiting that long anymore. I think the war has made us all more aware of time's passing. Howell's wife had scarcely been gone six months when he asked me to marry him. He said he didn't wish to 'act with unbecoming haste,' but he does have the children to consider."

Alexandra met her gaze. "My dear Mary, while you may believe whatever you like about Mr. Jackson's haste in marrying you, don't forget . . . I've seen the way the man looks at you."

Mary's eyes watered. "The same way David looked at you."

Alexandra nodded as her own tears welled.

Her friend leaned closer. "Is there anything I can do to help you through today? And to help you . . . move beyond this difficult season?"

"You've already done so much. Just remembering today along with me helps. But . . ." Alexandra raised a brow. "I *did* use your address today for correspondence regarding a possible position."

"You applied to teach somewhere?"

"I did."

Mary squeezed her hand. "David would be so pleased, Alex. And so proud of you. But what did your father say?"

"I haven't told him yet. Or Mother."

Mary made a face that aptly described what Alexandra was feeling whenever she thought of that exchange.

She was tempted to tell Mary more, but she knew that would only elicit questions she wasn't ready to answer. And might not even need to answer, if she ended up not getting the job after all.

She didn't think Mary would fault her for wanting to teach at Fisk. But her friend *was* the daughter of General William Giles Harding, and everyone knew where he stood on the subject of educating freedmen. Exactly where her own father stood.

"You'll likely receive a letter for me in the next day or two. And if you can either bring it or send it over to my attention, I'll be so grateful."

A gentleman approached the table, and Mary turned to help him, but not before she whispered, "I want to hear more about this. I hope it isn't too far away. I don't want to lose you!"

Alexandra nodded. Mary was the closest thing she had to a sister, and it was sweet of her to say that. But Alexandra knew that *she* was the one about to lose *Mary*. To a wonderful man, granted. But why was it that every time a friend married, a page turned and a chapter closed? It was about to happen all over again.

After distributing the remaining envelopes, the two women joined the crowd near the edge of the platform, where General Harding was speaking.

A moment passed, and Alexandra felt someone watching her. She turned to see Sylas Rutledge looking her way. He nodded and smiled, and she did the same before turning back. He *was* a handsome man, as Mary had said. And as it turns out, he had a sense of humor as well. He was obviously successful. And intelligent, even if in a less formal sense.

Alexandra felt a stab of guilt. How could she be having thoughts like that on this day? Her heart was still with David, as was her future now, in a way.

"To the fine citizens of Nashville," General Harding said, his voice carrying over the quieted crowd, "I pledge to do everything within my power to continue to rebuild this fair city alongside you, and to garner the much-desired attention it is due." He paused briefly as applause momentarily drowned out his voice. "As one whose roots go deep into the soil of this city . . ."

Alexandra eyed a certain stock car on the track, one with the gangplank lowered, surmising that's where the thoroughbred was being held until the presentation. Then she glanced back in Mr. Rutledge's direction, only to find him gone.

The discovery brought both relief and disappointment.

"So it is with deep remorse," General Harding was saying, "and heartfelt sympathy to everyone who lost a loved one exactly one year ago today . . . that we pause to remember." The general withdrew his watch from his pocket.

"In just a moment," he continued, "after the bell in the First Presbyterian Church strikes three o'clock, it will continue to strike one hundred and three times. Once for each life lost that afternoon on Dutchman's Curve. And though the pain of loss remains, let us focus today on lives well lived and love that was shared."

Alexandra felt her throat closing.

"Would you please bow your heads with me as we remember . . . and pray silently for one another?"

Heart pounding, she bowed her head, not having expected this. Seconds passed in tense, almost painful silence, then from a few streets away the bell in the church tower struck three times. And continued . . .

One . . . two . . . three . . . four . . .

She found herself counting along, feeling each strike resonating deep inside her.

Which toll was for David?

As she'd wondered many times . . . Had he died instantly? Or had he suffered beneath the weight of that train car, his body crushed and broken? Had he cried out for help? Only to die before they could reach him?

The ache in her chest sharpened with each toll.

Thirty-two . . . thirty-three . . . thirty-four . . . thirty-five . . .

Though General Harding hadn't mentioned it, the majority of the victims had been freedmen riding in the frontmost cars. Where David had been.

Not far from where she stood, soft sobs rose. Slowly she lifted her eyes to see an elderly woman, her face buried in her frail hands. Nearby, a young Negro woman stood with a small boy cradled to her chest as she looked heavenward, silent tears trailing her cheeks. Even some of the men wiped unshed tears from their eyes as the bell continued to toll.

Seventy-one . . . seventy-two . . . seventy-three . . . seventy-four . . .

Suddenly it felt as though they'd been standing there for such a long time. Too long a time.

Eighty-one . . . eighty-two . . . eighty-three . . .

Too many people, Lord. Too many lives senselessly cut short that day. Needlessly, carelessly. *Oh, David . . .*

How she missed him. Missed his laughter and the life they'd intended to share. Why had they not married sooner? If they had, he might never have been on that train that morning. But she knew why . . .

She'd bent to her father's will in that decision too. He'd wanted them to wait until after David began teaching at the university in Memphis. To make sure "the young man settles into the position well, Alexandra." But looking back, she wondered if her father had hoped she might change her mind.

Ninety-nine, one hundred. One hundred one, one hundred two . . . one hundred three.

The final reverberation of the bell seemed to cling to the heat and humidity, and to the almost palpable grief now hovering over the gathering. For a moment Alexandra doubted if the sound would ever completely fade away.

But it did, finally, and everyone drew a collective, audible breath. She felt a tug on her hand and looked over to see Mary, whose cheeks were also damp.

Her friend leaned close. "I see someone I need to speak with, Alex. Wait here for me?"

Alexandra nodded, grateful for a moment to collect her thoughts. Then she spotted him again. Sylas Rutledge. Standing across the way near the gangplank of the stock car. And his expression . . .

Pained best described it. Or even anguished. But why would he be feeling such a sense of loss? Had he known someone who'd perished in the accident that day too? Doubtful, his being from so far away.

Then again, he was a railroad man. Maybe that alone provided a strong enough link. After all, she'd read in the newspapers of train accidents in the Colorado mountains and of workers plummeting to their deaths while building trestles across canyons. She shuddered.

The railroad represented progress, she knew. But at what cost?

General Harding resumed his speech, yet all she could focus on was the thunder of those two massive locomotives as they'd met head-on in that cornfield, the grinding of metal on metal. From where she'd sat by the window in her railcar, she'd watched helpless as the forward-most passenger cars telescoped into one another, the wooden structures splintering like children's toys, the impact fanning out and over the remaining cars on both trains in a wave of destruction. Then everything went still. A sudden, unearthly silence, as if the entire world had gone mute.

Until the screams and cries arose.

"In conclusion of our remembrance," General Harding said, his voice strong yet compassionate, "thank you, dear neighbors, for honoring those who died that day. If they could speak to us, I believe they would challenge us to venture on with fresh courage.

To live out our days not shrouded in grief, but in the bold hope that, through the compassion and mercy of our Lord, we *will* see one another again someday."

A wave of subdued amens rose and fell, and Alexandra added one of her own, the determination to start living again steeling inside her. And to live the life *she* chose, not one chosen for her. She'd already taken the first major step in that journey. Now to figure out how to tell her parents about her decision.

Hot and tired, she found herself eager to get back home. Even if she didn't secure the position at Fisk, she wasn't marrying Horace Buford. She would tell them that much at least. And surely she would find someplace else to teach. A school that didn't demand the higher education she didn't have.

But whatever she did, she needed to plan her departure quickly yet carefully. With as volatile a topic as this was, especially for her father, everything could go terribly wrong if she didn't.

"So in the spirit of looking toward the future," Harding continued, "and also in the continuing vein of this city's nationally renowned blood horse lineage, allow me to share with you the most recent addition to Belle Meade Plantation . . . a world-class thoroughbred of which Nashville can be proud. The best three-year-old of 1870, the winner of the Kenner Stakes at Saratoga and the Phoenix Hotel Stakes at Lexington! I give you . . . Enquirer!"

Applause rose as all eyes shifted to the stock car where a tall, muscular Negro man was leading a massive horse down the gangplank. The magnificent bay stallion, standing at least sixteen hands high, snorted and tossed his head as the man coaxed him down to where Sylas Rutledge waited, Uncle Bob beside him.

The two men were conversing like old friends. Then again, Uncle Bob seemed like a friend to everyone he met. He'd certainly always made her feel welcome at Belle Meade.

"Alexandra!" Mary appeared at her side, breathless and face flushed. "You'll never believe what I just heard. And on today of all days!"

Alexandra might've been tempted to smile, if not for her friend's sober expression. "What is it, Mary?"

"It's about Mr. Rutledge, whom we were talking about only awhile ago. The man in your father's office yesterday." Mary grabbed her hand and squeezed hard. "Mr. Rutledge's father was the engineer driving the No. 1 that day, Alex. The train that you and David were on."

Alexandra blinked. She heard the words but couldn't get them to make sense. "That can't be right. His last name is Rutledge, and the engineer's name was Harrison—"

"Kennedy. Yes, I know. Harrison Kennedy was Mr. Rutledge's stepfather. Apparently one of the other bidders was privy to the information and shared it with a friend of mine."

Alexandra found her attention drawn back to Sylas Rutledge, who was still speaking, and even laughing, with Uncle Bob. Harrison Kennedy . . . his stepfather?

"Alexandra, are you all right?"

She heard Mary's voice from far away and nodded, her gaze still riveted. "Yes. I'm fine. But . . . I need to go, Mary. I need to get home."

"Would you like me to come with you? I will."

"No." Alexandra turned, numb inside and suddenly feeling unwell. "I'll be fine. You go see Mr. Jackson. He's waiting for you over there with your father."

Mary looked across the platform and gave her fiancé a brief wave as the crowd pressed closer. "Alex . . . I'm so sorry. But I thought you'd want to know. And I truly don't mind going along with you."

"I prefer to be alone, Mary. But thank you." Alexandra forced a smile. "Let me know if a letter comes for me?"

"I will." Mary hugged her tight. "I'll send it over myself. Take care going home."

Alexandra nodded, and as Mary maneuvered toward her father and fiancé, Alexandra felt herself being carried along by the crowd's momentum as they pressed closer in the direction of the thoroughbred.

How could Sylas Rutledge be here today? How could he be standing here among all these people, knowing what he knew? That his father was responsible for taking all of those lives? For taking David's life? The audacity of it. The disrespect.

It would seem her initial instincts about the man had proven true after all.

Tears in her eyes, she tried to push her way back through the throng toward the street, but it was no use. She'd have to move forward, press off to the side, and then cut back.

She hadn't noticed it before, but stacked crates connected with lumber formed a makeshift paddock around the horse, and a couple of General Harding's stablehands stood nearby as well. Measures to ensure the public's safety, she felt certain, but also the safety of the thoroughbred, which represented a sizable investment.

Makeshift paddock or not, Alexandra had no intention of getting any closer. She'd been around enough stallions to know they were dangerous animals. Handsome, to be sure, with a masculine strength and beauty that lured one in, then could crush a person in a single blow.

Not unlike Mr. Sylas Rutledge.

She looked back and found him looking in her direction. Their eyes connected, and he smiled at her. Then just as quickly, the expression faded. His brow furrowed, and a clear question showed in his features. But Alexandra looked away, and seeing a break in the crowd, she forced her way to the side, scarcely able to breathe for the pain in her chest.

Even when she heard him calling her name behind her, she didn't stop.

Chapter SEVEN

"M iss Jamison!"

Sy called her name again, knowing she'd seen him. But she continued walking. He cut a path between the railcars, Duke trotting close, and easily overtook her before she reached the street.

"Miss Jamison . . ." He fell into step beside her, trying to catch her attention, but she wouldn't look at him. "I was calling you, ma'am. Didn't you hear me?"

She quickened her pace. "Please excuse me, Mr. Rutledge. But I really cannot speak with you right now."

A harshness tightened her voice, similar to the distress he'd seen in her expression moments earlier, and he wondered again if she'd lost someone on Dutchman's Curve. For an abundance of reasons, he hoped not.

"Miss Jamison—" He didn't dare touch her, but did lean in a little in order to see her better. "Would you please slow down and tell me what's wrong?"

She suddenly veered to cross the street.

He hesitated for only a beat, then caught up with her again, Duke shadowing his steps. Sy didn't know what else to say. He only knew that earlier, things seemed to be fine between them, and now they were anything but. And to think he'd been planning on asking her for a favor.

"Miss Jamison, I truly don't wish to be a bother to you, but—"

"You don't wish to be a bother?" She stopped in the middle of the street. "You have the nerve to attend that gathering today knowing what you know." Fire lit her eyes beneath unshed tears. "And yet you say you don't want to be a bother?"

Sy searched her expression and went a little cold inside. "What do you mean . . . I have the nerve?"

A single tear trailed down her cheek before she wiped it away. "Harrison Kennedy. That's what I mean, Mr. Rutledge. That man was your stepfather? The engineer who was driving the No. 1."

Hearing his father's name from her lips felt like a punch to the gut, and Sy briefly bowed his head. How she'd found out, he didn't know. But if she knew, that meant that others likely knew as well.

"Yes, Miss Jamison." His voice was surprisingly even. "Harrison Kennedy was my father. And yes, he was the engineer of the train coming from Memphis that morning. But Harrison Kennedy was one of the finest engineers any railroad in this country has ever employed. There's—"

He stopped himself, not wanting to say too much. Yet he couldn't say nothing.

"Miss Jamison, there's no way that events happened as they say. That's the main reason I've come East. To find out the truth and to clear my father's—"

She took off again and almost walked straight into the path of an oncoming wagon. Sy signaled to the driver in time, and the freighter slowed so they could pass.

"Miss Jamison, at least do me the courtesy of hearing me out before you walk away."

"I don't need to hear anymore, Mr. Rutledge. Especially knowing that you came to see my father yesterday under false pretenses."

"False pretenses? I did no such thing."

She whirled to face him. "You just admitted that the main reason you've come East is to clear your father's name. I didn't hear anything about buying land. I could tell yesterday in the office that you were only there to gain information. You had no intention of enlisting my father's services. Well, I hope you got what you needed, because you'll be getting nothing else from me or from him. And furthermore, the railroad conducted a thorough investigation of that crash, Mr. Rutledge. And while I know it must be very difficult for you to accept, the officials found your stepfather responsible for the collision." Her eyes watered again. "His negligence killed over a hundred people that day and injured many more. People whose lives will"—her voice broke—"never be the same again."

She firmed her jaw, her chin trembling as fresh tears pooled in her eyes. Sy felt the same forming in his own and had to look away. When he looked back, she was still staring at him, a rawness to her pain that cut him down deep.

"I won't delay you further, Miss Jamison. Except to say this . . . Remember, ma'am, that I lost someone that day too. Someone very dear to me. So don't for a moment think that the people who gathered here today are the only ones hurting or the only ones still mourning. Not a day's gone by over the past year that I haven't wished I could speak with my father again. That I wouldn't give everything I own to know for sure what went on in that handful of moments before those two trains collided. But as certain as I'm standing here before you now, I'm going to do my best to find out the truth. No matter what it takes. Good day to you, Miss Jamison."

∽

Her stomach in knots, Alexandra fingered the letter in her hand and knew it was time. She couldn't wait any longer to tell her parents her decision. She'd slept fitfully last night, and a dull ache at the base of her neck throbbed even now.

When the letter arrived during breakfast she'd been alarmed, thinking that Mr. White had sent his response to her home address by mistake. But a closer look at the missive cleared up that misassumption, even as it forced her hand on another issue.

Seated at her dressing table in her bedroom, she still had trouble reconciling that the ornate, rather feminine-looking handwriting on the front of the envelope belonged to Mr. Horace Buford. But it matched the script within. And the romantic declarations the man had expounded upon . . .

She didn't dare read the phrases a second time for fear she'd unintentionally commit them to memory.

She sighed and slipped the letter into the top drawer and ran through her opening argument, as it were, for a second time. Now if she could only deliver it with the same calm and forthrightness she'd displayed moments earlier when she squared off with her dressing mirror.

She massaged her neck and shoulder muscles. It had taken forever to go to sleep last night, the day's events replaying again and again in her mind.

Yes, Miss Jamison. Harrison Kennedy was my father.

Mr. Rutledge's response echoed again in her mind with striking clarity. Not stepfather, but father, he'd said. Which revealed so much.

The pain in his expression . . .

For the past year, she'd not once, in all that time, considered the grief that Harrison Kennedy's family must have been enduring. The guilt and shame, yes. But that they'd lost a husband and father and were grieving his passing? No. And she felt so much smaller a person because of it.

Especially having stared that grief in the eye yesterday. And yet . . .

Sylas Rutledge's mourning and that of his family, sincere and heartbreaking though it was, didn't alter the fact that the fault of the collision had been traced back to his stepfather's negligence. To failing eyesight, the newspaper had recounted. And to the man's misreading the signs on the tracks. Oh, that the cause of the accident had been something more complicated than that.

Every time she thought about it, a wash of futility sluiced

through her. So needless. So preventable. In that vein, she and Mr. Rutledge shared a common desire. She, too, would like to know for absolute certain what happened in those final moments.

Something else occurred to her as well . . .

Hadn't the newspapers also reported that Mr. Kennedy had been a widower, and that his wife had preceded him in death by some years? Which meant that Sylas Rutledge was now without both of his parents. As much as she disagreed with her own father and mother and wished the three of them enjoyed more common ground, she couldn't imagine her world without them.

And yet, that's exactly what she'd spent the last few hours doing. Because she had a good idea of how they would react when she told them her news.

She took the framed picture of David from her dressing table and slipped it into the side of her satchel, then set the satchel and her reticule atop David's trunk, which she'd packed during the night. With a last look around the room, she headed downstairs.

She saw her father working in his office, then found her mother in the sitting room off the kitchen, knitting. "Mother, I'd like to speak with you and Father together, if you have a moment."

Her mother paused midstitch, a pleased smile lighting her face. "Of course, my dear." She hurriedly stuffed the half-finished scarf into her kitting basket. "Was Mr. Buford's letter to your liking? Is he as well-written a man as he is wealthy? And did he say anything about coming over later today? He told your father he might."

Hearing the happy expectation in her mother's questions, Alexandra knew better than to encourage it. She also guessed now why her mother had offered to help her dress that morning and had cinched her corset so tight.

Tiny waist, marry in haste.

Alexandra rolled her eyes at the quippy little rhyme maids whispered when pulling the strings taut. She'd always hated the phrase.

"No, Mother, Mr. Buford didn't mention anything about visiting this evening. And regarding the letter, let's simply say that the man is . . . verbose."

"Verbose." Her mother nodded, a twinkle in her eye. "Perhaps the more words a man needs to use, the more insistent his feelings."

Somehow believing quite the opposite was true, Alexandra led the way to her father's office and knocked on the open door. "Father, may Mother and I join you? I'd like to speak with you both."

Seated at his desk, he gestured for them to enter, the lines of his face appearing deeper than usual. The harsh morning light, no doubt. Alexandra closed the door behind them. Her mother claimed one of the two chairs in front of the desk, and Alexandra sat in the other.

Looking between her parents, she felt as though she were balanced on a ledge and the slightest puff of air would send her tumbling over the side.

"First, I want to say that I appreciate you both more than I've likely demonstrated in recent months. This past year has been a very difficult one, but it's also caused me to reexamine what's most important in life. And how I want to spend mine."

"Contemplation has its place, Alexandra." Her father shifted in his chair, his grimace like a forewarning. "But what's most important are our actions. What is your decision?"

She hesitated. So much for presenting her opening statement. The temperature in the room was warm, and she was grateful for the raised windows. "After much reflection—and prayer," she added hurriedly, "I recognize that Mr. Buford's offer of marriage, and even his letter this morning, demonstrate a very generous and even forgiving nature on his part."

"Indeed," her mother said softly, fragile hope composing her features.

"Especially when considering how I responded to him earlier this week." Sensing her father's growing impatience, Alexandra cleared her throat. "And yet, marriage to Mr. Buford is not a choice I wish to pursue. What I really want to do is to teach. In fact . . ."

Seeing her father's expression harden even as her mother's

began to give way, she hurried to get the words out. "I had an interview for a local teaching position this week. And if it comes to fruition, which I believe it will, I hope to—"

Her father rose so quickly his leather chair slammed into the cherry wood credenza behind him. Her mother jumped, her eyes going wide.

"So this is your carefully thought-out decision, Alexandra?" Restrained anger sharpened her father's tone. "You have the opportunity to wed a man who will take care of you, who will give you a home and children. Who will provide for you so you need never want. And yet after . . . reexamining what's most important in life, you decide to throw all that away." His voice rose. "And for what? To teach. Where, Alexandra? Where will you teach? You have no furtherance of education. At best, you can tutor children. It is a noble task at heart, but not one suitable for a woman of your station and privilege in life."

"But it could be, Father." Alexandra worked to keep her voice soft. "It could be, if I could teach at a school where I'm helping to shape lives for the better, to open new futures. Where I'm a part of something larger than myself. Something that will live beyond me."

He exhaled. "I'll tell you what will live beyond you, Alexandra. Children! And a heritage. That's what—"

A knock sounded at the door.

Already standing, her father crossed the room and opened it. "Yes, Melba, what is it?"

"A letter arrived, Mr. Jamison. For Miss Alexandra."

Heart catapulting to her throat, Alexandra rose to intercept it, but her father took the letter and closed the door. He studied the front of the envelope, then slowly looked up at her, and she was certain she felt the floor shift beneath her feet. Either that or the too-tight corset was getting the best of her.

"'Miss Alexandra Jamison,'" he read slowly. "But it was sent to Belle Meade."

She held out her hand. "Father, please. May I have the letter?"

He walked back to his desk and retrieved the antique letter opener that had belonged to his grandfather, and slit the envelope down the side in one swift motion.

Alexandra drew in a breath, all but feeling the cut, just as she felt the chasm widening between them. "I interviewed at Fisk University this week. For a teaching position in which I'll be instructing new students in their primary education. I haven't been officially awarded the position yet. I'm still waiting for word." Her gaze fell to the letter.

The disbelief in her father's expression was outdone only by that in her mother's.

"It's a salaried position," Alexandra continued, her stomach a tangle of nerves. "Though it doesn't pay much at present, because the school's finances are tenuous. Mr. White, the treasurer and the gentleman with whom I interviewed—"

"Mr. *White?*" A hint of derision edged her father's tone.

She ignored it. "Yes, Mr. White is his name. He's a teacher with the American Missionary Association. He said he doesn't think there's currently room enough in the teachers' barracks for me to live there on campus with everyone else—"

Her mother gave a small gasp.

"—but he's hopeful something will work out very soon."

Anger simmered in her father's features as he unfolded the letter. His gaze moved over the page with a patience that belied the crimson creeping up his neck. Finally he looked up.

"You're telling me that my daughter, a woman born to one of the most privileged and esteemed families in Nashville, is to teach at a freedmen's school?" His voice escalated, and her mother let out a sob.

"Barrett, please. Don't get upset."

He dropped the letter on the desk and turned toward the window. "I told your mother years ago that you were far too independent-minded. Too lacking in respect both for tradition and . . . it would seem . . . for your parents."

"Father, that's not true." Alexandra stepped closer. "I do respect you. Both of you. And I love you dearly. But this is something in which I believe strongly. When David came into my life, he showed me an entirely different way of—"

Her father held up a hand, his attention still focused out the window. "No more of this, Alexandra. David Thompson indulged you in this regard, I know. I did not approve of it then, and I do not now. I believe he did so foolishly and to your detriment. And perhaps to your mother's and my detriment as well, as I fear we soon shall see."

The silence in the room thickened as the grandfather clock ticked off the seconds, and Alexandra looked at the letter again, wishing she knew its contents. But from what her father had said, she gathered she at least had the job.

Her father turned to face her, his demeanor surprisingly calm. "Are you certain this is what you want to do, Alexandra?"

She searched his face, and her heart. "Yes, sir. I am."

"Very well, then. Every choice comes at a cost, and yours is no exception." He walked to the office door and opened it. "Alexandra, if you choose to teach at Fisk University, then you choose to leave your home—and your mother and me—behind."

"Barrett, no!" Her mother rushed to his side. "Don't do this. Please. Not now. Now with all that's—"

He silenced her with a look, then faced Alexandra again.

"Father," she whispered, looking between them. "It doesn't have to be this way. I don't want it to be this way."

"And if you choose *not* to teach at Fisk University, you will marry Mr. Buford at the earliest possible opportunity. Up until which time, you may live here with us. But beyond that, this house will cease to be your home. Along with everything in it."

Alexandra stared, the words harder to hear from him than she'd imagined. "I understand. I have my trunk and satchel packed upstairs."

"And they will remain in this house. As I said, Alexandra . . . you will take nothing with you."

"But, Father, those things belong to me. I need my clothes, my books, what money I've saved to—"

"I've made my decision, Alexandra. And now you must make yours."

He turned and strode into the foyer, her mother trailing. Alexandra quickly grabbed the letter from the desk and followed, starting to object a second time, thinking of everything she'd packed—David's books and papers, his photograph, so many tangible memories. Items she would need. Then she saw the anguish in her mother's expression, and in Melba's, who stood silent in the doorway of the kitchen, and she remembered what Mr. White had said about the sacrifices she would be called to make, and about the challenges she would face.

Only she hadn't expected this particular one.

Once again she wished that David were still here. Perhaps he would have known what to say to ease the moment. Then again, sometimes there simply were no words to bridge the gap or heal the wound. And struggling to find them only made the injury worse.

She hugged her mother tight, then walked to the front door and opened it. A hot summer wind hit her in the face. As she took the front steps to the brick walkway, her gaze dropped to the pots of daisies accenting each rise.

But the pretty little flowers of summer had already wilted in the heat of day.

Chapter EIGHT

*D*ust and dirt swirled around the hem of her skirt as Alexandra strode down the endless stretch of unpaved road leading to Belle Meade Plantation. An almost-six-mile walk from town. Sweat caused her chemise to cling to her front and back, and she licked her dry lips, wondering if she'd ever been so thirsty. And her corset! She could scarcely breathe.

She'd given herself ten minutes to cry. Which had turned into thirty. But that was all she would allow.

She wiped the last remnants of tears from her cheeks and focused on thinking of situations far worse than her own—an exercise Melba had taught her growing up.

But it still didn't lessen the pain of her father's ultimatum, or the manner under which she'd left home.

With her jacket slung over her arm, she spotted a rare bit of shade ahead and decided to rest. The large rock beneath the ancient poplar bid welcome and she sank down, almost as hungry as she was thirsty. She reached for the pocket watch pinned to her shirtwaist. Then remembered . . . She hadn't taken the time to pin it on that morning.

She blew out a breath. Something else she'd left behind.

She took inventory of herself—her dress covered in dust, her boots layered in dirt, strands of hair slipping from the pins, every inch of her dewy with perspiration. But that was only on the outside. Her real weariness lay within.

Fresh emotion threatened, but she stuffed it back down again, mindful of having exhausted her allotment of self-pity. She had much to be grateful for. She had a place to live at Fisk come Monday, and a friend in Mary Harding to turn to until then.

In his letter Mr. White had indeed confirmed her teaching position, for which she was grateful. Yet the other bit of news he'd shared took a chunk of her courage with it.

She withdrew the crinkled stationery from her pocket and attempted to smooth it again. He confirmed that the teaching position paid ninety cents a week, which she was especially glad for. The point of remuneration was far more critical now than it had been only a day ago.

As she scanned the lines, she could hear Mr. White's distinctive New York accent.

Dear Miss Jamison,

It is with utmost pleasure I write to inform you that the board sincerely welcomes you to the faculty at Fisk. As we discussed, we had no instructor for an incoming class of students beginning Tuesday next, so your joining the faculty is well timed. Your talent and knowledge will make it possible for thirty-five precious souls to not only learn their subjects but to grow closer to their Savior.

Alexandra sighed and stared across acre after rolling acre of Harding land. Thirty-five students! And *this* Tuesday! Only four days hence. How did she begin to prepare for that many? And without her books and teaching materials?

The largest group of children she'd tutored was six brothers and sisters, and all but two of them had already known how to read, write, and work their numbers. How would she handle thirty-five unschooled students in one classroom? How would she keep them all still in their seats?

In regard to your living in the teachers' barracks, I believe I have found a solution. A teacher here at Fisk University and my assistant, Miss Ella Sheppard, occupies her own room and has offered to share her quarters with you. All accommodations at Fisk are meager, to be certain. But I hold that you and Miss Sheppard will get along splendidly. You will need to provide your own mattress and bedding, as is customary for our teachers. My apologies, but we do not have the funds to purchase such.

Thank you again, Miss Jamison, for your kind heart and . . .

She scanned the remainder of the letter, the words—and her head—growing a bit hazy in the heat. Where was she going to secure the funds to purchase a mattress and bedding? Much less clothing? Necessities?

She would take all of her meals at Fisk University, so that was something. But still . . .

What did a woman do when she suddenly lost everything? Her home. Her means of support. Especially if she had no one to turn to?

The thoughts were sobering.

How many thousands of women in this city alone had gone through exactly what she was dealing with now? But with no other choices at hand, no friends. No Mary Hardings to come to their aid.

Alexandra glanced both ways down the road, then unbuttoned the top three buttons of her shirtwaist and fanned herself with the letter. She'd worn more comfortable boots today, but her ankles were still a little sore from negotiating the pebbled terrain in heels.

She loosened the laces on each boot and slid her stockinged feet out, feeling instant relief. She recalled Mary stating General Harding's desire to layer this road with macadam and—based on the dirt clinging to the hem of her skirt—she wholeheartedly approved that proposal.

Thirsty and hungry, she knew that resting here wouldn't get

her to Mary's any faster, but the heat was proving more difficult to abide than usual. She hadn't forgotten that General Harding was hosting his formal dinner tonight for the men bidding on his railway. But it was still early enough for her to get there before his guests began to arrive.

She lay back on the rock, wishing for even the softest breeze. Dappled sunlight penetrated the canopy overhead, and she closed her eyes.

Until the clomp of horse hooves brought her head up with a start.

The rider coming toward her at a good clip swam in her vision, his white mount eating up the distance at a pace that sparked her jealousy. She sat up and blinked repeatedly in an attempt to focus. The features of the man's face were shielded by his hat, but his dark duster—

No. It couldn't be.

She squinted, then swiftly looked for a place to hide. But other than behind the tree—or up in its branches—there wasn't one. And judging by the animal's slowing gait, she gathered Sylas Rutledge had already seen her.

Realizing her shirtwaist was still unfastened at the top, Alexandra turned and hastily secured the buttons again, then did her best to shove strands of hair back into place. All while thinking again of his bold insistence of his father's innocence. It set her teeth on edge even as renewed animosity began to build inside her.

"Miss Jamison!"

She turned back as he reined in. He'd shaved since yesterday, she noticed. No more stubbled jawline. An attempt, she assumed, to impress General Harding, and to appear more like a Southern gentleman. She could have told him it was going to take more than a shave to accomplish that.

"Good day, ma'am." He tugged at the brim of his hat. "What brings you all the way out here?"

"Mr. Rutledge." She did her best to appear confident beneath his wary gaze. "I'm on my way to see Miss Harding at Belle Meade."

He looked around. "Afoot? And without benefit of an escort?"

She trailed his gaze, then leveled hers. "As you can clearly see."

He shook his head. "I didn't know Southern women had it in them."

Her resentment ticked up a notch. "I enjoy walking, Mr. Rutledge. I find it invigorating. And I *am* a grown woman. Not some . . . debutante in her first season." As soon as she said it, she regretted it. Because it made her sound older than she was. "I believe I've earned the right to walk from town to Belle Meade on my own, if I so desire."

He leaned forward in the saddle. "I couldn't agree more, Miss Jamison. Still, it'd be my pleasure to offer you a ride."

"I prefer to walk, Mr. Rutledge. But thank you."

He proceeded to dismount.

"What are you doing?"

"Just stretching my legs a little." He looped the reins around a low-hanging limb. "As you said, it's a ways out here."

She eyed him as he removed a flask from the inner pocket of his coat, uncorked the bottle, and took a short swig. Her throat constricted. She licked her dry lips.

"*Mmmm* . . ." He wiped his mouth with the back of his hand and stared out across the countryside. "Beautiful land." He glanced over at her. "You want some?" He held out the flask.

"No." She swallowed, pride answering. "I do not."

"It's awfully hot out here."

She shook her head again. "I'm fine." Her throat felt like parchment.

"How many acres does Harding have?"

"*General* Harding owns close to six thousand acres, Mr. Rutledge. He's one of the wealthiest men in the South. But I would think you would know that since you're striving to do business with him."

He smiled. "'Know your enemy,' huh?"

"I didn't say General Harding was your enemy. But yes, it is wise to know one's opponent as well."

"Or business colleague."

He took another swig, and her throat all but closed for the wanting of whatever was in that bottle.

"Sure you won't have any?" he offered again.

She looked at the bottle, then back at him. And finally nodded.

He handed it to her and—grateful he looked back toward the hills to the west—she thoroughly wiped off the mouth of the flask, then drank. Only a tiny sip at first, to make sure it wasn't liquor. But when the delicious wetness touched her tongue, she tipped the bottle full tilt and drank. The water was sweet and satisfying, and she drank the bottle dry.

"Whoa there!" He covered her hand on the flask and gently urged the bottle from her mouth. "Let's slow down there a—" He turned the bottle upside down. "You drank it all?"

"I'm sorry. I was thirsty." She licked her lips, feeling only mildly guilty, considering who it was.

He smiled. "Yes, I guess you were."

"But I thank you, Mr. Rutledge. It was very . . . satisfying."

"That's one word for it." He slipped the bottle back into his coat pocket. "You sure I can't offer you a ride? Thunder here is awfully gentle."

The horse pawed the ground and snorted, and the timing of Mr. Rutledge's comment with the animal's movement struck her as comical. She smiled, feeling somewhat more refreshed. If not also a bit . . . heady.

"As I said, Mr. Rutledge, I enjoy walking. I find it—" What was the word? It was right there, on the tip of her tongue.

"Invigorating?" he offered.

"Yes! Precisely." She started to stand, then remembered her feet were still relieved of her boots. She reached down to slip them back on when the road did a funny little swirl. She blinked and grabbed hold of the rock.

At the same time, Mr. Rutledge caught hold of her upper arm. "You all right, ma'am?"

Alexandra nodded, then immediately regretted the decision when the road's little swirl turned to a sway. Her breath came short and she braced herself on the rock, wishing again that she could loosen the laces of her blasted corset.

"I think, Mr. Rutledge, that perhaps I *will* accept your offer of a ride. It's quite warm out, and . . . I believe the heat has taken a greater toll on me than I realized."

She tugged at the collar of her shirtwaist, then bent again to tie her boots, and her head swam. His arm came around her shoulders, and she caught the scent of bayberry and rum cologne. *He smells nice,* she thought. *Like bay rum and spice.* Then briefly wondered if she'd spoken the words aloud.

"Miss Jamison, would you like some help lacing those?" He knelt before her, but she waved a hand.

"No, thank you. I can manage."

And she did. Though it seemed to take a great deal longer than usual as the stays in her corset dug into her side. Finally she stood. A breeze, hot but heavenly, hit her face, and suddenly the lure of a cool feather bed held great appeal. She hadn't slept well last night, after all. In part, she remembered, due to this man.

He assisted her onto the horse, no small feat with so large an animal, then swung up behind her.

"Miss Jamison, how long have you been out here?"

She thought for a moment. "An hour. Maybe two."

"And you walked all this way from town?"

"As I said."

"When did you last eat?"

She thought for a moment. "Breakfast."

He made a noise in his throat but said nothing else, which was fine with her. Conversation wasn't the foremost thing on her mind. Rest, however, was.

On the horizon, puffy white clouds floated over the hills like tufts of cotton on a breeze, and as she watched them she found herself growing more relaxed. The rhythmic gait of the horse and the warmth of the sun didn't help. Neither did her lack of sleep in recent days.

Feeling herself leaning back into him, she sat straighter and attempted to put distance between them. But the very act of riding tandem sabotaged that goal.

A haze moved over her, and for just a moment, she gave into it and closed her eyes. Gradually she became aware of a distant humming, a melody she recognized. But from where?

She listened, following its cadence, drinking in the deep resonance. And soon those notes blended with others from her memory, and she could feel the years-gone-by love in Abigail's hands, could see it in her eyes.

You just climb yourself on up into that big ol' cloud of a bed and let Abigail sing you a go-to-sleep song.

The memory, clearer and closer than it had been in years, tugged on her heart even as fatigue coaxed her under, fast and deep.

Chapter NINE

When Sy reached the entrance to Belle Meade he reined in. Miss Jamison was still asleep against his chest, her breathing steady and deep. He gazed down the long tree-lined drive to where a mansion the size of a small mountain sat nicely situated, then prodded Thunder on down the road. He already had the sense that General Harding didn't think too highly of him, and riding up with Attorney Barrett Broderick Jamison's daughter napping on his saddle wasn't going to help that any. But what else could he do?

He peered down at her again.

He hadn't known what to think, coming across her lounging on that rock, face flushed, dirt smudged on her cheeks. And the misaligned buttons on her shirtwaist, as though she'd done it up in a hurry.

She'd said she was thirsty and he guessed she had been. Enough to down nearly an entire flask of Mrs. Taylor's Fancy Cordial, which he'd be hard pressed to admit to anybody that he drank. It wasn't wine so much as it was watered-down blackberry juice gone a mite wild. But it was right tasty and harmless enough, even when enjoyed in excess and on an empty stomach. For most people, anyway.

But as he was quickly learning, Miss Jamison was not most people.

He smiled to himself. "You are something else, woman," he whispered, enjoying the feel of her in his arms while trying not to enjoy it too much.

"What in tarnation?"

Sy glanced back to spot Uncle Bob striding toward him in the same white apron, or one like it, the man had worn before, his face pinched in a frown.

"It's not what it looks like, Uncle Bob." Sy kept his voice soft and indicated for the man to do the same. "I found her on the road heading this direction. She'd walked all that way from town in the heat of the day. Got a little too much sun and then . . . drank a little too much of what was in my flask."

The man scowled. "Which was?"

Sy glanced away. "Mrs. Taylor's Fancy Cordial," he said softly.

"Say again, sir?"

Sy turned back. "Mrs. Taylor's Fancy Cordial. I get it at the mercantile. It's not anything like you might—"

"I know what it is. I even know Missus Taylor. And you ain't tellin' me no fancied-up kinda berry juice did this."

"I give you my word, Uncle Bob. That's what it was."

Miss Jamison stirred, and Sy gestured.

"I best get her on up to the house. I know she's friends with the general's daughter. Miss Harding will know what to do."

"No, no, sir. You can't take her up there. Not slung over your saddle that way, and not with her lookin' like that. I hate to say it, Mr. Rutledge, but the general ain't takin' much of a likin' to you, sir. And you ridin' up with her ain't gonna help your case none." Uncle Bob sighed. "Seems he's favorin' that fella from New York City."

"Harold Gould?"

Uncle Bob nodded. "Somethin' 'bout him I don't like, though."

Sy scoffed. "With good reason."

"Anyway, sir . . . I been knowin' Miss Jamison since she was a girl, and she'll skin you alive if you let all them people see her in this state. No, sir. Don't you know nothin' 'bout women?"

Sy shifted in the saddle. "For your information, yes, I do."

"Uncle Bob . . ." Miss Jamison lifted her head, then groaned and pressed a hand to her temple. "My head is splitting."

"You done got too much sun, Miss Jamison." Uncle Bob spoke up quickly, shooting Sy a look. "You best come over to the cabin, and we'll get you some cool water and a powder for your head."

"Thank you, Uncle Bob, but . . . I think I'd rather go on up to the house. Is Mary home?"

"Yes, ma'am, she is." Uncle Bob glanced at Sy again. "She's helpin' the general entertain the visitors who are already here. I think they's sittin' in the front parlor, ma'am. So they'll see you comin', one and all."

Miss Jamison frowned and ran a hand over her hair. "Perhaps going to the cabin first would be a good idea. To get a powder for the ache in my head."

Sy had to admit, Uncle Bob's instincts had been right.

As soon as they reached the cabin, Miss Jamison drank her fill of water, along with the powder, then excused herself, only to return moments later with her shirtwaist properly buttoned and her color starting to return.

Wordlessly she moved to a shaded spot on the front porch and sank down into a rocker, her eyes closing almost immediately.

Sy paused in the doorway and studied her, trusting she'd begin to feel better soon. He still couldn't account for her being out there on the road like that, though. Even someone who liked to walk didn't walk on days like this. Not that far from town. And certainly not when her family had carriages galore at her disposal.

When he'd first spotted a woman on the side of the road, and then realized who it was, he hadn't been at all certain what kind of reception he'd receive. She'd been upset to learn about his father, and that was putting it mildly, which still made him wonder what personal connection she had to the accident. But at least he'd learned one thing today . . .

Alexandra Jamison thought he "smelled nice." And would be mortified if she knew he'd heard her say it.

With a smile, he grabbed the pail Uncle Bob had shown him and headed out back. He pumped fresh water into the trough, let Thunder drink, then tethered the horse to a nearby post in the shade. After filling another fresh pail he returned, admiring Uncle Bob's home.

The log cabin, rudimentary but well built, consisted of a small two-building structure joined by a dogtrot, with porches that ran along the front and back. According to Uncle Bob, General Harding's father had built the cabin some sixty years earlier after moving his family from the Commonwealth of Virginia. Having glimpsed the mansion on the estate, Sy had trouble picturing the General William Giles Harding he knew being raised in such a modest setting.

Yet he knew enough stories about successful, wealthy businessmen who'd had their start in humble beginnings, and he held the hope that his own story would have a similar ending.

He ducked into the left side of the cabin off the dogtrot, where the scent of brewing coffee greeted him. He spotted a ladder leading up to what he figured was a loft above them. The furnishings were sparse, but comfortable. And most decidedly those of a bachelor.

"Do you have anything she could eat, Uncle Bob? She hasn't taken any food since breakfast."

"Got some jerky in the jar over the stove. Or some cornbread left in the skillet from last night. Miss Alexandra's welcome to either."

Miss Alexandra . . .

Sy made a mental note and chose the latter. Somehow she didn't seem like a jerky kind of gal. He cut a triangle of cornbread from the cast-iron skillet and took it outside, pleased to find her eyes open and her color much improved.

"Feeling better?" He handed her the piece of cornbread and eased down onto the top step.

"Thank you, and . . . yes, I am." She ate the cornbread and drank her water intermittently, looking anywhere but at him.

"I have a favor to ask of you, Miss Jamison. Actually, it's more of a business proposition."

Her chewing slowed.

"I was going to ask you this yesterday, but we got a little . . . sidetracked. As you know, I'm not from here. And contrary to what I expected, I'm having some difficulty navigating the . . . Southern way of things, let's call it. Especially when it comes to business. I saw you work with your father, and I'm betting you know your way around a business meeting and how these Southern gents broker a deal. So I'd greatly appreciate it if you'd consider helping me. Giving me some tips and whatnot. I'd pay you for your work, of course, and don't foresee it taking up too much of your time."

She opened her mouth to respond when Uncle Bob walked from the cabin with two steaming mugs of coffee in his hands.

"Here you go, Miss Alexandra. Mr. Rutledge."

"Thank you, Uncle Bob." She smiled up at him. "I truly appreciate your help."

"Oh, I didn't do nothin' much, Miss Jamison. Just made some coffee, that's all. It was Mr. Rutledge here who toted you halfway from town."

Miss Jamison nodded and met Sy's glance fleetingly.

"Yes. Thank you as well, Mr. Rutledge," she said softly, the inflection in her voice not quite matching her words.

❧

Alexandra wished she could blink and be somewhere— *anywhere*—where Sylas Rutledge was not. *Embarrassed* didn't begin to describe how she felt. She'd managed to excuse herself earlier and had taken one look in the mirror over the washstand— and cringed. Her hair was a tumbling-down mess, her shirtwaist misbuttoned, her cheeks dirt-smeared. She'd cleaned up as well as she could, which wasn't saying much.

What exactly had happened to her, she wasn't sure. The combination of being exhausted and overheated, she guessed. Along with her blasted corset. She'd managed to loosen the ties, so she could finally breathe again. Amazing what a difference oxygen in the lungs made.

"Well, I best get on back to the stables." Uncle Bob grabbed his customary black bowler from a peg by the cabin door and slipped it on his head. "They'll be lookin' for me, I'm sure. Stay here for as long as you need, Miss Jamison. Mr. Rutledge said he'll stay with you."

"I'll consider it a pleasure, ma'am."

Alexandra nodded her thanks, careful not to look in Sylas Rutledge's direction. She *was* grateful to him for his assistance. That wasn't the problem. But every time she looked at him she saw David and was reminded of why he was no longer here.

Uncle Bob paused on the porch steps and looked back. "Miss Alexandra, it's been a whole lotta years since you and Miss Mary played out there beneath that old oak tree with your dolls and such, ma'am. It's been kinda nice havin' you back as my guest."

She smiled. "Thank you, Uncle Bob."

As he walked away, she felt Mr. Rutledge watching her, and the front porch seemed to shrink by half. He was no doubt awaiting a response to his business proposition. A response that—given every moment of her life up until this one—she would have flatly refused.

But considering what had happened that morning and her current financial situation—and that she wouldn't get paid from Fisk until after working two full weeks—she found herself strongly considering it. If she didn't choke on her swallowed pride first.

"So?" he said, looking back at her. "About that business proposition. I realize it's not exactly a—"

"I'll do it." Alexandra took a deep breath. "Under one condition. Or two, actually."

In a flash he stood, reached for a straight-back chair near her rocker, flipped it around, straddled it, and faced her square-on, smiling. The move was decidedly male. And decidedly disarming.

"First, Mr. Rutledge, I won't help you cheat anyone."

His smile faded. "I never cheat, Miss Jamison. And I never lie. If I tell you something, you can take it as truth. However . . ." He leaned forward. "Don't ever try playing poker with me. I don't visit the tables anymore, but I'm still very good at reading people. And weighing the odds. And I can bluff better than anyone you've ever seen."

"You say that as though it's something to be proud of."

"Actually, I believe it is. Holding your cards a little closer to the vest can be quite helpful at times. And is a trait, I wager, you know a little something about yourself, Miss Jamison."

Alexandra worked to keep the surprise from her expression, wondering if he knew more about her than she realized.

"Secondly," she continued, "I prefer that no one else know we have this . . . arrangement between us."

"And why is that?"

"Because while it's innocent, Mr. Rutledge, it's not wholly respectable. For a man to pay a woman in such a manner."

"Why isn't it respectable? You have information and knowledge I need. I have money to pay. It's an equitable exchange. How is that not respectable?"

She shook her head. "Because it goes against the grain of etiquette. The centricity of a gentleman and gentlewoman's association should never be founded upon a monetary exchange."

He paused, then patted his coat pocket. "Hold on, I think I'm going to need to write that one down."

She smiled despite herself and could tell he was pleased that she had.

"Tell you what, Miss Jamison. Why don't we just base our association on . . . friendship. Will that work?"

She looked into his eyes and realized—much to her

unease—that part of her would have liked that very much. If not for Dutchman's Curve. If not for his stepfather and what he'd done.

"Perhaps, Mr. Rutledge, we should simply view our arrangement as what you stated it was a moment earlier. An . . . equitable exchange?"

The light in his countenance dimmed, but he nodded. "Fair enough. So where do we start?"

She blinked. "You want to begin right now?"

"Now's as good a time as any. How about a dime per question answered?" He reached over, pulled a roughhewn table closer to them, and emptied the change from his pants pocket.

She stared at the assortment of coins, growing more uncertain by the second.

"You don't think a dime per question is enough?" he asked.

"I think it's more than fair, Mr. Rutledge. But—"

"Oh, I know what it is." His smile came gradually. "You don't like dealing with the actual exchange of money." Still straddling the chair, he tipped it forward slightly. "All money is, Miss Jamison, is a mode of trade. The way I view it, this money on the table can bring good or it can bring bad. What you get from it all depends on what you do with it."

She thought about that for a moment.

"Do you have a dream, ma'am?"

His question struck a painful chord. "Yes," she said softly. "I do."

"First, does it require risk? Because no dream worth having doesn't."

"Yes, Mr. Rutledge. It does."

"And secondly, does your dream require money?"

She thought of the life she and David had planned together. Then thought about all of his books, his papers, her teaching materials that she'd left behind, then about the lack of funding for Fisk University. "Yes again, Mr. Rutledge. It does."

"Then this money here"—he touched a dime, then a

quarter—"that you're earning in a respectable fashion between the two of us—a most definite gentlewoman and a not-quite-so-gentle man—isn't really just money anymore. It's a step in achieving your dream. And from what little I know of you, Miss Jamison, that dream of yours will end up contributing to other people's dreams. Which, frankly, is the only kind worth pursuing."

Alexandra stared, surprised by his response. And almost convinced. Yet she had to remember that this man wanted something from her and would likely go to great lengths to get it. And that included complimenting her in ways he thought she might want to be complimented. All to win her favor.

"Now, if you're ready, Miss Jamison, I have a couple of questions about tonight. Simple ones, granted. Having lived in Colorado all my life, and spent most of the latter years in mining towns, I haven't attended many Southern soirées. Dinner is being served, I know. But beyond that, what's expected? After-dinner dancing? Gentlemen's poker?" He raised an eyebrow. "Cigars and port in the study?"

"I'm relatively confident there will be no dancing, Mr. Rutledge. So no need to discuss ballroom decorum. And I can promise you there will be no gambling. Fine cigars and aged port, however, are a definite possibility."

"A threat I'll do my best to weather." Humor edged his handsome features. "Next . . . In Colorado, it's acceptable to discuss business at a dinner like this. In fact, it's considered a missed opportunity not to. Am I correct in assuming it's the same here?"

How tempted she was to say yes and be done with it. But her conscience wouldn't let her.

"Discussing business at a dinner like this is allowable within certain confines. It's acceptable as long as it's not a ploy to advance your own agenda. For instance, discussing how your bid is superior to another man's is not advisable. Of course, *any* topic that your host raises is always acceptable. Likewise, any topic he quashes should immediately be dropped."

He nodded. "You're very well spoken, Miss Jamison. And off the cuff, no less."

She merely inclined her head and said, "Thank you." But it crossed her mind to hope the same could be said when she stood before a class at Fisk in four days.

"Last question . . . Alexandra, if I may. We're much more informal out West," he added with a smile. "Is there anything you would suggest I do—or not do—to increase my chances at succeeding with General Harding? After all, one might say I'm more beer and bullocks, whereas the Hardings are champagne and thoroughbreds."

She narrowed her eyes slightly. "First, comparisons aside, I would suggest you present the most competitive bid you can. And second, honor the first condition of our agreement. Which was . . . I will not help you cheat. And cheating," she continued, as he opened his mouth to speak, "includes lending you an unfair advantage due to sharing personal information about General Harding that I may be privy to . . . *Mr. Rutledge*. Remember, sir, you're in Nashville. Where we still hold to proper Southern decorum," she added with a smile of her own.

A gleam entered his eyes. "Sharing that information isn't actually *cheating* in my book, Miss Jamison. It's called doing one's homework. But, fair enough."

A clock from inside the cabin struck four times, marking off the hour, and Alexandra seized the opportunity. She stood, mindful of the dull ache in her head. At least her legs were steady beneath her. "If you'll excuse me, Mr. Rutledge, I need to make my way to the main house."

He rose. "Would you allow me to accompany you there?"

"No, thank you. I can manage. But I am grateful for your help this afternoon. And that you came along when you did. I don't know what came over me. Nothing like that has ever happened to me before." She offered a cordial nod. "Good day to you, Mr. Rutledge."

"Aren't you forgetting something, ma'am?"

She turned back and saw the handful of coins he held out, yet hesitated, thinking of David and their dreams. And the fact that this man represented the loss of all of that. Yet she needed the money. She slipped the coins into her pocket.

"Miss Jamison?"

On the bottom step, she paused for a second time.

"Before you go, I must issue an apology for something." A sheepish look swept his face. "The flask I gave you today . . . It wasn't filled with water."

She stared. "Of course it was. I should know. I drank it."

"You drank it, all right. But it wasn't water."

"What was it then?"

He held up a hand. "You were very thirsty, and understandably so after being out there that long and having walked all that way. Which is probably why you didn't realize."

She climbed the steps to the porch. "If it wasn't water, Mr. Rutledge, what exactly did I drink?"

The look on his face was a mixture of remorse and chagrin. "You drank Mrs. Taylor's Fancy Cordial."

Alexandra stared. "I drank a flask full of wine?"

"It's not really wine. It's more like a fancied-up kind of berry juice."

"That you keep in your flask?"

As soon as she said it, she realized how silly it sounded. And his expression echoed that same thought.

He opened his mouth to say something else, but she held up a hand, remembering how sweet the water had tasted and how lightheaded she'd felt afterward. Which she'd attributed to the heat and fatigue. Then she imagined what might have happened if she'd shown up at the mansion in front of General Harding's guests in that state. She looked away, feeling so foolish. So . . . silly. Something she didn't often feel.

And especially didn't appreciate feeling in front of this man.

"Please, Mr. Rutledge, I'd prefer not to discuss it anymore. Let's simply . . . forget that it ever happened."

He smiled. "Act like something didn't happen when it did. Interesting way of handling it. Is that part of the proper Southern decorum you were telling me about, ma'am?"

Alexandra stared, and slowly realized she couldn't do this. Banter back and forth with him as though Dutchman's Curve had never happened. Besides, this was no way to honor David.

"Upon further reflection, Mr. Rutledge, I believe it would be best if I said, 'Thank you, but no thank you' to your earlier offer. Best wishes to you in your endeavors, sir, and good day."

"Miss Jamison, let's talk about this before you go. Please."

She turned and walked on toward the mansion, grateful when she heard no further argument coming from behind her. She desperately needed money. But considering Sylas Rutledge's connection to Dutchman's Curve, she needed not to be beholden to him even more.

Chapter TEN

A lexandra!" Mary pulled her across the threshold of the back door, her expression aghast. "What happened to you?"

"I'll tell you, but you won't believe it." Alexandra caught a quick glimpse of herself in a mirror over the side table and looked away. Mrs. Taylor's Fancy Cordial? She still wanted to throttle the man. "But I could really use your help."

"I should say you can." Mary smiled, then glanced toward the partially opened front door and pressed a forefinger to her lips. "Father's coming with some of his railroad guests who arrived early. Let's hurry up to my room!"

Following her, Alexandra raced across the entrance hall and up the cantilevered staircase, not at all eager to see Sylas Rutledge again so soon. She'd spotted him riding up the front drive a moment earlier and had made a point not to look in his direction.

They reached Mary's bedroom, and Alexandra collapsed on the half tester bed, still not feeling quite normal.

Mary plopped down beside her. "So tell me what happened!"

Alexandra sighed. "First I need to tell you something else that's far more important. It's about the teaching position I interviewed for."

Mary perked up. "Your letter came this morning, and I sent it right over. You did get it, didn't you?"

"Yes, I did. Thank you. Though it arrived at a most inopportune time. Through no fault of yours," she added quickly. "I was in the middle of telling my parents about my desire to teach."

"I take it your father didn't accept the news well."

Alexandra shook her head. "That's putting it mildly. And this is after what happened the evening before last." She quickly relayed the details about the dinner with Horace Buford.

Mary's grimace said what words couldn't. "Your father wants you to marry Mr. Buford?"

"I know. And yet I do see his perspective, Mary. I'm nearly twenty-six years old. I should be married, with a home and children, as he says. For reasons we both know, that hasn't happened. And I *don't* want it happening with Horace Buford."

Mary shook her head. "So . . . you got the teaching position?"

"Yes, I did." Alexandra smiled at the joy lighting her friend's face.

"Congratulations! But any school would be foolish not to hire you. Which school is it?"

"Well . . ." Alexandra smoothed a hand over the bedcovers. "I'll be teaching here in Nashville. At Fisk University."

Mary blinked, then frowned. "You don't mean the school for freedmen."

"The very one."

For a second time Mary's features dissolved into disbelief. "Fisk University," she repeated, then exhaled. "I can well imagine how your father reacted to that news. Much the same as my own would, I'm sure. Not that I agree with their opinion. You know I'm in support of freedmen's schools. But, Alex, you also know how most of the people in this city feel about Fisk. And about educating freedmen."

"I do. Which is why I packed David's trunk and my satchel last evening. I was relatively certain my father wouldn't allow me to live at home any longer after he knew. What I didn't expect was for him to give me an ultimatum." Alexandra teared up, thinking again about her father's words. "He said I must either agree to marry Mr. Buford or leave. Right then. With nothing."

Mary's face fell. "Not even what you'd packed?"

Alexandra shook her head. "The only place I knew to go was here. To you. So I began walking." She glanced down at her soiled dress. "As you can see."

"Oh, Alexandra." Mary drew her into a hug. "I'm so glad you did come here. But . . ." She pulled back. "What made you want to do this? Not the teaching part. That, I understand. But . . . at Fisk?"

"Ever since David died, Mary, I've . . ."

How to explain this to someone who stood poised on the brink of a fresh new life? One including instantaneous motherhood?

"I've felt an urgency to do something more . . . meaningful with my life. As David was doing with his teaching. I believe I'm capable of it, even if I've never taught before in a formal classroom setting."

She told Mary about happening upon the concert the night before last. "And after hearing about the school needing teachers, I simply felt led to learn more about it. And the doors began to open. Rather hastily, in hindsight."

Mary shook her head. "You really are something, Alexandra Jamison. So when do you start?"

"Tuesday."

"*This* Tuesday?"

"I know. I'm excited—and also scared to death."

"You'll do so well, Alex. I think I've always known that you would take a different and more . . . unconventional path with your life."

Alexandra frowned. "Why would you think that?"

Mary shrugged. "It's simply who you are. You're intelligent, level-headed. You have an inquisitive mind. And you're brave, too, in a way I so admire. You always have been. Even when we were little girls, you were always the first one to climb the tree or jump the ditch. And the way you've helped your father in his practice all these years."

Alexandra looked at her, already missing this relationship and mourning how it would change with Mary's upcoming nuptials.

"So where will you live? Since your father won't allow you to live at home."

"Teachers at Fisk live in the old army barracks." Seeing the doubt in Mary's expression, Alexandra nodded. "I know. The barracks are old and some even border on rotting, but it'll be fine. And actually, there wasn't a spot available there for me. But Mr. White—the man I interviewed with, the school's music director and treasurer—informed me that another teacher is willing to share her room."

"Have you met her yet?"

"No. Her name is Miss Ella Sheppard."

"Of the Samuel Winford Sheppards? From Memphis?"

Alexandra shrugged. "I suppose I'll find out soon enough. But there *is* a question I have for you. A favor, actually. I don't have a place to stay there until next week, so—"

"You don't even have to ask." Mary patted the bed. "You're welcome to stay here. Only *please* don't tell Father where you're teaching while you're here, or we'll both be in a world of trouble. Though I'm sure he'll find out soon enough. News like this seems to travel fast."

Alexandra nodded.

"I still can't believe you walked all the way from town!"

"Well, that's another part of the story. About what happened on my way out here." Alexandra squeezed her eyes tight. "If we weren't such dear friends, I don't think I could tell you."

"Oh my goodness! Now you *have* to!"

Alexandra took a breath. "It was so hot outside, and I was thirsty and tired, not having slept much last night. So I sat down to rest for a while. I fell asleep and then awakened to hear a rider coming. It was one of the men who's bidding for your father's—"

A knock sounded on the door. "Mary?"

Alexandra recognized General Harding's voice.

Mary rolled her eyes. "Don't begin to think you don't have to finish this story, because you do!" She crossed the room and opened the door.

"Hello, Father."

"Mary, I came to make certain you're—" General Harding looked beyond her to Alexandra. "Why, Miss Jamison, I didn't realize you were here." His eyes narrowed. "I hope you're not unwell, my dear?"

Alexandra smoothed the sides of her hair, as if that would make any difference. "Oh, no, sir. I simply became a little overheated on my way out here, so please forgive my appearance. I'm a bit . . . disheveled."

"Am I to understand that you walked all the way from town?"

"Yes, she did," Mary jumped in. "Quite the adventurer, our Miss Jamison. I've asked her to spend the weekend with us, Father. A spur of the moment plan. Mr. and Mrs. Jamison are . . . otherwise engaged this weekend, and Alexandra's going to help me with wedding preparations."

"Well, how kind of you, Miss Jamison. I trust this means you'll be joining us for the soirée this evening? Guests are arriving as we speak, and I would greatly appreciate another lovely young woman at the table to assist in lively conversation."

Alexandra hesitated. At that table was the last place she wanted to be tonight. "Well, sir, I'm not really—"

"Of course she's planning on joining us, Father. She'll wear something of mine. We were about to get ready, in fact. Don't worry. We'll be down shortly."

Mary closed the door and hurried back to plop on the bed again. "You were saying? One of the men who's bidding for Father's railroad project rode up and . . . ?"

Alexandra might have laughed, if not for what attending that dinner meant. She got a sick feeling in the pit of her stomach at the thought of having to face him again. "And then . . . Sylas Rutledge rode up."

Mary's mouth slipped open. "The man whose stepfather—"

Alexandra nodded. "Oh, Mary, it was so . . . frustrating. And then, embarrassing."

"What happened? He didn't act unseemly, did he? Because if he did—"

"No, it was nothing like that. It was . . ." She sighed. "As I said, I was hot and thirsty, and he offered to give me a ride. I said, 'No, thank you.'"

Mary looked at her as though she was daft.

"I know. But seeing him again only made me think of David and the accident. Anyway, he offered me something to drink."

Mary held up a hand. "Is he on his horse at this point? Or off?"

"Why does it matter?"

"I want to have the right image in my head."

Alexandra gave her a look. "He was off. And don't we need to get me cleaned up?"

"Oh! Yes, we do. There's a cloth and soap and water over there on the washstand. You freshen up, and I'll get a dress out of the trunk room for you. But you must continue the story the minute I'm back!"

Alexandra disrobed down to her chemise and began washing. First she scrubbed away every inch of dust and grime, then she took the pins from her hair and pulled a brush through the tangled mess.

"I'm back!" Mary closed the door and held up a gown.

Alexandra stilled. "Oh, Mary . . ."

"It is pretty, isn't it? I wore it not long ago to a gala in New York City."

"I can't wear that. It's far too nice."

"You *will* wear it. But not if you don't finish the story first!"

Alexandra continued, grateful that Mary had brought fresh underthings with her as well. "He offered me something to drink. From a flask."

"Would we expect anything less from such a man?"

As Mary brushed out the dress, Alexandra quickly changed into the fresh underclothes.

"At first I declined. Then I finally took a tiny taste. And it felt so good to my throat and tasted so sweet . . . I drank it all."

Mary's eyes widened as she motioned for Alexandra to sit on the dressing bench before the mirror.

"Wait! It wasn't what you might think 'such a man' would carry in his flask." Alexandra briefly closed her eyes so she wouldn't have to see Mary's smile in the mirror. "It was Mrs. Taylor's Fancy Cordial."

Mary laughed. "Why, that's nothing but sweet wine. And it isn't even that strong."

"It is if you don't have food on your stomach. And you're not already overheated and exhausted."

Mary paused, brush in hand. "You're not telling me that drinking that caused you to be . . . inebriated."

Alexandra grimaced. "Not so much that as . . . considerably lightheaded. Enough to fall asleep as we rode here together."

Mary's laughter rang. "Only you, Alexandra Jamison. Only you."

Alexandra handed her the pins as Mary arranged her hair.

"I feel so foolish, Mary. And I truly do not want to go down there and have to face him again."

"And if there were a way for you not to, I would happily encourage you to stay up here. But with Papa having—"

"No, no. I can't refuse your father. And you're all so kind to let me stay here. Of course I'll take part. But please, let's go down as soon we're ready so we can make sure I'm seated as far away from Sylas Rutledge as possible."

❧

"Good evening, Miss Jamison. I see we're seated next to one another at dinner." Sy read the complete lack of enthusiasm in her expression. "I sneaked a look on an earlier tour of the house."

A pasted-on smile if ever he'd seen one turned her lips.

"What . . . wonderful news, Mr. Rutledge."

He'd nearly choked on his sherry a minute earlier as she descended the staircase. Every eye in the room had turned, even those of the married men. After all, married or not, a man could still admire a beautiful rose.

"You look radiant this evening, ma'am." He tried to keep his gaze from dipping down to her modestly displayed—yet still lovely—*décolletage*. And managed it. Almost.

"Thank you, Mr. Rutledge. And—I beg your pardon—but would you please excuse me? I see someone with whom I need to speak."

"Be my guest, Miss Jamison. We'll have plenty of time to catch up over dinner." He raised his glass while lowering his voice. "To proper Southern decorum, ma'am."

Her smile never dimmed as she walked away, but her blue eyes told the truth of the matter.

He thought of the folded piece of stationery in his pocket. The letter he'd found beneath the rocker on the front porch of the cabin after she'd left. He'd opened it, only to read the first sentence, realize what it was, and swiftly fold it back again. So she was going to teach at Fisk. An interesting and most surprising choice for such a woman.

He looked around, unaccustomed to feeling out of place, but definitely feeling it here.

He had to assume that by now everyone here knew that Harrison Kennedy was his stepfather. Which more than likely meant that no one would say anything about it. To his face, anyway. His main concern was whether Harding knew, and whether that knowledge would influence the man's decision on the railroad project.

Along with a trip to the barber that morning, he'd purchased a new coat, shirt, and trousers. But the wrong style, apparently, based on what all the other men were wearing. But since when did a man's clothes prove what kind of man he was or what kind of railroad he could build?

To his relief, the before-dinner portion of the evening proved brief, which meant the amount of chitchat he had to endure was kept to a minimum. But it did give him an opportunity to scrutinize the competition. And the man heading that pack, according to Uncle Bob, was Harold Gould—who was currently escorting Alexandra Jamison to her seat at the table.

Sy followed and watched as Gould's hand lingered on the small of Miss Jamison's back. The urge to rip a man's arm off didn't come to him all that frequently, but it did now. With a vengeance.

Gould assisted her into her chair, then glanced around the table, apparently looking for the place card with his own name on it.

"Mr. Gould." Sy pointed. "You're seated on the other side of the table. Across from me and Miss Jamison."

Gould glared at him, which considerably eased his urge from a moment before. Sy waited for the ladies, and then his host, to sit, then took his own seat.

He spied the collection of forks and spoons and knives laid out on either side of his plate along with several glasses, and while he wasn't completely unaccustomed to fine dining, he knew he'd have to watch the others to get the lay of the land.

General Harding tapped his glass with a spoon, and all heads turned.

"A formal welcome to Belle Meade to all of our guests," their host announced. "My family and I are grateful to have you in our midst. And now, before dinner is served, would you please bow with me?"

General Harding began praying, and Sy bowed his head, feeling more like a boy of eight than a man of thirty-one. He couldn't remember the last time he'd sat at table with someone who paused to say grace. Including when he ate by himself.

It wasn't that he didn't believe in God. He did. Very much. A man couldn't hang off the side of a mountain by a rope and not somehow get a glimpse of the Almighty, and in that same frightening, exhilarating moment, experience a hankering for a better understanding of him. But once you reached the summit and hiked back down, and the mountain faded into the background, a certain measure of that hankering—or maybe it was the urgency of it—did too, it seemed. Not a fact he was proud of.

Sy tried to focus on Harding's prayer, but Miss Jamison's presence beside him made that difficult. Unlike his eyes, hers were closed, her hands folded neatly in her lap. Not a trace of dirt, dust, or aftereffects of Mrs. Taylor's Fancy Cordial anywhere in sight.

Remembering her as she'd been that afternoon made him smile. Stubborn woman, though. Ending their arrangement as she had. And yet, he enjoyed a challenge.

The prayer ended, and he echoed a belated amen along with the other men.

Conversation ensued around the table, and Miss Jamison practically turned sideways in her chair to engage a Mr. Fike from Boston—one of the five bidders—on her right. But Sy didn't mind. He could be a patient man, when it suited him.

Servants appeared through a doorway toting trays of food. He hoped Harding believed in serving hearty meals at this type of gathering, and not that womanish kind of food he'd seen served in some fancy restaurants in Denver.

Having put small talk off as long as he could, Sy finally turned to his left, to the foot of the table, uncertain what topic he and this particular woman could have in common. "It's Mrs. Jackson, isn't it? General Harding's eldest daughter?"

The woman nodded, a tiny smile coming to her face. "Yes, Mr. Rutledge, it is. And you're the gentleman from Colorado."

He raised an eyebrow. "Does it show?"

She laughed softly. "I actually adore Colorado, sir. I traveled there not long ago. For a time of respite."

"Really? Where'd you visit?"

"The town of Colorado Springs. It's some distance south of Denver. Do you know it?"

"Certainly do. I've been to Colorado Springs many times, ma'am. You ever walk through a place they call Red Rock Corral?"

Her eyes brightened. "Why, yes. I have. You've been there?"

He nodded. "It's a good place to walk and think."

"Indeed it is, sir. They say it's a fitting place for the gods to assemble."

"It's a good place for lying beneath the stars too."

"They somehow seem bigger out there. Don't they, Mr. Rutledge?"

"Climb Pike's Peak, and they'll seem even bigger."

She set down her glass. "You've climbed that mountain?"

"I have. Twice. And crawled it in some places too. There were moments when I thought that mountain was bent on killing me." He laughed.

She laughed along with him, and glanced down the table at her husband, General "Billy" Hicks Jackson. Sy acknowledged the man with a brief nod, then saw a special kind of affection pass between the couple.

He'd heard that General Harding was grooming his son-in-law to take his place on the plantation someday. And Mary Harding was betrothed to General Jackson's brother. They were certainly keeping it in the family.

An older black woman appeared by his side, and Sy nodded his thanks as she set a plate before him. The thick cut of juicy steak nearly hung over the rim, and his mouth watered in response. Belle Meade beef, no doubt. From what he'd seen so far, Belle Meade was as self-sufficient an operation as they came. With its own dairy, blacksmith, quarry, greenhouse, and acres of crops and herds of livestock, General Harding's estate was impressive.

Still, Sy was homesick for Colorado.

A young woman came around serving buttery whipped

potatoes piled high in a china dish, followed by another with green beans—cooked in bacon, smelled like. Sy waited for Mrs. Jackson to begin eating, then followed suit. The steak was tender, and the blade of his knife all but sank right through it.

He listened to the conversations circulating around the table, more than content to take in what bits and pieces of information were helpful, while savoring the meal.

Not once did Miss Jamison turn his way, so apparently intent was she on the descriptions of Boston with which Mr. Fike was regaling her. Regaling a bit too enthusiastically, Sy thought, and with ever increasing volume.

"Mr. Rutledge," Mrs. Jackson said after a moment passed. "Speaking of Red Rock Corral . . . Do you remember seeing a particular rock balanced on its tip, right on the end of a ledge? Where it looks like only God himself could have put it there?"

"I do, ma'am. That's a sight that tends to stay with a person."

"It is, isn't it. My maid and I have picnicked in the shadow of that rock many times. And I've marveled at how it stays perched so precariously near the edge."

"Well, that was mighty brave of you, Mrs. Jackson. Taking your lunch right by it, as you say. I recently heard that rock just slid right off. Took twenty men to get it back up there again."

She stared, shock gripping her expression—until Sy smiled a little. And then she laughed.

"Oh, Mr. Rutledge! You entirely had me believing you!"

"Yes, he's very good at getting people to believe him, Mrs. Jackson," Harold Gould said from across the table. "So you best mind what you take as truth from Sylas Rutledge."

Gould smiled as he said it, as though he were making jest, and Sy responded in kind. But he caught the tip of the blade in Gould's tone. Tempted to respond, he held back.

"Tell me, Miss Jamison," Gould continued, looking across the table, "has your family been in Nashville long?"

"Yes, sir, we have. For quite a long time, actually."

"Miss Jamison is being modest." General Harding wiped the corners of his mouth with his napkin. "The Jamisons are one of Nashville's founding families. And also one of our finest." He raised his wine glass, and everyone else followed suit. "To Nashville's founding families and to the continued prosperity of this fine city for which they sacrificed so much."

"Hear, hear!" Boston's Mr. Fike said more loudly than anyone else. "Fine toast, General. *Fine* toast!" The man drained his wine glass and snapped his fingers for the servant behind him to refill it.

Sy carved another bite of steak, sneaking a look at Harding, who sat at the head of the table. Sy couldn't be certain, but he'd bet that Boston had just been dropped from the running. Because that's what this dinner was about, at least in part. It was a test. Or maybe more like a culling.

He wished again that he'd been able to get more personal information from Miss Jamison that afternoon. Details that would help him navigate his way around General Harding. But she'd shot down that possibility pretty quickly.

Seeing her momentarily freed from Mr. Fike's charms, Sy spoke softly to his right. "From a founding family, Miss Jamison. Quite impressive."

She took a sip from her stemmed water glass. "Not at all, sir. I don't believe a person's lineage should mandate a special recommendation. That should be determined by the person himself."

"So you're saying there's hope for me yet."

She offered a smile. "I'm not certain I'd go that far, Mr. Rutledge."

He grinned as she turned her attention elsewhere. At least she was talking to him.

"Tell me, Mr. Maury . . ." General Harding addressed the bidder from Pennsylvania.

Though Sy didn't look up, he honed in on their exchange.

"You expressed a desire, sir, to provide transport for my thoroughbreds on your railway. I've got an upcoming yearling sale in

Philadelphia. But I'm curious . . . Precisely what type of railcar would you provide for my fine blood horses?"

"Well, General Harding—" Mr. Maury, a hefty beef of a man, cleared his throat. "We have newly constructed cattle cars that I believe would do the job quite nicely, sir. We could get as many as eight horses in each car. Very efficient."

"*Cattle* cars?" General Harding echoed, eyes narrowing. "For my prize-winning thoroughbreds?"

Sy smiled to himself and deposited his fork and knife on the edge of his plate. There went Philadelphia. Two bidders down, two to go. He almost felt sorry for Mr. Maury as the man attempted to claw his way out of the hole he had dug for himself.

"Excuse me, Mr. Rutledge. But is you finished, sir?"

Sy looked up to see a young black man. "Yes, I am. Thank you."

As soon as the man took his plate, he heard a soft clearing of a throat to his right and looked over.

"Problem, Miss Jamison?"

"When one finishes one's meal"—she kept her voice low—"one's fork and knife should be laid parallel on the plate, pointing toward the eleven o'clock position. Not placed haphazardly on the rim. The placement signals to the server that you're finished and that he or she may remove your plate . . . so you don't keep the rest of the table waiting. Consider that lesson complimentary, Mr. Rutledge."

Only then did Sy realize that all other the plates had been cleared away. When he looked back, Miss Jamison had focused her attention across the table, acting as though she was captivated by a conversation about train couplers and air brakes.

He downed the last of his wine, suddenly feeling far less like the successful railroad owner from Colorado and more like the son who'd been abandoned along with his mother in a shanty-town outside Boulder. A young woman stepped forward to refill his glass, but he shook his head.

Hearing Miss Jamison's laughter and resenting her for it—as

he did her decision not to help him—he looked over at her and remembered the letter in his pocket he needed to return.

He leaned toward her. "You're quite the teacher, Miss Jamison. I'm curious, though. Do you plan on using that same tone with your students at Fisk?"

Chapter
ELEVEN

*A*lexandra went cold inside. How did he know about Fisk? Regardless, she read a challenge in Sylas Rutledge's discerning blue eyes and knew her last comment had pushed him too far. But his manner had seemed so smug.

"*Please,*" she whispered. She glanced down the table at Mary, whose heightened expression hinted that perhaps she'd heard him too. "I beg you, Mr. Rutledge, don't say anything else about—"

"Did I hear someone say Fisk?" Mr. Walker, the gentleman bidder from Indiana seated on the other side of the table, looked in her direction. "As in Fisk University? The school for freedmen?"

Alexandra threw Sylas Rutledge a pleading look. A keenness now sharpened his features that told her he hadn't anticipated such a response to his question.

"I've heard a great deal about the Fisk school," Mr. Walker continued, his gaze moving around the table as all other conversation fell away. "From what I've been told, it's quite impressive how well the students are learning. I find it most heartening, considering the Negroes' plight and how they were—"

"*Mr. Walker!*"

General Harding's tone shed its cordiality, and Alexandra winced at the cost this unassuming guest from Indiana was about to pay. And she felt more than a little responsible.

"I do not believe, sir," the general continued, "that the topic of that school is a proper subject for dinner conversation. Especially considering that women are still in our company."

Mr. Walker stared, his expression revealing both surprise and wariness. "But surely, General Harding, with the war being long over and the outcome so profoundly in favor of—"

The general's gaze hardened. "I *said* this is not a suitable topic for the dinner hour, *sir*."

Mr. Walker blinked, looking as though he'd been struck in the face. "My deepest apologies, General Harding. I didn't realize that such a topic was so . . ."

As his voice trailed off, Alexandra prayed—heart in her throat—that the man would let the moment die its terrible, awkward death. And that Sylas Rutledge wouldn't say anything further.

The twitter of birds drifted in through the open windows, contrasting with the sudden, jarring silence until, finally, Selene leaned forward in her chair, her smile overly bright. "I believe it's time for dessert, Father."

"Quite right, daughter." General Harding nodded.

Selene rang the silver bell at her place setting, and servants entered the dining room carrying trays. Even before Alexandra saw what was on the plates, she smelled the mouth-watering blend of homey spices and guessed which dessert Susanna had made for the occasion.

"Your favorite, Miss Jamison," Susanna said softly when setting Alexandra's plate before her, a smile in her voice.

"Yes, it is." Alexandra eyed the generous slice of warm carrot cake slathered in creamy frosting, then looked back up at Belle Meade's head housekeeper and cook. "Thank you, Susanna. It's so kind of you to remember."

Now if only she had an appetite to enjoy the confection.

Mr. Gould, the gentleman from New York who had escorted her to dinner, smiled at her from across the table. He seemed like a nice enough man. Intelligent, well spoken. And most definitely a better fit for doing business with General Harding.

Once dessert and coffee were served, conversation gradually resumed around the table. All except for poor Mr. Walker, who sat silent, the truth of his outcome in the bidding process etched in the bewildered lines of his face. And no matter how Alexandra tried to focus on the exchanges around her, she couldn't. Not with Sylas Rutledge in the room.

As though reading her mind, he leaned close and spoke in a whisper. "To be clear, Miss Jamison, I had no idea what response my question would—"

"So, Mr. Rutledge," she interrupted, aware of Selene watching them, "tell me about your business in Colorado, sir. Mrs. Jackson here has often told me that Colorado is exceptionally beautiful country." She indicated Selene Jackson with a glance.

Sylas Rutledge stared at her, and his eyes narrowed the slightest bit. "Yes, ma'am. Very beautiful country."

Alexandra did her best to look impressed. "How exciting it must be to live there. Precisely what do you do in Colorado, Mr. Rutledge?"

A languid smile tipped his mouth, telling her he knew she was redirecting the conversation.

"Thank you, Miss Jamison, for taking such an interest. I started my first railway out there. It was only a small railway, mind you. From one town to the next." With a glance, he included Selene in the conversation. "But over time the railway proved successful. Then after a while, I started running cattle. For the miners."

"Oh, you're a cattleman." Selene gestured toward the head of the table. "Father will appreciate knowing that."

"Yes, ma'am, I am. And I appreciated the fine cut of meat served tonight. I take it that came from Belle Meade stock?"

Selene nodded. "My father would serve nothing less."

Mr. Rutledge smiled. "Tasted almost as good as what I raise out West."

Selene laughed, and Alexandra joined in as best she could.

She watched Sylas as he tasted his cake, then took another

bite and chewed more slowly. He followed with a sip of coffee, appreciation in his expression.

The ease with which he conversed with Selene was impressive. What was it he'd told her about himself earlier that day? That he was beer and bullocks, and the Hardings were champagne and thoroughbreds. That was certainly true. And though the coat and trousers he wore were not the black tails and tie every other man had known to wear, he still cut a dashing figure. And stood out from among the crowd.

Yet even as charming as he could be, she didn't think he would be the man General Harding would choose to build the rail line to Belle Meade. And once the general found out about the man's stepfather, surely he would send Sylas Rutledge packing.

Which couldn't happen soon enough to suit her.

∽

Scarcely a word from General Harding all evening, which Sy knew didn't bode well for his standing.

He slowly sipped his port and listened, nodding on occasion, as the ill-fated Mr. Walker regaled him, Mr. Fike, Mr. Maury, and Harding's son-in-law, General Jackson, with recent woes regarding railroad hires.

After Mr. Walker's serious miscalculation at dinner, General Harding's opinions on freedmen had been made perfectly clear. Not that Sy planned on backing down if asked directly about the subject. But just as he'd told Miss Jamison that it was wise for a person to hold his cards close to the vest, likewise it would be foolish for him to show Harding his entire hand as it was being dealt.

Best wait until the time came to lay his cards down.

Sy glanced through the open door of the study across the entrance hall to the central parlor, where the ladies had retired following dinner. No doubt Alexandra Jamison was wishing she could wring his neck. An occurrence that might not be all that unpleasant, when he thought about it.

"Why, yes, General Harding. I'm certain I can build your stretch of railroad within a couple of weeks."

Sy glanced across the room to see Gould leaning, hand braced against the mantle, swirling the brandy in his glass as though he were railroad king Cornelius Vanderbilt himself.

"Or even one week," Gould continued, "if your schedule demands it. I have supplies and men standing by simply waiting for my command."

General William Giles Harding regarded him. "That's an aggressive pledge, Mr. Gould. I'm not a man who likes to be disappointed."

"And I'm not a man who ever disappoints, General Harding."

Sy shook his head. Harold Gould was always overpromising and underdelivering. The man was a lying, scheming, overinflated, pompous—

"So you don't agree with that assessment, Mr. Rutledge?"

Sy pulled his attention back to Mr. Walker, who was eyeing him. He had no idea what the man was talking about, but the look of discomfort and even embarrassment on the faces of the other men in the circle proved most intriguing.

"The facts are clear, sir," Mr. Walker continued, "and have been substantiated. There is a slight grade and plenty of curve along that stretch of track outside of town, not to mention a bridge that reduces the line of sight. All of those factors, when combined, mean that stretch of railway is definitely not a track for straight-line speeding. And though both trains were running full out that morning, the engineer of the No. 1 was clearly at fault, as the jury found. How could you not agree with that finding?"

"I'll tell you why he doesn't agree," Gould interrupted, walking toward them. "You're apparently unaware of Mr. Rutledge's close and rather embarrassing connection to the tragedy."

Sy's grip tightened around his glass.

"See here now, Gould." General Jackson cut the man a stern look. "Now is not the time or place to—"

"It's all right, General Jackson." Sy glanced back at Gould, and at General Harding standing beside him. Then he turned to Mr. Walker.

"It would seem, Mr. Walker, that everyone here but you knows that my father, Harrison Kennedy, was the engineer driving the No. 1 that morning. As I'm sure you understand, it *is* most difficult for me to accept the jury's findings. Their rendering is especially challenging in light of the fact that my father was one of the most dedicated and conscientious engineers in the history of the railroads. Not a single blemish on his record, not even a reprimand in nearly forty years of service. But of course"—he forced a smile— "you would expect me, Harrison Kennedy's son, to say that."

To a man, Sy met each of their stares, and to their credit and decency, each looked away. Except for General Harding, who held his gaze, unwavering. And Harold Gould, who feigned compassion.

"It must be hard, Rutledge"—Gould shook his head—"to live with that hanging over your head. And to show your face in public. In this town, especially. I don't think I could do it."

Sy checked his tone. "I'm certain you couldn't, Gould. Because you would've had to have a father like Harrison Kennedy."

The door to the central parlor opened then, and like moths drawn to a flame, every man's gaze trailed in the direction of the women. Sy caught Miss Jamison's eye as she entered the foyer, but she quickly looked away.

Mr. Fike cleared his throat and smoothed a hand down his lapel. "If you'll excuse me, gentlemen, there's a certain young woman I'd like to—"

But Harold Gould had beaten him to it.

"Miss Jamison!" Gould strode ahead into the foyer and offered his arm. "Would you care to take a stroll this fine evening? General Harding has offered to show us all the stallion stable, and I'd be most obliged if you'd allow me to accompany you."

To Sy's frustration, she accepted.

The entire party strolled from the mansion toward the stable, the setting sun sinking over the hills and bathing the estate in a golden glow. The stable ahead was an impressive structure, to be sure. Clearly Harding's blood horses lived a fine life. Better than most people, Sy wagered.

Mr. Maury came alongside him. "I appreciated your response back there, Rutledge. Regardless of my own opinion on the matter."

Sy looked at him. "So you share the prevailing opinion."

"I do, sir. Though I can clearly see how you would not."

Maury's pace slowed and Sy matched it, sensing that the man wanted to say something more. Soon they fell to the back of the party.

"I didn't want to say this back in the study, for obvious reasons, Mr. Rutledge. But I was made privy to the court files on Dutchman's Curve."

Sy paused. "You've read the actual court transcripts?"

Maury nodded. "A colleague of mine was serving on Tennessee's Railway Board at the time. He knew of my interest in railroad safety, and discreetly allowed me to review the documents."

"You wouldn't still happen to have access to them, would you?"

"I don't. I can tell you, though, that considering the testimony I read, there's little doubt in my mind where the fault lay."

"You say 'little.' So in your mind, is there some question?"

"Without the witness of someone who was there at the scene that day, how can we ever know for certain? But based on the evidence in the files, I hold full confidence that the final rendering was accurate. I'm sorry to disappoint, Mr. Rutledge."

"You don't disappoint, Mr. Maury. On the contrary, I appreciate your telling me this. By chance, would you share with me the name of your colleague who let you review the files? With your permission, I'd like to contact him."

"I would, but it won't do you any good. He passed on four months ago. Cancer." He briefly bowed his head. "I wish I could've been more help."

Sy nodded.

"And for what it's worth, Mr. Rutledge, I don't think I stand much of a chance of winning this bid now. But I think you do. And I hope you get it. Anybody but that Gould fellow," he whispered under his breath as they caught up with the others. "Took me awhile to see it, but . . . what a buffoon."

Appreciating the man's vote of confidence, Sy still fought a fresh wave of discouragement. Maury's opinion didn't exactly inspire hope. Yet his gut told him there was truth waiting to be discovered. Or maybe it was his love and gratitude for a man who had changed the course of his life—and his mother's too—that was blinding him to the facts.

Sy watched for an opportunity to speak with Miss Jamison alone, to give her the letter and ask her to reconsider their arrangement. But the woman seemed bent on avoiding him. She had yet to learn how persistent he could be.

He caught a glimpse of Enquirer in a stall not ten feet away. The animal seemed to be faring well and was receiving the bulk of attention from the guests.

"My daughter tells me you're a cattleman, Mr. Rutledge."

Sy turned, surprised to find himself face-to-face with General Harding. "Yes, sir. That's correct. Though my small spread isn't nearly as impressive as what you've established."

"We all have to start somewhere, Mr. Rutledge."

Sy nodded.

"In your bid, Mr. Rutledge, you stated it could take up to six weeks, perhaps even eight, for your company to construct the railway from town to Belle Meade. I realize your bid included laying the macadam road as well, where the others didn't. But even then, I'm curious as to why the longer period of time on the railway. The other bids estimate two to four weeks at most for that portion."

"I've ridden every mile where the railway will be laid on your property, General Harding. And I've walked it too. There are some grade issues in a couple of places, so we're not talking laying track on a straightaway. There's also a stretch about halfway between town and Belle Meade where, if you're willing, we could extend the track about a quarter mile south and build a bridge over the creek. That would give a first-time visitor to Belle Meade a nice view of your deer park. I caught a glimpse of some buffalo there the other day too. I think that's a sight people coming here would enjoy. Kind of sets the stage, so to speak. Of course, it does add to the cost. And to the schedule."

"Yet your plan was moderately priced, Mr. Rutledge. Not the lowest bid, but not the highest either."

"Good to know that, sir." Sy glanced over at Gould, who had Miss Jamison's hand firmly tucked in the crook of his arm. "I hope I can conclude from your comments that I'm still in the running."

Harding smiled. "It's not always the horse with the biggest lead that crosses the finish line first, Mr. Rutledge. He can fall behind and another takes his place."

Prospects boosted, Sy nodded. "Thank you, General Harding."

"Then again"—Harding fingered his long beard thoughtfully—"sometimes that first horse does come back to win, son."

Sy caught a glint of humor in the older man's eyes, yet couldn't quite share it. Talk about a man wanting to hold his cards close.

"Interesting bit of news I got today, Mr. Rutledge, about the Silver Line in Boulder. You did say you own that railroad, is that correct?"

Curious, Sy nodded. "Yes, sir, I do."

"My sources tell me that the Silver Line has quadrupled its track in the past three years. Along with its profit."

"You certainly do your homework, General Harding."

"Any man worth his salt does."

Sy had to agree, and wished Miss Jamison understood that.

"Would you be available next week, Mr. Rutledge, to have lunch with me and a select group of my colleagues? Men influential in the city of Nashville. I'd like to introduce them to you."

"I would, sir. But is this about the railroad?"

"Several of them own stock in the industry, yes. So they'll enjoy meeting you. But this is more about an old man paying a debt forward." Harding smiled. "I was young once. I remember what it's like to struggle to raise capital, to find investors. So if I can help out a younger man who I believe holds great promise, then I believe that's worthy of my time."

"Thank you, sir. I appreciate that."

Harding extended a hand. "We'll speak again soon, Mr. Rutledge. Come ready to share any ideas you may have. And about what happened in the study earlier. Opinions notwithstanding . . ." His grip tightened. "Well done."

As Harding walked away, Sy pondered the exchange, then turned in Alexandra Jamison's direction, more determined than ever to speak with her. She was still flanked by men on either side, and as the party returned to the house, he hung back a bit.

"Mr. Rutledge . . ."

Sy turned and saw Mr. Maury holding out a piece of paper.

"I thought of this a moment ago. It may prove to be nothing, but here's the name of one of the judges my late colleague mentioned as having worked on the trial, along with his address here in Nashville."

Encouraged, Sy read the name on the paper. "Thank you, Mr. Maury. I appreciate this more than you know."

Sy shook the man's hand again. Maury started for his carriage, then paused, his gaze earnest.

"Mr. Rutledge, I hope that if I'm ever accused of having done something beyond the pale—whether I'm guilty or innocent—that my son would stand proudly beside me and still claim me as his father . . . as you did yours tonight."

Sy swallowed hard. "Thank you, sir."

With a quick nod, Maury walked on and didn't look back.

Sy waited until the other guests were in their carriages, then approached Miss Jamison as she and Miss Harding climbed the front steps.

"A quick word, Miss Jamison, if you don't mind."

She reached the front porch and turned. "It's been a long day, Mr. Rutledge. And I promised Miss Harding that I would—"

"Five minutes of your time, ma'am. That's all I require."

Miss Jamison gave him a look that said she doubted that, but Miss Harding offered him a smile.

"It's fine, Alexandra," she said softly. "Take your time."

Liking Miss Harding more by the minute, Sy read displeasure in Miss Jamison's demeanor as she descended the steps.

She stopped a few feet before him. "Yes, Mr. Rutledge?"

He held up a hand. "Please don't say no until you give me the chance to lay out my case."

"Mr. Rutledge, if this is about helping you—"

"General Harding invited me to attend lunch with him and some of his colleagues next week. It's an opportunity that could mean a great deal to my future, and that of my railroad. And as I said, I'm willing to pay you for your time. I simply need some insight into how to negotiate with these men in a manner that will translate well."

Her eyes flickered with an emotion he couldn't define.

"I realize you don't care for me, Miss Jamison. Or at least you don't care to be around me. And I have a good idea as to why. What I don't know is what happened for you at Dutchman's Curve. And I'm not asking you to tell me. But whatever it was, I'm deeply sorry. Not only for your loss then, but for the sorrow you still carry around inside you. That I can see in your eyes even now." He took a step toward her. "I know you hold my father responsible for that . . . horrible morning. I understand. But I don't believe he was responsible for the accident. And as I've told you, I'm working to uncover the truth."

She said nothing. Only stared, her beautiful features carefully composed. Only the sharp rise and fall of her chest revealed the emotion she was struggling to contain.

Sy waited, sensing her pain from where he stood. But seeing

her clenched fists and the firm set of her jaw, he finally nodded. "Well . . . you let me say my piece as I asked, so I'll leave you now. Thank you, Miss Jamison. And good night to you."

He'd taken five or six steps down the brick walkway when she whispered his name. He paused and looked back.

Arms at her side, she was trembling. Though not from cold, he knew.

"You're correct, sir, in saying that I do not care to be in your company." She took a shaky breath. "It's what you represent that makes it so difficult."

He took a step toward her, but she held up a hand.

"You speak of that horrible morning as though you were present. You weren't. You didn't feel that train shudder beneath you like a beast writhing in pain. You didn't hear the scream of steel on steel as the brakes tried to catch but found no purchase. I was on the No. 1 that morning," she whispered, tears falling. "I was riding in the ladies' car in the back, so I lived. But my fiancé, my life . . ." She took a shuddering breath.

"While we were waiting to board in Memphis, he overheard workers talking and learned they couldn't read their contracts. So he chose to ride with them in one of the freedmen's cars, right behind the engine. To help them, so they would know what they would be signing once they got to Nashville. Only . . ." She shook her head. "They never did. Everyone in that car died. Either crushed by metal and steel, or pierced by splintered wood that acted like spears. Or scorched by steam from the locomotive or boilers that ripped open on impact." She took a sharp breath. "So when you say that you understand . . . Please know, sir, that you do not!"

Sy watched as she struggled to catch her breath. He wished he could go to her, comfort her somehow, console her. But he didn't dare move. Her grief held him bound.

How long they stood there, he couldn't say.

Finally she lifted her gaze, and with a single look she laid waste to every thought in his head but one. He had to find out the truth about his father, not only for his father's sake, to clear his good name, but for this woman. For Alexandra Jamison and the love in her heart for a man who was gone. A love Sy envied more than he would've thought possible, even as he realized it was a treasure out of reach.

He tried to think of something to say, but "I'm sorry" seemed too feeble and frail for the weight of the moment. She wiped her face, and he was certain she was about to excuse herself and go back inside when she sought his gaze.

"I will help you, Mr. Rutledge, as you've requested. But only if you agree to a third condition."

He waited.

"Whatever you learn about Dutchman's Curve, about the trial, about the evidence . . . you must share with me. No matter if it exonerates your father of his guilt or if it condemns him. You'll hide nothing. Because I, too, want to know what happened on that train. Do we have a deal, Mr. Rutledge?"

Sy nodded. "Yes, Miss Jamison. We do."

"Very well then. Good night, Mr. Rutledge."

Chapter
TWELVE

Granger Mercantile was busy for a Monday morning, but Alexandra managed to find the handful of personal items she needed, as well as sheets and a pillowcase. She looked, but didn't see either a blanket or the ticking she needed to sew a mattress. Perhaps they kept those in the back.

A queue was forming at the front counter so she joined it, awaiting her turn. Mary's generous gifts of toiletries and clothing had minimized the list of what she needed to purchase. Which was good, considering her finances. Mary had also insisted on sending the satchel containing those items on ahead to Fisk, and Alexandra was grateful now that she had. Carrying all of this, in addition to the satchel, across town would have proven a challenge.

She took the coins from her pocket and discreetly counted them again. She had enough for everything in her basket thus far, with a little to spare. So depending on the cost of the ticking and the blanket, she should have enough.

It wasn't until she emptied the coins from her dress pocket late Saturday night that she'd realized Sylas Rutledge had overpaid her by at least twenty-five cents. But considering what the man had put her through at Saturday night's dinner . . .

And then their private exchange out in front of the mansion afterward. His look of shock when she'd told him about being on the train, and about David, still resonated inside her. She hadn't planned on telling him. Nor had she intended to offer to help him again. But how many times in the past year had she longed to know more about what led up to that fateful moment?

She wanted to know the full truth. If, indeed, there was more to be known.

But what had tipped her decision was what Mary had told her about Mr. Gould. Apparently the man had challenged Mr. Rutledge about his stepfather, and in front of all the other men, no less. A tasteless decision on Gould's part. But it was Sylas Rutledge's response that had left the lasting impression.

"My brother-in-law told Selene the exchange could have gotten quite heated," Mary had whispered in the stable, "but for Mr. Rutledge's show of restraint. He handled himself with the utmost decorum. And even in the face of the accusations laid upon Harrison Kennedy, Mr. Rutledge defended him, as an engineer and as a father."

Alexandra stared at the coins in her palm. Such steadfast devotion from a son to a father. To so publicly stand by a relationship even when the person one loves has made a grave and costly mistake. Or perhaps made a decision one doesn't agree with.

Had her father regretted his decision at all in recent days? But she already knew the answer to that question.

"May I help you, miss?"

Alexandra looked up to see a woman staring expectantly at her from behind the counter. "Oh, yes, thank you." She stepped up and placed her purchases on the counter. "Along with these items, I need ticking for a single bed. And also a pillow. Down, if it's not too expensive."

"Down pillows are a special order. Takes two to three weeks. We got bags of feathers, or you can visit the livery and buy fresh hay."

Hay didn't sound at all appealing. "Two bags, please. And I need a light blanket as well."

"Only got one kind of blanket without special ordering." The clerk thumped the catalog.

"Whatever you have in stock will work nicely, I'm certain." Alexandra heard a heavy sigh behind her and turned to offer an apology when she spotted Sylas Rutledge standing near the back of the line. She hurriedly faced the front. But not soon enough.

Recognition flashed in his features, and he smiled and tugged the brim of his hat. She nodded politely, then turned back around, hoping he would take the subtle hint.

The clerk returned and hefted two large sacks up to the counter. "You're getting the last two bags of feathers, miss. And here's your ticking. You got needle and thread to sew the tick?"

Alexandra didn't, but she hated to admit it. Yet she needed both. She shook her head, and the clerk frowned and trudged back to the storeroom. From close behind her, Alexandra heard another exasperated sigh. Yet she didn't dare look around.

A moment later the clerk returned with a package of needles and a spool of thread and set to working the figures. "That'll be . . . one dollar and forty-six cents."

So much? Alexandra quickly reviewed the cost of each item, then gently nudged the blanket aside, smiling to cover her unease.

"I believe I'll wait and get this later. Fall isn't quite upon us yet." But she was still thirty-seven cents short. And everything else, she needed. "Here you are." She laid her coins on the counter. "I'd like to put the remainder on my account."

"What name is the account under?" The woman reached for a ledger.

"Alexandra Jamison. But I don't have an account yet. I need to open one."

"Oh, we can't do that today, miss. The man who does them is out sick. You'll have to come back tomorrow."

"But . . . I need these things today."

"Then you need to come up with another thirty-seven cents."

Feeling the prickle of other patrons' stares, Alexandra leaned forward, keeping her voice low. "Which I don't have right now, I'm so sorry."

"Which means," the clerk said in full voice, "you need to step aside and let me help these other people who've been waiting."

Her face heating, Alexandra set the bottle of hair soap aside. "There. That should do it."

The clerk looked at her. "Still sixteen cents short."

Flustered, Alexandra turned the receipt around in order to read the individual prices, but the numbers blurred in her vision.

With a sweep of an arm, the clerk moved her items to the side. "Why don't you come back later, miss, when you—"

"Miss Jamison . . ."

Alexandra recognized the voice from behind.

"I'm sorry, I didn't realize you were already checking out." Mr. Rutledge laid aside a bottle of saddle polish and pulled his wallet from his coat pocket. He withdrew a wad of bills and placed a dollar on the counter, then added the blanket and bottle of hair soap back to the pile. "If you'll tally all this, please, ma'am. That'd be appreciated."

"Why, of course, sir." The clerk's demeanor altered instantly. "Would you like everything wrapped as well?"

"Yes, we would. Thank you."

"Very good, sir." The clerk returned Mr. Rutledge's change and set to work wrapping.

Meanwhile, Alexandra wished the floor would open and swallow her whole. "Thank you," she said softly.

"No need to thank me," he whispered. "I'm glad we ran into each other."

The clerk returned. "Here's your first box, miss. I'm wrapping the second now."

"If you don't mind, Miss Jamison—" Mr. Rutledge glanced behind them. "I'll get the packages if you'll check on Duke. He's been waiting out front for a while now."

Grateful to have an excuse to leave, Alexandra made a beeline for the door, careful not to look at any of the other patrons in line.

Outside, she shielded her eyes from the sun and looked for

the foxhound. She spotted him lazing beneath a tree across the street. His head came up as she approached, then his tail swiftly engaged as well.

She knelt, mindful of Mary's borrowed reticule hanging from her wrist. "Hello, Duke. It's nice to finally meet you." In the absence of his master, she petted the animal without fear of reprimand.

The dog gave a doleful whine, as if trying to tell her something, its gentle brown eyes silently imploring. Alexandra smiled and nuzzled the dog's head.

"Thank you for commiserating, Duke. It *was* a most humbling experience in there. Even if what your master did was kindly meant."

The dog's ears suddenly perked up, and Alexandra glanced behind her to see Sylas Rutledge exiting the mercantile.

She gave the pooch one last pat and rose.

"Here you go, Miss Jamison." Mr. Rutledge set the bags of feathers and a second, larger box tied with string at her feet. "All wrapped up and ready to travel. And before you say anything, there are worse things than being caught short of cash. Besides, I look at this as a down payment on what I'm going to owe you anyway. For the . . . tutoring, let's call it. So really, the way I see it, you've saved us both some time."

Still feeling foolish, Alexandra realized he had a point, even if her pride didn't like it. She glanced down at Duke. "Mr. Rutledge, your dog and I have not been properly introduced."

"Beg your pardon, ma'am. Miss Jamison, meet Sir Duke Rutledge Kennedy, my faithful companion for going on nine years now. And, Duke, meet Miss Alexandra Jamison." The dog wagged his tail as if on cue. "I found him when he was just a hungry pup wandering the alleys of a mining camp, so I took him in. We've been inseparable ever since."

Not missing the dog's last name, she smiled. "He's a handsome companion. And loyal, it would appear."

"To a fault." His gaze settled on the foxhound. "Everybody

in this life will eventually let you down, Miss Jamison. That's a truth you can count on. But not a dog. Dogs love you even more than they love themselves, it seems. And without their saying a word, you can read everything they're feeling just by looking in their eyes."

Alexandra stared. "Why, Mr. Rutledge. You're a romantic."

He laughed. "Only about dogs, ma'am. And maybe trains." He removed his hat and ran a hand through his hair. "I don't know how you Southerners abide this heat. It sure gets to a man after a while. I'm missing the cool of the mountains about now."

"It's cool there even in the summer?"

"Sure is. Not on the plains so much. But even then, come nighttime, there's always a breeze to settle things down. You open your windows and let in the cool at night." A satisfied look came over him. "You ever been West?"

"I've been to Memphis."

He laughed, and too late she realized how silly that sounded. Yet the humor warming his gaze said his laughter hadn't been meant at her expense.

Dappled sunlight slanted through the tree and accentuated the subtle laugh lines at the corners of his eyes and mouth, and she was certain she caught the familiar scent of bayberry and spice mixed with sunshine and leather.

He hadn't shaved that morning—hardly a surprise—and standing this close to him, she saw traces of silver at his temples.

"Well . . ." She smoothed a hand over her skirt. "I need to be on my way. Thank you again for—"

"Miss Jamison . . ." He studied her for a moment. "May I please call you Alexandra? I believe we've reached a place of familiarity with one another to sustain such informality. And to satisfy even the most staunch revelers in proper Southern decorum."

Hearing the gentle teasing in his voice, she nodded. "I agree . . . Sylas. And yes, you may."

"Actually, I prefer Sy, if you would."

"Sy, then."

"And while I'm thinking of it . . ." He pulled a folded piece of paper from his shirt pocket. "I found this after you left the cabin the other day. I opened it to see what it was, but only read the first sentence before stopping."

She nodded, glancing at Mr. White's letter. "I hadn't even missed it, but I would have, eventually. Thank you for returning it. This explains how you knew about Fisk."

He nodded. "And about what happened at dinner Saturday—"

She shook her head. "I could tell by your expression you had no idea what kind of ire your comment would draw."

"That's for sure."

Movement beyond him drew her attention, and Alexandra peered down to the end of the street—and saw her mother standing near the corner. Their eyes met. Alexandra knew her mother had seen her by the subtle tilt of her head. Instinctively Alexandra waved, and thought she saw her mother's arm move— but then she quickly looked away and walked on without further acknowledgement.

Alexandra slowly lowered her hand.

Sy, who'd turned around and followed her gaze, looked back at her. "Someone you know?"

She swallowed the hurt aching at the back of her throat. "Yes," she whispered. "My mother."

Uncomfortable beneath his gaze, Alexandra reached down and picked up the bags of feathers, eager to take her leave. "In light of your meeting with General Harding later this week, Sy, and my need to repay my debt, would you like to schedule our next lesson?"

He nodded, graciously accepted the obvious bait. "Yes, I would. How about tomorrow evening?"

She thought quickly. "I believe that will work. I would imagine there's a place where we could meet at Fisk. If that's convenient for you?"

He nodded again.

"Let's say, after dinner? Around seven o'clock? When you arrive, simply ask someone to direct you to the teachers' barracks. I'll be waiting out front."

"Sounds good. And, Alexandra?"

She looked back, purchases in hand and heavier than she'd anticipated.

"About what we discussed the other night . . ." His gaze never wavered. "I'm deeply sorry for what you went through that morning. And for your loss."

Unable to speak, she gave a quick nod and started in the direction of Fisk, emotion knotting in her chest even as her heart somehow felt inexplicably lighter.

Chapter THIRTEEN

*I*t wasn't as he'd imagined it would be, this stretch of track known as Dutchman's Curve. Sy stood at the edge of the cornfield, Duke quiet at his heels, and looked out over the countryside.

So still, so serene, compared to the mental picture of this place etched in his mind. A scene stitched together from reporters' descriptions in newspaper clippings that would never be pried from his memory. Horrible moments his father had lived through, however briefly.

> The impact propelled both steam locomotives off the track. Engines went airborne, straight up, before slamming mercilessly back to the earth. Bodies thrown like rag dolls, smashing into glass, steel, wood, and dirt. Passenger cars telescoped one into the other. Body parts strewn across the blackened cornfield. Blood running down the aisle of passenger cars like water pouring from a pipe.

He swallowed, the images, raw and real, appearing before his eyes with excruciating clarity even as they blurred in his vision.

He glanced back behind him, noting again how—at the curve in the track just before the bridge—he could see only a few feet down the railway. A train traveling at any speed on that curve, much less full out at fifty to sixty miles an hour, would be careening through a blind spot. How had his father reacted when he'd looked up and seen the other engine bearing down hard, coming straight for him. *If* he'd even seen it. There would have been no time to react, at least not in a way that would've made any difference in the outcome.

Sy took a deep breath, then exhaled slowly as he walked along the track, feeling a closeness with his father he hadn't felt since receiving the telegram almost a year ago.

What was it about visiting the place where a loved one died that somehow made you feel more connected to the person? Maybe you were looking at the same piece of sky he last looked at, or the same rolling hills rising in the distance. The very air around him seemed different, as though the breath he just drew might have passed through his father's lungs in that final moment.

Sy shook his head and gave Duke's neck a rub. His imagination was running away with him, and he was grateful no one else could hear his thoughts.

Looking back, he was grateful his father had made the trip out to see him after the Transcontinental Railroad was completed in '69. What a good time they'd had. He only hoped his father had realized how much he appreciated his daring to love an outcast woman and her little boy with a strength that changed the course of both their lives.

Sy swiped at his eyes, a heaviness inside him that seemed tied to something more than just this moment and this place.

He paused beside the familiar ribbons of steel and listened to the rustle of the wind through the cornfields, to the distant ringing of a church bell, and to his father's honor that seemed to call out from the grave. And woven through them all, he heard the distant but familiar lyrics . . .

Brightly beams our Father's mercy, from his lighthouse evermore.

*But to us he gives the keeping of the lights along the
shore.*

Surprising, how easily the words to a song his father had loved
returned to him. "I'll see your name cleared, Pa," he said aloud.
"And I'll make sure everyone knows that—"

"Who you talkin' to there, son?"

Sy jumped and turned, his hand going to his gun belt.

"*Whoa*, whoa there, young'un!" The gnarled-looking codger
stopped dead in his tracks and lifted shaky hands in the air, looking from Sy to Duke then back again. "Don't go shootin' a fella just
for bein' neighborly."

Sy relaxed, and Duke wagged his tail.

"Best not sneak up on a man that way, mister," Sy said. "Good
way to get yourself killed."

"Lucky for me you ain't foolhardy with that snapper on your
hip."

Sy smiled. "Lucky for us both. Killing you would've put a
damper on my day."

The man let out a high-pitched laugh, and Sy took a closer
look, wondering if the old guy wasn't a bit touched in the head.
Duke wandered over and sniffed at the man's raggedy pant legs.
The fellow bent to pet him, though judging by his grimace, the
effort cost him.

"You a good dog, ain't ya there, boy. Ain't got nothin' for ya to
eat, though, so don't go sniffin' around too personal like."

Sy glanced up and down the tracks, wondering where the
man had come from. The woods, most likely. A drifter, to be
sure. The presence of a train always seemed to draw that type.
The lonesomeness of it, maybe. Or the thirst of a wanderlust spirit
searching for peace.

Sy shook his head, remembering what Alexandra had said
earlier about his being a romantic. He'd never thought of himself
in that light before.

Thinking of her stirred the heaviness inside him, a sense of regret he couldn't seem to shake. She'd been on the train that day. Had she seen his father as she boarded? And her fiancé. What kind of man had he been? Worthy of her affections, no doubt, judging by the way she spoke of him.

He would see her again tomorrow night. But Dutchman's Curve was hardly a subject to be broached easily.

"Lose someone out here, did ya?" the man asked, peering up through rheumy eyes. "Most folks who come out here stand like that, lookin' 'cross the cornfield . . . That's their story. 'Tis yours too, son?"

Sy took a minute to answer, then nodded. "Lost my father here."

The man's brow furrowed even more. "The Great Cornfield Meet."

"Beg pardon?"

"That's what folks 'round here took to callin' it. That mornin' when them two trains met like thunder. Right about where you're standin'." The man pointed.

"You were here that day?"

"Oh, yes, sir. Saw it all. Still do when I close my eyes too long. The sounds, they all come back. The voices too."

"The voices?" Again Sy looked at him with uncertainty.

"Can't seem to quiet 'em most nights. The cryin', awfulest sound you ever heard. Worst thing was them little ones laid out in the dirt, not makin' a peep no more. Their Sunday-best clothes all bloody and soaked."

Sy winced, the man's descriptions prodding his imagination in directions he preferred it not go.

"But it was them angels," the man whispered, his watery eyes narrowing. "Hundreds of 'em, just walkin' about. That was the real sight. Fiercesome lookin' things too. I's right scared at first, I'm not afeared to say. 'Til I figured out what they was and settled in to watch."

Sy nodded slowly, certain now of what he'd only guessed before. "So you watched angels that day, did you, sir?"

The man nodded. "Most every one of them bodies laid out that day had one standin' over 'em. Even the colored folk!"

Sy smiled at how the man's eyes widened in disbelief. Then he suddenly turned and looked back over his shoulder as though he heard someone calling him.

Sy felt a bit of a prickle on the back of his neck.

When the man turned back, his gaze fixed on Sy. "I hope ya find your peace, son." Sadness filtered across his face. "Though I'm thinkin' ya ain't gonna find it here. But you'll find it soon enough."

A slow smile pushed aside the sadness and revealed even fewer teeth in his mouth than Sy had imagined at first glance.

"Yes, sir." The old man winked. "You'll find it . . . if you look hard enough. And in the right place!" He reached down and rubbed Duke's head again, then turned to go.

Resisting the urge at first, Sy finally gave into it and reached into his shirt pocket. "Hey, old-timer!"

The man paused.

Sy pressed some coins into his palm. "Get yourself something good to eat in town. But no liquor, you hear me?" He bent down a little to make sure the man saw his eyes. "You need to promise me."

That toothy grin again as he accepted the money. "I ain't had me a drink in two years, son."

Sy nodded, not believing it for a second. But he knew from watching too many of the miners what a troublesome road that was to travel. The man headed for the woods some distance away, and Sy snapped his fingers at Duke. The dog fell in step beside him, and they walked the short distance together to the bridge.

When Sy neared the curve in the tracks, he turned back in case the man had done the same, and he readied a wave.

But the field was empty. The man was gone.

"Thank you again, Mrs. Chastain." Alexandra wiped her forehead with the back of her hand. She'd had her fill of the summer heat, same as Sy. "I so appreciate your help."

"It's no trouble at all, Miss Jamison." Mr. White's administrative secretary gestured toward the barracks where Alexandra would live. "I'm sorry to have to leave you, but I need to prepare for a meeting this afternoon. And please don't fret for one more minute about tomorrow. You're far more prepared than you think you are. Remember, most of your students have never even set foot in a classroom. You'll do splendidly, I'm certain. Mr. White and President Spence believe the same."

"Thank you." Alexandra drew strength from the kind words as she climbed the stairs to the teachers' barracks, her bundle from the mercantile in one hand, cloth sack in the other. And tucked beneath her arm a thin folder containing Fisk University's rules that she was to "thoroughly digest" before her first class tomorrow morning at eight o'clock.

Hungry and tired, she set down the sack and opened the door to the barracks. An odor similar to that which had welcomed her the first day she'd visited Fisk greeted her when she stepped inside. She guessed one grew accustomed to it.

A shadowed hallway stretched before her, doors appointed on either side, some open, some closed. Mrs. Chastain had said her fellow teachers would be in class this time of day, but Alexandra didn't mind. She hoped for time to freshen up before meeting her colleagues.

Mary had wondered whether the teacher who'd offered to share her sleeping quarters was of the Samuel Winford Sheppards of Memphis. Alexandra figured she would find out soon enough. How nice it would be if it turned out she already knew a little about the woman generously sharing her room.

One foot in front of the other, she told herself, until she reached the last room on the right, per Mrs. Chastain's instructions. Alexandra pushed open the partially closed door and spotted a young Negro woman—a slender little rail of a thing—sweeping the floor beneath the wooden skeleton of an old hospital cot on the far wall. A soldier's blanket provided the rug for the room, a remnant bequeathed from a former tenant of the camp, no doubt. Such Spartan-like austerity described every corner of this school.

Not wishing to startle the woman, Alexandra gently cleared her throat. The young woman turned, and her face lit up.

"You must be Miss Jamison!" She set aside the broom and dusted off her hands.

"Yes, I am." Alexandra set down the bundle of bedding. The sacks of feathers had proven far heavier than she'd imagined feathers to be, after lugging them all the way across town. "Thank you for cleaning beneath my cot. I appreciate that."

"I'm happy to do it. And it needed it!" She smiled. "I think it's wonderful that you've decided to teach here."

Alexandra attempted a confident smile and thought again of the Fisk students she'd heard at the concert and how well-spoken they were. Same as this woman. "I hope I'm able to do some good."

"Oh, there's no doubt about that, I'm sure."

Alexandra pointed to the twined bundle on the floor. "I've brought all my bedding. You should find everything you need in here to make up the cot. But"—she winced playfully—"I'm afraid I'm arriving with my mattress not yet sewn. I don't suppose you're any more handy with a needle and thread than I am, are you?"

The young woman held her gaze, then gradually, unmistakably, the friendliness in her countenance drained away. "You're asking me to sew the tick for your bedding?"

Alexandra offered a conciliatory smile, suddenly feeling as though she'd asked something she shouldn't have. "Well, if it's not too much of an imposition. I assumed you might—"

"You assumed that since you saw me sweeping beneath your cot, that I must be the chambermaid."

Alexandra blinked, looking into eyes that were a striking gray color. And a stormy gray, at that. She felt the unnerving prickle of comprehension moving through her, and she swallowed.

"You're . . . Miss Ella Sheppard," she managed, the weight of her mistake bearing down hard. "A teacher here and . . . Mr. White's assistant."

"Yes, Miss Jamison, I am. And I'm sorry to be the one to inform you, but there are no chambermaids here at Fisk University. If you pee in a pot, you empty it. Same for anything else you choose to do in it. This isn't the Clarendon Hotel."

"No! No, of course not. I'm so sorry, Miss Sheppard. I simply walked in and saw you . . ." Alexandra fought to find the words to rectify her mistake, but there weren't any. Because no matter what she thought of to say or how she might explain her request away, she knew it was useless. The young woman had every right to be upset.

The sting of embarrassment rose to her eyes, and Alexandra fought the urge to turn and run. Yet something held her there, as surely as if her boots were nailed to the plank wood floor.

"Please, Miss Sheppard." Alexandra steadied her voice. "I made a very wrong and . . . ignorant assumption. And I offer you my sincere apology."

Alexandra waited, breath held, heart pounding. But Miss Sheppard didn't move, didn't bat an eye. If not for the voices drifting in through an open window somewhere, Alexandra might have thought that time had frozen. Then . . .

Miss Sheppard smiled. Only the tiniest bit. Scarcely even enough to qualify as a smile. But Alexandra clung to its possibility.

"It was the broom, wasn't it, Miss Jamison?" Miss Sheppard whispered, leaning in, giving Alexandra a look she didn't completely follow.

Yet she was terrified to say anything else for fear of offending the young woman further.

"It was the broom I was holding," Miss Sheppard repeated, a sparkle showing in her lovely gray eyes. "Not the color of my skin that caused you to think I was the chambermaid. Isn't that right?"

Watching the way the young woman's lips slowly tipped up at the corners, Alexandra suddenly recognized the olive branch the woman was extending to her, and she grabbed it for all she was worth, even as the gentle grace the woman offered her shined a light on hidden places in her own heart that still desperately needed grace applied.

"*Yes*," Alexandra whispered, her voice strained, her teary eyes revealing the real truth. "It was the broom, Miss Sheppard. It was the broom." She took a deep breath. "And . . . *thank you*, most sincerely, for sweeping beneath my cot."

Later that evening, back in the bedroom, Alexandra grabbed the needle and thread and set to finishing her mattress. Miss Sheppard had escorted her to dinner and introduced her to the other teachers. All of them much older, as Mr. White had said. And all from the North.

She thought again of the assumption she'd made about Miss Sheppard that afternoon and felt queasy. And already the bland and watered-down vegetable soup—at least that's what Ella Sheppard said she thought it was—wasn't settling too well. According to teachers and students alike, this was the typical aftereffect of most of their meals at Fisk.

Even so, Alexandra still felt a pinch of hunger.

She set down her sewing and retrieved the cloth sack, recalling the soda crackers she'd purchased at the mercantile that morning. Or rather, that she'd *attempted* to purchase at the mercantile.

Sylas had actually done the purchasing.

Her hand closed around the crackers and she pulled them out. Only it wasn't a package of crackers that emerged. Cheese? She hadn't added a block of cheese to her basket. She peered inside the sack and frowned, then pulled out another package. Mrs. Waverly's Ladyfingers? Her mouth watered. She loved these delicate little cookies.

She lifted the sack and carefully emptied the contents onto the desk, the only other piece of furniture in the room besides a small wardrobe washstand and the two cots. And what she discovered both delighted and distressed her.

In addition to the cheese and ladyfingers, there were packages of sugared pecans, hard candy, dried apples, and—a laugh escaped before she could catch it.

A lady's flask.

Alexandra shook her head, fingering the beautiful oval sterling flask embossed on the front with a pair of butterflies amidst flower-filled cornucopia and floral swags. And on the reverse side, two more butterflies and a small space reserved for monogramming, she assumed. No more than four and a half inches, the decorative bottle would fit easily inside a woman's reticule. And might actually produce quite a nice-sized goose egg when thrown at a man's head.

She sighed, then twisted open the lid and sniffed, just in case. But thankfully, no Mrs. Taylor's Fancy Cordial. The flask was empty. And would remain that way until she returned it to Sylas Rutledge tomorrow night. But the ladyfingers and the cheese . . .

She opened both packages and relished the treats, alternating between savory and sweet as she returned to her task at hand.

Awhile later, she spread the unstuffed mattress out to survey her progress. One long seam remained to be sewn, besides the opening at the top. She finished stitching the side, then began stuffing the mattress with feathers. And none too soon, because she was exhausted.

The door opened, and Miss Sheppard entered.

To Alexandra's delight, the young woman accepted her offer to share the cheese and cookies, then immediately set to helping with the feathers. After a matter of minutes, the two sacks were depleted—and yet the mattress was still almost flat.

Miss Sheppard stepped back. "That is the saddest-looking mattress I've ever seen in my life, Miss Jamison."

Alexandra firmed her lips. "It *is* sad looking, isn't it?"

They both started laughing.

"You're not going to get a wink of sleep on that flat old thing."

"I know!" Alexandra attempted to make a sad face, which only got them even more tickled.

"Come on!" Miss Sheppard motioned to the door. "Let's go pilfering."

"Pilfering? For what?"

She smiled. "You'll see."

Alexandra looked at the clock on the desk. "But it's almost nine," she whispered. "We're supposed to be quiet and in our rooms. To be examples to the students. I read every word of the rules, per Mr. White's orders."

Miss Sheppard raised a perfectly arched brow. "I'm sorry, but there is simply no way I'm letting you sleep on that flapjack of a bed. You have an introductory class to teach tomorrow, Miss Jamison. You need some rest. Now grab your mattress and come on."

Miss Sheppard quietly opened the bedroom door, but Alexandra still hesitated.

Hand on hip, Miss Sheppard shot her a look. "I never knew white women could be so skittish and scared."

With a grin, Alexandra grabbed the mattress tick and practically pushed past her new friend and out the door.

Chapter
FOURTEEN

*H*er stomach a flurry of nerves, Alexandra shook the jitters from her hands, finished arranging her hair the best she could, and returned to buttoning her shirtwaist. Thirty minutes until she taught her first class.

Ella looked over at her from where she sat on her cot giving Tuesday's lessons one last review. "Surely a woman who can sneak into the Fisk president's stable and borrow a couple of bales of hay isn't nervous over teaching a class of new students . . . Is she?"

Alexandra giggled. "How can you look so sweet and innocent, Ella Sheppard? When you have such mischief in you!"

Ella laughed and gathered her papers from the cot. "And how can you run so fast holding a stuffed mattress up over your head? I could scarcely keep up with my end!"

"Terror is a tremendous motivator."

They both started laughing again.

"But truly, Ella. Thank you." Alexandra nodded toward her relatively comfortable if a tad prickly mattress. "I wouldn't have gotten a wink of sleep last night without your help."

Ella curtsied. "My pleasure, ma'am." Then she grew more serious. "And thank *you* for sharing with me last night. Have you told Mr. White yet . . . about your parents, I mean, and what happened when your father found out you'd decided to teach here? Because Mr. White will want to know, so he can be praying."

Alexandra shook her head. "Not yet, but I will."

Ella gathered her satchel and waited by the door, singing a hymn softly beneath her breath. Alexandra had heard her doing the same thing last night as they were getting ready for bed.

"You have a beautiful voice, Ella."

A heartfelt smile lit the young woman's face. "Thank you. I love to sing!"

"I would imagine so. With talent like that, though, why are you not singing with the group of singers from Fisk?"

"Oh, I do sing with them."

"But I don't remember seeing you last week in the concert at the Masonic Hall."

"Actually . . . I wasn't feeling well that night, so I didn't take part." As they walked down the hallway, Ella's demeanor turned more solemn. "You'll learn this soon enough, Alexandra. I get sick quite often. It's not the kind of sick where I shouldn't be around people," she added quickly. "I simply don't have a very strong constitution."

"I'm sorry to hear that." Alexandra couldn't say she was surprised, though. After all, Ella was so thin. And if last night's meal was any indication of the customary fare, it didn't boast a very nutritious regimen for the students and faculty.

She and Ella had finished up the cheese and ladyfingers for breakfast that morning, and Ella said it was the best breakfast she'd had since coming to Fisk. Alexandra was grateful to Sy for those added treats and planned on giving him as thorough a lesson on negotiations with Southern gentlemen as she could.

Together she and Ella walked the short distance from the teachers' barracks—formerly the Union officers' quarters, she'd learned last night—to the barracks housing the classrooms.

She breathed in the humid morning air, so eager for fall and cooler weather she could almost taste it. She smoothed a hand over her borrowed shirtwaist and skirt, grateful again for Mary's generosity. What would she have done throughout this transition without her friend? She glanced beside her at Ella.

Both the old and the new.

"I'll try to find you at lunch," Ella whispered as they neared the classroom barracks. "But I might be a little late. The other singers and I give half of our noon hour every day to study under Mr. White, and all our spare time too!" She glanced at the barracks ahead. "That's your building!"

She gave Alexandra a good-bye squeeze on her arm and continued on, nodding hellos to students as they passed.

Alexandra greeted them as well, hoping she appeared more confident than she felt. So many students. And some surprisingly young. But Mr. White had said Fisk admitted younger scholars. Thankfully, at twenty-five, she would be older than all of them.

She noticed the students watching her, and their dark eyes and eager expressions radiated an excitement she'd rarely seen in the children she'd tutored. Many of the students had apparently brought along their parents to see them off, and the hallway leading to her classroom was full of people.

The long narrow classroom on the left side of the building was hers, Mrs. Chastain told her yesterday, and the closed door loomed ahead.

Lord, help me to give these young scholars my best. And please . . . remove every false assumption from my heart.

"Excuse me, please," she whispered, turning sideways to better slip past the groups huddled waiting in the narrow corridor.

As she maneuvered her way through, she had the same sensation she'd experienced last night at dinner. She felt so very . . . white. And not a part of the same world as these people around her. Even her borrowed clothes—more than adequate, but not what she and Mary usually wore when visiting about town—were far nicer than the missionary barrel hand-me-downs that clothed her students and their siblings and parents.

"Please, excuse me," she said again, and noticed a girl around thirteen or fourteen reaching out to touch the lacy edge of her sleeve. Alexandra smiled at her, and the girl's dark brown eyes warmed with affection.

"You the new teacher?" the girl asked.

"Yes, I am."

"I'm in your class. I'm Lettie. This here's Brister, my little brother. He ain't much for talkin'."

Alexandra glanced up at the girl's "little" brother. "It's good to meet you, Lettie. And you as well, Brister." Though the young man said nothing, Alexandra loved the way his eyes sparkled when he looked at his older sister. "I'll see you both inside, all right?"

Nodding, Lettie scrunched her shoulders and grinned.

Her nerves lessening bit by bit, Alexandra hoped there were seats enough for all the students. She'd heard of schools where the pupils sat on the floor. Perhaps they could take turns, if it came to that.

She reached the door to her classroom and pushed it open, only to see Mr. George White standing at the front of a classroom full to overflowing. Her face went hot.

"Oh, I'm sorry, Mr. White. I-I must have confused my classroom assignment. Please excuse me." She hurried to close the door.

"Miss Jamison!" he called, rushing over. "You're in the right place, ma'am. This is your classroom."

Alexandra looked at him, then at all the students and their parents staring back. And grandparents, judging by their ages. "But"—she lowered her voice—"all those people in the hallway. In your letter, you indicated there would be thirty-five!"

His smile held a note of regret. "I know. We always have more students show up for an introductory class than we can grant admittance. Sometimes *far* more. But they're accustomed to the process and to the lack of teachers. Most of the students in this room have tried to attend a session like this before. Hence, many of them were waiting outside since the wee hours of the morning."

Alexandra looked into their faces and felt such a weight of responsibility. Then she glanced toward the open doorway and thought of Lettie and her brother outside in the hall. It hurt to think of their being turned away. But maybe there would be room once the family members left.

Mr. White led her to the podium at the front of the room and offered a kind introduction. Alexandra placed her loose stack of lesson papers atop the table, wishing she had her teaching satchel from home. It lent a far more professional appearance.

As soon as the thought came, she realized how inappropriate it was. Because this wasn't about her. It was about something so much larger.

"And though Miss Jamison is new to Fisk University, she comes very highly recommended. She's taught many students in her lifetime, and I know that in the next six weeks, for those of you who are admitted, if you'll study hard, which I *know* you will, you'll benefit from her knowledge. Which is of utmost importance. Because remember, anyone devoted to his books is on the road to freedom, while anyone ignorant of books," Mr. White continued, many within the room saying the words along with him, "is on his way back to slavery."

Hearty amens rose from the gathering.

"So I know that all of you will leave Miss Jamison's classroom with the ability to read and write, and to work your sums. And most importantly, with a thorough knowledge and understanding of Christian citizenship. And with the ability to read your very own Bible . . . all by yourself!"

Several of the parents actually started applauding until soon everyone joined in, and the spontaneous gesture overflowed into the hallway.

Mr. White leaned closer, but even then Alexandra could scarcely hear him over the clapping. "God has brought you here, Miss Jamison, to do a very good work. And we're most grateful to have you among our staff."

"Thank you, sir." She smiled and moved to the podium, then quickly stepped back toward him. "How long do the parents usually stay?" she whispered. "And is there anything specific I need to say to them in regard to their students?"

Mr. White's expression went slightly blank before gentleness overtook his sharp features once again. "My dear Miss Jamison . . . Everyone in this classroom and in the hallway, both young and old, is a student who has come hungry to learn, with a precious soul eager to be fed."

⌒∞⌒

"I'm sorry, Mr. Rutledge, but as it happens, those specific court files aren't available for public viewing at the present time."

Sy glanced past the secretary to the office she'd reemerged from a moment earlier. "I find that difficult to believe, ma'am. Because when I first arrived, you told me *all* public court files were open to the public. And . . . I'm the public."

Despite his even tone, he heard the impatience in his own voice. But after the name of the judge Mr. Maury had given him led to a dead end, and after wasting the majority of his day digging through layers of bureaucracy, being sent from one end of Nashville to the other, he'd had his fill of civil "servants" and dead ends. Especially when the dead ends felt intentional.

Seemed no one on the legal side of things was eager to talk about the accident at Dutchman's Curve—until he happened upon a young female clerk who'd been on the job for all of three days. She'd been more than willing to search the Davidson County court rosters and give him the information he needed, and far more.

Including the name of the judge who'd presided over the civil trial following the accident—the judge who'd ruled that the fault of the accident on Dutchman's Curve was his father's.

The secretary firmed her lips. "Mr. Rutledge . . ." Condescension thickened her tone as she reached for a pencil and pad of paper. "Why don't you write down your specific questions, and I'll make certain Judge Warren receives them. He's an extremely busy man, as you may imagine, but he'll review your inquiries at his earliest convenience and will respond accordingly. Be sure to include your address so he can post his letter to you in a timely—"

Sy nudged the pencil and pad back in her direction. "As I

already told you"—he glanced at the nameplate on her desk—"Mrs. Meeks, I'm here to speak with Judge Warren in person. Not leave him a note."

Her nostrils flared. "And as I have attempted to explain to you, sir, His Honor is in extreme demand. In fact, he's due in court in the next few moments. So I'm afraid he will *not* be able to—"

The office door behind her opened and out walked a man, cloth napkin stuffed inside his open collar, sandwich in hand. "Mrs. Meeks, once I finish this, I'm going to leave early and—"

Sy locked eyes with the man who, he assumed, was the Honorable Judge Warren, and would've sworn the older man was about to choke on his last bite.

"Judge Warren," the secretary said hurriedly, "I was explaining to this . . . gentleman, Mr. Rutledge, for the second time that the files he's requested to see are not available for public review at the present time."

Sy didn't have to guess whose inflection she was parroting.

"I've told him you're very busy, Judge," she continued, "and are due in court any time now, as you told me."

The judge threw her a scathing glare, then turned it on him.

"Mr. Rutledge, this is an office of the law. Hence, we abide by rules. Rules that apply to everyone. Because if they do not apply to everyone, then they apply to no one. Your persistence in forcing this issue shows a gross lack of respect for the law and for those who have dedicated their lives to upholding it. It is the very bedrock upon which our great nation is founded!"

Sy looked at him, wondering if he was done. "If the files of a public trial aren't open to the public, Your Honor, then who does have the authority to look at them?"

Still breathing heavily, the judge leveled a stare. "In this instance, members of the Tennessee Bar Association, the Interstate Commerce Commission, and the United States Federal Railroad Administration." He smiled insincerely. "Are you by chance a member of any of those associations, Mr. Rutledge?"

Sy held his gaze. "No, sir. I am not."

Judge Warren nodded, his look one of regret. "I thought not." He tossed his napkin and sandwich on the secretary's desk. "Mrs. Meeks! My robe, please."

The woman raced to the coat rack in the corner as though her life depended on it, then returned with equal haste.

Sy watched them for several seconds, then glanced at the clock on the wall. "It's half past four, Judge Warren. My understanding is that the courts officially close at three o'clock on Tuesday afternoons. So exactly where are you holding court . . . sir?"

The man's face flushed crimson. Mrs. Meeks's went a little pale.

"A judge's responsibilities do not cease, sir, simply because he is not presiding over a trial. Now I will take my leave in order to fulfill my obligation to the people of this fine city." He strode to the door and held it open. "And may I suggest, Mr. Rutledge, that you take your leave as well."

Sy crossed to the door, tipped his hat, and walked to the hallway. He descended the ornate limestone staircase to the vast marble lobby. As he passed a statue of a barefoot maiden seated on a marble base, he slowed. In one hand she held a set of scales, in the other, a mighty sword that rested atop a large volume on her lap.

Lady Justice.

He'd seen statues similar to this before, only the other maidens had always worn a blindfold. How timely that he should see this particular statue now.

He left the court building, whistled to Duke, who waited in a piece of shade to the side. Together they walked in the direction of Fisk University, Sy heartened by what—and who—awaited him that evening, even as what he'd discovered here rankled him. But he'd confirmed his suspicion.

Now to discover exactly what it was that was being hidden. And why.

Chapter
FIFTEEN

Famished, Alexandra finished every bit of her soup. It tasted oddly similar to what had been served for dinner the night before. Then she savored every bite of her thinly sliced bread, as everyone else around her was also doing.

She paused and scanned the faces of the other teachers, then looked across the room over the long rows of makeshift tables filling the barracks that served as the dining hall. So many students. So many "precious souls," as Mr. White had expressed that morning.

Her first day at Fisk University had passed in a blur of activity and questions and frustrations, but most of all—excitement. And though she knew without a doubt that she was where she needed to be, she couldn't account for the persistent lump that kept wanting to lodge at the base of her throat.

How could she feel so joyful in one sense, and yet so inadequate and heavyhearted in another? A pang of homesickness hit her.

Not for her house here in town or, sadly, not even for her parents. Though she did wish she could speak to her mother after that painful parting. But after seeing her in town, Alexandra wasn't certain her mother would welcome that conversation.

No, she was homesick for David and all the plans they'd had. Plans he had inspired her to dream in the first place. She wouldn't be here now if not for him.

She stifled a yawn, eager to get back to the barracks and do her reading and preparation before tomorrow's class. And not even the thought of her lumpy, itchy mattress could dampen her desire for sleep.

"A full day, Miss Jamison?"

Alexandra looked down the table to see Miss Frieda Norton watching her. Frieda was a twenty-six-year veteran American Missionary Association teacher she'd met briefly at lunch.

The woman was in her early fifties, Alexandra guessed. From New York City. A serious sort of woman, same as every other teacher she'd met so far. And also not in very good health, Alexandra gauged, based on the crackling sound of her cough.

Alexandra nodded. "A full day, but a very good one."

"Have you checked the chore sheet yet? To see what your responsibilities are for the week?"

Alexandra hesitated. A chore sheet? "No, I haven't. But I will."

"Never mind. I make the assignments. You're responsible for cleaning and sweeping your classroom, as well as the lobby area of your barracks. You also need to help with breakfast duty on Thursday, Friday, and Saturday mornings."

Alexandra felt a weight settle inside her but nodded, not wanting to get off on the wrong foot with anyone. "I'll be sure to get it all done." Although where she'd find the time to do "chores," along with everything she needed to do, she didn't know.

"Very good, Miss Jamison." Miss Norton nodded smartly. "We always give new teachers a week or two to settle in before giving them their full load."

A bell clanged, and Alexandra turned to see Mrs. Chastain standing by the back door signaling that dinner was over and study time awaited.

Of the over two thousand students who attended Fisk, only about a hundred actually lived on campus. And those scholars boarding at Fisk—in "the Home," as she'd heard the separate men's and women's barracks called—were students from outside

Nashville. Mr. White said they could have filled those boarding slots ten times over. There simply wasn't room for all of the students who wanted to live here.

Alexandra rose and was making her way toward the exit when she noticed Mrs. Chastain motioning to her.

"Turn around," the woman mouthed.

Alexandra did and saw Mr. White waving to her. What could he be wanting at this—

Then she saw who was with him.

Sy.

Oh . . . She'd completely forgotten about meeting with him tonight. Yet she couldn't refuse. She must pay the piper, after all. She forced a bright countenance and nodded to him.

"Who is that, Miss Jamison?"

Alexandra turned to see Mrs. Chastain looking in Sy's direction, her expression one of curiosity and womanly admiration. Did Sylas Rutledge have that effect on women of every age?

"He's . . . a student of mine. I'm tutoring him."

"You're tutoring that gentleman? In precisely what subjects, may I ask?"

Alexandra caught the jesting in Mrs. Chastain's tone and shook her head. "In etiquette, Mrs. Chastain. Specifically, protocol for how a gentleman is to conduct himself in business dealings."

The older woman nodded. "Impressive."

"Not at all. I'm simply sharing with him what little knowledge I have on the subject from having helped my father for several years."

"Actually . . . your knowledge wasn't what I was referring to, Miss Jamison." A glint slid into the woman's eyes.

"Mrs. Chastain!" Alexandra whispered.

"I'm married, Miss Jamison." Mrs. Chastain leaned closer. "But I've still got the eyes the good Lord gave me."

Alexandra smiled—until she looked back at Sy and realized she had at least an hour, if not more, of teaching yet ahead of her.

And knowing him even as little as she did, she guessed he would prove to be her most challenging pupil of all.

❦

She'd forgotten all about their meeting tonight. Sy could tell from the surprise in her expression, which she tried in vain to mask. And here he'd looked forward to being with her again almost since the moment she'd agreed to meet with him. Realizing that bothered him more than he cared to admit, even to himself.

"So, Mr. Rutledge," said Mr. White. "Are you familiar with Fisk University?"

"No, sir, I'm not. Or at least I wasn't until recently."

"Are you in support of the freedmen, sir?"

"Yes, sir, I am. I'm for every man—and woman—doing everything they can to better themselves. I wouldn't want anybody telling me what I could or couldn't do."

The man nodded in earnest. "Precisely. Well stated, sir." White glanced toward Alexandra, who'd paused to talk to a young woman. "And exactly what is your relationship with Miss Jamison?"

Sy looked at Mr. White, a little startled.

"Forgive me, Mr. Rutledge, if the question seems impertinent. But we here at Fisk hold our teachers to the highest possible moral conduct. Our scholars look to them for guidance and as an example. Hence, they need to meet certain qualifications. Which I'm happy to expound on for you, should you desire."

"Thank you, sir, but that—"

"First," the man continued, "are the individuals willing to sacrifice for the cause of Christ? Second, are they physically equal to the task? Third, do they have the drive that will compel them to go beyond what is expected . . ."

As the man talked on, Sy wished he'd waited out front of the teachers' barracks as Alexandra had suggested, instead of following a student's advice and coming to look for her.

"And lastly, do the applicants have the required experience?

In other words, have they proven their mettle?" A satisfied smile swept the man's face. "And I am pleased to say that Miss Jamison has met all of those requirements and more, sir."

Sy nodded. "As I would have assumed, sir."

Seconds passed, and Sy sensed White's continued attention. Then he remembered that the man had asked him a question.

"Ah . . . Miss Jamison is a friend, Mr. White."

"A friend?"

"Yes, sir. I've come by this evening to visit with her for a while." Call it pride, but he wasn't eager to admit to this man that he'd come for lessons.

"I trust you will conduct this visiting in a public place, sir."

It wasn't a question, and Sy suddenly felt as though he were speaking to the woman's father. "Yes, Mr. White. Of course we will."

"Very good. As men, we must always be vigilant to guard the reputation of a woman in our charge."

"Words I heard from my father from a very young age."

"A wise and godly man, I take it?"

"Yes, sir. He was."

White looked over, his brow knitting. "God rest his soul," he said quietly, then turned as Alexandra approached. "Ah . . . Miss Jamison. I've been enjoying the company of your fine friend Mr. Rutledge. Who has a keen interest in Fisk as well, as it turns out."

Alexandra looked between them, more than a hint of curiosity in her gaze. "Is that so?"

Sy simply nodded.

"Well." She gestured. "If you're ready for our—"

"Visit," Sy said quickly. "Yes, I am. I've been looking forward to it. And I'm certain we can find a public place that will be suitable." He tossed Mr. White a look as they walked away, and the man fairly beamed.

"I see Mr. White's already instructed you on at least a few of the rules here," Alexandra said as they left the dining hall.

"That he did. Shy man, though. He needs to learn how to interact with people more."

He enjoyed the lilt of her laughter. He whistled for Duke, and the hound came bounding.

Alexandra reached down and gave the dog a rub. "Mr. White can be quite straightforward. And even demanding."

"I could see that."

"But he's also a wonderful man, Sy, who cares very much about this school and its students." She glanced around them and dropped her voice. "I've also learned that he recently put up his own personal savings to help keep Fisk afloat. Even so, I'm afraid the school is still in dire financial straits. But as Mr. White and some others prayed in chapel this morning, we need to trust that God will make a way."

Sy watched her as she shared what she'd learned about Fisk, beginning to see who she was a little more clearly. Her decision to teach here made more sense following what he'd learned about her fiancé. How he'd been riding in a freedmen's car, helping those workers. And it hadn't escaped Sy that, at the mercantile, the amount of money she'd laid on the counter to pay for her purchases was the exact amount he'd given her. Then there was Alexandra's mother in town the other day, and how the woman hadn't returned her daughter's wave. Yet it had sure appeared to him as if she'd wanted to.

Having met Barrett Jamison, Sy could easily guess what—or who—was responsible for her hesitation. Yes, he was gradually putting together the pieces of the puzzle named Alexandra Jamison.

"Why don't we sit here." She motioned to the steps of the teachers' barracks where he'd started out. "Which reminds me . . . How did you know to come to the dining hall this evening?"

"I got here a little early, and a student saw me waiting. He told me where I might find you."

She nodded, situating her skirt over her ankles. "For our lesson this evening, why don't we discuss what you—"

"Whoa!" He held up a hand. "First, tell me about your first day of teaching."

A slight frown creased her forehead.

"What was it like? How many students were in your class? This was a big day for you, wasn't it?"

"Well . . ." She paused, and then a smile he wished he could bottle up and carry in his pocket spread across her face.

"All in all, it was . . . an exhausting but wonderful day. I was so scared this morning, though. You should have seen me. I was shaking! Mr. White had told me to prepare for thirty-five students." She exhaled. "Seventy-two showed up! And they're all ages, Sy. I even have a grandfather, his daughter, and *her* daughter in my class. A grandfather and a granddaughter who will share the same primer, can you imagine?"

He watched her as she talked, and her enthusiasm somehow reached down inside him and gave his heart a firm tug. He really enjoyed watching her—the way her eyes twinkled when she laughed, how she kept absentmindedly twirling that strand of hair that had escaped a pin, the way she pursed her lips when she paused and looked off in the distance. He could all but see the thoughts forming.

And the more he saw of her, the more he wanted to see.

She described her day from start to finish, leaving out few details, it seemed. And she would've kept on going too, he wagered, and with no complaint from him, except the daylight was starting to fade. Suddenly she paused.

"I'm sorry for having gone on so long. We best get to your lesson, Sy."

"Just finish telling me what you and Mr. White decided on. With teaching that many students."

"We're dividing the students into three classes. The first will meet for the morning, the second for the afternoon, and a third class will meet in the evenings. That will be the biggest one of all."

"And you'll teach all three? Sounds like a challenge. But nothing you can't handle."

"I will, but I'll have help. There are already classes that meet at night, but the evening class I'll teach will be a little different. It was my idea, actually." She smiled shyly. "We're recruiting some of Fisk's students to assist me. The idea is that, as I teach the class, I'll also be patterning *how* to teach to those students helping me. So they'll be assistant teachers, if you will. Which Mr. White says reinforces one of the fundamental principles of this school—to educate freedmen so they, in turn, can educate each other."

"That sounds like Mr. White." He smiled, admiring how quickly she'd adopted the mission of this school. Admiring her.

"What?" She looked at him.

"This was your dream, wasn't it? The one you told me about at Uncle Bob's cabin that day."

She fingered the edge of her sleeve. "Yes. It was David's and my dream to teach. He had a position at West Tennessee State School in Memphis. It's a university."

"Your fiancé was a scholar then."

A warmth moved into her eyes that made him envy a man he'd never met.

"Yes. David would teach anyone and everyone. Whoever wanted to learn. I wanted my university degree, and he had been teaching me for a while. The only formal education I've had is what I received from my governess."

"So who says you can't still pursue that? Can't you get a degree?" He looked around. "You are working at a school, after all."

She hesitated. "Yes, but an education at Fisk isn't free, remember. And anyway," she added quickly, "I believe God led me here to teach. As David had been doing. As we would have done together."

Sy heard the silent ending of her sentence: *if not for what happened at Dutchman's Curve.* He felt a defensiveness rise inside him.

"Well, it's getting late." She took a breath. "Perhaps we should move on to what brings you here this evening. To begin with, I'll detail the customary etiquette between gentlemen conducting business affairs. Some of it may seem elementary, but I'll cover it quickly, and you can stop me if you have any questions. If there are cultural differences, which I'm certain there are, those will surface as we discuss things back and forth."

He nodded, listening as she continued, but still wondering about her fiancé, David. A man who wouldn't have needed these lessons, for sure. A man who would have fit perfectly into her world.

Or . . . what her world had been.

As daylight gave way to dusk, he spotted a young woman approaching them at breakneck speed. She looked first at him, then at Alexandra, curiosity clear in her expression. A student, he first thought. But judging by the way she carried herself—with maturity and purpose—he leaned more toward teacher.

Alexandra paused midsentence and followed his gaze, then her face lit. "Ella!"

The two women exchanged greetings, and Sy stood as Alexandra made introductions. He was grateful when she referred to their reason for meeting having to do with "discussing business relations" instead of *tutoring.*

It was obvious from observing them that the two were friends. What surprised him was to learn they'd only met each other the previous afternoon. And they were roommates, to boot.

"Pleasure to meet you, Miss Sheppard."

"The same to you, Mr. Rutledge. And hello to your fine canine friend as well." Miss Sheppard's gaze slid to Duke, then back up to Alexandra. "Forgive me for interrupting your discussion. I'll see you inside shortly, Alexandra."

A hint of expectation lingered in the woman's voice. Alexandra apparently heard it too, because she hesitated.

"Is everything all right, Ella?"

Miss Sheppard nodded, an excitement about her that not even

approaching nightfall could mask. "We'll talk inside," she said softly, then went on in.

Alexandra sat once again on the top step and promptly continued where she'd left off. But Sy sensed her focus was with whatever news Miss Sheppard had to impart.

"Alexandra," he finally said when she paused to stifle a yawn some moments later. "It's late. Why don't we pick this back up tomorrow evening?"

"Yes." She gave him a quick smile. "That might be best. It *has* been a long day."

He stood and offered his hand to help her up. It felt good to hold her hand in his, however briefly.

"One more thing before you go. I promised to keep you updated if I learned anything about Dutchman's Curve."

Her brow furrowed.

"I went to see a judge earlier today. Long story short, I spoke with him, or tried to. In the end I didn't get any new information. But I did leave feeling as though there was more to be learned."

She nodded. "Thank you for sharing that. And for keeping your word."

"And thank *you* for taking the time to meet with me tonight. What you shared was very helpful."

"I'm so glad. Until tomorrow night then." She turned to go.

"Oh . . ." He reached into his shirt pocket. "I almost forgot. I saw this today and thought of you."

She stared at the tiny bag he held out.

"Come on," he urged. "It won't bite." *And I won't either,* he thought, sensing her wariness.

She shook her head. "You shouldn't be buying me things, Sy. It isn't proper."

"I already bought you a lot of things. All that stuff from the mercantile."

"Yes, I know. But I needed those things due to . . . extenuating circumstances."

"So . . ." He shrugged. "Since we've already burned that bridge." He nudged the sack toward her.

She looked up at him and smiled, then shook her head.

So he set the little bag down by her feet, patted his leg for Duke, and started back to town.

Chapter
SIXTEEN

Alexandra watched him walk away, already knowing what she was going to do. How could she not? She knelt, picked up the bag, and peered inside. Unable to see the contents in the fading light, she tipped the bag end-up into her palm.

Out fell . . . three coins?

Then she caught a whiff of chocolate and smiled. "You're paying me in chocolate dimes?" she said loudly enough so he would hear.

He turned and bowed at the waist like a proper gentleman. "I always pay my debts, Miss Jamison."

Though she couldn't see his features, she knew well enough the roguish grin he was wearing.

"Thank you, Mr. Rutledge."

"My pleasure, Miss Jamison."

She turned and entered the barracks, letting the door close behind her. But she stood at the edge of the window watching him and Duke until the shadows enveloped them. Then she unwrapped a chocolate coin and popped it into her mouth—and savored the silky sweetness on her tongue as she hurried down the hallway.

As soon as she opened the door Ella turned, looking as though she'd been pacing the small bedroom.

"Oh, Alexandra, I have such hopeful news!"

Alexandra tossed her a coin, and Ella caught it, frowned, then smiled and did exactly as Alexandra had done.

"*Mmmm* . . ." Ella leaned her head back. "Do you know how long it's been since I've had chocolate?"

"No, I don't. But if you don't go ahead and tell me the news, I'm not going to give you another one."

"Mr. White wants to take the troupe of singers on tour up North. To raise funds for Fisk!"

Alexandra's thoughts flew. The idea seemed like an incredible undertaking, especially considering the already tenuous finances. How would Mr. White pay for such a journey? And would such a tour prove profitable?

And yet, the hope in Ella's face—and Alexandra's desire to see Fisk continue—swiftly won out.

"What a wonderful idea, Ella! You're all such gifted singers, I'm certain the audiences will love you. The same as I did when I first heard the group!" She took great pleasure in tossing Ella the last coin.

Ella caught it and, judging from her expression, savored it as much as she had the first one.

"Now, Miss Sheppard! Tell me all the details!"

"I will, but first you need to tell me yours. Who is this Mr. Rutledge? And why are you discussing 'business relations'?"

"Mr. Rutledge is a businessman from Colorado. It's a very long story that I will not go into—" She held up a hand when Ella's gaze turned probing. "But I *will* say that he did me a good turn, and now I'm doing him one. He's meeting with a group of businessmen to negotiate some sort of a deal. And since he's from Colorado, and apparently we do things quite differently here, I agreed to help him. I've assisted my father for years so I know a little about it. Mr. Rutledge will be here twice more. Then we'll be done."

"And after that you won't be seeing him anymore?"

"That's right."

Ella smiled. "Does Mr. Rutledge know that?"

Alexandra looked at her. "Of course he does."

Ella just pursed her mouth and nodded.

"Now tell me what Mr. White said!" Alexandra got comfortable on her own cot, and Ella did the same.

"There aren't that many details to share at present. Other than the troupe would consist of the ten singers, including me, and then Mr. White. I would also act as his assistant and be the pianist. It would be a lot of work, certainly. But it's exciting to think about."

"Of course it is. And imagine, you'd be sharing that beautiful music with hundreds, if not thousands, of other people."

Ella nodded. "Which would be important, but secondary to raising funds for the school. Because I don't know how much longer we can keep functioning unless we bring in more money."

Alexandra thought back to the confrontation between Mr. Granger and Mr. White and wondered how many other vendors had given Mr. White the same ultimatum.

"Who knows . . ." Alexandra tried to sound especially hopeful. "Perhaps this is the opportunity everyone has been praying for."

"I hope so."

The hour getting late, they both turned to reviewing their lessons for the following day. An hour later, Alexandra finished and closed her books, and readied for bed. She peered over at the title of the book Ella was still poring over.

The Rise and Fall of the Roman Empire. It made her lesson preparations on grammar, sentence structure, punctuation, and penmanship seem even more elementary. She recalled the deep discussions she and David used to have about history, the history of Rome included. He'd possessed such a wealth of knowledge.

Lying in bed, she waited until Ella was finished writing her notes, which consisted of several pages of elegant script, before posing her question.

"What's the lesson you're presenting tomorrow?"

Ella stood from her cot and stretched. "What we can learn from the rise and fall of the Roman Empire, and how we can apply those lessons to current-day America."

Alexandra let her jaw drop open for dramatic effect, which

drew the desired laughter. "I bet your discussions with the students are interesting."

"They are. And thought provoking. The scholars here, especially those about to take their finishing exams and earn their degree, are especially bright. It's a challenge to stay one step ahead of them."

Alexandra started to ask something else, then stopped herself.

"Go ahead," Ella coaxed softly.

Alexandra smiled. "I'm not sure if this is proper, but . . . Would you mind if I were to read your lesson notes from that class sometime?"

"Mind? I'd be happy to share. In fact . . ." Ella pointed to two boxes beneath her cot. "Those are full of lessons from the last five or six years. Mostly my own, but some of them from professors I've studied under in the past. World history, geography, philosophy, biology. Enough to keep you busy for months on end. We can discuss them as you finish reading them, if you'd like."

"I'd love that! Thank you."

"Would you like to start with tomorrow's? On the Roman Empire?" Ella pointed to her satchel.

Alexandra nodded, feeling both honored and excited. Ella handed her the notebook, then crawled into bed.

Alexandra opened the notebook and began to read, then sensed that she was being stared at. She looked over at her roommate.

"Go ahead," she mimicked. "Whatever it is, you can ask."

Ella hedged for a moment. "Where did you receive your education? Did you attend a school here in town?"

"I had a governess until I was twelve. That's all the education my father thought I needed. In a way, though, he countered his own opinion, because soon he enlisted me to help him in his practice as an attorney. At first it was simply office work. Filing, writing letters, and such. But after copying countless contracts, taking minutes for his meetings with clients, and reading his law books—"

"How old were you when you began reading his law books?"

"Ten."

They both giggled.

"I was curious to know what the legal terms he used meant. Then I became fascinated with the lawsuits the books cited. And then the law itself. It's actually quite interesting. What about you? I mean, I know you received your education here at Fisk, but . . . You have such a keen mind, Ella. You're so intelligent. And musically talented as well. Have you always had such a thirst for learning?"

Ella lay down, then turned onto her side to face Alexandra.

"Yes, I've always had that thirst, as you call it. But that wasn't what drove me to learn. And even though my life has changed drastically since I was a little girl, I find that the memory of what I'm about to tell you still serves to motivate me even now."

Feeling as though she'd been allowed entrance into a room where few were permitted to go, Alexandra closed the notebook and lay perfectly still. And listened.

"My mother, Sarah Hannah Sheppard, was a slave. She belonged to Phereby Donelson, here in Nashville. Andrew Jackson's grand-niece." Ella's voice was strong and even, yet held tenderness. "When Miss Donelson married Major Sheppard, Mama eventually became her head nurse and housekeeper, which was an esteemed position for a house slave. Mama was generally treated kindly. When she was seventeen, she met my father, Simon Sheppard, and married him right in the parlor of Miss Phereby's mansion not far from here. Almost seven years later, I was born."

Ella's voice took on a smile even though the gesture didn't reach her face. An occurrence Alexandra was becoming accustomed to with her friend.

"When I was a little girl, about three years old or so, Miss Phereby taught me to spy on my mother—it was common practice, I later learned. She bribed me with buttered biscuits and sweet cakes. Then she took what I'd told her and used it against Mama, and threatened to punish her. Mama knew that Miss

Phereby would likely do it again, and might even use me as a real pawn against her one day. And that, eventually, our own relationship could be torn asunder." Ella inhaled, then slowly let out her breath. "Some of my earliest memories are of my mother's tears over the cruelties of slavery, as she realized that its degradation fell heaviest upon the young Negro girl." Ella's voice grew softer. "So one afternoon Mama settled me on her hip and set out for the Cumberland River. She'd decided it would be better for me to meet a watery grave than to be a slave."

Only then did Alexandra realize how tense she'd become, and how very still the room was.

"As Mama reached the banks of the river, Old Mammy Viney saw her and called out to her. Somehow the old woman knew what my mother was about to do. Old Mammy Viney told Mama she'd seen a different future for me. She said, 'Look, honey, don't you see the clouds of the Lord as they pass by? The Lord has got need of this child.'"

Something in Ella's voice, or maybe in what Mammy Viney had said, further stirred Alexandra's heart.

"So Mama turned back from the river and gave up her plan to 'spare' me. She took courage, instead, she said, and walked back to slavery to await God's own time. For as long as I can remember, Mama has told me that story. So even though I've always held a curiosity within me to know new things, it's knowing what it's like to be enslaved that motivates me to learn. That motivates me to do everything I can to help Fisk succeed. Because I don't ever want to go back to that. We can never go back."

Alexandra swallowed, not bothering to wipe away the tear that trailed her temple.

"I study the histories of civilizations past, like Rome," Ella continued, "and see how slippery a slope it can be. As Mr. White so often preaches, and rightly so, 'Anyone devoted to his books is on the road to freedom, while anyone ignorant of books is on his way back to slavery.'" Ella took a deep breath, held it, then slowly exhaled. "Education is the key to unlocking not only a person's future, Alexandra, but to helping to create a new world. For everyone."

Alexandra nodded, but a long moment passed before she could speak. "The Lord *does* have special plans for you, Ella Sheppard," she whispered. "Very special plans. And, along with everyone else here, I'll do whatever I can to keep Fisk open."

"Jesus is with us in this, Alexandra. I know he is. He must be." She briefly closed her eyes. "But . . . whatever the Lord wills . . ."

Long after Alexandra heard Ella's soft, rhythmic breathing, she stayed awake reading her roommate's lecture notes about the Roman Empire, and thinking about all Ella had said. She was right. They had to find a way to keep Fisk from being closed. Same for the rest of the freedmen's schools around the country.

When Alexandra finished reading, she turned from her back onto her side, wishing for sleep and knowing morning would come all too soon. And yet the gentle echo of someone else's voice kept sleep at bay even as it lit a hope inside her. *So who says you can't still pursue that? Can't you get a degree?*

She stared into the darkness. Yes, who indeed.

Two days later, following her afternoon class, Alexandra hurried to Mr. White's office, overjoyed to share with him the progress her students were making. Anyone who said Negroes weren't capable of learning need only visit Fisk University to have their ignorant opinions proved wrong. Her students were not only learning, they were excelling in ways that—

"You are set on ruining us, Mr. White!"

"I am doing no such thing! I am following the will of God Almighty and the way he has provided to save this school!"

Alexandra stopped stone-still in the hallway, only feet from Mr. White's office. The door was closed but the raised voices carried. And considering how shabbily these barracks had been constructed, she'd be surprised if the argument couldn't be heard from outside the building.

Clutching her papers to her chest, she hastily turned to go when the floorboard creaked beneath her boot. She cringed at the possibility of being discovered by Mr. White and whoever the other man was with him.

"Save the school? We're nearly out of money, Mr. White. Not to mention food! And what we're eating now is execrable! Our teachers are sick! Their health is considerably weakened. You're pushing them all beyond their limits!"

"God demands nothing less than our best, Mr. Spence! Or have you forgotten that?"

Alexandra felt a weight sink in her chest. *President Spence?* And the two men were arguing so viciously!

"You must discard this foolish concerting scheme, George." President Spence's voice lowered to a more normal tone. "Your personal ambition is clouding your judgment. In my heart, I cling to the thinning hope that you truly do mean well for this school. But as its president, and the one who answers to the American Missionary Association, I cannot sanction moving forward on this ill-founded idea of yours. You want to take all of the remaining money in the school treasury to take your group of singers to the North? And what will those of us remaining here do for funds? The association does not support this idea. Nor do they support the tour. They are against your plan as much as I am."

"Which goes to show how little faith you all have. These singers are the best I've ever heard. Their talent is—"

"Standing these students up before white audiences is more likely to make them targets than stars, George, and you know it!"

"What I know, sir—"

White's deep voice thundered. And Alexandra, her heart racing, hurried back down the hallway—only to hear the front door open. She froze. Caught either way.

"—is that the Good Lord put these voices and this talent in

these students. Then by his divine providence he brought these students together at Fisk University, the least, some would say, of any of the freedmen schools. Surely any God-fearing man can see that the Lord is paving the way before us, Mr. Spence! He is parting our Red Sea."

Though the volume of their voices had diminished, the anger in them had not.

"The missionary board and I view this endeavor as excessively risky and born out of your own self-interested opportunism, Mr. White. And I'm telling you, if you persist in forcing this issue—"

"You are a weak man, Adam Spence! And I am weary of it!"

Wincing at the brutal exchange, Alexandra watched for whoever had come in a moment earlier to walk around the corner and find her seemingly eavesdropping on the president and treasurer of Fisk University. Oh, why had she come by here now? She should have gone straight to dinner. She was seeing Sy right afterward for their final meeting, so she didn't have much time to—

The door to Mr. White's office opened.

Seeing no other choice, Alexandra bolted around the corner—and ran straight into Sy himself.

Chapter
SEVENTEEN

Well, good evening, Miss Jamison."

Alexandra motioned frantically toward the door. "Go! Go!" she whispered, hearing Mr. White and President Spence continuing their exchange in the hallway. "Hurry!" She shoved him toward the door, nearly dropping her papers.

He grinned. "What are you—"

"I'm telling you for the very last time, Mr. White! If you pursue this idea, I'll be forced to—"

Still urging Sy toward the door, Alexandra saw understanding dawn in his eyes, and in a blink he had the door open.

He grabbed her by the hand and pulled her out, then closed the door noiselessly behind them. But Alexandra didn't stop. She hurried down the steps, took the path at a run, then ducked around the corner, Sy matching her stride for stride as she watched for anyone who might have seen them.

But it would appear that everyone else was already at dinner.

She finally stopped and pressed back against the building, working to catch her breath. "Oh my goodness." She squeezed her eyes tight. "That was one of the most uncomfortable moments of my life!"

"What was going on back there?"

"I came to see Mr. White to share with him . . . how well my students were doing when . . ." Between deep breaths, she recounted the conversation she had overheard. "I heard him shouting, saying that God has provided a way to save the school. Then President Spence shouted back that they're nearly out of money—and food! And that what we're eating now is execrable! Which"—she made a face—"I would have to agree with. Still . . . when I heard the front door open, I was certain it was another teacher, or a student, or even Mrs. Chastain. And they'd see me and think I was listening."

"Which . . . you were."

She nudged him. "Not intentionally!"

He smiled.

"Which raises the question . . . What were you doing in there, Sy?"

He briefly glanced away. "I was coming to speak with Mr. White."

"About?"

One side of his mouth tipped. "Just because you eavesdrop on everyone else's conversations doesn't mean you get to know my personal business too."

She gave him a droll look.

"I was coming to ask Mr. White about going to school here. How much it costs, how much you need to know before you can start."

Alexandra sobered. "Sy . . . are you thinking about—"

"No! It's not for me!" All humor faded. "I may not be the most educated man you've ever known, Alexandra, but I do have a fair amount of learning. Especially when it comes to things that can't be taught in school."

He started walking in the direction of the teachers' barracks, and she hurried to catch up with him.

"I didn't mean anything by my question, Sy. But when you said that, I simply assumed you might be—"

He held up a hand. "Let's just forget it, all right?"

Recalling an afternoon at the old Harding cabin when he'd

poked fun at her for wanting to do just that, she started to do the same. Then saw the firm set of his jaw and decided she best not.

"You go on to dinner." He gestured. "I'll wait on the steps."

"Actually, it's too late for me to go into the dining hall—everyone will be seated and served by now. But honestly, that's not too terrible a thing. Because the meals here . . . leave a lot to be desired." She grimaced, hating to say anything disparaging.

"So I take it that's what *execrable* means?" His smile resurfaced. "What President Spence said about the food."

She looked at him and, for the first time, noticed how kind his eyes looked when he smiled. Honest. Kind and caring.

"Yes, that's what it means. But I don't think I've ever used that word in all my life."

"And I'm sure I've never heard it before in all of mine."

They laughed together. He glanced down the road, then back at her.

"Do you have time to walk over to town with me? Get some dinner? There's a place not far from here that serves barbecue. It's nothing fancy, but it's good. And they typically have musicians playing too. It'll be my treat."

"I don't know if I should . . ." Alexandra debated, her stomach arguing with her head.

"It's just dinner, Alexandra. Not a lifetime commitment."

She heard the humor in his voice and acquiesced. "In fact, I would enjoy having dinner elsewhere. Very much. Let me stop by the teachers' barracks, put my papers in my room, and then we'll go."

∽

He enjoyed the way she closed her eyes after she took a bite of barbecue.

"Oh . . . This is delicious!" She savored another bite. "It's surprising how wonderful food can taste after eating the watered-down soup they serve at Fisk. Same for the porridge in the mornings."

Her smile faded. "Although I feel a little guilty eating this when all the staff and students are back there eating that."

He nodded to her across the table. "There have been plenty of times I've been without, so I know what that's like. But the tour you told me Mr. White is planning should eventually turn the finances around. Is that right?"

"If it comes to fruition." She lowered her voice, glancing at patrons at nearby tables. "But President Spence vehemently disagrees with him, remember. Still, something must be done or the school will be forced to close."

He gestured to her plate. "For now, please . . . Enjoy your meal. You work hard, and you're sacrificing a lot. And you'll be back to that soup soon enough."

Still looking slightly guilty, she took another bite, then dabbed at the corners of her mouth.

The group of four musicians playing in the corner by the front window were quite good, and Sy was enjoying their music. Appalachian, they called it, deftly blending guitar, banjo, fiddle, and dulcimer in unique fashion.

"Do you like it? The music?"

He looked back to see Alexandra watching him. "I do. Very much."

"I'm guessing you don't have music like that back in Colorado."

"Yes, because we're not civilized like you Southerners are."

She smiled, then her expression grew timid. "I saw you that night. At the concert with the singers from Fisk."

"You were there?"

"I came in late and sat in the back. I saw you leave right after the concert ended."

"And did you enjoy it? The concert?"

"Oh, very much."

"I did as well. Be sure and let me know when they perform again. I'd like to hear them." He wanted to add, *Perhaps we could even go together,* but didn't feel at liberty to. Not with Dutchman's Curve standing between them.

He slathered butter on a piece of cornbread. "I think I'm ready for my meeting with General Harding and the other men tomorrow morning, but I was hoping you might've had a chance to think more about what we discussed last night. About things I could do to make my bid stand out."

She nodded. "I have thought more about it, and I do have some ideas. You may like them, you may not. We'll see . . ." She set her fork aside. "As best I can judge, given the blueprints you showed me last night, your plans for the railroad and for the Belle Meade depot in particular are exemplary. You're taking advantage of the best vistas the plantation has to offer, and we already know General Harding is impressed with the design of the depot. So as far as contributing anything else to that part of your proposal, I'm afraid I can't. However . . ." Her blue eyes took on a gleam. "I do think there are ways to make your presentation more . . . unique. And memorable."

He smiled inwardly at her enthusiasm and the way her hands fluttered on occasion as she talked.

She withdrew a piece of paper from the folder she'd brought with her. "My idea is to enhance the train ride from the Nashville station to the Belle Meade depot by offering certain amenities to the passengers. For instance . . ."

She turned the page around so he could see it.

He took it in, then looked back up at her. She'd obviously gone to a lot of trouble, and he didn't want to hurt her feelings, but . . .

"This is . . . really something, Alexandra."

She smiled. "Well, don't sound so surprised! After all, I'm the one who knew what *execrable* meant!"

He smiled. "No, I didn't mean it that way. I meant . . . that it's very kind of you to have done all this work."

She waved a hand. "I enjoyed it, actually. Now, let me explain . . ."

He followed along on the page—that, to her credit, looked remarkably like an actual printed handbill. The handwriting was neat and evenly spaced. She'd even drawn fancy little curlicues to decorate the margins.

But how this could help his proposal was another thing altogether.

"At the top here I've included a brief history of Belle Meade for first-time visitors, along with what they'll see along the route to the plantation. The deer park, the bison, a glimpse of the limestone quarry, the high pastures. Next, I thought it would be nice to offer some refreshment."

"Refreshment?" Sy looked from her to the page, then back again.

"So next is a brief menu with some delectables that could be offered to passengers once they've boarded. You'll remember Susanna Carter, Belle Meade's head cook?"

He nodded, already imagining how hard it was going to be to abide Harold Gould's gloating once Gould won the bid.

"Susanna has some signature dishes, you might say, that she makes often. One of them is the carrot cake we had for dessert the night we were there. And she makes wonderful beaten biscuits with country ham. Also a delicious blackberry cobbler. I've listed a couple of other options here. And lastly—"

Despite being skeptical about her ideas, Sy found himself watching her, imagining what a man could do with this woman beside him. As his wife, his partner, his friend . . . his lover. How much more rewarding and enjoyable life would be for that man.

"—I thought that perhaps at the Belle Meade depot itself, you could suggest that certain items be made available for sale to the passengers. For instance, General Harding could commission a local artist to draw the house or the stables and corrals, then those likenesses could be framed and sold. Or have a photograph made instead. The same for the champion thoroughbreds. People come from all over the country to see those blood horses. I think they would enjoy taking home a souvenir of their journey."

Sy just stared for a moment, taking it all in. "You really think people would take the time to stop and look at paintings? And that they'd want cake on their way to see thoroughbreds?"

The instant he asked the questions, he knew he'd made a mistake.

"I do, but . . ." She pulled the paper back. "You apparently disagree."

He covered her hand. "Alexandra . . . I'm not saying I don't like your ideas."

"Your face is saying exactly that!"

He had to work not to smile. "What I'm trying to communicate is . . ." He struggled to find the words.

Meanwhile, a feminine eyebrow arched in none-too-subtle warning.

"It just seems to me that these ideas might appeal more to women than to men."

"And how is that a bad thing? Do you think only men come to visit Belle Meade? Or that only men come to yearling sales? Or that only men buy blood horses? And as far as the refreshments . . . I saw how much you enjoyed that carrot cake the other night." Her chin lifted a notch. "I think a lot of people would be interested in knowing the history of Belle Meade. And I think General Harding would be impressed that you think enough of his home, his thoroughbreds, and his life's work to share them with visitors as they're on their way there. And furthermore—"

This woman was even more fetching when riled. And though he hated to admit it . . .

"I think you've got a point there."

She stopped and looked at him more closely. "So . . . you're saying you agree with me now? I've won you over?"

If she only knew. "I'm saying that I also believe your ideas are very good. And I think you're right about how General Harding will respond." He tapped the page on the table between them. "So thank you, Alexandra."

The sun that was setting outside suddenly rose again in her

features. "I'm glad you're pleased." But she gave him the tiniest sideways look to let him know she hadn't forgotten how ornery he'd been at first.

She returned the handbill she'd designed to the folder and slid it across the table to him. His eyes never leaving hers, he placed it on the empty chair beside him.

Truce offered and accepted, conversation came easily between them as they ate.

"So tell me, Sy—"

She laid her fork and knife parallel on her plate, both pointing toward the eleven o'clock position, just as she'd taught him, and he couldn't help but smile. Then did the same with his own utensils.

"—you said you were coming to ask Mr. White about enrollment at Fisk. Is it too personal a question to ask for whom you're inquiring?"

"Not at all. It's for a friend . . . an employee of mine. Vinson and I were thick as thieves as boys. And still are. I couldn't do what I do without him."

She looked at him across the table. "So," she whispered, water glass in hand, "Vinson is a freedman?"

"Actually, he was never enslaved. His parents were, but when their owners moved to Colorado years ago, they allowed them to buy their freedom. Vinson is one of the finest men you'll ever know."

A moment passed before she spoke again.

"And the two of you were close growing up?"

He nodded, then took a long drink of lukewarm coffee, remembering the last winter he and his mother endured before Harrison Kennedy came into their lives.

"Somehow, when it's the dead of December and you're huddled in bed beneath a thin quilt, watching the snow come down through the cracks in the roof of the cabin, and you're hungry and cold . . . it doesn't matter to you what color the person is who brings food to your door. You're just grateful that they came."

The server chose that moment to approach. "More water, ma'am? Coffee, sir?"

They both nodded, and the woman obliged.

As she poured, Sy sensed Alexandra weighing the newly discovered knowledge about him. He didn't fully know why he'd told her, since he usually kept those details about his life to himself.

Before the server left, Sy glanced quickly at the menu. "And could we have two pieces of pie, please?"

"Certainly, sir. We have peach, apple, buttermilk, chocolate chess, and rhubarb."

He looked across the table.

Alexandra's eyes widened. "Chocolate chess, please."

"The same for me, please."

The woman left, and Alexandra leaned forward. "One more idea, and then I'll stop."

He winked, grateful for the change in topic. "I could listen to you all night."

She gave him a doubtful look. "At dinner the other evening I recall General Harding mentioning something about a yearling sale in Philadelphia. He asked one of the gentlemen what type of railcar he would provide for the blood horses."

"To which Mr. Maury replied *cattle* cars. Which did not go over well."

"Understandably." She nodded. "A practice my father has always pursued is to gain as much of a person's business as he can—to 'make yourself indispensable' to them, he says. So my suggestion, if it's possible with the current routes on your railroad, is that—"

"I mention to General Harding tomorrow that I'd like for him to consider my railway for that contract as well. It is possible, and I've already got that on my list."

She looked impressed. "Very good, Mr. Rutledge."

He feigned a frown. "Yes, as I've bumbled my way through

life, I've somehow managed to learn a few helpful things here and there."

"Your pie, ma'am. Sir." The server set the desserts and forks before them. "It just came out of the oven not long ago, so it's still nice and warm."

Alexandra took the first bite. Sy had thought her expression with the barbecue indicated delight, but that had been nothing compared to this. And her gentle sighs of pleasure tempted his own appetite in directions decidedly not related to chocolate chess pie.

"This . . . is . . . delicious!" She licked her lips. "Make sure they have this at the Belle Meade depot as well."

He nodded, his gaze going briefly to her mouth. "I'll see what I can do to satisfy that desire, Miss Jamison."

No sooner had he turned his attention to his own piece of pie than Alexandra let out a little gasp.

"Oh no!" She looked past him toward the door.

He turned, but could see little through the darkened window.

"What time is it, Sy?"

He glanced at his pocket watch. "Half past nine. Why?"

She winced. "Teachers are supposed to be in their rooms by nine o'clock!"

"You're not serious."

"I am. It's study hour."

"But you're a teacher, not a student."

She scooted her chair back. "I know. But it's one of the rules!"

She paused for an instant and looked at what remained of her piece of pie. For a second, Sy thought she might wrap it up in the cloth napkin and take it with her. But, of course, that would mean taking the napkin, which belonged to the café. Which, in her mind, would be tantamount to murder. Or at the very least, anarchy.

She suddenly sat back down and began forking the dessert into her mouth, her jaw working furiously. The sight was entertaining enough. But that she still insisted on cutting the pie into tiny lady-like bites was especially amusing.

"Nobody will say anything about you getting back a little late, Alexandra. Nobody will even know. I'll sneak you back in."

She shook her head, eyes widening, and washed down the last of her pie with a gulp of water. The woman could really put it away when properly motivated. She took a deep breath.

"That would be even worse." She wiped her mouth, then tucked her napkin neatly beside her plate. "I can't be seen walking back with you at this hour."

"But we sat on the steps until nearly dark two nights ago."

"Yes, in front of everyone. We weren't . . . skulking about like—"

"*Skulking?*"

She made a face. "It means to sneak or to—"

"I know what it means!" He looked at the bill, pulled money from his pocket, and left it on the table. He rose. "I just can't imagine *skulking* as something you would ever do."

"Thank you for dinner, Sy." She skirted past him.

He followed. "I'm not letting you walk back by yourself."

She turned at the door. "If Mr. White or one of the older, more . . . mature teachers sees us together, they'll—"

"If that happens, I'll take care of it. Trust me." He opened the door for her.

He had no trouble keeping up with her, but was surprised at how quickly she could cover ground in that skirt. And after downing a hearty dinner and a piece of pie, no less.

It was a good fifteen-minute walk back to Fisk. But at this brisk stride, they'd make it in ten. Only when the faint outline of the barracks came into view did Alexandra finally ease up on her frantic pace.

She glanced over at him. "If we see anyone, we need to act as if we haven't done anything wrong."

"But we *haven't* done anything wrong."

"You know what I mean!"

He grinned—and made sure she saw it.

The hasty tread of boots on dirt filled the silence between them, along with the chirrup of crickets and the occasional hoot owl. They were nearly back to the teachers' barracks when Sy spotted a figure swiftly moving toward them from the shadows.

Chapter EIGHTEEN

M iss Jamison, is that you?"

Sy recognized the voice immediately. And as the man stepped from the shadows, his tall, lanky frame, reminiscent of the late President Lincoln, left no doubt. "Mr. White!" Sy took the lead, as he'd promised Alexandra he would do.

"Good evening, sir. It's Sylas Rutledge. And yes, Miss Jamison is with me. We're both so grateful you're still out and about this evening."

"Well, I, along with others, have been greatly concerned about our Miss Jamison here." Darkness cloaked the man's features, but didn't disguise the disapproval in his tone. "It's nearly ten o'clock! No one had seen her since before dinner. And I'm certain I don't have to tell you both about the nightriders that often frequent schools such as ours. We can take no chances. Especially with our female teachers."

"No, sir. You're right. You can't." Sy shook his head.

"Mr. White." Alexandra bowed her head. "I'm so sorry, sir. I was—"

"Helping me prepare for a very important meeting I have in the morning, sir." Sy stepped forward. "It's my fault she was out so late. She was sharing her ideas about how I could include freedmen in my new venture, to improve their lives, increase their wages, perhaps. We simply lost track of time. But the fault, Mr. White, is entirely mine."

"Including freedmen in your venture, you say. Precisely what *is* this venture, Mr. Rutledge?"

"As you and I were discussing the other day, sir, I own the Northeast Line Railroad. Tomorrow morning I meet with General William Giles Harding about the possibility of—" Sy stopped, then forced a laugh he hoped sounded genuine. "Look at me, Mr. White. Here I go again. And at this hour, keeping you both from your studies and your sleep."

"I would very much like to hear more about this venture. However . . ." White nodded. "You're right, of course. This is not an appropriate time."

Sy felt Alexandra watching him. "Mr. White, maybe we could talk more about this at lunch one day soon. My treat, of course. Also, I have an employee who may be interested in attending the evening classes at Fisk. So we could discuss that as well."

"Splendid idea, Mr. Rutledge! As I frequently tell Fisk scholars, 'Anyone devoted to his books is on the road to freedom, while anyone ignorant of books is on his way back to slavery.' So yes, please. Let's do meet soon. When our schedules allow."

"Yes, sir. And now, with your permission, I'll walk Miss Jamison to the teachers' barracks. Unless you're headed that way?"

"No, I'm not, Mr. Rutledge. You see her safely there, please. I'll continue my prayer walk around the campus. It helps me sleep at night to have walked the grounds and prayed. Miss Jamison, fine work on assisting Mr. Rutledge with this venture. You continue to prove yourself both tenacious and resourceful, and a welcome contribution to Fisk. Though in the future, please see that you inform someone of your comings and goings. We must always be vigilant in our care and concern for each other."

"Yes, Mr. White. And again, my apologies, sir."

"Well . . ." The man dipped his head. "Good evening to you both."

Mr. White left as stealthily as he'd come, the darkness swallowing him whole.

Alexandra exhaled. "That was . . . impressive, Sylas Rutledge."

Sy took a mock bow. "We best get you back before he runs out of prayers."

She laughed softly. "I don't think that's possible."

He walked her the rest of the way and expected her to go right inside, but she paused at the base of the steps and looked up.

"Sy, I hope your lunch with General Harding and his colleagues goes well tomorrow. And that you overwhelm them with your newly acquired Southern charm."

He laughed. "I'll try to do you proud."

"And please be sure and tell me as soon as you know about the bid!"

"You know I will." For all the world, he wished he could kiss her good night. That he had earned the liberty to draw her close, to touch the curl at her temple. That she would even want him to.

It was a fool's wish, he knew. Instead, he settled for a bow. "Good night, Alexandra."

Sy knew better than to interrupt her Friday-night class, yet he couldn't wait until tomorrow. And he knew she wouldn't want him to. Not with this news. But it was the happenstance conversation he'd had with a porter earlier that afternoon that truly had him hopeful.

Alexandra had pointed out the barracks where she taught before, so he let himself in and quietly walked down the darkened hallway. He heard her speaking before he reached the open doorway, the glow of lamplight in the schoolroom spilling into the corridor.

"Next, please retrieve the primers from the shelves. Remember, there aren't enough for everyone, so please form groups of six or seven and share. Begin with the assignment on the board, and I'll come around to check on you. If you get stuck, raise your hand."

He stood for several moments by the doorway, hidden in the

shadows, and listened as she answered questions. Her voice confident yet nurturing, corrective yet encouraging.

Once she fell silent and he heard the crinkle of pages turning, he stepped around the corner and discreetly caught her attention. The way her expression lit when she saw him did his heart good.

"I need to step outside the classroom for a moment, but please continue. Lettie will be in charge until I return."

No sooner did she round the corner than she whispered, "How did the meeting go? Did you get the bid?"

He only hesitated for a second. "I did."

She squeezed his arm tight. "I knew you would! Congratulations, Sy."

"Thank you. And thank you again for all your help. General Harding was very impressed by your ideas. I think that's what finally won him over."

She beamed. "I'm certain that's not the case, but thank you for saying it. And what about the luncheon? Did you form any worthwhile associations there?"

"I would say so. Harding and two of his colleagues expressed a desire to invest in my next venture."

Her jaw went slack. "I would say those are worthwhile associations indeed. What is your next venture?"

He hesitated to tell her too much. Not because he didn't trust her, but because he still wasn't certain the deal would come together as he hoped. "There's a stretch of land between Charlotte, North Carolina, and Charleston, West Virginia, that isn't serviced by rail yet. And since the Northeast Line already travels through Charlotte Station—"

"Then connecting north to Charleston," she jumped in, "would be a profitable run, considering that's coal country. And the South is still rebuilding."

He looked at her. "I should have asked if you could attend that luncheon today."

She laughed softly.

"But I think I've saved the best news for last, Alexandra. I spoke with a porter at the train station today, and he told me the name of the community in Memphis where most of the freedmen workers who were on the No. 1 had lived. Some of the survivors hailed from there too, of course. I don't want to get your hopes up, or mine either, because it may turn out to be nothing. But I've got some traveling to do anyway, so I'm going to go to Memphis and see if any of them are willing to speak to me. I leave in the morning and could be gone for a couple of weeks."

Her expression clouded, and that alone endeared her to him even more.

"I'm almost finished with class. I only have another twenty minutes or so. If you can stay, I have something I want to share with you too."

She could have asked him for almost anything in that moment and he would have said yes. "I'll be waiting on the steps."

∽

"Thank you for waiting for me, Sy."

"My pleasure. You've got me curious."

She enjoyed that certain roguish smile of his, especially now that she knew he wasn't the rogue she'd originally pegged him to be. She started down the steps when he reached for the stack of books and papers in her arms. She relinquished them gratefully, and they started in the direction of the teachers' barracks, occasional oil lamps hanging from posts lighting their path.

She looked over at him. "Something you said to me recently has inspired me, and I wanted you to know."

"And what was that?"

"About pursuing my degree, and about what—or who—is keeping me from it. So . . . I've decided to do it." She appreciated the pride showing in his eyes. "Ella's lending me her textbooks, and she's also letting me read her collection of lecture notes. And,

Sy, it's so interesting. She's so intelligent and has notes on every subject imaginable."

"And you're devouring them all." He smiled.

"I am. I'm not getting much sleep these days. But there'll be time for sleep later." She gave a happy sigh. "Mr. White said he wants me to take a brief teacher exam, one they routinely administer to instructors who haven't earned their degrees yet. Usually before they begin teaching, of course. But he said since he was confident in my ability to teach the introductory level classes, and we were under such time constraints he didn't mandate it in my case. But it's required for all teachers, so I'll be taking that in coming weeks."

"And I have no doubt you'll do well."

When they rounded the corner to the barracks she heard singing, and knew from his expression that he had too. They looked at one another and she grinned.

"Would you like to go listen? They won't mind. I've done it before, several times."

"Lead the way, Miss Jamison!"

She deposited her books inside her room, then met him back outside, and they covered the short distance in the dark to the dining hall. They entered through the back of the barracks, the beautiful blend of voices singing "Beautiful Dreamer" growing much stronger.

Alexandra offered a tiny wave to Ella, who was playing the piano, and the others when they looked their way. Mr. White, who was directing, never turned around.

"Let's sit over here," she whispered.

They took seats in a far corner, so as not to disturb, and Sy settled in beside her.

"They may be almost done," she whispered, "but we're sure to catch another song or two. They're practicing for the tour Mr. White is hoping to take them on."

The singers didn't disappoint. They sang three more popular

tunes of the day, a song from Handel's *Cantata of Esther*—which Sy seemed to especially enjoy based on the way he leaned forward, forearms resting on his knees as he listened—and closed with "How Can I Keep from Singing."

Mr. White concluded the rehearsal with prayer, and Alexandra and Sy bowed their heads as well. Following the director's firm amen at the end, Thomas Rutling began to sing softly, tenderly, and Alexandra's throat threatened to close.

It was the song she'd heard the group singing in hushed tones from the back hallway after the concert that night. The song from her childhood, which Abigail had sung to her. Her "go-to-sleep song," as Abigail had called it.

> *In the morning when I rise, in the morning when I rise,*
> *in the morning when I rise, give me Jesus ...*

Listening to Thomas, Alexandra realized that what a local reporter had recently penned about the young man's golden voice being "by far the best tenor voice ever heard in Tennessee" wasn't hyperbole.

"He's especially good," Sy whispered beside her, and she nodded, glad he was here with her.

One by one, the other singers joined in, and the blend of their voices was nothing short of transcendent. Even . . . holy.

Benjamin Holmes, the other tenor, glanced in their direction, his gaze seeming at once alert and askew, and he nodded, as though aware of what she was feeling in that moment.

Ella had shared with her that Benjamin's cleverness had once earned him the title of a slave who "knew too much." But from what Alexandra knew of Benjamin, the depths of knowledge he could acquire had only begun to be plumbed. The young man had a wealth of talent.

How could anyone not see that these people were fashioned in the image of their Creator? The color of one's skin had no bearing on that immutable fact. And for that matter, she thought with a smile, the same could be said for one's gender. Why should being a woman preclude her from teaching at a university? Or from pursuing any other dream she wanted to pursue?

> *Give me Jesus, give me Jesus, you can have all the rest,*
> *give me Jesus ...*

Jennie Jackson caught Alexandra's eye and flashed a sweet smile before closing her eyes again. Jennie had a voice that possessed power beyond her years. But it was the consistent kindness in Jennie's nature that Alexandra found most endearing.

> *And when I am alone, oh when I am alone, and when I*
> *am alone, give me Jesus ...*

In her mind, Alexandra could hear Abigail's sweet voice. Not as cultured and refined as these, but no less precious or moving. It was a voice that had shaped her youth, and resonated inside her even now. What had happened to Abigail? One day the woman had been there, a house slave in the Jamison home. And the next, she hadn't. Alexandra remembered asking her mother about her.

"Alexandra, we do not question the decisions your father makes about the slaves. That's his business. Abigail is gone and isn't coming back. That's the end of it."

But it hadn't been the end of it. Not for her. Barely ten years old at the time, Alexandra remembered crying for weeks. She'd even asked Melba about it. But all Melba had said was that Abigail had been sold.

> *Give me Jesus, give me Jesus, you can have all the rest,*
> *give me Jesus ...*

Maggie Porter, the powerful soprano who'd performed the

role of Queen Esther in the cantata, slowly raised a hand as her voice ascended so beautifully that Alexandra bowed her head in response. Ella had confided in her once that Maggie's voice was arguably the strongest and best-trained among the singers. And Alexandra couldn't deny it.

Fifteen-year-old Eliza Walker, an alto whose customary horse-shoe braid only accentuated her spherical brow, took the lead on the next verse.

> *And when I come to die, oh when I come to die, yes,*
> *when I come to die, give me Jesus ...*

Alexandra found herself wanting to sing along with them. And if she was perfectly honest, she was a little jealous of their abilities. Her voice was nothing like any of theirs. Phebe Anderson, another contralto, softly sang the chorus again as the others hummed along, and Alexandra would have sworn the veil to heaven lifted ever so slightly. She could all but feel the brush of it against her face.

She looked into the faces of the extraordinary men and women standing before her. Did they have any idea how special they were? How gifted? Only God himself could have brought all these voices, all this talent, together in one place.

For a purpose, Lord. Please, for a purpose.

She looked over to see that Sy had bowed his head. His eyes were closed. But as if sensing her stare, he looked up, then reached over and gently took hold of her hand.

"Thank you, Alexandra," he whispered. "For sharing this with me."

Her eyes watered. He brought her hand to his lips and kissed it—once, twice—then covered her hand between his. The warmth from him traveled the length of her body. And as calm as she'd been only a moment before, now her pulse raced. Not since David had she been touched like this.

David ...

She still loved him. Would always love him. At times she still felt the heartbeat of that love deep inside her. So much so it took her breath away for the longing of it. So how could she have the feelings for Sy that she did? And yet she couldn't deny having them.

It felt like a betrayal somehow.

She'd once told Sy that when she looked at him all she could see was Dutchman's Curve. And while that was still true in part, it wasn't the whole truth. Not anymore. And the realization was startling.

Taking a deep breath, she wiped the corner of her eye and gently tugged her hand free from his. He looked over at her, but she didn't look back.

The song ended, and after making quick introductions between Sy and the singers, she walked with Sy back to the barracks. But the silence between them felt stilted now. She kept her hands conveniently clasped at her waist.

They reached the steps, and she bid him good night and started inside.

"Alexandra?" he said softly.

She turned.

"Is everything all right?"

"Yes, everything is fine," she said quickly. But even as she said it, she heard the false note in her voice. And judging by his expression, he did too. She realized then how she might have given him the impression that she felt more than only friendship for him. Because she did. And yet, she couldn't. "I hope your trip goes well, Sy, and that your time in Memphis is successful."

He stared, his gaze far too discerning. "I appreciate that. But I sure would like to know what's wrong. If it's because I took your hand a moment ago, then I—"

She shook her head. "No, it's not that. It's . . ." She briefly bowed her head, unable to look him in the eye and say this. "I'm grateful that we're friends, Sy. Truly. And again . . . I hope you find the answers you're looking for. That we're both looking for."

He said nothing for a moment. Then he nodded. "Take care of yourself while I'm gone, Alexandra. I'll see you when I get back."

She heard the hint of a question there at the end and simply answered with a smile, then walked into the barracks.

Awhile later, with Ella asleep on her cot, Alexandra lay awake, the churning inside her keeping sleep at a distance.

This was her world. She'd found the purpose and meaning for her life that she'd been searching for. That David's love had prepared her for. Sy's life was in Colorado. A world away. A world where she didn't fit. She saw that so clearly now.

She simply needed to make sure that he saw it too.

"Miss Jamison? Miss *Jamison*?"

"Yes, Lettie, I hear you!" Alexandra looked across the classroom, forcing patience into her tone while blowing a strand of hair from her face. She felt worn to the bone. And . . . restless. The hunger gnawing her stomach didn't help.

But as Ella had said recently, the meals served at Fisk, though lacking in nutrition, still constituted more sustenance than most of their students enjoyed.

Ella Sheppard constantly seemed to be looking for the blessing in every circumstance. A trait Alexandra appreciated but had yet to master.

The thermometer outside hovered at near ninety degrees, and the threat of rain hung heavy in the air. A threat that—if the angry skies made good on their bluster—would churn the sun-packed dirt surrounding the barracks to muck and mire, while challenging the already leaking roof of the old structure to what could likely be the final showdown.

But something else was contributing to her restlessness. Sy had been gone for nearly two weeks, and despite every moment of every day being spoken for, his absence had left a bigger void in her life than she'd anticipated.

"Thank you, Alexandra," he'd whispered to her the night they'd listened to the singers. "For sharing this with me." As it turned out, the two of them had more in common than she'd originally thought. And yet—

"Miss Jamison?" Lettie said again.

"Yes!" Alexandra answered, grateful for the distraction. "Just one moment please, Lettie, and I'll be right there."

Lettie nodded, the young woman's excitement about her studies evident in her insatiable enthusiasm. She was older than Alexandra had first thought. Seventeen. And more mature. Lettie had also come into class already knowing her letters and able to sound out words.

The young woman would make a fine teacher one day—if Alexandra could only help her focus that exuberance.

Alexandra surveyed the classroom to make sure the other students were on task, then bent again to help the seventy-year-old Miss Henrietta who, in only six days' time, had mastered the alphabet. These students' thirst for knowledge ran deeper than any she'd ever seen. And with good reason. As George White stressed again and again, education meant freedom. The same, when she thought about it, as it meant for her.

Alexandra pulled her attention back. "Miss Henrietta, you're doing so well. Simply take your time and sound out the letters of this word one by one."

Eyes bright, the older woman nodded and bent back over the text—and did exactly as Alexandra instructed.

"Very good!" Alexandra gently touched her shoulder, aware of other students watching, listening. And learning. "Now, Miss Henrietta, I want you to put all of the letters together. But slowly this time. And remember, there are only three syllables in this word." Alexandra held up three fingers. "And the *e* and the *r* in this word are pals. They like to stick together!"

The older woman smiled, nodding. Then looked back at the page. "Mmm . . . eh . . . nnn . . . i . . . sss . . . t . . . er . . . e . . . d.

Min . . . is . . . ter . . . ed." Miss Henrietta looked down at her three outstretched fingers and counted. "*Mi . . . nis . . . tered.*"

"Excellent!" Alexandra felt a rush of joy as unmistakable pride brightened the creases in the woman's cheeks and brow.

Miss Henrietta had been a house slave all her life, so she'd seen "scores o' paper plumb full o' odd scratchin's before," as she'd put it. But as a slave, she'd never been taught to read or write. Those were privileges strictly forbidden to slaves, and punishable by whipping, imprisonment, or worse.

"Now try the entire sentence again," Alexandra urged. "I know you can do it."

"For . . . even . . . ," Miss Henrietta began. "The . . . Son . . . of . . . man . . . c-came . . . not . . ."

Several fellow students sitting in adjacent desks and on the floor leaned in as she—slowly, painstakingly—read the passage.

". . . and . . . to . . . give . . . his . . . life . . . a . . . ransom . . . for . . . many."

Claps and congratulations abounded when she finished, as they always did when someone succeeded. And Alexandra joined in.

"Now it's my turn. Right, Miss Jamison?" Jacob reached for the Bible on Miss Henrietta's desk.

"Yes, Jacob. It's your turn." Alexandra gave the young boy a smile, then chose a new verse in the gospel of Matthew and set him to sounding out the words, the others looking on.

She regretted that they didn't have enough Bibles and spellers to go around. As it was, in this class alone six students had to share the same Bible and spelling book, and the bindings on the Bibles were split and cracking, the pages torn and some missing. The spellers were no better.

She'd actually considered taking the Bibles apart book by book and then passing them out, but Mr. White had greatly frowned upon the idea.

Thinking of the trunk of pristine books back in her bedroom

at her house, she got the same sick feeling she did every time she thought about leaving them behind. How was her mother doing? Worried about her, no doubt. Alexandra needed to make contact with her, and had an idea about how to do that. But she'd need to enlist Ella's help.

Young Jacob began sounding out his letters. After making sure he was on track, Alexandra crossed the room to help Lettie.

The students rarely complained about having to share the Bibles and books, but it slowed their overall progress, and Alexandra had told Mr. White as much. Still, the school's finances were in a shambles, and the debate over the potential tour for the singers raged on.

Only yesterday she'd again overheard Mr. White arguing with gentlemen from the missionary board in his office. She and Ella had lain awake on their cots last night wondering if the ferociousness of the disagreement itself might actually portend the end of Fisk University.

Neither of them had gotten much sleep.

If Fisk ended up closing its doors, what would she do? She'd heard a couple of the other teachers talking in their room a few nights earlier saying they'd either move to Atlanta to help with the freedmen school there or go back home, to the North.

But there would be no going home for her. Bridges had been burned that could never be crossed again. At least, not with her father. But far worse for the students if Fisk closed. What would happen to them? To their futures? To Ella and the other singers? Surely God hadn't brought all this together only to see it fail.

"Miss Jamison." Lettie held up one of the spelling books. "I'm just wonderin' if I can go ahead and be startin' on the next one."

"The next one? Do you mean you've already worked through all these lessons?"

"Yes'm." Lettie smiled, then lowered her voice. "I been sneakin' in and readin' before class. Me and Brister both."

Alexandra glanced at Lettie's brother, who towered above

nearly every other student, young or old, in the school. He was bright as well, though not as bright as his sister. Alexandra had known almost from the first day that keeping Lettie challenged was going to take some doing. If only she had her books from home. She had several advanced readers in her collection.

"I'm afraid this is the only speller we have. At the present time," Alexandra added, seeing the cloud pass over Lettie's pretty face. "But . . . I'll see what I can do."

Lettie was looking past her, and the young woman's eyes suddenly went wide as the classroom fell silent. Alexandra turned in the direction of the door and felt her breath leave her lungs.

Chapter

NINETEEN

He was a fierce-looking man, and what he was doing here, in her classroom, she couldn't guess. And yet something about him seemed vaguely familiar. "May I help you, sir?"

Another couple of inches, and the man would have had to stoop to get through the doorway. The shirt he wore strained against the muscles in his arms and chest, and his skin, glistening with sweat, was black as coal. He cradled three long, shallow wooden crates in one arm, the containers looking almost toylike in his grip.

"Yes, ma'am," he said in a voice as deep as still water. "I believe you can. You're Miss Jamison?"

She moved to the front of the classroom, aware of the students watching. "That's right. And you are?" Despite being certain they'd never met, she couldn't shake the feeling she'd seen him before.

He smiled then, only the slightest bit. But enough that she felt the tightness in her chest lessen by a degree.

"My name is Vinson, ma'am. I'm here with a delivery for you."

"A delivery?" She frowned, looking at the wooden crate he placed with care on the worktable serving as her desk. "I'm afraid there's been a mistake. I didn't order anything." She could only imagine what Mr. White would do if she accepted a shipment for which the school couldn't pay.

"I know you didn't, ma'am. But these are for you, all the same."

Alexandra drew closer and noticed a cloth draped over the top crate. She caught the sweet aroma of chocolate and looked up at him, bewildered. Curiosity getting the better of her, she peered beneath the dishcloth—and had to smile, despite her suspicions. "These . . . are for me?"

"That's what the boss said, ma'am."

"The boss?"

"Mr. Rutledge, ma'am."

She shook her head, looking at the four chocolate chess pies nestled in the top crate. And there were two other crates beneath it. *Twelve pies?*

"He said all this comes to you. Same as the rest of everything I've got out there," the man added.

Alexandra looked up. "The rest?"

She followed him into the hallway where she saw four crates stacked alongside the wall. She peered inside. Primers! For every grade. And not the used primers they had now, with dog-eared corners and pages missing. Brand-new primers with bindings that had never been creased. *Sylas Rutledge* . . . The man was not playing fairly.

"I'm to give you this too, ma'am." He pulled an envelope from one of the crates.

She opened it.

Dear Alexandra,
   Try not to rush your piece of pie this time.
                     As ever,
                     Sy

   P.S. Headed to Memphis next. Would appreciate your prayers.

She read the note a second time, his post script especially surprising. "By chance, do you know when Mr. Rutledge will be returning?"

"I'm sorry, ma'am, but I don't. You want me to carry these crates in for you?"

After some inward debating, she nodded. "Yes, please."

She followed him back into the classroom and saw the huddle of students gathered around her desk. She whispered to Lettie, who then set off on the errand, but not before the young woman tossed Vinson a subtle smile.

The man simply nodded in return, but Alexandra didn't miss how his gaze followed Lettie as she left the room.

Vinson turned back. "Good day to you and your students, Miss Jamison."

"To you as well, Mr. Vinson." She briefly considered offering her congratulations on his starting classes at Fisk, then thought better of it. She wasn't certain if Sy had confirmed it with Mr. White yet or not.

Minutes later, Lettie returned with a knife from the kitchen, and Alexandra cut the first four pies into slices enough to feed her entire class. Then she sliced another three pies and shared them with the classroom across the hallway. There were no plates, no forks, no napkins, but no one cared.

She marked the remaining pies to be taken to dinner that night and shared with the entire staff and all the boarding students, making note to be certain Mr. White received a piece and was told about the primers. And the benefactor.

After her last student was served, she cut a sliver for herself and enjoyed the creamy chocolate custard and buttery pastry, and prayed for Sy's meeting in Memphis, as he'd requested. Only another prayer surfaced. One that brought her up short. And almost felt as if it hadn't come from her.

How could she be praying that the evidence Sy found would clear his stepfather of any wrongdoing? And yet, that's precisely what she wanted. For Sy. For his peace of mind.

Taking a deep breath, she wiped the corner of her eye, then looked around to make sure no one was watching. The students were all laughing and talking, the joy in their faces evident. As was something else.

This, indeed, was her world. And she was grateful for it. No matter how much she missed Sy Rutledge.

∽

Sy knocked on the door, mindful of the time. Only two hours before his train departed. The last daily run from Memphis to Nashville, and he aimed to be on it.

This house was like all the others in this community of freedmen on the lower southeast side—a small, narrow shotgun style, put up hastily with more attention given to getting it done than seeing it last.

He'd been gone for two weeks now, but the time had been productive. He'd managed to secure an attorney in Charlotte who would handle the purchase of the four parcels of land. But what he still lacked was the full slate of committed investors. Harding and two of his colleagues had signed on, but he was still waiting on three others who had indicated interest but had yet to seal the deal.

Next he'd traveled to Chattanooga and St. Louis, and now was here in Memphis coordinating supplies for the Belle Meade depot and railroad and finalizing the details of the new venture. Everything had taken longer and cost more than he'd estimated. Meanwhile, he'd also been working every step of the way to learn more about the accident and to uncover any new bit of information that might clear his father's name.

But no matter who he'd talked to at the Nashville, Chattanooga and St. Louis Railway offices, he'd gotten the same answer: the official fault for the accident lay with Harrison Kennedy, the engineer who drove the No. 1 train from the Memphis station. It was as if every last one of them were reading from the same script.

He'd thought that being on the inside of railroad operations, being the owner of the Northeast Line, would give him a leg up on gaining information. But that wasn't turning out to be the case.

So he hoped his conversation with the porter back in Nashville that had led him here—to the heart of the community where many of the freedmen who'd died in the accident had lived—would prove fruitful. A good number of those were farmhands who had taken interim work in Nashville last summer, only planning to be there for two or three months before heading back to harvest crops. They'd simply been providing for their families as best they could.

Sixty-eight of the one hundred and three people killed had been freedmen. He'd known that from one of the first newspaper accounts he'd read. But not until he'd seen the list at the Chattanooga office of all the names of the victims—along with their race, ages, occupations, and the towns they'd hailed from—had it really sunk in with him how unjust that number was.

But he knew how things worked on the railroad. Passenger cars for white people were always placed at the end of the train to lessen the risk of injury and to escape the annoying soot and cinders, while cars carrying black men and women were placed right behind the baggage cars, which sat directly behind the steam locomotive.

Frustrated by his own nearsightedness in that regard, he knocked a second time, harder than the first. He was tired and more than ready to be back—

He caught himself. *Home* had been the next word in his thoughts. And yet Nashville was not his home. So why did it feel as if the hub of his world, of his future, resided there? He knew the answer.

Alexandra Jamison.

The woman lingered behind every thought. When he had an idea or an obstacle to work through, it was Alexandra he wanted to discuss it with. Their last evening together in Nashville, when they'd sneaked in to listen to the singers, remained foremost in his mind. And that song . . .

The lyrics, though simple, wouldn't leave his head. *In the morning when I rise, give me Jesus. When I am alone, give me Jesus. You can have all the rest . . . Give me Jesus.* The words kept returning at odd intervals, bringing comfort in one moment and discontentedness in the next. Perhaps it was the soulful way in which the singers had sung the song. He didn't know.

He only knew he was grateful that Alexandra had come into his life. And that he had to find a way to remove the barrier of Dutchman's Curve if he wanted her to stay in it. That much was clear.

But it was the article he'd read earlier that morning in the newspaper that had pushed her to the forefront of his thoughts today.

A female schoolteacher in Alabama, teaching at a freedmen's school, had been attacked by nightriders. A group of extremists, the reporter had labeled them. Men who dressed up in robes and masks and conical hats. Sounded like the teacher had been been badly beaten—and worse. All for "seeking to instruct Negroes and for associating with them publicly." The thought that someone would lay a hand to Alexandra like that made his blood boil.

Footsteps sounded beyond the door, and Sy straightened, wrestling his focus back to the moment and hoping this next-to-last person on his list would prove to be a better lead than the others he'd visited that afternoon. He was running out of prospects.

The door opened, and a black woman peered up, her dark eyes immediately distrusting. "Help you, sir?"

"I hope you can, ma'am. My name is Sylas Rutledge, and I'm here to see Luther Coggins."

Her gaze ran over him. "What you wantin' Luther for?"

"I'm with the railroad. We're looking into a collision that happened about a year ago. Just outside of Nashville with the Nashville Chatta—"

"I know what train crash you talkin' about. Gotta be livin' under a rock not to. But what you think that's gotta do with my Luther?"

"Ma'am, we're talking with some of the people who were on the No. 1 and No. 4 that day. I understand Mr. Coggins had been working in Nashville and was on his way home on the No. 4 bound for Memphis. We're wanting to learn from past errors. Perhaps see if maybe there's something that was missed in all the details the first go-round."

"Luther don't know nothin' he ain't already told you people. Besides, he ain't home." She started to close the door.

"Well . . ." Sy held out a fifty-cent piece. "If Mr. Coggins did happen to be home, I'd sure be obliged if you'd tell him I'd like to speak with him. I won't take but a few moments of his time."

She reached to take the fifty-cent piece, but Sy closed his palm around it. "Once you make sure Mr. Coggins is home."

She eyed him. "Wait here." She closed the door.

A minute later a man opened it. "You wantin' to talk to me, sir?"

"I am. Thank you, Mr. Coggins. I'm Sylas Rutledge."

Sy held out his hand, but the man just looked at it, then raised a stump where his right hand should've been.

"No. 4 took it from me that day, Mr. Rutledge. Never could find it either. Found others, but not mine."

The man said it so matter-of-factly. Sy had read of the extent of the injuries sustained that day. Similar to frequent tragedies he saw in mining. He quickly changed the coin to his other hand, then extended his left to the man. Luther Coggins stared at it for a second, then slowly smiled and took hold.

"I have a few questions, Mr. Coggins, about—"

"The crash. I know. My wife told me. But I done said my piece to all of you last summer."

"I realize that, but I'm hoping you would simply go over some of the details with me again."

Sy held out the coin and the man took it, then gestured for him to enter. They sat in a sparsely furnished parlor, and for the first few moments Sy focused on asking him general questions. Facts Sy knew about the accident, just to gauge the fellow's knowledge and to get a reading on the man himself. Did he tell the truth? Did he stretch it any? Did he make up parts to cover what he didn't know?

To Sy's pleasure, he found Luther Coggins to be as candid and forthright as they came.

"So when you came to after the crash, Mr. Coggins, you said a man was standing over you."

"Yes, sir. He was feelin' of my throat to see if I was still alive. Said he didn't think I would be, based on the blood. He tied my arm off real good to help stem the bleedin'."

"You didn't happen to get his name, did you?"

"Hank."

Sy hesitated, not having expected that. "Hank," he repeated. "Did you get a last name?"

Coggins shook his head. "But I know he works for the railroad. Or did back then, at least. 'Cuz he told me he saw the crash from his perch."

"His perch?"

"Yes, sir. The one with them flags."

"The signal tower. So Hank was a signalman."

"I guess. If that's what you call 'em."

Sy was fairly sure he already knew the answer to his next question based on where the wreckage of the No. 4 had been. "Did you happen to see this tower?"

"Yes, sir. He pointed it out. It was over by the bridge."

Sy nodded, having seen the tower himself when he was out at Dutchman's Curve.

They talked awhile longer, Sy aware of the time slipping by, then he thanked the man again.

Coggins walked him to the door. "Don't know if I helped any."

"Oh, you did. That you knew the name of the man who assisted you is a start. Most people I've spoken with about the accident were so shaken at the time, understandably so, they didn't get many details."

Coggins shrugged. "Seemed wrong, somehow, not thanking the man by name who saved my life."

"Yes. It would, wouldn't it?"

Sy walked on but stopped around the corner, pulled a notebook from his pocket, and jotted some quick notes. He had one more address to visit before he headed to catch the train.

He found the residence with little difficulty, but no one came to the door. He'd known better than to get his hopes up, yet he still felt a sinking disappointment at the lack of information he'd uncovered. With no time to spare, he hurried back across town to the train station.

Passengers were already boarding when he arrived, so he retrieved his satchel from the hold and climbed aboard. He found an empty bench toward the back of the passenger car and hunkered down to get some rest.

He nudged his hat over his eyes, the week and its frustrations catching up with him. He was beginning to seriously doubt whether he'd be successful in uncovering the truth about his father's role, if any, in the accident. Plus, he knew Alexandra was hoping for news as well, so she could reach some peace about her late fiancé, David.

David *Thompson*.

He'd learned the man's last name while scanning the official roster of the deceased from the accident while at the offices of the Nashville, Chattanooga and St. Louis Railway in Chattanooga. There was only one passenger with the first name of David on the list.

What had David Thompson been like? Even more thought provoking, what had his relationship with Alexandra been like? But as soon as Sy's thoughts headed down that pike, he knew it wasn't a direction he wanted to go.

"Mind if I sit here, friend?"

Sy opened his eyes, the frustration and weariness in him prompting an emphatic *Yes, I mind*. But the heavily bearded, suited fellow appeared harmless enough, and the train was full, so Sy gave a sluggish nod toward the bench opposite him and closed his eyes again.

The train left the station and he settled in; the rhythm of the rails always seeming to coax him to sleep. But today, sleep eluded him. After a while he sat up, took off his hat, and ran his hands through his hair.

"No matter what you do, friend, sometimes sleep simply won't come."

At the voice, Sy looked over at the man sitting across from him and nodded.

The fellow offered his hand. "Philip Paul Bliss."

Sy shook it, wishing now he'd kept his eyes closed. "Sylas Rutledge."

"Well, Mr. Rutledge, you're headed to Nashville?"

"I hope so. Because if I'm not, I'm going in the wrong direction awfully fast."

Bliss laughed. "What's your line of work, Mr. Rutledge?"

"Railroad."

Bliss nodded, then eyed him as though trying to imagine what role he played.

"I own the Northeast Line," Sy finally offered, hoping to cut the exchange short.

"Owner of a railroad! Now that sounds exciting!"

Sy gave a noncommittal nod and glanced back out the window at the countryside speeding past. But as he sat there, the silence lengthening, he heard Alexandra in his head, along with her counsel. *When someone introduces himself to you in a social setting and inquires about your profession, etiquette demands that you reciprocate and show an equal interest in his as well. Southern gentlemen expect it. It's a way of broadening one's sphere of influence.*

He sighed. So much for putting the woman out of mind.

"And what is it you do, Mr. Bliss?"

"I'm a missionary singer! I sing and write church music."

Sy stared, wishing he could throttle Alexandra about now. Because the man obviously loved his work and was eager to talk about it. And all Sy wanted to do was sleep.

But he did love music . . .

"I work for a music publisher," the man continued. "In addition to singing and writing, I conduct musical conventions, singing schools, and concerts for my employer. But my favorite pastime is composing hymns."

"Hymns . . ." Sy nodded.

The man laughed. "I know. It's not as romantic or colorful a life as the railroad, I'm sure. But it *can* be exciting, at times. Do you have any favorites?"

Sy hedged a little. "I'm afraid I don't know many church songs, sir." Plus, he didn't want to prime the conversation any more than he already had.

"Well, I'm working on a hymn right now for an upcoming prayer meeting. But I can't seem to get the right words to come."

"I'm sure you'll think of them soon enough." Sy shifted in his seat toward the window, hoping to send a subtle hint.

"Are you a God-fearing man, Mr. Rutledge?"

Sy didn't know whether to laugh or cry. "Listen . . . Mr. Bliss," he offered as politely as he could, "I've had a long week. Two weeks, actually. And all I really want to do is get some rest. So if you don't mind . . ."

The man held up a hand. "Say no more! I understand completely. You go on and get some sleep. I'll sit here and write and give you the quiet you need."

"Much obliged." Sy pulled his hat back over his eyes and settled into the seat, grateful to be spared that particular conversation. He took a deep breath and—instead of focusing on the scribbling going on two feet away—he willed the tension to leave him and tried to concentrate on the gentle rocking of the train, the almost hypnotic way the steel wheels had of lulling a person to—

Nope. It was hopeless. He'd never get to sleep. And he didn't dare shift positions, knowing that as long as he kept still, he at least stood a chance of enjoying a measure of peace.

As the train rumbled down the tracks, he squinted from beneath the brim of his hat, looking to make sure Mr. Bliss couldn't see his eyes. Safe. And besides, the man was busy writing in a notebook. Sy stared out the window and watched the sun setting on the distant horizon while it bathed the wheat fields in a golden blur.

He hoped Alexandra had gotten a smile from the pies, and he was confident the students were making good use of the primers. He'd wanted to do something special for her after all she'd done for him. And he planned on doing more, despite her clear signal that he not.

He'd known that taking her hand like that had been risky. But he also knew she cared for him more than she let on. A woman like Alexandra Jamison didn't open herself to a man as she had unless she cared for him on some level.

I'm grateful that we're friends, Sy.

He'd warned her never to try to bluff him. But that's exactly what she'd done that night on the steps. And he'd seen right through her. While also seeing that if he rushed things, she might bolt for good.

Talk about needing to play his cards close to his vest . . .

He spotted a herd of deer in the distance, running and leaping about. It was the first day of September, and fall would be here soon, though not soon enough for him. Especially with the upcoming construction. He'd won the bid . . . That still felt good to dwell on. As did the look of disgust on Gould's face when the man found out he'd lost. Sy allowed himself the tiniest smile. Some things just never got old.

He'd assured Harding that, once supplies were on the ground, he'd have the entire project completed—Belle Meade depot, railway, and macadam road—in no more than two months. By the first of November at the latest. A tall order, considering everything that had to happen between now and then. But doable. Especially with Vinson overseeing things in his absence.

Sy shifted on the bench, his back aching from being in one position too long. And he was hungry too. He should've planned better. No sooner did the pain in his back lessen than another began, on a different level. What if his father *was* responsible for that accident, even in some small way?

But that simply wasn't possible.

For nearly forty years, Harrison Kennedy had been one of the most respected engineers on the Nashville, Chattanooga and St. Louis Railway. Proven experience like that didn't simply disintegrate overnight.

Sy pushed himself upright, deciding that what faced him across the bench was better than the questions burning a hole inside him. He reseated his hat and massaged the back of his neck.

"Good rest?" Bliss asked, his easy smile in place.

"Great." Sy rubbed his temples, then checked his pocket watch. Only thirty minutes or so outside of Nashville.

Bliss stood and reached into a leather satchel on the rack above and withdrew a cloth sack. He sat again and stretched out his long legs, then unwrapped a sandwich and held out a half. "My wife makes the best chicken mash you've ever tasted."

It did look and smell good, but Sy shook his head. "I'm fine, but thank you."

"You'll be doing me a favor." Bliss grinned. "She gave me two of these, and if they're not both gone when I get back tonight, I'll be in big trouble."

Hunger winning out, Sy accepted. "Much obliged, Mr. Bliss."

They ate in welcome silence, staring out the window. Then did the same with the second sandwich. It really was the best chicken mash Sy had ever eaten.

"Please give my thanks to your wife, sir."

"I'll do it. She packs an extra sandwich every time I travel. She can't stand the thought of someone going hungry."

"Sounds like a fine woman."

"Oh . . ." Bliss's expression grew gentle. "She is." He reached into his coat pocket and withdrew a worn photograph that had been folded down the middle. "Here's my Lucy. And here're our sons, George and Philip Paul. Ages four and one, respectively."

Sy took the picture, assuming from its condition that Bliss always carried it with him. "Handsome family."

"They mean the world to me," Bliss said softly. "I truly don't know what I'd do without them." Then he laughed. "Odd how you can live the bulk of your life without someone. Then once you meet her and she becomes part of your life, you can't imagine living another day without sharing it with her."

Sy stared at the image but was picturing another face entirely. "I know what you mean."

"So you're married, too, Mr. Rutledge? Have a family?"

Sy laughed. "No . . . Not yet anyway."

"Well, it'll come. And when it does, you won't regret it."

The train whistle blew—two long blasts—signaling the approach to Nashville.

Bliss glanced at his notebook again and shook his head.

"Words not coming?" Sy offered.

Bliss sighed. "No, and that prayer meeting is this weekend. Say . . . you wouldn't be interested in coming, would you? Dwight L. Moody himself will be speaking. Powerful man, full of the Spirit."

Sy did his best to look impressed, not having a clue who this Moody fellow was.

"There'll be dinner on the grounds with plenty of food, good fellowship, and"—the man's smile grew wide—"some mighty fine singing."

"Or maybe only a little humming, if you don't get that hymn finished." Sy laughed, and was glad when Bliss did too.

Bliss went back to work, and Sy was grateful. Because they were coming up on the place where his father had taken his last earthly breath. Sy stared out the window, imagining what it must have been like, how quickly the world had changed for the people on both of those trains that morning. How quickly it had changed for Alexandra . . .

Everyone in that car died. Either crushed by metal and steel, or pierced by splintered wood like spears. Alexandra's vivid descriptions rose to his memory with force, the sacred ground passing beneath him. *Or scorched by steam from the locomotive or boilers that ripped open on impact.*

She'd been right. Though he'd told her he understood, he hadn't.

As the train pulled into the station, Sy looked across at Bliss. The fellow's brow was furrowed in concentration, and Sy decided that perhaps the man wasn't so annoying after all. The train came to a stop, and they stood along with the other passengers and retrieved their satchels.

"I'm sure if I tell Lucy you're coming to the meeting, she'll make more of her chicken mash. Just for you."

"You're kind, Mr. Bliss. And I thank you. But I need to decline." Sy stuck out his hand. "You almost had me persuaded, though, with that chicken mash."

Bliss shook his hand, then grew still. And frowned. "That's it," he whispered, as though to himself. "Almost persuaded." He grabbed his notebook and began scribbling something down. "That's perfect, Mr. Rutledge! Sad and . . . so despairing, in a sense. But perfect."

Sy looked at him, not really knowing what he'd done. "Glad to be of service, Bliss. And again, I appreciate the sandwich. And . . . our meeting."

"As do I, Mr. Rutledge. May the Lord Jesus bless you and keep you, sir. May he guide you to the life he has for you." Bliss leaned closer. "Which I earnestly pray includes the woman who, I dare say, has already caught more than only your attention."

Sy laughed and continued on down the aisle. As they waited to disembark, Sy heard the man softly humming a tune behind him. A tune he recognized. And he was reminded of his father, and of standing there at the edge of the cornfields on Dutchman's Curve. Again, the lyrics returned with surprising clarity, and though he wasn't about to burst forth in song, Sy couldn't resist turning around.

"Brightly beams our Father's mercy," he said, enjoying the surprise in Bliss's expression, "from his lighthouse evermore. But to us he gives the keeping of the lights along the shore." He smiled. "Turns out I do know a hymn after all."

A smile swept the man's face. "You have made my day, sir. I *wrote* that song. After hearing a story about a shipwreck on a starless night. But . . . How do you know it?

Sy quickly sobered. "It was my father's favorite hymn in recent years." He glanced away. "We just passed over the place a few minutes ago where he died. In the train accident about a year ago."

"On Dutchman's Curve," Bliss said, the light dimming in his eyes. "I remember reading about that accident in the paper. Heartbreaking. So many fatalities, so many injured. My deepest condolences to you, Mr. Rutledge."

Sy nodded his thanks, then disembarked, wondering if Bliss's attitude would change, as others' did, if the man knew his father had been the engineer of the No. 1.

Bliss came alongside him on the platform. "You have encouraged this poor hymn writer's heart, sir. Please, allow me to buy you dinner. I'd love to hear more about your father, if you're willing. And though I'm not sure you have any interest, I know someone who was on the train that morning and survived, by God's mercy. A woman I met in Ohio at a church meeting a few months back."

Sy bent to the unexplained prodding inside him. "I'd appreciate very much sharing a meal with you. But it'll be my treat."

Later that night Sy walked back to the hotel in the dark, his conversation with Bliss having gone long. He thought of Alexandra and knew she would be asleep by now. And that Mr. White would likely be circling the campus on his nightly prayer vigil.

He'd told Bliss about his father being the engineer of the No. 1, and Bliss had listened patiently, not a trace of judgment in his eyes.

The city was quiet for a Friday evening, and once back in his room, Sy didn't bother lighting a lamp. He stripped to his drawers, edged his window open a little more, and fell into bed, the sheets a welcome cool against his skin. But still his thoughts raced.

He needed to meet with the three straggling investors and convince them to commit to the North Carolina–West Virginia venture. It was past time. Then as soon as the funds were secure, he'd wire the Charlotte attorney and tell him to move forward on the offers to the landowners.

He turned onto his side and thought again of the parishioner Philip Bliss had told him about. Miss Riley Glenn. He hoped the connection between Bliss and the woman would prove to be more than merely coincidental. That it would lead him to the answers he sought.

Because it felt like he was running out of resources. And time.

The gentle thump of rain hitting the roof filled the silence, and from some distance away the low, mournful cry of a train whistle moved toward him, filling his room, filling him. He swallowed hard, thinking of his father and of honor lost that yearned to be restored.

How empty the past two weeks had felt without Alexandra's presence. He couldn't pinpoint when it had happened, but she'd become a part of his life, and he didn't welcome the thought of not sharing a future with her. She'd stated that she cared for him as a friend, but he didn't buy it.

Yet he knew there might be some wisdom in giving her a little time, a little room to miss him, perhaps. However difficult that would be for him. Still . . . He determined in that moment, no matter the outcome of his efforts surrounding Dutchman's Curve, he would find a way to win Alexandra's heart.

Even if he had to wager everything to do it.

Chapter
TWENTY

The low, mournful cry of a train whistle drifted in through Alexandra's bedroom window. Maybe it was the late hour, or the dimly lit bedroom in the aging barracks, or the way the rain hit the roof above—a lonely *pitter-pat, pitter-pat, pitter-pat*—but the sound tugged at her heart.

And also sent a tiny shiver up her spine.

Sitting still on her cot, she could make out the distant thrum of the locomotive, and she closed her eyes, memory taking over, as she heard the echo of the explosion that shook the ground last summer, and shook her world to its core. She swallowed, seeing David's face so clearly in her mind. Then seeing his broken body, so badly burned, in the cornfield when she'd had to identify him to the authorities.

She dragged in a breath and rose from the cot, needing to move, needing to clear her mind. She was grateful it was Friday, and she had the weekend to prepare for next week's classes.

She'd seen Mary in town recently—an unexpected meeting but so welcome. Until Mary reminded her of the train trip they were to take together "sometime soon." Alexandra had hastily responded that her teaching position at Fisk wouldn't allow for any travel in the near future. Which was a valid enough reason.

But Mary knew the truth. As did Alexandra. Would there ever come a day when she'd be able to put that fear behind her and board a train again?

Needing a diversion, she crossed in stocking feet to the satchel Mary had loaned her and reached inside for her friend's copy of *Little Women*. And saw the sterling flask beside it. Holding the flask in her palm, she ran her fingertips over the butterflies embossed on the front.

She'd intended to return this to Sy that first night he'd come to Fisk for lessons. But in the course of that week she'd forgotten all about it. And hadn't thought of it since. She would return it at her first opportunity. If he ever got back. Of course he might be back already, for all she knew. He might simply be—

"You're still up?"

Alexandra turned to see Ella in the doorway. "Oh . . . I didn't hear you come in. How was your day?"

"Long, but good." Ella deposited her books on the desk. "So . . . You haven't given that back to him yet?"

Alexandra shook her head. "But I will."

"It's been a few weeks since Mr. Rutledge has been by."

"He's been out of town. But he should be back any day now." Eager to change the subject, Alexandra slid the flask back into the satchel. "How was practice this evening?"

"It went well. We're working on a few new songs. Two of them hymns." Ella unlaced her worn boots, dropped them by her cot, and collapsed onto her mattress.

Alexandra looked over. "Does that bode well for the tour happening after all, do you think?"

"Mr. White still hasn't mentioned anything, and we've all decided not to ask. Best not stir that hive of bees." Ella pointed. "I brought a newspaper with me. It's inside the book on the top. It's a few days old, but it's still news. One of the other singers shared it with me tonight."

Alexandra claimed it and settled back on her lumpy cot, working to get comfortable. This was a part of her old life she missed—staying up with current events, reading about what was happening on the other side of the world. But it wasn't the only thing. The sparse life here at Fisk was taking more adjustment than she'd anticipated. And as hot and muggy as it was in these barracks now, she could only imagine how cold it would be come winter.

She scanned the front page, surprised to find the column headings only mildly interesting. A few of them even seemed familiar. She checked the date on the paper, wondering if she'd read this edition before. But she hadn't. Seemed the *new* news was really only more of the same.

She flipped through the pages, then stopped when an ad caught her eye. She held the paper closer to read the smaller print.

"What is it?" Ella rose from her cot and began unbuttoning her shirtwaist.

"Maybe a way to raise a little money." Alexandra folded the newspaper back on itself and held it up, pointing to the ad.

"'Will pay money for iron,'" Ella read aloud, then looked back at her. "And where, Miss Jamison, do you propose you and I get iron?"

"Well . . . tomorrow after class, we could walk along the railroad tracks. I've seen old scraps of metal and even nails lying along there before."

Ella frowned. "Precisely how long has it been since you've walked the railroad tracks?"

Alexandra tried not to smile. "About . . . thirteen or fourteen years."

They both laughed.

"I can assure you, Alexandra, any scraps of metal and nails are long gone by now. Taken either by a Johnny Reb or a Yankee. But it was a nice thought."

Alexandra returned the newspaper to the desk. It was still raining, but she edged the window up a little more, hoping for a breeze to cool down the stickiness in the room. She lay back down on her cot.

"Have you heard from your mother yet?" Ella asked a little later, crawling into bed.

"No, but your idea was brilliant. Far better than mine. Hopefully, I'll receive a reply soon."

She'd originally asked Ella to pen a letter to her mother on her behalf, knowing her father would recognize her own handwriting but wouldn't suspect Ella's. But Ella had suggested—very wisely so—that the letter be penned to one of the servants in the household instead, with instructions that a message be safely conveyed to Mother when the time presented itself.

The only servant in their household who could read was Melba. Alexandra had taught her years earlier. In fact, it was teaching Melba and watching the world open up for her that first made Alexandra want to become a teacher.

She had posted the letter last week, trusting the woman without reservation to handle the request as she saw best. She only hoped her father wouldn't intercept the servant's mail as he had her own.

Ella blew out the oil lamp, and Alexandra was reminded yet again of how she used to simply turn down her own oil lamp in her bedroom at night, leaving it burning low, not worrying about conserving oil.

But here at Fisk one conserved everything, not knowing if there would be more the next time or not. Which, she'd learned, wasn't an oddity to the people here; being missionaries or freedmen, they were accustomed to living frugally. Not that it made sacrificing any easier for them. But it did make her keenly aware of how much she'd once had. And of how, even having owned so much, she hadn't really been aware of her wealth, or appreciated it as much as she should have. Something she vowed to change.

She pressed her face into her pillow—and earned a sharp jab. Wincing, she rubbed her cheek, questioning her decision to supplement the meager feathers with hay.

Perhaps she could ask Sy about the iron. Or . . . perhaps she needed to do what she'd promised herself she would do and stop thinking about the man at every—

She sat up. "Ella! Are you asleep?"

There was a rustle of bedcovers. "I *was* . . ."

"I know where we can get iron!"

A yawn. "You're really craving a piece of that pie, aren't you?"

"No, Ella. I'm serious!" She struck a match and relit the lamp.

Ella slowly turned over. "I can tell you're serious, Alexandra, but—"

"I can't believe I didn't think of it earlier." She climbed from bed.

"Wait." Ella held up a hand. "You're thinking of going *now*? And . . . Exactly *where* are you going?"

Alexandra sat back down, wondering how Ella would respond when she told her. "It's a place not far from here. It's been closed for years now, though. It was called—" Suddenly she wasn't sure she could say it. "Porter's . . ."

"Slave Pen," Ella finished.

"Yes," Alexandra said softly. "I remember, years ago, after the war . . ." And she told Ella about the article she'd read in the newspaper.

"Does someone still own it? The building? The land?"

"I don't think so. Mr. Porter died some years back. No family to speak of, and the building's been abandoned since before the war ended. Same as other shops on that street."

A moment passed before Ella spoke again. "How do you know that what was buried is still there?"

"I don't. But I'm hoping that maybe it was forgotten."

Ella looked at her, a spark of possibility lighting her eyes. "There's only one way to find out."

Chapter
TWENTY-ONE

The next morning following breakfast, Alexandra met Ella at the gardener's shed as planned. Not ten minutes later, four male students whom Ella had enlisted to help arrived as well. She and Ella had discussed waiting until that night, but decided it was best to carry out their quest in the light of day. Where anyone could see. Alexandra only hoped they weren't going to all this trouble for nothing.

Because what if there wasn't anything buried in that lot after all? What if someone else had remembered that same newspaper article and had gotten there before them? What if someone in town saw them and objected?

The what-ifs fired at rapid speed, and with every forward step Alexandra prayed not so much for the success of their endeavor but that "whatever the Lord wills," Ella's oft-repeated prayer, would be done.

Ella made certain that the men—DeWitt, Johnnie, Rodgers, and Jeb, all in their late teens and strongly built—knew precisely what they were setting out to do, so there would be no misunderstanding.

They agreed without hesitation.

Ella distributed shovels and trowels, and they set off. The air had smelled of moisture earlier in the night, and the overcast skies hinted at a dreary day. When they finally reached Porter's, the clouds made good on their threat and a light mist fell in a patchy drizzle.

The six of them stood before the old auction stand.

"Where do we start, Miss Ella?" DeWitt asked.

Ella walked a few steps and sank her shovel into the dirt. "Let's all spread out and simply start digging. If you think you've found something, call out."

Alexandra moved a few paces away, knelt, and shoved the trowel into the earth, then scooped and emptied. And scooped and emptied. And scooped and emptied. Her damp hair kept falling in front of her face, and she kept shoving it back.

After digging down about a foot with no results, she moved over a couple of feet and began again. Then, a few minutes later, did the same thing. As the others were doing.

Every few seconds she peered up, expecting to see someone standing on the street watching them. And wondering what she would say if someone approached and asked her what they were doing. She would tell them the truth, she guessed. *We're digging for iron to help change the futures of those who were chained in the past.*

She dug with a fresh intensity and focus she didn't know she had. And by the time she'd dug her eighth hole, her palms ached and her back screamed.

"Miss Sheppard!" one of the students called out, excitement in his voice.

Alexandra looked behind her and saw DeWitt, the only one of the four students she'd met before tonight, holding up a chain. She abandoned her own efforts and joined the group. And soon, each of their shovels and trowels were striking iron against iron.

Alexandra gripped a half-buried chain and pulled, but it wouldn't budge.

"Here, Miss Jamison." Jeb moved in beside her. "Let me help you with that, ma'am." He pulled and the earth reluctantly released its hold.

"Let's make a pile over here." Ella pointed. "We'll take all we can carry, and then come back if we need to."

Alexandra lost track of time as they kept digging and unearthing rusty manacles and chains, now piled in a heap beside a hole at least six feet wide and four feet deep. The misty rain had ceased, and it looked as though the sun was trying to peek through the clouds.

"Do you think that's all of them, Jeb?" Ella stood at the edge peering down, her damp skirt and shirtwaist filthy.

Jeb and DeWitt plunged their shovels into the up-churned earth again and again, until DeWitt finally turned back.

"I do think we got the last of them, Miss Sheppard. No sign of any more."

"Good, then." Ella nodded. "Now let's all get these holes filled back up. Leave it like we found it. Then we'll be on our way."

Nearly an hour later, holes filled and the sun growing more insistent, Ella turned and lifted a rusty chain from the pile and draped it about her slender neck. For as long as Alexandra lived, she knew she'd never forget that image. Tears in her eyes, she watched as DeWitt, Johnnie, Rodgers, and Jeb followed their teacher's lead. Then she did the same, feeling her friend's gaze.

The chains were cold and rough and dug into skin and muscle, and were far heavier when manacles were still attached. The young men worked especially fast to pick up the chains and place them around their own necks, as though wanting to lessen the load she and Ella would carry.

Each chain weighed about four pounds, maybe a little more, Alexandra estimated. And by the time she'd draped five of them about her neck, the tears that had only risen to her eyes moments before now spilled over. Not so much from the physical pain. But from the fact that scarcely more than a handful of years ago, these people standing with her—these warm, intelligent, caring people—would have been subjected to this. And for all she knew, they had been.

Rodgers lifted the last chain and manacle, the heavy iron links already spanning the width of his broad shoulders and draped over both arms. "We have them all, Miss Sheppard."

"Praise Jesus," Ella whispered, her own voice thin with emotion. She looked at each of them, her gaze finally settling on Alexandra. "Let's head home, friends."

The young men walked a few feet ahead, their conversation dotted with laughter every now and then. But Ella walked quietly, not desiring conversation, it seemed. So Alexandra let the silence settle between them.

As they passed through town, passersby looked their way, and Alexandra felt certain one of them would say something. But most of them, upon looking, quickly averted their gazes. And even those who didn't, didn't speak. They simply watched, expressions somber, as the unlikely band passed by, the clink of chains marking every step.

A breeze picked up, and the air felt considerably lighter and cooler than before. And as Fisk came into view, whether it was the morning sun or the touch of fall in the air or the experience they'd shared together, Alexandra saw the rows of ramshackle buildings differently. Suddenly they didn't seem so dilapidated anymore. *Thank you, Father, for allowing me to be a part of this.* As quickly as the prayer rose, it seemed to fall flat.

Because up ahead was a gathering of students—with Mr. White front and center, as though they'd been waiting. A look of concern—or was it anger—lined the man's face.

Ella looked over. "It's all right. I told him last night about our plan. He wanted to come along, but I convinced him it would be best if he stayed here. In the event anything went awry."

"So we're not in trouble?"

Ella smiled and gestured. "What do you think?"

Alexandra looked back to see the students running toward them, Mr. White leading the charge. And as whoops and hollers rose in the air, Ella wordlessly reached over and took hold of her hand.

∽

Sy leaned down and looked through the lens of the surveying level on the tripod, then pulled the pad of paper from his pocket and made some notes. "Looks good, Ben." He stepped to one side and gestured for the surveyor to peer through the lens. "Watch that elevation to the north, would you? And then that angle up ahead as we take the curve toward the creek. I want a gentle rise along that stretch. Not one that throws people back in their seats."

Ben laughed. "Yes, sir. I'll watch it, Mr. Rutledge."

"Otherwise, everything looks fine. We're making good time too."

Ben glanced at the cloudless skies overhead, his tanned face a testament to decades of railroad work. "Weather looks like it's going to cooperate, sir. Rains have moved out. That always helps."

Turning to leave, Sy remembered something Alexandra had said to him about always shaking the hand of an older man out of respect for his age. So he offered Ben his hand. The older man paused, then smiled and accepted.

"I'm grateful to you, Mr. Rutledge, for hirin' me for this job. It's good to work. And good work is hard to come by."

Sy tightened his grip. "You do good work, Ben. That's why I hired you. It's good to have you working on this project."

The old surveyor smiled and set back to his task.

Sy walked the ridge, looking in the distance at the workers who were already laying track. And making good time of it too.

He'd only been back in town for three days, but it already felt like a month or more. So much for giving Alexandra time to miss him. Being out of town and away from her was one thing. But he'd underestimated how difficult staying away from her would be when he was so close. If not for the work, and plenty of it, he'd have been over at Fisk the first day.

At least his meeting with the three investors yesterday had gone well. They assured him they'd make their decision sooner rather than later, which was what he needed. As soon as they committed their capital, he would head to Charlotte, extend offers to the landowners—who would, if all went well, accept them without a glitch—and the building would commence straight away. They needed to get the dirt work done before the ground froze hard.

He'd be gone three to four weeks at least on that trip. And he wasn't about to leave town again without seeing her. He was determined to give the woman time. He felt the touch of a smile. But his patience only went so far where his desires for her were concerned.

An eagle's cry drew his gaze upward, and he paused and watched the majestic bird from beneath the brim of his hat as the creature soared across the cloudless blue sky. Such a sighting had been common in Colorado. Not so much here. And though he was eager to see his mountains again, he hadn't accomplished what he'd come here to do. Not hardly.

"Hey, Boss!"

Sy turned to see Vinson walking toward him, determination in his stride.

"General Harding's come to see you. But first . . ." Vinson held up an envelope. "Just got a letter from Fisk University."

Sy tried to read the glimmer of emotion in the man's eyes, but couldn't decide if it was good news or bad.

"The man I interviewed with, Mr. White, he says I can start my schooling come January." A muscle flinched in Vinson's jaw. "He also says my tuition's already been paid. And I know you did it. But I can't take that from you."

Sy gripped his shoulder. "You can and you will. Because I wouldn't be here now, Vinson, if you and your parents hadn't come to me and my mother that winter. We would've either starved or frozen to death, if not for your family."

Vinson grabbed him in a bear hug, just like Vinson's father used to do to both of them growing up. Then just as quickly he stepped back.

"I'll do you proud . . . Sy."

"I know you will, Vinson. Because you don't have it in you to do any less. Just to be clear, though . . ." Sy eyed him, trying to curb a smile. "I still expect you to help run the Northeast Line. You'll have to get your homework done on your own time."

Sy headed in the direction of Harding's carriage, hearing Vinson's laughter behind him. He didn't know what Vinson's future held or whether he'd go back West after Fisk. He only knew he couldn't hold the man back. No matter how much he depended on him.

"Mr. Rutledge!" Harding climbed down from his carriage.

"General Harding! Come to see the progress, sir?"

"Come to marvel at the progress, Mr. Rutledge."

Sy managed a smile, accepting the man's handshake. "We're on the straight and clear right now, as you can see. So we're making good time. But those hills are waiting, as is the creek. Still, at this rate, we'll finish within the schedule I gave you."

"That's what I like to hear, Mr. Rutledge. I see that the Belle Meade Depot is already under construction too. When you undertake a project, you attack it straight on, with zeal! I admire that in a man."

"Thank you, General."

"And the stock cars you're refitting for my thoroughbreds. How are those coming along?"

"Nearly finished. They're at the train yard if you'd like to see them."

"I might stop by while I'm in town this afternoon." Harding turned toward the carriage, then paused. "My colleagues and I have been discussing extending the railway past the Belle Meade depot and on down south across my land and across some of theirs toward Mississippi. That translates to a lot of track, Mr. Rutledge. And though we won't be ready to proceed until spring, from what I'm seeing right now, I believe you may be the man for the job."

Sy knew his surprise showed on his face. He'd hoped for this, but for Harding to mention it even before this project was finished . . .

"Thank you, General Harding. I appreciate your confidence."

As the carriage drove away, Sy marveled at how quickly things were falling into place. And that he might be here in Tennessee for longer than he thought. But what struck him even more was how little all that mattered when he imagined not having Alexandra Jamison in his life to share it with.

✑

Glad it was Wednesday night, which meant no kitchen duty for her this week, Alexandra was studying for her upcoming teacher's exam when the bedroom door burst open.

"I think he's going to announce it!" Breathless, Ella gestured toward Alexandra's boots by the foot of the cot. "Mr. White has asked the singers to gather in his office. Ten minutes from now. And he wants you there too!"

"Me?"

Ella nodded. "Your guess is as good as mine! I'd say it's because you've been so supportive of Fisk. And of him. He admires you, Alexandra. Especially after what we did the other day, and because of all the new Bibles and notepads the money from selling the iron will buy." Ella smiled. "He said he found a gentleman willing to come and get the iron and take it to the smelter for us too. At no charge. Which is another answer to prayer."

Alexandra slipped her boots on and laced them as quickly as she could, then followed Ella down the hallway. Together, they hurried to Mr. White's office, where they found the other singers already gathered, waiting in the area by Mrs. Chastain's desk.

"Mr. White said to stay here," Minnie Tate offered, her eyes round with excitement. "He'll come get us in a moment."

Alexandra looked around the room, already acquainted with everyone. The four men were huddled together, speaking in hushed tones. Greene Evans, who sang bass and worked as a grounds-keeper to pay his way through Fisk, motioned them over.

"Miss Sheppard, do you have any idea what he's going to tell us?"

Ella shook her head. "He hasn't said a word to me."

Alexandra listened as they discussed the possibilities, noting again what a sober and industrious sort of young man Greene was.

Quite the contrast to Isaac Dickerson, who also sang bass, and who was fun loving and sometimes even flirtatious. Isaac possessed an extraordinary gift for extemporaneous speaking as well, and often spoke in chapel. Alexandra wagered he knew as much, if not more, about the Bible as any learned preacher in a Nashville pulpit.

"If Mr. White says yes to the tour, do any of you think your parents are going to object?" Thomas Rutling's gaze circled the small group.

Isaac shrugged. "It's hard to say. But I think we all know that the decision will have been baptized in prayer. Surely our parents will know that as well."

They all nodded.

Phebe, who stood next to Ella, looked over after a moment. "Miss Sheppard," she whispered, "I'm not certain my father will allow me to go on the tour. Even if Mr. White demands it."

"We'll cross that bridge when we come to it, Phebe."

Phebe nodded, just as footsteps drew their attention to the hallway.

Mr. White appeared from around the corner and gestured for them to follow him. His customary stony expression revealed nothing. They all crowded into his office.

Alexandra was surprised to find no one else there. Not President Spence nor any of the board members.

"Thank you for coming to meet with me so late this evening." White moved to stand behind his desk. "I'm sorry to interrupt your studies, but . . . I've come to the end of a very difficult and gut-wrenching season of reflection and consideration." He gripped the back of his chair.

Alexandra felt a sinking inside her, and judging from the others' expressions, they felt the same. So this was it. No fund-raising tour? Did this mark the beginning of the end for Fisk? After only five years?

If she felt this great a sense of loss, she could only imagine what the others were experiencing.

"As you all are aware, President Spence and I have not seen eye-to-eye on the idea of this troupe's tour. Same for the board members from the American Missionary Association. I have wrestled with those men both in personal arguments—and with their opinions in hours upon hours of prayer." White's expression was one of enmity. "So many naysayers. So many who do not believe in the mighty power of our God, and who have *refused* to take the necessary steps to save this school."

Alexandra felt a burning behind her eyes.

"And yet, I'm here to tell you that by God's mercy and the much-needed determination of some of his most stubborn creatures, the Fisk Singers *will* be going on tour!"

For a moment, no one said anything. No one moved. Then Isaac Dickerson gave his deep-throated, funny little laugh, and they all began to cheer and hug.

Alexandra turned. "You're going, Ella! You're *going*!"

Ella beamed. "God is so good! There's hope for Fisk yet!"

Alexandra laughed as she looked into the eyes of these extraordinary people, and she felt a depth of gratitude to Mr. White for having included her in this moment.

White held up a hand. "I have a few more words to say, please."

The group fell silent and attentive.

"I've long believed that this troupe is an appointed agency of God for the salvation of Fisk University. And now we shall take the definitive step to prove it! Despite," he added quickly, "those who still do not agree and have chosen not to support us. We will step forth in faith and depart Nashville for the North by train the first week of October! And with full faith in God's ability to deliver, I believe our journey from town to town will be met with great success."

Again, excited whispers skittered through the gathering, and Alexandra felt a thrill of excitement for them all. Sobered nods and amens rose in response, and she nodded in agreement, then found Mr. White's gaze settling surprisingly on her.

"Miss Jamison, I, along with Miss Sheppard, my assistant, and everyone else here, are most grateful for your recent contributions to Fisk. Your skills in organization and leadership are exemplary, and are qualities that will greatly benefit this endeavor."

Alexandra smiled. "Thank you, sir. I'll be honored to support this group, and your tour, in whatever way I can."

"I expected no less from you, Miss Jamison. Which makes this next announcement even more gratifying. You, too, will be joining us on the tour, as the trip's preceptress. Arranging train schedules, hotel stays, and being our publicist as we venture North!"

More laughter and celebration. Alexandra felt congratulatory pats on her back. But her smile faltered even as her pulse edged up a notch. "I-I . . . don't understand, sir. I h-have classes to teach and—"

"No worries, Miss Jamison! Your introductory classes will be completed by the time our train departs for Cincinnati on the first Friday in October! You'll be traveling with us as a fellow ambassador for Fisk University . . . and for the Lord Jesus Christ!"

The room ignited again in excitement, but all Alexandra could hear was the grinding of metal on metal and the splintering of wooden passenger cars.

Chapter
TWENTY-TWO

*A*lexandra hesitated in the hallway outside Mr. White's office, her stomach a taut bundle of nerves. Same as it had been since his announcement of the tour three days ago. She'd waited for Saturday so he would, she hoped, have more time to talk to her. Though what she had to say wouldn't take that long.

She simply had to find a way to tell him she couldn't accompany them on the tour. And she'd have to tell him why. She'd tried twice to tell Ella, but couldn't. The image of Sarah Hannah Sheppard carrying her daughter down to the river prevented her from it. Ella had faced more challenge and struggle in her lifetime than Alexandra ever would.

She bowed her head, ashamed.

Yet she *could not* get on that train. Every time she thought about it, she broke out in a cold sweat. And the one person she wanted to talk to most, who would understand, she hadn't seen or heard from. She missed Sy more than she would have thought possible. Then again, admitting this paralyzing fear to him wouldn't be easy either.

Squeezing her eyes tight, she knocked on the door.

"Come in."

She stepped inside, and Mr. White looked up from his desk.

"Greetings, Miss Jamison! I only have a few moments before the next rehearsal. But what I have is yours. Have a seat, if you like."

She shook her head. "No, I'm fine to stand. This won't take long."

"Music to my ears." He smiled. "And to my ever-full schedule." He rose from his desk and began gathering files and stuffing them into his satchel.

"Mr. White . . . This isn't an easy thing for me to say, but—" She swallowed. "I'm afraid I won't be able to travel with the troupe on the tour. I so wish I could . . ." Which wasn't a falsehood. She would do near anything to move past this. "But something happened to me. A year ago. Something I haven't talked about with anyone here, and that left me very much afraid of—"

"Sit down, Miss Jamison."

His firm tone and countenance brooked no argument, so she did as he bade.

"You may not realize it, Miss Jamison," he continued, moving around to her side of the desk. "In fact, I'm certain you do not. But I was once a man ruled by fear. Allowing fear to dictate what I would do and what I would not do. Fear of failure, fear of not living up to my own expectations, much less others' expectations of me. Until I—"

She stopped him with a shake of her head. "Mr. White, I appreciate all that, but my fear is not one of failure or of others' opinions. It's far more . . . tangible in nature. And its talons sink deep."

He stared. "Go on."

"To state it aloud feels so foolish." Her laughter came out flat. "But the reason I can't go on this tour is that I . . ."

She couldn't get the words to come. It felt as though some invisible hand were tightening around her throat.

He eased into the chair beside her. "Miss Jamison." His voice was gentle. "Whatever this fear may be, know that you will receive no judgment from me. There is a reason why our Lord repeatedly told his disciples to 'Fear not.' It is precisely, of course, because they were afraid. Just as you and I are at times. He knows. He understands."

She nodded, thinking of Ella, Maggie, Thomas, George, and the other singers, as well as the students and teachers. "So many people here have endured so much more hardship than I have, Mr. White. Which makes me even ashamed to admit this to you. Or to anyone else."

"Oh, Miss Jamison . . ." His gaze held both understanding and censure. "I fear the Enemy has entangled you in one of his most deceitful and yet successful lies. I cannot count the times I have been ensnared by him in this regard." His expression held discernment. "There will always be someone who has suffered more—or less—than you. To think the person who has suffered more, in your estimation, is somehow more worthy is just as prideful in nature as thinking that the person who has suffered less, in your estimation, is not quite as holy as you are." He smiled. "God alone sees our lives from start to finish and ordains what your suffering and mine will be. For he alone sees what we each must endure to become more like his Son and to be made ready for eternity. For though we all are his, we are not all the same. As you and I have discussed before in this very office."

She nodded, feeling herself begin to calm.

"Now. You said something happened to you a year ago. Why not begin there? Just as it's easier to pluck a seedling from the ground rather than to uproot a mighty oak, I've found it's often less difficult to speak of where the fear first took seed rather than of the fear itself."

Alexandra took a deep breath. "You've heard of Dutchman's Curve, Mr. White."

He nodded, expression somber.

Her eyes filled as her mind took her back to the scene. "I was on the train that morning, the one from Memphis. With my fiancé." Myriad emotions flashed across his face, and as she described the awful seconds, moments, and hours as that day aged into night, his gaze grew glassy. Finally, grateful to have it past her, she sighed. "And I haven't been aboard a train since."

He bowed his head for a long moment, then finally looked up. "Oh, my dear Miss Jamison. But for moments like this, we none of us know the weight the other is carrying within, do we? I am deeply sorry for your losses that day, and for the pain they still inflict."

She offered the semblance of a smile.

He rose. "So now I know why you feel as though you cannot accompany us on the tour."

She nodded, grateful he understood, and relief filtered through her.

"What I do not think *you* yet know, Miss Jamison, is the cost to you if you do not." Though his voice held its usual strength and frankness, his expression held compassion. "God showed me long ago that I must not allow my fear to rule me. Because I have his almighty power dwelling within me. The same power that raised Christ from the dead, the Word says, resides in me, and in you, to carry out his good will. Whatever that may be."

He reached for his satchel, and Alexandra stood, the anvil back on her chest and even heavier now than before.

"One last question for you to pose to yourself, Miss Jamison. And it in no way is meant to diminish your sorrow or to belittle your fear. Because there is nothing little about it. Your fear is real and it is warranted. Because I cannot guarantee that another situation like Dutchman's Curve will not intersect with your life again. I wish I could. But then . . . I would be God, and I clearly am not." He smiled briefly. "My question is a simple one, and it's one I often ask myself when prone to fear over a decision or a direction to take . . . Is the Lord leading me to do this?" He stared into her eyes. "Because if the answer to that question is yes, then you and I have no choice but to do his will. We are the clay, after all. And he is the potter."

He opened the office door, then paused, the hint of a smile at the corners of his mouth. "You see, I believe that if the Lord tells me to jump through a wall, it is my part to jump—and the Lord's to put me through it."

Feeling beaten yet comforted, Alexandra followed him down the hallway.

He stopped by Mrs. Chastain's desk and pulled a piece of paper from his coat pocket. "Mrs. Chastain, I have a wire that needs to be sent today. And my dear wife is in need of some soup bones from the butcher. I fear she's ailing at present. I need to attend to troupe practice and won't be able to get there before the shopkeepers close. Would you be so kind as to—"

"I'll go," Alexandra volunteered, needing to get away for a while, to stretch her legs. To breathe. And maybe even to see Sy, if she could find him.

✑

"So you were personally responsible for the alterations to this stock car, Mr. Rutledge?" General Harding strode around the inside of the specially refitted railcar that had transported Enquirer some weeks back. He took it in from every angle.

"I was, sir." Sy sneaked a look at his pocket watch, needing to get to some shops in town before they closed, then out to Fisk before it got too late.

He'd waited an entire week after returning to town before going to see Alexandra, and he'd only been able to do that because the last three days had been nothing but problems. One step forward and five back. Rail had to be pulled up and laid again due to the ground being softer than the soil tests had first noted. Supplies hadn't come in on time or were back-ordered. It'd been one thing after another.

Yet he was also eager to get an agreement from Harding about the yearling sale. Anything to get the deal closed.

Feeling Harding's attention, he looked over and realized the man had asked him a question he'd only half heard.

"Ah . . . yes, sir." Sy nodded, pulling his thoughts back. "We could easily fit six stalls on this side of the car to transport your yearlings to the sale in Philadelphia, and still have room for the handlers, the feed, the water, and such over here. You could squeeze in eight stalls, but I wouldn't recommend it. Traveling that distance is hard enough on the horses, and if we crowd them up, it'll be even more so."

Harding nodded. "I agree, Mr. Rutledge. And I like what you've done. If we're talking six yearlings per car, then I'll need . . . five cars total."

"That many?" Sy didn't even try to hide his surprise.

"Will that be a problem?"

"No, sir. I was just thinking about how busy those Belle Meade studs of yours must be."

Harding laughed and offered his hand. "I enjoy doing business with you, Mr. Rutledge."

"Much obliged, sir, and the feeling is mutual. I'm honored you've entrusted me with your railroad project. And with your yearlings."

"*And* my investment. Let's not forget that."

Sy laughed. "No, sir. I'm not forgetting that."

"As for the yearlings, Uncle Bob speaks most highly of you, Rutledge. And that man's trust isn't easily won."

Harding bid him good day, and Sy turned toward town, eager to get out to Fisk before the day wore on. But as soon as he entered the butcher's shop, he saw that Fisk had come to him.

Chapter
TWENTY-THREE

Alexandra was waiting in line, fourth in the queue, and every bit as beautiful as he remembered. Sy started to approach her, then saw another young woman and what appeared to be her mother glance Alexandra's way. He sensed familiarity in the way they looked at her, so he stepped to the side, figuring he'd let them visit with her before he did.

But it was Alexandra who turned and saw them first.

"Maribelle! Mrs. Johnson!" Beaming, she crossed to where the two women stood. "It's been weeks since I've seen you. How are you both?"

The older woman's expression instantly turned sour. "Come, Maribelle!" She skirted around Alexandra, shunning her entirely.

But her daughter hesitated, looking at Alexandra, then back at her mother. She opened her mouth to say something, but her mother gave her a look and hissed, "Maribelle!"

The daughter swiftly clamped her mouth shut and hurried to her side, leaving Alexandra to stand alone.

"We do not consort with Negro schoolmarms!" The older woman cast a hateful glance in Alexandra's direction. "Of all the insults to which the fine families of Nashville have been subjected . . ." She huffed and turned toward the counter.

If the old bat had been a man, Sy knew exactly what he would've done. But as it was . . .

Seeing the hurt on Alexandra's face twisted his gut.

Then she turned and saw him. For an instant, her features

cleared. Then just as swiftly, they clouded again. He started to go to her, but her look told him to wait.

Once Mrs. Johnson and her daughter left the shop, she quietly moved back to the line, and Sy joined her.

"Good afternoon, Alexandra," he said softly, stealing a look at her. "I was coming to see you after this."

She looked over at him, doubt in her eyes. "When did you get back in town?"

The question, a simple one, carried weight. He sensed that his absence, even at her request, so to speak, had hurt her. If only she knew how much it had cost him too.

"A week ago. But it's been so busy and believe me, I've wanted to—"

"Help you, ma'am?" The butcher waited behind the counter.

Alexandra stepped forward. "Yes, please." She glanced at the meat, then at the coins in her hand. "How much for a soup bone? Preferably one with a good amount of meat left on it."

"I got a few I ain't stripped yet. They'll run you a nickel each."

"I'll take two, please."

The man wrapped up the bones, took her coins, then looked pointedly at Sy.

"Wait for me," Sy whispered as she headed for the door. "I need two bones as well. Same as hers. And give me about a pound of that summer sausage." Sy pointed, glancing behind him to make sure Alexandra hadn't taken off without him. "And a pound of the cheese there, and the same for the jerky."

She stood to the side with her back to the customers who'd come in behind them. Sy paid for his purchases, opened the door for her, and followed her out.

"Walk with me?" He held out his arm, and she hesitated only a second before accepting. That was something, at least.

"But I need to stop by the telegraph office for Mr. White before it closes."

They walked in that direction, and Sy sensed something

simmering beneath the surface. Something other than his absence. He started to try to pry whatever it was out of her, then decided it was best to let it come of her own volition. Based on the tension he felt coming from her, he gave her about twenty paces, or until they reached the end of the street.

He managed to count to seven.

"Mr. White has asked me to go on the tour with the singers."

"So they're definitely going? That's wonderful news." He looked over. "Or do you not want to go?"

He sought her gaze, but she wouldn't look at him.

"With how you feel about Fisk, Alexandra, and how close you and Ella are, I would've thought you'd be thrilled."

"Sy . . ." She stopped and pulled her hand away. "Don't you see? I'm terrified of getting on a train again! Even the thought all but paralyzes me." She squeezed her eyes tight. "And yet I want to help. If I could somehow blink and be there from city to city, I would. But—" She shook her head.

The conflict within her was so evident, the tension so taut, he wondered why it hadn't occurred to him before that she'd been dealing with this. But what he realized most of all was that she was talking to *him* about this. No, she was practically yelling.

Which meant there was hope for them yet.

"Of course you're frightened, Alexandra. After experiencing what you did—and I've only read about it; you've lived through it—it would concern me if you *didn't* have second thoughts about traveling by rail again. When my train from Memphis returned the other night, and we passed that spot . . . I couldn't help but feel something akin to a shiver pass through me, wondering at how quickly life can change. You're sitting there, visiting, reading your paper, staring out the window, and then—"

"Your world turns upside down. And takes you with it."

She stared at him for the longest time, and he would've sworn he saw a portion of her apprehension melt away.

"Thank you, Sy," she whispered. "For understanding."

He chose his words carefully. "Have you spoken with Mr. White about this yet?"

She nodded. "Earlier this afternoon."

"And?"

She all but rolled her eyes, then gave him a look worthy of Mr. George White himself. "He said the kind of thing he always says. He said he understood why I felt as though I couldn't go. And yet he questioned whether *I* understood the cost of deciding *not* to go." She frowned. "You know how he is."

Sy held back a smile. "But?"

"But I'm still scared! And I don't see how I can do this. Yet how can I not? I'll be letting everyone down."

Tears rose in her eyes, and he fought the instinct to comfort her. "Tell you what . . . Some afternoon this next week, why don't you and I spend some time on a train. Parked. In the train yard," he added quickly. "Then I'll ask Carson, our engineer, to take us for a little ride. A *slow* ride. Not far. On one of the tracks that circles the maintenance depot. And we'll take it step by step from there. We can get together a time or two this next week, if you want. And then over the next month. How does that sound?"

"It sounds like you're trying to get me to do something I don't want to do without letting me see you do it."

He smiled. *This woman.* "After we're finished at the telegraph office, we'll head back toward Fisk. Maybe pick up some barbecue on the way."

She nodded.

"I've missed you, Alexandra," he said softly.

She looked as though she might cry again. But she didn't. "I've missed you too," she whispered, her tone almost begrudging. "Oh . . ." She reached into her skirt pocket and pulled out the flask. "I've been meaning to return this to you."

Sy frowned. "But it was a gift. You don't like it?"

"My liking it is of no consequence. As I told you before, it's not an appropriate gift."

"So . . . you *do* like it."

"Sy." She paused.

He stared.

"Please, just take it."

He did as she asked and stuck the flask in his shirt pocket without another word.

She smiled, looking genuinely surprised. "Thank you."

"You're welcome."

They continued on to the telegraph office.

"Did you discover anything on your trip to Memphis?" she asked.

"Unfortunately, no. But on my way back to Nashville I made an acquaintance on the train. All because of you, I might add. And your lesson on Southern Reciprocation."

She laughed, and the sound of it, the pleasure that came with being in her company again, gave him a joy he would've been hard-pressed to put into words. He proceeded to tell her about meeting Philip Bliss.

"Then as we were getting off the train, I heard him humming a song. One that, as it turns out, he happened to write. I know the hymn because it was—" He caught himself, realizing he was about to share something about his father, something very personal. And he wasn't at all certain how she would react, given the circumstances.

"What?" she asked softly.

"Because it was my father's favorite."

She stopped and looked up at him, the softness in her eyes a blend of understanding and uncertainty. "What's the name of the hymn?"

He told her and she nodded, touching his arm.

"I know that song, Sy. 'Let the Lower Lights be Burning,'" she repeated. "It's beautiful. And the lyrics . . . so powerful."

Grateful to her in a way she couldn't know, he tucked her hand into the crook of his arm and they walked on.

"In a twist of fate that I hope proves to be providential, Mr. Bliss knows a survivor from the accident and has agreed to contact her. To see if she'd be open to speaking with me."

"That sounds promising." She looked at him. "Was she on the No. 4 or the No. 1?"

"The No. 1," he said softly, aware of her hand tightening on his arm.

He held open the door to the telegraph office for her. There was no line, so she walked directly to the counter.

"Mr. Rutledge?"

Sy looked over and saw the clerk who had helped him yesterday.

"We have two telegrams here for you, sir. We were just about to deliver them to the hotel."

"Much appreciated." Sy tore open the first envelope, read the brief message from his supplier, and felt his frustration from earlier in the day returning. A delay in shipment? This would mean another trip to Memphis to straighten things out. And if that didn't work, to find a new supplier. And each day he delayed leaving meant the Belle Meade project was getting further and further behind.

He tore open the second envelope, saw Philip Bliss's name at the top of the telegram, and hurried to read it.

Miss Glenn gravely ill Stop Time short Stop

"I hope it's not bad news, Sy."

He looked up and saw Alexandra's concern. "It is, unfortunately. On two counts. A supply shipment that's delayed on the Belle Meade project. And a note from Mr. Bliss. The survivor I just told you about . . . She's gravely ill. Bliss says the time is short."

"So . . . you need to leave town again."

The disappointment in her voice tugged at him. Especially after he'd promised only moments earlier to try to help her overcome her fear.

He tucked the telegrams into his pocket. "When is the tour scheduled to leave?"

"It's all right, Sy. I know you're busy. You have responsibilities and—"

"When, Alexandra?"

"The first week of October."

He sighed. That gave them not quite a month, but he still hated to cancel his offer for this next week. If he put it off too long she might decide definitely not to go on the tour. But maybe there was another way. "Have you ever seen a Pullman Palace car?"

Chapter
TWENTY-FOUR

*T*hey reached the train station and made their way across the platforms toward the train yard. To Sy's pleasure, Alexandra had reluctantly accepted his challenge back at the telegraph office, but with this clear understanding: she could change her mind at any time, back out on their agreement, and still get to see the newest Pullman Palace car—unhitched and sitting in the train yard.

She was good at negotiation, he'd give her that. But she was on his turf now.

He gave a whistle and heard a bark in the distance. Then braced himself. Duke bulleted around the corner of a passenger car, headed straight for him. Sy dropped his cloth sack and caught the hound midair.

"Hey there, boy!" Sy welcomed the dog's affection, hearing Alexandra's laughter. After a minute he set Duke down, and the dog promptly rolled onto his back. Sy gave his belly a good rub.

"For heaven's sake, how long have you been gone?"

"Since about seven o'clock this morning."

Alexandra shook her head. "What happens when you've really been gone? Say, for a week or more?"

"Then he really gets excited."

Duke wriggled his way over to her and, laughing, she bent to scratch him behind the ears. "Who keeps him for you while you're out of town?"

"Vinson. Who spoils him something crazy. Hence, I bring Duke these on occasion. So he won't forget me." Smiling, Sy grabbed the sack, unwrapped one of the bones, and tossed it to the dog, who caught it before it hit the ground.

"Hello, Boss!"

Sy looked up to see Vinson striding toward them.

Vinson nodded to Alexandra. "Miss Jamison. Good to see you again, ma'am."

"You as well, Mr. Vinson. I hear from Mr. White that congratulations are in order."

He smiled. "Yes, ma'am. Come January, I'll be sitting in your classroom. Ready to learn."

"I'm already looking forward to it. Although I have a feeling you won't be with me long. Mr. White says your test scores on the entrance exam were some of the highest they've seen."

"Thank you, Miss Jamison. But maybe we should tell Mr. White to check those tests of his." Vinson laughed. "Say, Boss . . . Carson's finishing up with the maintenance on the No. 2 engine. Says she's running like a dream now. And that new Pullman's ready. Not hitched yet, but we'll do that in the morning."

"Good. That's why we're here. That, and maybe to take a little ride." Sy shot Alexandra a look.

Which she shot right back. "Or maybe not. We'll see."

"Oh, you're going to like that Pullman, Miss Jamison." Vinson reached down and petted Duke. "She's a beaut! No better way to travel than in a Pullman."

Alexandra smiled, but Sy sensed she was already having second thoughts. Best move things along before she changed her mind.

"Vinson, you're still headed in the direction of Fisk this evening, right?"

"Yes, sir, Boss. Got an errand to run over that way."

Sy knew good and well the man had no errand to run. Unless a young woman by the name of Lettie could be considered an errand. "If you don't mind, Miss Jamison has something that needs to be delivered to Mr. White for dinner, and it may be a little longer than that before we get over that way."

"I'll be glad to deliver it for you, Miss Jamison." Vinson stepped forward.

"That's very kind of you, Mr. Vinson. Thank you." She handed him the butcher sack.

"Boss, the Pullman's back there on the No. 3 track."

Sy nodded. "And, Vinson . . . I'd appreciate it if you'd tell Mr. White that Miss Jamison is with me and that I'll bring her home directly."

Sy took the long way to the back of the train yard. It was quieter, away from in- and outbound trains, and Alexandra wouldn't have to climb over multiple couplers and navigate so many rails in her heeled boots.

He glanced back to make sure Duke was following, knowing that fresh bones could sometimes challenge the foxhound's loyalty. But the dog was trotting behind them, bone clutched in his teeth.

"How is General Harding's railway progressing, Sy? Delays in supplies notwithstanding."

"It's going well overall. We've already made good progress with the grading on both the railway and the road. And he's pleased, which is saying a lot." He slowed and held out a protective hand. "Watch your step through here. The gravel can be loose. And about seeing that new Pullman *after* our ride . . . Have you ever been inside a Palace car before?"

"I have. But not one of the newer models. In fact . . . I've met Mr. Pullman. He and my father are colleagues, of sorts. They've invested in projects together and served on various company boards. But that's some years back now."

They turned the corner, and Sy spotted Carson up ahead conversing with a worker near the locomotive. But no passenger car was attached as he'd thought it would be. He looked. No other passenger car on that switch rail either. "Wait here for me?" he asked.

At her nod, he ran up ahead and talked to Carson briefly, then returned. "Carson says our timing is perfect. Are you ready to do this?"

Alexandra shook her head no. "But . . . yes."

He smiled and offered his hand. With a fleeting look up at him that said so much, she accepted and held on for all she was worth. He decided it was a feeling he could quickly become accustomed to.

He led her forward, hoping his instincts proved right. He could already see her determination faltering.

He leaned close. "I'll be with you every step of the way. If you want to get off, we'll get off. Even before we start moving."

She nodded. "I'm fine."

But her death grip on his hand told a different story.

Sy gently coaxed her on. But when she spotted Carson standing beside the steps to the locomotive, engineer cap in hand, ready to greet them, she pulled away.

"You didn't say we were riding in the engine!"

"I know. Because I thought there would be a passenger car attached. But, Alexandra . . . I think this is even better for you. Because riding in the engine of a train is unlike anything else. It's where I first discovered, years ago, that I wanted to be a railroad man."

"No!" She shook her head.

He slipped an arm around her shoulders. "This isn't what we agreed on, I know. So if you want to turn around right now and go back to Fisk, we will. After seeing the Pullman, as promised." He smiled. "But this will give you a different perspective. Something to replace the scene that's been playing over and over in your mind for the last year. And riding in another passenger car won't do that the way this will. Trust me. Please," he whispered.

Her complexion decidedly more pale, she stared at the iron beast as if it might lunge for her at any moment. "I can't."

"And that's the difference, Alexandra. I know you can." He gently angled her face toward his. "If you don't go on this tour, someone else will step up and do the job White has offered to you. But I think a time will come—maybe soon, maybe not until years from now—when you'll look back and wish you'd done it. When you'll realize the strength was right there with you all along. You just had to reach out for it." He smiled. "Like Queen Esther."

Her brow furrowed, and she narrowed her eyes. "I'll tell you what I'm wishing right now, Sylas Rutledge. I'm wishing you'd never attended the concert that night."

He laughed and caught a speck of humor in her expression too. That was swiftly extinguished.

"Welcome aboard, ma'am!" Carson called out over the churn of pistons and the roar of the smokebox.

Sy quickly climbed the steps, Duke bounding up beside him, and held out his hand to Alexandra. She looked up at him, eyes full of fear. And determination.

✑

Alexandra stared at Sy's hand reaching down to her and wanted to take hold of it, even as she wanted to turn and run from this place and never look back.

You must ask yourself . . . Is the Lord leading me to do this?

In the space of a breath, the events of the past year flitted before her mind's eye. One year ago, she would never have been able to imagine that she would be a teacher at Fisk University. That God would have given her the courage to face the obstacles she'd faced, and that she would have found such purpose and meaning in her life after feeling so lost and without direction.

Acknowledging the answer to Mr. White's question, she suddenly felt the tug-of-war inside her yank decisively one way, and she grabbed hold of Sy's hand for all she was worth. He pulled her up beside him, and his arm came around her waist.

"Looks like we're ready to ride, Carson!"

Chapter
TWENTY-FIVE

A week later and Alexandra could still feel the surge of power beneath her feet, the rumble of the engine as the train lurched forward. She'd been certain her legs would give way. But they hadn't. Perhaps due in large part to Sy's arm around her waist, holding her close, something else she could still feel. And that, in some ways, had proven more powerful than the locomotive.

"You're doing great," he'd yelled, his voice all but drowned out by the churn of the engine and the roar of the smokebox as the iron behemoth crept forward, then gradually gained steam. She'd held on to him and the train with a white-knuckled grip.

Exhilarating. Terrifying. Unlike anything she'd ever done before. A tumult of emotions had pounded through her. She was glad she'd done it, while at the same time wondering if she'd be able to do it again when the time came.

The door to Mr. White's office opened and she stood, her stomach doing tiny flips. It being Saturday morning, the office and teaching barracks were quiet.

He gestured. "Miss Jamison, we're ready for you now."

We? Alexandra rose, under the impression he alone administered the teacher's exam. She'd spent every spare minute in recent weeks honing her knowledge in various subjects in preparation for this test. Sy had left for Memphis Sunday afternoon after treating her to breakfast in town. And though she'd hated to see him go, she'd welcomed every moment of studying afforded to her in his absence.

She couldn't explain how it had happened, but somehow they'd fallen back into rhythm right where they'd left off the night they'd sneaked in to listen to the singers. And she was grateful.

She prayed again that he'd reach Miss Glenn, the survivor from the train wreck, in time. And that the woman would hold some piece of information that would aid Sy in discovering the truth and in clearing his father's name. Surely it wasn't a coincidence that Sy had met Mr. Bliss on the train from Memphis that day. And that Bliss had been the author of his father's favorite hymn.

The longer she lived and the greater number of years she had to look back on her life, the more she saw God at work in hindsight where she had missed him in the moment. She hoped this trip to Ohio to see Miss Glenn would prove to be one of those moments for Sy.

She entered Mr. White's office and saw Miss Frieda Norton standing almost at attention beside his desk. The twenty-six-year veteran teacher gave her a solemn nod, and even though Alexandra liked the woman, she felt more than a little intimidated by her. She sensed Miss Norton wasn't quite convinced of her ability to teach. Which, on some days, Alexandra wouldn't have argued. Especially if the teaching involved advanced mathematics. Not her strongest suit.

She wanted to do well on this test. Not only so Mr. White wouldn't regret hiring her, but to make Ella proud too. Ella had such unwavering faith in her abilities, and Alexandra wanted to be worthy of it.

"Good morning, Miss Jamison." Miss Norton nodded.

Alexandra smiled. "Good morning, Miss Norton."

"I trust you're prepared for your examinations."

Alexandra looked between them. "Examinations? You mean . . . there's more than one?"

The older teacher drew her shoulders back; Alexandra thought

she caught the hint of a smile from the woman, then swiftly realized she was sorely mistaken.

"If you will allow me to continue, Miss Jamison." Miss Norton
leveled a stare. "It is of utmost importance that we ascertain a
candidate's cognitive abilities before allowing them to begin shap-
ing and influencing the lives of Fisk scholars. As you know, we
customarily make this determination before a faculty member is
hired. However, Mr. White made an exception in your case, which
was within his purview. Now, to my original statement . . . I trust
you're prepared for your examinations?"

Alexandra blinked, hearing unequivocal sanction in the woman's tone. "Yes, Miss Norton. I-I believe I'm prepared." Oh, what if
she failed? And after all the late nights Ella had spent quizzing her
on various topics.

Mr. White pointed to a table in the corner by an open window. A fall-like breeze stirred the curtains. "You may sit there, Miss
Jamison. Miss Norton will be proctoring the six one-hour exams,
which will be graded by various members of the faculty."

Six one-hour exams? Alexandra swallowed. She'd never
dreamed the exams for an introductory level teacher would be so
involved. Once again she wished she'd had the opportunity for a
formal education. Had she known what to expect, she could have
studied more, and she might not be so nervous now.

As soon as the thought came, she dismissed it. She'd studied
as much as she could in the time she'd had. And further, she knew
herself well enough to know that if she *had* known there were
multiple examinations, she would've only worried more.

"I'll be in and out throughout the day," Mr. White continued.
"Miss Norton knows where to find me should any questions arise."

Mr. White closed the door behind him, and Alexandra took a
seat. She removed her freshly sharpened pencils from her reticule
as Miss Norton withdrew a thick stack of pages from a professorial-
looking, if worn, leather satchel.

"As Mr. White said, there are six exams, Miss Jamison. You'll have precisely one hour in which to complete all the answers. Not a moment more. As soon as I announce, 'Pencil down,' you are to place your writing instrument on the table and lower your hands to your lap. Is that understood?"

Alexandra nodded, her stomach graduating from tiny flips to full-out somersaults. "Yes, Miss Norton."

I can do this. I can do this. She kept repeating the phrase, much as Sy had done: *You can do this, Alexandra. I know you can.* Embracing borrowed courage, she sat up straighter.

"Your first examination, Miss Jamison"—Miss Norton placed the test face down on the table before her—"advanced mathematics."

And just like that, all courage fled.

∽

Sy knocked on the door of the clapboard house, making the door rattle on its hinges. After a moment, he checked the address again: 121 East Main. The address Philip Bliss had given him.

He glanced at his pocket watch. He needed to be on the last train to Nashville at five thirty, and still had to run back by his hotel. He'd already been gone from Nashville nearly two weeks and was eager to get back to the Belle Meade project. But mostly to get back to Alexandra—and to give her what he'd seen in a shop window earlier during the week. She'd told him it was improper for a man to give a woman gifts. But he didn't think she would balk in the least at this.

She'd surprised him at how well she'd done on the locomotive the weekend before last, although it had taken a day or two for the marks on his arm where she'd dug in her nails to disappear. He smiled, imagining what she would say if she heard that thought.

He knocked on the door again, harder this time, recalling Bliss's telegram about Miss Glenn being gravely ill. He hoped he wasn't too late. Before coming today, he'd made sure Bliss had told her who he was and that it was his father who had been driving the No. 1. Bliss had wired back that Miss Glenn was still willing to meet.

The night he and Bliss had dinner, Bliss told him she'd been riding in the second freedmen's car on the No. 1 and had sustained severe injuries. It was a miracle she'd lived through it. Most had not.

Still no answer. He sighed and started back down the walkway.

"Hold on! I'm coming!"

Sy turned back as the door opened.

"Mr. Rutledge!"

"Mr. Bliss?" Sy stared. "I didn't realize you were going to be here too."

"Come in, come in." Bliss gestured. "I didn't realize it either, until the Avondale Church here in town invited me for a concert. Knowing you were coming, I hopped on a train this morning and came a day early. The wonders of the world in which we live."

Pleased to see him again, Sy shook his hand and stepped inside, catching the promising aroma of coffee. The man possessed what seemed to be a perpetually sunny disposition. Which might have been annoying if Bliss were not so kindhearted.

"So tell me, Mr. Rutledge, has anything new turned up in your inquiries with the railroad?"

"Please, call me Sy. And no, unfortunately not."

"Only if you'll call me Philip. And I'm sorry to hear that. But don't be discouraged. I'm still praying you'll find answers. More than anything, though, I'm praying you'll find real peace, Sy. Because the former may disappoint, but the latter never will."

Sy heard the certainty in the man's voice and wished he shared the same optimism. "Did you ever finish that song?"

Bliss smiled. "I did. But you're going to have to come to a church meeting to hear it."

They laughed.

"Actually, the sheet music is currently being printed. I'll have my publisher send you a copy when it's ready, if you wish."

Sy nodded. "I'd appreciate that. And the next time you're in Nashville for a prayer meeting, Bliss, let me know, if you would. I'd . . . like to attend."

Bliss held his gaze for a moment, then smiled. "I'll do that, Sy. And Lucy will make you some more of her chicken mash too!"

They laughed again, then silence crowded close.

"Miss Glenn is eager to meet you, Sy. In fact, I think part of the reason she's still with us is because of this appointment. The woman who takes care of her has stepped out for a while, so it'll be just the three of us. Come on back, and I'll introduce you."

Sy followed Bliss down a narrow hallway, still marveling at how his path had crossed with that of this man. Having done a fair share of gambling, Sy was familiar with figuring the odds. And he knew the odds were slim to none that his meeting Bliss on the train that day had been happenstance. That much had been made clear to him in recent days. The very man who'd penned his father's favorite hymn? And who knew a survivor from the train accident? He and Bliss on the same train, same passenger car, seated across from each other. It hadn't been a coincidence.

Sy felt a stirring within him. *In the morning when I rise, in the morning when I rise, in the morning when I rise, give me Jesus. You can have all the rest . . . Give me Jesus.*

How often those words returned to him, along with the memory not only of the Fisk singers' voices, but of their conviction behind the words they were singing. It had been a humbling thing when he'd realized years back that the Almighty knew his name. But even more humbling of late, he'd come to realize that Jesus knew the inner workings of his life, of his business, and all that was going on inside him.

And instead of finding that bothersome, as he would have in earlier years, Sy found it a comfort and wanted more of what Philip Bliss seemed to have in spades.

At the end of the hall was an open door, and Bliss gestured for Sy to precede him into the bedroom. Sy entered, and though he hadn't really known what to expect, he certainly hadn't expected this.

A young black woman sat propped up in the bed, nestled

beneath a pile of blankets. She smiled when he came in. Or he thought she did. The scarring on her face made it difficult to tell.

"Miss Riley Glenn, I'd like to present Mr. Sylas Rutledge. Mr. Rutledge, Miss Riley Glenn."

Sy had difficulty speaking at first. "It's an honor to meet you, Miss Glenn."

"And you as well." She spoke slowly, her voice fragile and raspy. She looked toward two chairs situated by the bed, and Sy took a seat. Bliss didn't.

"If you'll both excuse me for a moment, I'll get us some coffee."

As the man's footsteps receded down the hallway, Sy grew somewhat uncomfortable under the woman's gaze.

"Mr. Rutledge, Mr. Bliss tells me . . ." She paused and swallowed, the act deliberate, patient. ". . . that you have come to ask me questions . . . about the accident."

"Yes, ma'am, that's correct. But if it's too much for you, then please, we don't have to—"

She shook her head. "If I can help you . . . I want to."

He nodded. "I appreciate that." He'd brought his notepad with him, full of questions, but he didn't need to take it out. He knew them by heart.

Bliss returned with the coffee, Miss Glenn's in a special cup with a lid and a spout to aid her in drinking.

Sy asked her many of the same questions he'd asked Luther Coggins and the others, and she answered in her slow, patient cadence. She didn't recall hearing or seeing anything out of the ordinary before the second her world exploded, the wooden passenger car around her disintegrating and scalding water from the boiler raining down.

"Those of us still alive . . . were trying to get out . . . away from the fire . . . but my leg was stuck . . . I couldn't move . . ."

Sy listened, emotion burning his eyes, as she described what she'd been through.

"There was a man . . . I'd seen him earlier . . . riding in my car . . . He crawled over . . . and freed my leg . . . so I could get out . . ."

As he listened, Sy felt an ache inside him for the pain she'd endured and for his father, again, for how he must have suffered too.

After a while Miss Glenn's eyes started to close. Bliss gave Sy a subtle nod and stood. Sy followed his lead, able to see that their visiting had come at a cost.

But Miss Glenn held up her hand. "One more thing . . . please . . . before you go."

Sy paused.

"Do you know if . . . anyone else . . . from my railcar . . . survived?"

"I'm afraid I don't, Miss Glenn. I'm sorry."

She nodded. "I wanted to . . . thank the man . . . who saved me . . ."

Sy thought of Luther Coggins and how important that had been to him too. "I wish I could tell you, Miss Glenn. But I'm afraid there's no way of knowing."

One side of her face edged up. "It's just that I'd . . . never seen a . . . white man traveling . . . in a freedmen's car."

Sy went still inside. His throat tightened. "A . . . white man, you say?"

She nodded. "I overheard him talking . . . with the workers . . ."

"About their contracts," Sy finished for her, and watched the smile that couldn't quite touch her face bloom in her eyes. He cleared his throat. "In fact, I do know that gentleman's name, ma'am. David Thompson," he said softly. "He's . . . a very fine man, from what I hear."

She reached for his hand, an urgency in the act. "Could you . . . tell him . . . thank you . . . for me?"

Sy hesitated, her hand in his, as he struggled to find his voice. "I believe I can do that, Miss Glenn." He leaned down and barely brushed his lips against the scarred skin of her hand, not wanting to hurt her any more than she was already hurting. "Thank you, ma'am, for meeting with me today. I wish you comfort . . . and peace."

"I wish you . . . the same . . . Mr. Rutledge."

Rushed for time, Sy ran back by the hotel and grabbed his bag from his room, still trying to wrap his mind around what had just happened. David Thompson—Alexandra's David—hadn't died in the accident immediately. But what last moments he'd had, he'd used to save another's life. Again Sy felt the push of emotion in his chest. This was the man Alexandra had loved. Still loved, for all he knew.

He checked out at the front desk and was nearly to the door when he heard his name and turned back.

"A telegram came for you, sir."

"Thank you." Sy grabbed it and headed toward the station, hoping it was from his suppliers, informing him they'd corrected the problem as they'd assured him they would when he was in Memphis last week, and that the new shipment would be in Nashville tomorrow as promised.

He opened the envelope and read the name of his Charlotte attorney at the top.

Investor Funds Confirmed Stop North Carolina–West Virginia Project Ready to Proceed

Not the news he'd been expecting, but welcome news all the same. At least in one regard. But it also meant he wouldn't be headed back to Nashville today, or possibly even that week. He only hoped he could get back in time to say good-bye to Alexandra before the singers left on their tour—if she hadn't changed her mind about going along. Which he hoped she hadn't.

Certain opportunities only came around once in life. And once they were gone, they were gone for good.

Chapter
TWENTY-SIX

Alexandra paused beneath the shade of the familiar sycamore trees in front of her parents' home, which somehow
seemed larger and finer than she remembered. The past three
weeks had been a whirlwind of finishing her introductory classes
at Fisk and helping prepare for the upcoming tour. But she
couldn't leave town in the morning with Mr. White and the singers
without saying good-bye to her parents.

She didn't feel comfortable entering by the front door, so she
skirted around to the back.

While recent days had flown by in some ways, they had also
crawled. Because Sy had yet to return to Nashville.

He'd wired her from Cleveland saying the land deal was moving forward and he was headed to Charlotte for a week or two.
He'd written her not two days later saying he'd do his best to be
at the station in the morning when the train left, but he'd stopped
short of promising. And she understood.

She could still feel the surge of the locomotive beneath her
feet. He'd been right. The experience was one that had stayed
with her. Yet as the days had passed, the exhilaration had ebbed
and old fears lurked in the shadows.

But she was doing her best to keep them at bay.

Sy had written that the meeting Mr. Bliss had arranged with
the survivor in Ohio had had been encouraging, and he would

relay more details when they were together. As for this Mr. Philip Paul Bliss—Sy spoke so highly of him, she couldn't wait to meet him. Which apparently wouldn't be long from now. Mr. Bliss and his wife were scheduled to attend one of the concerts on the tour.

Alexandra hurried across the backyard to the kitchen door and peered inside. Empty. She had no way of knowing whether or not her father was home. But it being Thursday, the day of his standing luncheon with fellow attorneys, she felt certain it was safe.

The knob turned easily in her hand.

Her mother had never responded to the message she'd sent through Melba—twice. Melba hadn't responded to the missives either. So Alexandra could only hope her visit would be welcomed.

Scents of home greeted her and tugged at emotions worn thin in recent days and weeks. On the counter, Melba's sour cream pound cake sat on a cooling rack warm from the oven. Beside it, an early pumpkin rested on the worktable, no doubt destined to be blended with savory spices and baked into one of Melba's flaky pie crusts.

Alexandra paused, listening. The house was quiet.

She crossed to the door leading to the family dining room when she heard footsteps coming down the staircase. She peered around the corner, ready to bolt if it was her father.

Dr. Phillips?

Medical bag in hand, the doctor let himself out the front door, and Alexandra walked into the hallway, the carpet muting her steps. Her first thought was for her mother, and guilt prodded her. She should have visited sooner. Her mother tended to worry too much and took care of others before taking care of herself. Something that had always escaped Father's notice.

Voices drifted down from the second-floor landing, so she headed up—and met Melba at the top of the stairs. The woman's eyes went wide.

Alexandra lifted a forefinger to her lips and gave her a quick hug before drawing back. "Is Mother ill?" she whispered. "I saw the doctor leaving just now."

"She's in your parents' room, Miss Alexandra. And no, ma'am. She's not ill." She paused. "Have . . . you two talked at all in recent days?"

"No. That's why I'm here. I couldn't leave town without seeing her again."

A frown creased the woman's brow even as her gaze took Alexandra in. "Sure is good to see you again, ma'am."

"You as well, Melba. Which reminds me . . . Did you not receive either of my letters? I wrote twice."

"Oh, I got 'em, Miss Alexandra. But your mama, she . . ." Melba glanced in the direction of the master bedroom. "She said it wouldn't be fittin' to answer back, since it'd be goin' against Mr. Jamison's wishes. And I just couldn't risk that he might—"

"I understand." Alexandra nodded. "I do. Truly."

"I heard what you doin' over there at Fisk. I even know about where you're goin' tomorrow. Word of that sort sprouts legs real fast, ma'am. Me and the others will be prayin' for you all."

"Thank you. You, of all people, Melba, understand my not wanting to get on that train in the morning."

"Yes, ma'am, I do. Some memories, they never leave a person. But that don't mean you gotta stay stuck back there with 'em."

Alexandra smiled. "I'm learning that. Do you know if my parents are aware of the trip?"

"Oh, yes, ma'am." Her smile faded. "They know. But not from us."

"Well . . ." Alexandra breathed deep. "I best get this done." She knocked on the bedroom door.

"Come in, Melba."

Alexandra opened the door to find her mother sitting on the edge of the bed, but quickly realized it wasn't her mother who was ill. Her father lay in the bed, eyes closed, skin pallid, unmoving.

"Mother?"

Her mother turned, then quickly rose. "Alexandra!"

Alexandra moved to the end of the bed. "Mother, what's wrong? Why didn't you send for me?"

Her mother made a shushing sound and gestured toward the hallway. "Please, let's not wake him. Dr. Phillips was just here and gave him something to help him rest. Your father had a difficult night."

Alexandra didn't move. "But what's wrong with him?" she whispered again. "What did Dr. Phillips say?"

Her father stirred, and his eyes opened. He tried to lift his head, but the act seemed too much for him. "Laura? Are you here?"

Her mother immediately went to his side. "Yes, Barrett, I'm here, dear. It's all right."

"I thought that . . . you'd gone away." He coughed, the sound deep and raspy.

"No, dear. I'll never go away. Would you like a drink?"

Her father shook his head.

The scene was so surreal, so foreign, Alexandra moved to the side to see him better. And when he looked in her direction, she smiled.

"Hello, Father." She kept her voice soft. "I came by to say—"

"No . . . ," he whispered, his pale features contorting. He looked back at her mother. "I told you . . . She is not welcome in this house. And against my wishes, you—" He started coughing again.

"No, Barrett, I didn't. She came of her own volition. Alexandra didn't know you were ill. But now that she's here, perhaps the two of you could—"

"She has disgraced us!" Her father tried to sit up, but fell back against the headboard. "I will not—" The coughing returned in a fitful spasm.

"Get Melba. Quickly!" her mother ordered.

Alexandra started for the stairs, only to meet Melba in the hallway.

"I got the medicine, Missus Jamison!"

Alexandra watched from outside the door as they tended him. She tried to remember a time when she'd seen her father so vulnerable, so weak. And couldn't.

Finally, after several moments, the coughing subsided and her father's breathing became less labored.

"Melba, would you stay with him until I return?"

"Of course, Mrs. Jamison."

Her mother ushered Alexandra out and closed the bedroom door behind them. She motioned for Alexandra to sit with her on a cushioned bench down the hall. "He should sleep for a while."

"Mother, why didn't you tell me?"

"I've wanted to tell you for a long time, but your father insisted that I not."

"A long time? Do you mean—"

"Yes, your father has been ill for several months. Dr. Phillips says it's his heart. That's part of the reason your father moved his office here to the house. So he could rest when needed."

"But . . . you never said anything. Even when I was still here."

"That was your father's decision. He is my husband and the head of this home. So as much as I disagreed with him in not telling you initially—and still do—I followed his wishes. I'm sorry if that hurts you, Alexandra."

"What hurts me is seeing my father lying sick in bed and my not knowing about it."

"My dear, that is part of living with the choice you made. If you had been here in recent weeks, you would have known. And don't think for a moment that you're the only one paying a price for your decision."

Alexandra searched her expression, and remembered only too well the incident with Mrs. Johnson and Maribelle at the butcher's shop. "Have you and father been ill-treated by people in town?"

A bewildered expression swept her mother's face. "Of course we have, Alexandra. Did you think us so esteemed by other families that they would simply lay aside their own opinions for your father and me? It has been difficult. We have lost dear friends, some of whom we've known for many, many years. On the other hand . . ." Her mother paused, her gaze discerning. "I've discovered that many of the women who shun me now I don't miss in the least." She gave a soft, surprising laugh.

"Will Father get well? What does Dr. Phillips say?"

"He says there's reason to believe your father could live several more years, provided he rests and doesn't overtax himself. However . . . Dr. Phillips was also quick to explain that there's much they don't know yet about the heart. So time will tell. But for certain your father becoming distressed, as he did just now, is not good for him."

Alexandra bowed her head. "I'm sorry. Perhaps I shouldn't have come."

Her mother lifted her chin. "I'm glad you did. I wanted to go to you that day we saw each other in town, but I couldn't. Not and honor my promise to your father. Whom I love with all my heart."

Alexandra brought her mother's hand to her lips and kissed it, tears close. "I've missed you."

"I've missed you too, my dear."

"And you're doing well? I mean . . . aside from taking care of Father."

"I *am* doing well. Truly."

And she looked it. Her mother looked strong and healthy. And happy. And she exuded a confidence, a contentedness that Alexandra hadn't seen since . . . well, perhaps ever.

"Your father needs me, Alexandra. And that's something that hasn't happened in a very long time." Her mother smiled. "How are *you* faring, my dear?"

"I'm doing well too. Very well," she whispered, a tear slipping down her cheek.

The bedroom door opened. "He's askin' for you, Mrs. Jamison."

"I'm coming, Melba." Her mother rose. Alexandra did too, and they hugged. "You take care of yourself on this . . . singing tour."

Alexandra heard no accusation in the comment, only resignation. "I will. And, Mother? If anything happens here—" The words caught in her throat.

Her mother nodded, her own eyes misty. She walked toward the bedroom, then paused. "You'll be busy on your travels, I know. But as you have opportunity, I'm certain Melba would enjoy hearing from you while you're gone. And would even appreciate knowing where you are."

Hearing what her mother wasn't saying, Alexandra nodded. Her mother quietly closed the bedroom door, and Alexandra reached the stairs before she remembered and turned back. She hesitated only a moment before opening the door to her own bedroom.

Everything appeared to be as she'd left it.

Except that David's trunk had been placed once again at the foot of her bed and his picture adorned her dressing table. She treasured his smile, his eyes. She could still hear his laughter. She crossed the room and opened the trunk. What clothes she'd hastily packed the night of her planned departure had been removed. She ran a hand over the stacks and stacks of books and papers, the thin bundle of letters that David had written, and mementos she'd saved of their time together. She spotted a familiar title—*The Fundamentals of Biology*—that she'd wished she had when studying for the teacher's exams, that Mr. White kept saying he would meet with her about.

But she knew he'd been busy with preparing for the tour, as had everyone else. She'd taken the fact that he'd allowed her to continue teaching as a good sign.

She picked up the textbook and skimmed through the pages, reading David's handwriting in the margins along with notes she'd made. How she could use this now. Could use all of these books. For herself in her own studies, but also for the students at Fisk.

Every choice comes at a cost, and yours is no exception.

Thinking of her father that day in the study and now of him lying in the bedroom down the hallway, she gently closed the textbook and tucked it back into place, then closed the trunk. She walked to the dressing table and picked up the photograph and pressed a kiss to the glass.

"Thank you," she whispered, then set it back down, took one last look around the bedroom, and closed the door behind her.

Early the next morning at the Nashville station, Alexandra stood amidst the gathering of Fisk students, staff, and a contingent of sobbing parents—some even wailing—and attempted to focus on President Spence's benediction for the tour.

If she didn't know the history between President Spence and Mr. White, she would think from hearing the president's prayer that Spence was in full support of the tour. But apparently the two men had decided to present a unified front.

As she'd learned that morning, for many of the parents the tour was less of a wonderful opportunity and more of an interruption to their children's education. And a dangerous one at that. Mr. White couldn't guarantee when the group might return, and the open-endedness of the venture left many of them uneasy. Alexandra among them. Especially when she thought of working toward her own degree.

A blast of the train whistle, and she clenched and unclenched her hands. The trembling she'd somehow managed to stave off in recent hours broke through again. She'd slept little last night—same as Ella who stood beside her—and kept searching the crowd for Sy.

She'd so hoped he would get back in time. But . . . she would have to do this without him.

"O Lord," President Spence continued, "if the thought behind this journey comes from thee, prosper the going out of these young people. Care for and protect them, and bring them back to us bearing their sheaves with them, and we shall give thee the glory. Amen."

A flood of amens followed, bracketed by hugs and more

tears. But Alexandra was still focused on how President Spence had phrased part of this prayer. *If the thought behind this journey comes from thee . . .*

In that single little word *if* she caught hint of the argument yet lingering between himself and Mr. White, and of Spence's true feelings about this venture. It was difficult enough leaving on such a venture with everyone's support. But knowing that Spence—and apparently many of these parents—weren't in favor of this tour made it even more difficult.

As families began hugging and saying their final good-byes, Alexandra scooted to the side to make more room. Still she searched the platform for Sy's face, his dark duster and hat. She knew it was foolish, but she even looked for her mother. Or Melba. And though she knew so many of the people here, and smiled when her gaze brushed theirs, the sea of faces blurred in her vision. And an emptiness opened inside her.

"Every dollar was raked and scraped for them to go."

Recognizing President Spence's voice, she turned slightly and saw him speaking in low tones to an older woman off to the side.

"It cost about a thousand dollars to get to this point, Mother. So now we have no money, no steward, no treasurer! It requires some courage to face the situation, which I now have to do. If money does not come in, we will soon have nothing to eat. Though I for one am glad to be rid of White for a while. And glad at all events that this music is finally to be tested, and the thing settled in one way or another. I do not care much which. If that is the Lord's way, may it succeed. If not, may it fail. And they will have to get home as best they can. Meanwhile, I'm left here in the lurch."

If not, may it fail?

Alexandra felt a surge of anger, which swiftly gave way to trepidation when she saw the singers start to board the train.

Mr. White paused at the door to the passenger car and addressed those still gathered. "In God's strength," he called out, "this little band of singers will sing the money out of the hearts and pockets of the people! Cincinnati is our first stop, and I am confident that the power of the singing will tug at the hearts and generosity of their listeners."

Only a smattering of amens rose this time.

The train whistle sounded again, and Alexandra spotted Ella working her way toward her through the crowd. Her roommate reached her and took hold of her hand.

"We're going to do this together, Alexandra. Just as we talked about."

Alexandra nodded, knowing she'd made the right decision in sharing her fear with Ella, who had only been supportive.

"Something my mother used to tell me, and still does," Ella whispered, taking a step forward in the queue and pulling Alexandra along with her. "No matter where you're going, God is already there. He's already on the train. He's already waiting for us at the first stop in Cincinnati. There is nowhere we can go—by carriage, wagon, ship, or train—where he is not already there, holding us in the palm of his hand."

Alexandra nodded again, believing her. She only wished her nerves would show greater faith.

She held tight to Ella's hand and followed the dwindling line of passengers boarding the railcar, her heart hammering as though she'd just run a footrace full speed downhill. Nearly to the door, she took a deep breath—*I believe you're leading me to do this. I believe you're leading me to do this*—when she felt a sharp tug on her arm and turned.

Chapter
Twenty-Seven

Y ou came!" Alexandra knew the relief in her voice gave away any hope of a courageous pretense, but she didn't care.

"Of course I came." Sy smiled. "Any gentleman knows it's only proper that he see a lady off at the train station." He sounded winded, as if he'd been running. He looked at Ella and tugged the brim of his hat. "Would you mind, Miss Sheppard, if I have a word alone with Miss Jamison?"

Ella's eyes sparkled, and she looked between them as though she knew a secret they didn't. "I wouldn't mind in the least, Mr. Rutledge. I'll save you a seat, Alexandra."

Ella climbed the stairs, and Sy offered Alexandra his arm. She grabbed hold and wanted never to let go.

"Thank you for coming, Sy."

He smiled. "Duke and I got you a little going-away gift." He nodded toward the foxhound, sitting a few feet away, guarding a beautiful brown leather briefcase. Sy led her over and picked it up. "We're not very good at shopping for a woman, but we did our best to fill it with things you might be able to use."

"It's beautiful!" She ran a hand over the soft leather, then started to look inside, but he covered her hand.

"The briefcase can only be opened once you're aboard, Miss Jamison."

Whether it was the warmth of his hand on hers or the thoughtfulness of his gift, or both, she felt a rush of emotion that had less to do with gratitude and far more with wishing she could kiss him. Right here on the platform. To feel his arms around her. His gaze dropped to her mouth and lingered, causing her former imaginings to take on vivid life.

The train whistle blasted.

"It's time," he said softly, fingering a strand of hair at her temple. "It'll be all right."

She nodded quickly. "I know." But she didn't move. She started shaking. But deep inside this time. "I'm frightened," she mouthed, her voice barely audible. "Not for the tour, but of—"

"I know." The muscles in his jawline tightened. "But you're going to be fine, Alexandra. I know you are. You're strong. You're brave. And you've ridden in a locomotive."

She attempted a smile, but couldn't hold it.

His grip tightened on her hand, and the next thing she knew, he'd set the briefcase down by Duke and was leading her away from the crowd. The whistle sounded again—two long blasts— and smoke from the engine billowed onto the platform.

"Sy, where are we—"

He turned and pulled her to him. His mouth covered hers, his kiss tender, his embrace wonderfully less so. And what she'd only imagined a moment earlier came to life and was headier and more delicious than she'd dared dream. She slipped her arms around his neck, wanting to be even closer. As if reading her mind, he cradled the nape of her neck and deepened the kiss. She melted against him.

Far too soon he pulled away and looked down at her, his face still close, the thickness of the smoke dissipating. Desire warmed his eyes and she felt it all the way to her toes. And then some.

Smiling, he grabbed her hand, and she ran with him back down the platform. He snatched up the briefcase as they passed, and she reached down and gave Duke a quick pat on the head.

Sy lifted her onto the step of the passenger car just as the train gave a little lurch, then he climbed up beside her, opened the door, and ushered her inside.

"My addresses are in the briefcase. Both here in Nashville and in Charlotte at the new project. As is some money to wire me if you need anything, Alexandra. *Anything*," he said again, and pressed a quick hard kiss to her forehead. "Be watching for me along the way." He closed the door to the railcar behind him and stepped off the moving train onto the platform with enviable ease.

Holding on to a seat back, she spotted the porter ahead and reached into her skirt pocket, making certain she still had her ticket. Her hand brushed something cool and hard, and she pulled the object from her pocket. And smiled.

The flask? How on earth had he managed to—

The train surged forward, and in the space of a blink her world narrowed. She slipped the bottle back into her pocket and scanned the passenger car full of people. She heard the churn of the locomotive, felt the rumble of steel wheels on rails—and her body went weak.

"Alexandra!"

She forced herself to focus and spotted Ella, Jennie, Mr. White, and the others sitting toward the back. Clutching the briefcase, she somehow made it to the empty seat beside Ella and sank down, the hard wooden bench unforgiving.

Ella leaned close. "I see Mr. Rutledge gave you a parting gift."

Alexandra fingered the buttery brown leather. "Yes, but he told me I couldn't open it until I was on board."

Ella's mouth slowly tipped. "I wasn't referring to the briefcase."

Two hours into the four-hour train trip, Alexandra had read Sy's note nine times. She'd already memorized certain parts. *The briefcase, while lovely, is to aid you not only in your classes but also as you earn your degree. Which I know you will do posthaste, Professor Jamison.*

If it was possible, she still felt the tingle of his lips on hers. She didn't know if part of his plan in kissing her at that precise moment was to sweep every shred of fear from her body, but that's what he'd done. Until the train had picked up speed.

But between Ella close beside her and forcing herself to picture again riding on that locomotive with Sy, his arm securely around her waist, the fields bathed in sunlight and the wind on her face, she'd somehow made it through the tense moments following their initial departure.

But the flask . . .

How he'd gotten that into her pocket she didn't know. She pulled it out and unscrewed the lid. Then looked closer. He'd filled it with something, but she wasn't sure—

She sniffed. He didn't.

She tasted. He did! Mrs. Taylor's Fancy Cordial.

Glancing around and seeing everyone either dozing, reading, or otherwise occupied, she took a quick swig. Then another, wishing she'd known about the cordial an hour ago. It had taken her twenty minutes into the trip to loosen her hold on the bench seat. This would've helped considerably. But having already learned her lesson in this regard, she screwed the lid back on and put the bottle away.

Ella was asleep beside her, as were Jennie and Maggie on the bench opposite them. And even though it took concentration, Alexandra closed her eyes too and leaned her head back, under no illusion that she would sleep. She reviewed a mental list of to-dos instead.

Upon arriving in Cincinnati, the troupe needed to disembark swiftly, check in to the hotel, then locate the Congregational Church for their first concert that evening. The minister she'd exchanged letters with had said the community was enthusiastic about the Fisk singers coming, so they were all hopeful for a large crowd.

Mr. White had laid out the route for the tour, which wisely, in her estimation, somewhat followed the course of the Underground Railroad, the network of secret routes by which slaves had escaped to freedom. He'd placed her in charge of managing hotel reservations and train travel, visiting and corresponding with editors at local newspapers, writing press releases for each concert, looking after the health of the singers—Ella especially—and generally making certain the troupe had everything they needed before a concert. No small task. But she was thrilled to be part of it.

Sy had been right. Even now, having only embarked on this journey, she knew she would have deeply regretted it one day had her choice been not to come. She opened her eyes and looked out the window at the passing countryside, every passing moment taking her farther away from him.

But he'd made it to the station that morning. She'd been so excited, so flustered she hadn't thought to ask him about his trip. About the parishioner and whether his visit had turned up anything of consequence. And if the challenges with the railroad had been resolved.

"Are you faring well?" Ella whispered beside her.

Alexandra looked over to find her friend awake, and nodded. "Thank you. Without you and Mr. Rutledge, though, I don't know that I could've gotten aboard."

Ella patted her arm. "You would have. None us knows what we're fully capable of doing until God leads us to a place where we realize our strength is nothing compared to his. He says to take a step, yet you look out and see nothing but thin air in your path. Yet, he calls you on. And only when you finally trust him and take that step into nothingness do you discover you're standing on solid ground."

Alexandra smiled. "What if your knees are still knocking when you take that step?"

Ella laughed softly. "Then you're in good company with many a saint who's gone before."

Alexandra nodded, then let her gaze roam the cabin to the other members of the troupe. Her attention came to rest on Thomas, who was poring over a copy of Nashville's *Colored Tennessean*, his expression intense.

Ella leaned close. "Thomas's mother was sold away from him when he was two years old. He's been looking for her ever since the war ended."

Alexandra looked over at her.

"In every issue," Ella continued, as though sensing her unspoken question, "people place ads asking the whereabouts of long-lost kin, in the hope that perhaps someone will recognize a name and that somehow families separated years ago might find each other."

Alexandra looked back at Thomas, the handsome young man with the golden tenor voice—a voice his mother had never heard. And the prick of truth deepened her understanding yet again of the world in which she lived.

When the train finally pulled into the Cincinnati station unscathed, they disembarked, and Alexandra paused briefly on the platform and offered silent thanks, along with a prayer for Thomas and his mother.

Mr. White gathered the troupe and they continued down the platform. At first she noticed people looking their way, then gradually people stopped to stare. She glanced beside her at the others, yet they seemed not to notice. But by the time they reached the street, she didn't know how the other members of the troupe could miss it.

Everyone was turning to look.

"Pay them no mind, Miss Jamison," Greene Evans said softly and indicated for her to proceed him down the stairs to the street.

"Black cloud *rising!*" someone called out.

Alexandra looked up, not understanding. Then she heard the cackle of laughter and sneers off to the side and turned. A group of young men on the street were eying them, grinning. One of them hopped up and down and scratched his belly, making noises. And when she realized what he was doing, an anger shot up within her so hot and fierce she felt the heat of it behind her eyes.

"As Mr. Evans said, Miss Jamison," Thomas Rutling whispered, his voice even, controlled, "pay them no mind, ma'am."

With no small effort she looked away and continued down the street. Mr. White led them in the direction of the hotel, head held high, stride confident. She attempted the same, until a few blocks later, a sign in a store window caught her attention, and the anger simmering inside her stirred again.

Though she read the sign only once as she passed, the words seared themselves into her memory, and her chest tightened with the injustice and ignorance behind them. *Nigger read and run!* the sign had read. Then scrawled in writing below it, *And if you can't read, run anyway.*

"Do you see all the people?" Maggie whispered, peering out at the auditorium. The Congregational Church was filled, and Mr. White was beyond pleased. His plan, he'd explained, was to offer the concerts for free, then he would make an appeal at the end after the audience had been moved by the masterful blend of voices.

Travel from Nashville had made for a long day, but everyone was running on excitement, Alexandra included. Thirty minutes before the concert was to begin, she checked with each of the singers to make sure they had what they needed, then took her seat in the audience. She swiftly realized that no matter how many times she had the opportunity to hear these singers, she would never grow tired of listening to them.

Through the first four songs—"Down by the River," "Beautiful Dreamer," "Grace," and "I've Been Redeemed"—Alexandra sneaked looks across the auditorium and saw expressions ranging from awe-filled appreciation to what she could only term as utter shock. But nearly an hour and a half later, with Jennie Jackson's rendering of the "Old Folks at Home" as a finale, there wasn't a dry eye that she could see.

Following a standing ovation, Mr. White took the stage and gave an emotional plea about Fisk University that even stirred Alexandra's heart, and she already knew about the school's dire circumstances. The collection was taken and monies presented to Mr. White.

Later, in the lobby, she greeted guests and answered questions about Fisk University and their mission.

"Never in all my days did I imagine Negroes could be so well behaved!" a voice said behind her.

"Yes! That school must spend an inordinate amount of time on discipline."

Alexandra turned and spotted the two women conversing behind her. She smiled as she approached. "I'm Miss Alexandra Jamison, a teacher at Fisk University. Do you have any questions for me about the school? Or the exemplary students whom I have the honor of teaching? I'd be most happy to instruct you."

With chins slightly lifted, the women shook their heads and walked on. Feeling mildly victorious, Alexandra felt a touch on her arm.

"Mr. White."

"Miss Jamison," he said softly. "Your . . . forthright response to those women was well meant, I'm sure. But I believe it would be best to remember that actions speak far louder than words. And that a kind answer truly does turn away wrath."

All sense of victory swept aside, Alexandra nodded. "I'm sorry, Mr. White."

"No need to apologize. I have done precisely the same thing, Miss Jamison. Though perhaps not with quite such . . . sweet Southern meanness."

Alexandra might have felt even worse if not for the twinkle in his eyes.

After staying to visit with concert attendees, they returned to the hotel fatigued but also thrilled at such a successful first night. Until Mr. White paused briefly in the hotel lobby to count the contribution, and Alexandra read the disappointment in his face.

"Fifty dollars," he said quietly, looking from singer to singer. "That entire auditorium was filled. Every person listening to that blessed gift of music from you heavenly inspired singers, and this is representative of their gratitude?" He sighed. "This sum is barely sufficient to defray our expenses for the concert—travel, hotel, meals, publicity. How are we supposed to send money back to Fisk from this?"

They all went to their rooms somber rather than celebratory, and as Alexandra readied for bed, she could tell that even Ella had been affected by the news. She wanted to encourage her, and herself too.

"It will be better tomorrow night, I'm sure. The minister said they're expecting a large crowd as well."

"Whatever the Lord wills," Ella whispered, slipping beneath the covers of her bed and giving a sigh. "A real bed. Heavenly."

Alexandra saw signs of fatigue in the shadows beneath Ella's eyes, and she feared this trip would take a further toll on her friend's already weakened constitution. She vowed, as Mr. White had requested, to keep close watch over her health.

Alexandra climbed onto the single bed beside Ella's and pulled a file and a textbook from her lovely leather briefcase.

"You're staying up?" Ella asked.

"For a little while. I want to check the details for tomorrow's concert in Chillicothe. And Maggie loaned me a book." She held it up.

"*The Art of Civilizations*," Ella read out. "Some light reading at the end of a relaxing day."

Alexandra smiled, then thought again of something she'd wanted to ask her friend. "About the paper Thomas was reading today . . . Do you have anyone you're searching for?"

"I'm fortunate in that I was able to stay with my mother. And my father worked on a nearby plantation, so I was able to see him from time to time. He eventually bought his own freedom, then saved up enough to purchase Mama and me as well. Mrs. Phereby Sheppard, who owned us, always promised Mama that she'd allow my father to buy us when the time came. But once he had the money, Miss Phereby refused. Mama overheard her talking to her husband that night saying that Miss Phereby had simply pretended to agree to sell Mama to my father so as not to prolong Mama's grief at their pending separation. Miss Phereby told Major Sheppard that Mama was hers. That Mama had *been* hers and would *die* hers. And that my father could get himself another wife."

Alexandra stared. "I'm so sorry," were the only words she could manage.

Ella held her gaze. "You already know enough about my mama to know she wasn't going to stand for that. She told Miss Phereby that her daughter would never be a slave, and that if Miss Phereby would allow my father to buy me, then Mama would remain her faithful servant. But that if Miss Phereby refused"—a look came into Ella's eyes both fiery and sad—"Mama told her she'd kill us both. And Miss Phereby knew that was no idle threat. Because we all knew about the mother from a neighboring plantation who had been sold and was to be separated from her three small daughters. The mother gathered them together, slit their throats, and laid them out side by side. Then killed herself as well. It happened more than you might think," Ella finished softly.

Alexandra tried to imagine herself and her own mother in that situation. Further, she felt a deeper appreciation for their relationship, however imperfect and flawed. "Your mother must be an incredible woman, Ella."

"She is that." Ella smiled. "But she comes from a strong line of women. My maternal great-grandmother, Rosa, was the free, full-blooded daughter of a Cherokee chief."

Alexandra felt her eyes go wide, and Ella laughed. They stayed awake talking until after midnight, then Ella yawned and pulled her pillow closer to her face.

"One more question," Alexandra said, "then we'll go to sleep. I'm hesitant to ask Mr. White again because I've already inquired twice. But you being his assistant, do you happen to know whether or not my introductory teacher examinations were graded before we left? I'm not asking you to tell me the marks I earned, mind you. I'm simply wondering if they've been scored."

"He hasn't said anything about them to me. But I do know an inordinate amount of students are preparing to graduate in December, so perhaps the teachers charged with scoring the exams simply fell behind. But I wouldn't worry about it. I'm certain you passed everything with ease or Mr. White would have said something."

Alexandra smiled. "While I do not share your confidence, Miss Sheppard, I do so appreciate it."

Tired, Alexandra managed to stay up a little longer to check the details for tomorrow, then she pulled pen and paper from her briefcase and wrote Sy a short note. She addressed the envelope and set it by her reticule to be mailed, then turned down the lamp.

With the exception of the disappointing receipts from the night's concert, the day had gone as smoothly as she could have imagined. Which boded well for the coming days.

She reached to turn down the lamp and looked across to the other bed where Ella lay sleeping. How very little a person knew about someone simply from looking at her. Yet how much people decided about others at a single glance. Herself included. Ella's great-grandmother had been full-blooded Cherokee. and Ella's paternal grandfather, as she'd shared earlier, had been a white planter.

Perhaps it was all the studying about civilizations and histories of the world Alexandra had done of late, but it occurred to her that the blood flowing through Ella Sheppard's veins perfectly captured the history—and heartache—of this nation.

"*You*, my dear friend, are Esther," Alexandra whispered, extinguishing the lamp on the bedside table. "Born for such a time as this."

The next morning she and Ella awakened early and joined the troupe downstairs for breakfast, only to find Mr. White waiting for them in the dining room. His features were even more somber than they'd been the night before.

"My dear friends," he announced, "the city of Chicago is burning."

Chapter
Twenty-Eight

*F*rom what I read in the newspaper this morning, Uncle Bob, three hundred people have been killed." Sy watched the yearlings being loaded onto the wagons. "Over one hundred thousand homes were destroyed."

"That's hard to get your mind around, ain't it? Whole town just goin' up like that. They know what started the fire?"

"Not yet." Sy couldn't imagine the grief hanging over that city right now. So much destruction in so short a time. He hoped the tragedy hadn't hampered the Fisk singers' tour in any way. So much was riding on the success of those concerts and Mr. White's vision for them.

The group had only been gone a week, but it felt like much longer to him. Alexandra had already written him twice, and though he wouldn't admit it to just anyone, he carried her letters in his coat pocket. Right next to his flask. He'd especially appreciated her post script about sneaking a drink of the cordial on the train.

Since writing her back, he'd managed to fix his schedule so he could leave at the end of the week. He planned on surprising her in Columbus on Sunday evening in time for the concert. The Blisses were going to be in attendance that night too, and he hoped the four of them could meet afterward for dinner.

"All loaded up!" Uncle Bob slid the lever into place on the last wagon, then hefted himself up to the bench seat. Sy climbed up beside him.

Uncle Bob gave the reins a slap, and the team responded. The other four wagons fell in behind them.

Sy had grown to appreciate the time he and Uncle Bob spent together when he was out here working on the project. On a couple of occasions he'd watched the man training the stallions, including Enquirer. Everything he'd been told about his giftedness with horses was true. Uncle Bob had a connection with them unlike anything Sy had ever seen.

He checked his pocket watch. Just enough time to supervise the yearlings being loaded onto the train before heading to his meeting with General Harding and the investors.

The timing of the North Carolina/West Virginia project was working out perfectly; he couldn't have planned it any better. And while he didn't wish to tempt fate, a part of him kept waiting to receive a telegram about something having gone wrong. Land deals and railroad projects never ran this smoothly.

He'd wagered everything on this deal, investing all he had. And though he was a little strapped for cash right now, come late spring or early summer when the railroad between Charlotte and Charleston opened up, he'd be a rich man. And that ranch outside of Boulder would be his.

After seeing Alexandra, he planned on heading to Charlotte next week to check on things.

"You hear my news, Mr. Rutledge?" Uncle Bob eyed him.

"Your news?

"Yes, sir. This ol' man's gettin' married."

"You? Married?"

Uncle Bob feigned an injured look. "What? You don't think any woman in her right mind would wanna be hitched to this fine figure of a man?"

Uncle Bob puffed out his chest, and Sy shook his head.

"How could any woman *not* want to be married to that?"

They both laughed.

"So what's her name? This woman you're going to marry. And does she know it yet?"

"Yes, she knows it! Her name is Ellen Watkins. She's as pretty as pretty can be, and she done said yes to me two days ago. We already plannin' the weddin' too." Uncle Bob beamed. "I told her the sooner, the better. We'll live right here at Belle Meade, in the old Harding cabin."

"Sounds like a good life's ahead of you."

Uncle Bob nodded. "Mmm-hmm. I'd be fine to live and die right here on this land. Been here since I was two years old! Come with my parents. We was a weddin' gift to the first Mrs. William Giles Harding."

The man stated it so matter-of-factly, and Sy found his thoughts returning to what Alexandra had told him about how they'd dug up rusty chains and manacles at an old slave auction site in town. Then had sold them to a smelter and bought supplies of Bibles and paper for the Fisk students with the money. There was something poetic—and right—about the shackles that had once bound these people now being used to set them free.

"That depot's lookin' mighty fine, Mr. Rutledge. Mighty fine."

Sy had to admit, the Belle Meade Depot had turned out well. Some of the carpentry work still needed to be finished on the inside, but they'd easily meet the November 1 deadline two weeks away.

Uncle Bob slowed the wagon as they maneuvered onto the completed portion of macadam road, then snapped the reins again. "You build a nice road too, Mr. Rutledge. Smooth as glass. Just in time for winter snow and cold too."

Sy spotted something lying in the field. "What's that out there? You see it? About two o'clock. Looks like one of your horses didn't make it."

Uncle Bob laughed. "That's just Old Gray. A gelding who's been around here forever."

"*Old* Gray? He looks more like Dead Gray."

"Aw, he ain't dead, sir. He's just sleepin'. And come to think of it . . ." Uncle Bob grinned. "Him bein' a gelding, there ain't much left for him to do but sleep, now is there?"

Sy laughed. Then smiled again as they passed Alexandra's rock, as he'd come to think of it each time he passed it. And he'd passed it plenty in recent weeks. He thought of how she'd responded to him when he'd kissed her. About knocked him off his feet.

He hadn't come South looking for a wife. But as he'd learned through the years, sometimes the best things were found when you weren't looking for them.

∽

"I'm sorry, Miss Jamison. There are no rooms available in the hotel."

"But that's not possible, sir. I wired ahead and reserved these rooms three weeks ago, and received this confirmation in response. On your hotel stationery." She held up the paper and pointed to the name Springfield Inn. "We're tired and hungry, and we have a concert to give this evening. So please, check your register again."

The man looked down at the register, then immediately back up again. His attention flitted beyond her to where Ella and the other singers stood waiting inside the lobby. "And I'm telling you again, ma'am, that there are no rooms available."

She bristled, knowing exactly what was happening. And she struggled for patience, her own worn thin in recent days from low concert attendance, low contributions, and even lower spirits among the group. Hotel and travel expenses were consuming far too great a portion of their dwindling purse, and they weren't even raising enough money to cover costs. And this after seventeen concerts in fifteen days.

Plus, Ella was sick. She refused to admit it, but Alexandra saw the signs of fatigue and headaches. And young Minnie had a troubling cough.

And yet, even as their own funds were swiftly diminishing,

everyone had agreed without exception to donate the entire proceeds of that very first concert—all fifty dollars—to the Chicago relief fund. She couldn't have felt more proud to be part of this generous group.

Which made this situation even more infuriating.

"I'd like to speak to your manager, please, sir."

The man leveled his gaze. "I am the manager, ma'am. And now I'm asking you to leave my hotel. Right now."

She glanced back at Ella, who had quickly become the matriarch of the group—especially when Mr. White was gone, as he was now, working to book more concerts in the area. Ella gave an almost imperceptible shake of her head.

So they left, and went to three other hotels before they found one willing to allow them to stay.

"There's one stipulation, ma'am."

Alexandra looked up from signing the register.

"My other guests will not appreciate me allowing you to"—he smiled briefly—"well, not you specifically, but . . ."

She stared, not about to help him.

"The stipulation is, ma'am, that you must all take your meals before the usual hour. And please, I would ask that you not . . . linger in the lobby."

If the hour hadn't been so late and they hadn't been so bone tired, Alexandra might have left and gone looking for another place. But there wasn't time. And she couldn't be assured there would *be* another place.

With no time to rest, they quickly changed clothes for the concert. And since patrons were already in the dining room, they ate standing up in a back hallway of the kitchen, then walked the twelve city blocks in a misty rain to Black's Opera House.

The chilly October wind made it feel colder than the temperature actually was. And not one of them had an overcoat. Not due to an oversight in bringing them along, but because none of them owned one.

Ella led the group through scales and warm-up exercises, sticking closely to Mr. White's instructions. And in Mr. White's absence, Thomas Rutling prepared to give the plea for support at the end of the evening. But when the time came for the concert to begin, they found fewer than twenty people gathered to hear them.

Thomas spoke up first. "Miss Sheppard, I believe, under the circumstances, with some of us not feeling well and all of us weary, that Mr. White would with a heavy heart announce that we would postpone the entertainment for another evening."

Alexandra could see the struggle on Ella's face, but in the end she nodded. On the way back to the hotel, Alexandra insisted they stop by an apothecary, where she purchased medicine for Ella and Minnie. And once back at the hotel, they all went straight to their rooms and to bed.

Ella was asleep in seconds. Alexandra determined not to be far behind her. But first she had to write out several more press releases to be delivered to the local papers and churches.

Part of her wondered if perhaps it was her fault that more people weren't showing up to hear the singers. Maybe she needed to reword her description of the group or list different songs. She sighed.

When she finished her task she turned down the lamp and pressed her face into the softness of the pillow. Mr. White had painted the North to be a far more accepting place than they had found to be the case. Many here resented the "invasion" of freedmen, alleging that they depressed wages and competed for jobs. It was difficult navigating friend and foe in this randomly segregated North.

One of the churches last week had insisted they give separate concerts—one for whites, one for blacks. In the face of the group's mission, such a request defied belief. Mr. White had flatly refused, so there had been no concert at all.

She turned over, unable to get comfortable. She missed Nashville. She missed Fisk. She missed her students and teaching.

And most of all she missed Sy. "Be watching for me along the way," he'd said. And she had been.

But she had yet to see his face in the crowd.

∽

Sy entered through the front door of the Columbus Bible Church and could already hear the singers. He'd hoped to make it before the concert started, but problems with construction of the bridge over the creek at Belle Meade had forced him to take a later train. And he was only here overnight. Tomorrow would see him traveling on to Charleston, West Virginia, to settle escalating labor issues with the railroad workers.

He removed his hat and raked a hand through his hair, not eager to have to tell General Harding and the other investors about the possible delay. But knowing he was about to see Alexandra helped to lift his spirits.

The auditorium was full. That was a good thing. In her last letter, she'd said the group had been a little discouraged due to low attendance.

He looked around, but didn't see her. Didn't see Bliss or his wife either. But again, it was crowded. Sy opted to stand in the back. Too much sitting on the train. Plus, it offered better perspective.

The song ended and Thomas, one of the singers he'd met before, stepped forward to speak. Sy looked around again, searching for Alexandra.

He'd gotten a letter from Bliss earlier in the week confirming their attendance tonight and their eager acceptance for dinner following the concert. Their train from Ashtabula should have arrived about an hour ago. Bliss had also included a note about Miss Glenn, who'd died peacefully at her home two days after their meeting. Which, after all the woman had been through, Sy had been grateful to hear.

He still marveled at what had come out of their meeting. He'd thought he'd been going there to get information that would benefit his own search, and then she'd told him about David Thompson. The discovery still weighed heavily on him.

Or maybe what weighed heavily was knowing he still needed to tell Alexandra about it. That, and whenever he thought about David Thompson and how Alexandra spoke of him—as such a kind and compassionate man, intelligent and so well-educated— the greater the contrasts he saw between himself and her late fiancé.

The Fisk group began singing again. A song he didn't recognize, but he did know who they were singing about. Even hidden back in the mining towns of Colorado, he'd heard about John Brown and his armed insurrection against slavery. And about the man's hanging. Sy liked the song, and apparently the audience did too, because when it was over, they stood and applauded enthusiastically.

He took that opportunity to look for Alexandra. And finally spotted her near the back on the far side of the auditorium. He just stared for a moment, drinking her in, wondering exactly when she'd managed to so thoroughly capture his heart.

Now if he could only find a way to capture hers.

Chapter
TWENTY-NINE

When Thomas stepped forward and announced the last song, Alexandra was relieved. She still enjoyed listening to the troupe, but her mind was on other things.

Mr. White had added four more concerts that morning, but the venues were quite a distance south, which meant more expensive train tickets—which meant more money. Money they didn't have. And when she'd tried to explain her concerns to him, he'd merely said, "The Lord will provide, Miss Jamison."

She rubbed her temples. She believed the Lord would provide. But she also knew that sometimes her ideas of provision and his did not match up. And there'd risen some contention within the group. Petty bickering where there once was unity. Hurt feelings over the least little thing. But she knew the root of it.

Everyone was worried about Fisk's survival. And about what they would do if they had to return home empty-handed. Especially after having taken such a gamble with this venture, and with so many of the parents and the entire missionary board against them.

There was a restlessness inside her she couldn't define.

Unable to sit still any longer, she rose, needing to get back to the lobby anyway to prepare to greet guests and answer any questions.

Halfway down the aisle she stopped stone-still, unable to believe what she saw. But that languid smile tipping one side of his mouth told her she wasn't dreaming. She hurried to the back of the auditorium, accepted Sy's outstretched hand, and followed him into the lobby.

He pulled her to him and she held him tight. Head against his chest, she relished the strength of his arms and the solid beat of his heart. He let her go too soon.

"What are you doing here?" she whispered, hearing Mr. White deliver his plea from within the auditorium.

"I think that should be obvious," Sy said softly, and touched her face in a way that stirred emotions far too close to the surface. "Let me know when you can leave. I'd like to take you to dinner. Philip Bliss and his wife are here too. Somewhere. They're going to join us."

Pleased more than she could say, Alexandra found that for a moment she could only stare. "It's so good to see you."

He smiled. "I've missed you too."

Something stirred inside her. "How long are you here?"

"Only until the morning. But," he said quickly, as if sensing her disappointment, "I'll try to stop back through whatever town you're in on my way back to Nashville in a week or so."

She nodded, willing to take a few hours with him over nothing. She saw people begin filtering out of the auditorium and whispered, "I only have to stay for a few minutes, answer any questions people may have about Fisk, then we can leave."

"I'll find the Blisses and we'll meet you back here. And, Alexandra? It's good to see you too."

The moments couldn't pass quickly enough. Finally the attendees began to leave, and Alexandra joined Sy and Ella as they spoke together by the front door.

Ella looked her way. "Imagine my surprise when I looked up and saw Mr. Rutledge here."

Alexandra caught the subtle lift of Ella's brow. "Yes, I was as surprised as you were, I'm sure." She looked about. "Sy, could you not find Mr. and Mrs. Bliss?"

"I don't think they came." He shrugged. "They must have had a change of plans. But I know they were excited about hearing the singers, so my guess is they'll try to attend a concert in the future."

"I surely hope so." Ella inclined her head. "The other singers and I would love to meet him as well. We're all admirers of his work. Perhaps when you correspond with him next, Mr. Rutledge, you could let him know how much we appreciate his hymns."

"I'd be happy to, ma'am." Sy nodded.

"Well." Ella looked between them. "It was nice to see you again, Mr. Rutledge. And to you, my dear roommate"—Ella looked every bit the schoolteacher she was—"I'm going back to the hotel to read your paper on the Intellectual Standards Used for Critical Thinking, so be ready to discuss my comments when you return later."

Alexandra laughed. "Be lenient, please."

"Never! Especially not with so bright a pupil."

To Alexandra's surprise, Ella gave her a quick hug, a glint in her eyes.

"Enjoy your evening discussing 'business relations,'" Ella whispered, then walked on without a backward glance.

Sy eyed her. "You're writing papers while on the tour? And Miss Sheppard is grading them? You have time for that?"

"She's helping me earn my degree. Several of the other singers are helping me too, actually. We all study during our spare time, what little there is. They've been so helpful. And"—she gave a little shrug—"I've known the answers to a few of their questions too."

"I believe we call that Southern Reciprocation, Miss Jamison."

Happier than she could remember in a long time, Alexandra accepted Sy's offered arm, and they walked outside. The cool October evening was a welcome change from the warmth of the church building.

"Do you have a preference of restaurant, Miss Jamison?"

"I do not. We only arrived here this afternoon, so I've not been out. But I warn you, Mr. White said it would be best for appearance's sake if you have me back to the hotel no later than ten o'clock."

"Then we'd better find a restaurant fast."

They decided on a small Italian restaurant a few streets over, a quiet and out-of-the-way place. Sometime into their meal, as she shared with him all the things she'd wished she could have shared with him since she'd been gone, Alexandra noticed him smiling at her from across the table.

"What?" she asked, dabbing the corners of her mouth just in case.

He looked at her plate—still laden with spaghetti and meat-balls. Then at his, which was completely empty.

She winced. "I'm talking too much."

"Not at all. I'm enjoying hearing all about the tour. But I also don't want you to go back to your hotel hungry."

"So now it's your turn." She picked up her fork. "Tell me what's happening with your railroad projects. Oh! And about the meeting with the parishioner. The one Mr. Bliss arranged. You said you were able to speak with her."

A shadow passed over his face. "Yes, I was. She passed away a couple of days after our meeting."

"I'm sorry to hear that. Was she able to tell you anything about what caused the accident?"

He hesitated, then shook his head. "Not about the accident, no. But she told me what happened to her right after."

A pained expression came over his face, and although Alexandra sensed he wanted to tell her about it, she found she didn't want to hear it. She'd already lived that experience a thousand times over.

The server brought the check, and she seized the moment. "You know, it is getting late. Perhaps we should start back to the hotel. You said you have an early train."

He held her gaze, then nodded. "Yes, perhaps that would be best."

✐

Sy awakened early the next morning, got ready, packed, and walked the short distance to the hotel where the Fisk group was staying. He'd invited Alexandra to join him for breakfast this morning, with the goal of telling her what he had failed to share with her last night. Although he honestly hadn't tried that hard.

He stopped at a newsstand on the corner and bought a paper for the train. The older man behind the counter nodded his way as he took his nickel, heavy in conversation with another customer. Sy slid the newspaper into his briefcase and walked on.

The dining room in the hotel was small, but it was early yet, so only a couple of the tables were occupied. He chose a table in the corner where their conversation would be more private.

"Coffee, sir?"

"Yes, please."

Seeing he had a few minutes before Alexandra was supposed to come down, he pulled the newspaper from his briefcase and opened it to the front page. He read the headline and his gut knotted tight.

Chapter
THIRTY

ASHTABULA TRAIN DISASTER CLAIMS 92 LIVES

*S*wallowing hard, Sy stared at the headline and—somehow, deep inside him—knew what he feared was true. His gaze devoured the text, skimming for details. And for the name he prayed not to see.

> Yesterday, the outbound Pacific Express from Ashtabula, Ohio, comprising two locomotives and eleven railcars, was buffeted by high winds as it pushed its way across the Ashtabula Bridge. The lead locomotive cleared the bridge just as the undergirding of the trestle snapped beneath the weight. The bridge gave way, sending one locomotive and eleven carriages crashing into the ravine seventy-six feet below. Before the wooden cars slammed into the bottom, witnesses say they were already aflame, set afire by kerosene heaters . . .

Sy closed his eyes, a terrible sense of having lived this moment before passing through him. He saw flames devouring passenger cars like kindling and could hear the raspy, fragile voice of Miss Riley Glenn.

Initial reports from investigators, still pending confirmation, claim that the bridge, designed by Amasa Stone, the railroad company president, had been improperly designed and inadequately inspected. Among the dead are Ashtabula resident and beloved hymn composer—

Sy's lungs emptied.

—Philip Paul Bliss and his wife. Witnesses report that Mr. Bliss initially escaped the wreckage, but returned to the consuming conflagration to extricate his wife. The Blisses are survived by their two young sons, George and Philip Paul, ages four and one, respectively, who were initially thought to have been with their parents on the train. Ninety-two of the 159 passengers are believed to have perished in the crash.

The reporter then listed the names of the known deceased, but Sy couldn't read them. He could barely breathe.

"Sy?"

He didn't look up. Alexandra said his name again.

He wiped his eyes and lifted his gaze to see her standing by the table, her expression stricken.

"Sy, what's wrong?"

Wishing he could spare her, and knowing what this would do to her, he stood and pulled her to him and whispered into her ear. And felt her tense.

"No," she said in a rush, shaking her head. She pulled away and, eyes pleading, sought his gaze. "What happened?"

He handed her the newspaper and she read, the paper trembling in her grip. Then for the longest time she stared at the print, tears trailing down her cheeks. Finally she looked up.

"He went back for her," she whispered in a broken voice.

"Yes," was all he could manage. Then conviction hit him square in the chest, and he took a sharp breath. "There's something I need to tell you, Alexandra. About my meeting with Miss Glenn."

Same as last night, a look came into her eyes that said she didn't want to hear it. He took the newspaper from her, pulled out a chair, and she sat, back ramrod straight, hands clenched in her lap. He sat beside her.

"Miss Glenn was riding in the second freedmen's car that day. She told me that following the crash her leg was pinned beneath something." He paused, the tightness in his throat making it difficult to speak. "She couldn't move. She said there was a man she remembered having seen earlier, riding in the same car."

Alexandra drew in a ragged breath.

"He managed to crawl over to her and free her . . . so that she could get out. She asked me if I knew if anyone riding in that same passenger car had survived. She wanted to know because she wanted to thank the man for saving her life." He shook his head. "I told her I had no way of knowing. Then she smiled and said that before that day . . . she'd never seen a white man traveling in a freedmen's car before."

A strangled sob rose in her throat, and Alexandra leaned forward, her shoulders shaking. Sy knelt beside her chair and held her as she wept.

∞

That night, following a more somber but well-attended concert, Alexandra walked with Sy back to the hotel. With Mr. White and the singers walking some yards ahead, she reached over and tucked her hand into the crook of Sy's arm.

"Thank you for staying," she said softly.

He looked over, then covered her hand on his arm. "I needed to stay, Alexandra."

She nodded, hearing what he wasn't saying. He'd been quiet

all day. Understandably. And no matter how she tried not to, she kept thinking about that bridge giving way.

When they entered the lobby, Mr. White was waiting.

"We're meeting in the dining room. Would you two please join us?"

Alexandra sneaked Sy an apologetic look, but he shook his head as if to say, *It's all right.*

It was late and the dining room was empty. Two oil lamps provided the only light in the room. Mr. White had already delivered a beautiful tribute to Philip Paul Bliss in his remarks following the concert, having met the man at a prayer meeting some years before. So she knew that couldn't be what this was about.

"Dearest friends," Mr. White began when everyone had been seated. "It pains me to say it, but we once again find ourselves in the same situation as so many times before. The auditorium tonight was nearly full, and yet the contributions totaled only eighteen dollars."

The air seemed to evaporate from the room. Alexandra felt a weight in her chest even as Isaac Dickerson leaned forward, head in his hands. Several of the others bowed their heads. She glanced beside her, but Sy didn't look over.

"As you are aware," White continued, "we are running very low on funds. I want you to know that I am going to seek God's face tonight. I will not sleep. I will stay awake and pray and ask for his guidance. For his intervention. For with all my heart, I know you, dear singers, are Fisk's salvation. My belief in that has not—and will not—waver. I only ask that before retiring to your beds, you pray for me to hear the Lord's voice clearly. I do not ask you to join me in this night of prayer. In fact, I implore you not to. You need your rest in order to minister to those who need to hear your songs."

Alexandra didn't wait for her bed, but started praying right then.

"Also, as I shared with you last evening, we have three cities a good ways south from here that have requested concerts. They have stated with great confidence that we will be well received and that the contributions will be most generous. It will take the remainder of our funds to get there. But again, I believe this direction is from the Lord."

Alexandra's prayer trailed off. She still thought it a risky decision to travel that far with so little money. And yet, if Mr. White felt such conviction . . .

"Would you bow your heads with me," he said softly, "and let us silently thank the Lord for the richness of his blessings, the chiefest of those being his Son?"

Alexandra bowed her head and saw Sy do likewise. Moments passed, the only sound the *ticktock* of a clock somewhere behind them. Then the soft intake of breath.

"Steal away," came a feather-soft voice, the vibrato powerful even in a whisper. "Steal away . . ."

Maggie Porter, Alexandra knew without even looking. She knew each of these singers' voices as well as she knew her own. But she'd never heard this song.

"Steal away . . . to Jesus."

Slowly, one by one, the others joined in, humming along, a soulful longing in their tone, the rise and fall of their voices seeming to reach all the way to heaven even as the music sank deep into the heart.

"Steal away. Steal away home. I ain't . . . got long . . . to stay here."

Maggie's voice rose, no longer feather-soft, and it captured an urgency that tugged at Alexandra's heart. Then just as quickly it quieted again, powerful even in a hush.

"My Lord . . . he calls me, and he calls me by the thunder. The trumpet sounds within'a my soul. I ain't . . . got long . . . to stay here."

The song ended and another began. But this one Alexandra knew, and she softly joined in.

"In the morning when I rise, in the morning when I rise, in the morning when I rise . . . Give me Jesus. Give me Jesus, give me Jesus. You can have all the rest, give me Jesus."

To her surprise, Sy joined in on the second verse, his deep voice hushed but filled with emotion as it blended with the others. As they sang, a sweetness filled the room. And she couldn't think of anywhere else she'd rather be than in that room, right then, with those people.

The song ended, and quiet amens rose as people stood and left the room.

"Mr. White." Sy caught him as he passed. "Which cities down south were you referring to? The Northeast Line doesn't come this far north, but it does swing up through Kentucky and West Virginia. If you can get as far south as Portsmouth, I'd be more than willing to help with transportation for those specific cities, if you'd let me."

Mr. White smiled. "Before I have even bowed the knee, the Lord is already answering, Mr. Rutledge."

Tired, Alexandra stayed seated as they spoke, her mind going again to the accident in Ashtabula, then to Dutchman's Curve.

David . . .

So he had lived through the accident, only to die sometime later. Tears rose again as she thought about what he must have suffered, thought about him saving that young woman. She wished now that she could have met Miss Glenn as well. Then it occurred to her that perhaps, by now, Miss Glenn *had* had the chance to tell David thank you after all.

Mr. White bid them good night, and Sy walked with her as far as the staircase leading up to the second-floor landing. He looked down at her, then gently drew her to him. Alexandra breathed in the scent of him—bayberry and spice, sunshine and leather. And wished he didn't have to go. Even more, she found herself wishing she could go with him.

"I'm already missing you again," she whispered.

"And I've never stopped missing you."

The next morning when Alexandra and Ella entered the dining room, they found everyone already seated, and Mr. White's face aglow. As they took their seats, Alexandra sensed a renewed energy and excitement among the group.

"My dear children," Mr. White began, "I have spent the entire night in prayer and have decided upon a name for our group." His gaze slowly touched upon each of them. "You will be called . . . the Jubilee Singers. In honor of the Year of Jubilee!"

Alexandra was familiar with the Year of Jubilee as described in the Old Testament. She remembered learning about it in church in earlier years, but had heard the story much more recently at Fisk during chapel. The commandment was part of the law given to Moses by God, stating that every fifty years, the Israelites were required to observe the Year of Jubilee. To follow God's instructions for release from slavery, for redemption of property, and care of the land.

And as Mr. White continued to speak, she felt something stir inside her. She looked at the faces around the table and sensed they felt the same.

White leaned forward, his sharp features earnest. "Within the Jewish nation's struggle for freedom and our own humble work here within this small band of believers and at Fisk University back home, we share a kinship. And I can think of no better name than this to lift up our cry to this nation and to be the banner for our call for freedom."

Chapter
THIRTY-ONE

Seated at the head of a makeshift conference room table, Sy felt the tension pouring from the railroad workers packed tightly into the room.

He'd arrived into Charleston, West Virginia, a day later than planned due to the train accident in Ashtabula—which he was still having trouble accepting—and he found the tempers here volatile. The workers were frustrated over labor issues. Most of the issues not with the project at hand, Sy quickly realized. These were years-old grudges.

Nevertheless, it fell to him to deal with it if he wanted the North Carolina/West Virginia railroad built. And he did.

So he allowed the spokesman for the laborers to continue having his say.

"We want better pay, Mr. Rutledge! Better equipment and better food. We've spent our lives blastin' our way through the mountains of West Virginia and North Carolina. We've been diggin' trenches through rock-hard earth with picks and shovels and kegs of black powder. I done lost count of how many friends I seen buried in landslides and explosions, sir. And while all of us sittin' 'round this table this mornin' know you ain't to blame yourself, 'cause you wasn't our boss then, we're still comin' to you now askin' for what we believe is right! And we're willin' to strike for it too, if need be."

Assenting nods and rumbles of "That's right!" rose from those gathered.

Seated at the head of the table, Sy studied the face of each of the railroad men. Not suited executives who sat in offices far away from the grit and grime of laying ribbons of steel, but laborers who had bent their backs to the work, the years of toil etched in their faces.

Along with seeing them, he also saw countless images burned into his memory. Not only from the many railroad accidents he'd witnessed in Colorado firsthand, but from the stories all the railroad workers he'd spoken to in recent weeks and months had told him, including those from Dutchman's Curve and the Ashtabula Bridge.

He also saw his father. Harrison Kennedy. Who had started out as a laborer himself, then worked his way up. Railroading was dangerous work. Nothing would change that. But so much of the tragedy he'd seen was due to negligence, carelessness. Or someone sitting in an office far away and only too eager to make a quick fortune at the risk of other men's lives.

"Gentlemen, I hear your concerns." Sy slowly rose from his chair and sensed the tension in the room rise with him. "And I agree. Changes need to be made. And it's high time we make them."

He walked to the other end of the table, where the spokesman sat wary-eyed. "And starting today, we'll begin working toward those changes. Mr. O'Grady, would you and two of your men be willing to partner with me and my supervisors to address these concerns? And to build the best—and safest—railroad this country has ever seen?"

Sy held out his hand, knowing this was going to take more money and more time and would require his going back to his investors for more capital. But it was the right thing to do. And as his father had taught him, the right thing, be it more difficult and more costly, was always the right decision.

O'Grady stared at his outstretched hand for a moment, as

though not certain he could trust it. Then he stood and took firm hold. "Yes, sir, Mr. Rutledge. We would."

∽

They canvassed the city of Xenia, their last night here before heading south tomorrow. But one hotel after another refused to give them shelter. With each rejection, Alexandra realized more and more that although she'd thought she understood the realities of her friends' lives due to the color of their skin, she'd been wrong.

With no place to sleep for the night, the group returned to the railway station under Mr. White's counsel. A chilling November wind blew hard from the north, and with no overcoats among them, they huddled together to stay warm while Mr. White ventured out for food.

The past two weeks of concerts had seen better contributions than the week previous, but the Jubilee Singers were still living hand to mouth. And with every day that passed, Fisk University was sinking deeper and deeper into debt.

Mr. White returned some time later with sandwiches. "I implored several ministers to give us aid," he told them as they ate. "But without exception, all of them said they would need to seek the direction of their congregation before accepting us into their midst."

Huddled close to Alexandra, Ella coughed, a deep rattle in her chest. Alexandra put an arm around her, and Ella smiled her steady smile. Benjamin softly began to pray, and Alexandra followed along in her heart, her petition rising from a place of desperation she'd never prayed from before. Had never needed to.

A month into their travels and already the troupe had performed over thirty-six times. And had little to show for it.

She reached into her skirt pocket and briefly fingered the empty flask, the bottle cold to the touch. She'd almost tried to sell it to a street vendor today, knowing it would bring at least a little money. And every coin counted. But Ella had encouraged her to wait.

Around midnight, a man in a dark overcoat burst through the door of the station and strode toward them. Alexandra tensed, and felt Ella do the same beside her.

Mr. White rose, his thin frame looking even more so in recent days, and Isaac, Greene, Thomas, and Benjamin rose to stand shoulder-to-shoulder alongside him.

"Mr. George White?" the man called out.

"Yes. I am George White."

"I've been sent to gather you and your singers, sir. I'm to bring you to the church building where we'll offer you shelter for the night."

Tears rose in Alexandra's eyes, and she saw them mirrored in the other young women too.

"God is faithful, Alexandra," Ella whispered. "He is faithful."

The train pulled into the station at Portsmouth, the southernmost city on their tour to date. Alexandra, satchel in hand, disembarked with the rest of the troupe. She paused briefly on the platform—as she still did every time—and acknowledged with gratitude their safe arrival to yet another step of their journey.

Accustomed to the routine now, she and the others followed Mr. White, his tall frame making it impossible to lose him in a crowd, and with other travelers stopping to stare. She glanced across the tracks and spotted the words *Northeast Line* on the side of a train and felt a wave of longing. And almost felt like she was home.

She'd received two letters from Sy in the last week, both mailed from Charlotte. He'd said he would do his best to stop through one of these cities to see her on his way back to Nashville, and at every stop she found herself scanning the crowds for him.

They waited outside the ticket office for Mr. White. He returned a short time later with a glimmer in his eyes that drew Alexandra's curiosity. Ella just shrugged and smiled, her cough considerably better and the light returning to her eyes.

"Follow me, friends!"

They walked almost the full length of the platform, passing the third- and second-class cars before Mr. White finally stopped—in front of a Pullman Palace car. *Northeast Line* on the side. And Alexandra could only smile.

Sylas Rutledge.

Mr. White handed their tickets to the porter, who greeted them each as they boarded. She turned to check and found people not only staring, but gawking.

Ella leaned back and whispered before she boarded, "I don't think they've ever seen colored people riding in such a fancy car before."

Alexandra laughed and gave her a little shove.

Bold patterns in burgundy and gold covered the upholstered bench seats, and the rich scent of well-oiled leather and beeswax only added to the beauty. Black walnut finishes gleamed in the afternoon sunlight, and accents of crystal and silver graced the gas lamps affixed to the walls and ceilings. George Pullman never did anything halfway.

And neither, apparently, did Sylas Rutledge.

The luxurious car was stocked with drinks and refreshments, head pillows and lap blankets. The train whistle blasted, and minutes later the Northeast Line pulled away from the station with no sign of Sy.

And yet Alexandra felt him right next to her.

For the first half of the two-hour trip, she and Greene discussed a book he'd loaned to her about agriculture and husbandry. His knowledge was extensive, as was his generosity in sharing it.

"If you'll excuse me now, Miss Jamison, I'm going to get some shut-eye while I can." He leaned closer. "Isaac snores up a storm!"

She laughed, read for a while longer, then before she knew it her thoughts began to wander and her eyelids grew heavy. She closed the book, then closed her eyes. Then just as swiftly opened them again, realizing what she'd been about to do.

She sat up straighter, but the plushness of the seat and the warmth of the lap blanket plotted with the gentle rocking rhythm of the Pullman to lull her to sleep. And succeeded.

Awhile later, from far away she heard her name being called, and snuggled deeper into the warm cocoon of the blanket. But when a firm hand gripped her shoulder, she came wide-awake to see Ella standing over her.

"We're here." Ella smiled. "I never thought I would congratulate someone for falling asleep on a train. But . . . I'm so proud of you."

"Oh, listen to this one!" Jennie held the newspaper aloft as the troupe settled in to the Pullman Palace car the next day. The railcar was at their disposal, Sy had written, as long as they were traveling on his railroad. "And it's a national paper! The reporter writes, 'The assembly was as rapt as any concert audience has ever been, emotion flowing down their cheeks and even into the whiskers of old men.'"

The group responded with skitters of laughter and approval.

She held up a hand, continuing. "The singing was really fine, and that it was much enjoyed by the audience was evidenced by the hearty rounds of applause that greeted the close of each performance!' Oh wait!" Jennie looked up from the newspaper. "He mentions us traveling in a Pullman Palace car! And on the Northeast Line"—she looked over at Alexandra—"owned by the handsome Mr. Sylas Rutledge from the Colorado Territory, but lately of Nashville, Tennessee."

"It doesn't say handsome!" Alexandra leaned over to see the paper, but Jennie grabbed it away.

"No, it doesn't." Jennie smiled. "But I do."

All the women laughed. The men just shook their heads.

The train pulled into the station right on time, and true to what Mr. White had been told, the church auditorium holding the concert that night was filled to overflowing.

Later, when they returned to the hotel, Mr. White's countenance was more pleased than Alexandra could remember.

"Dear singers," he said as they met after hours in the dining room, "our contribution tonight was . . . one hundred and three dollars."

Whoops and hollers rose in response.

"And," he added quickly, "they've invited us to stay and give another four concerts, believing they will all be thus attended and supported."

Alexandra couldn't wait to get upstairs and write to Sy. She finished the letter just as Ella returned to the room from the special practice Mr. White had called.

They both readied for bed and talked late into the night, and Alexandra thanked God again for allowing her to be a part of this. And for Sy, who had given her a much-needed nudge.

"Alexandra?" came a soft whisper.

Alexandra stirred and opened her eyes, having slept hard. She pushed the hair back from her face and looked up to see Ella sitting on the bedside.

"I'm sorry to wake you, but Mr. White was just here."

Still foggy, Alexandra saw pale light through the window. "Is everything all right?"

Ella took her hand. "I'm sorry, Alexandra. Your mother has called you home."

Chapter
THIRTY-TWO

*D*og tired, Sy unlocked the door to his hotel room, grateful the labor issues with the Charleston railroad crew were improving. Not as quickly as he wanted, but at least they were moving in the right direction.

He stepped into the room and something crinkled beneath his boot. He lit the lamp on the desk, then spotted the envelope that had been slipped beneath his door. He picked it up, read the return address, and couldn't sit down fast enough.

Philip Paul Bliss.

Sy stared at the name, his throat constricting. It wasn't possible. And yet here it was. In his hand.

Nearly three weeks had passed since the Ashtabula accident, and not a day went by that he didn't think of Philip and his wife, Lucy. And their precious boys, now without their parents.

He fingered the envelope, the hand-stamped date "November 9" tempting his thoughts toward possibilities he knew were not possible, before reason swiftly took charge and settled on the only explanation that made sense. Bliss had either mailed this before he died, or someone had mailed it afterward on his behalf.

Sy slid his finger beneath the sealed flap, his conversations with the man coming back in a wash of memory. The shared laughter, the easy manner in which Bliss had talked about his life and dreams, the way he'd had a knack of getting to the very heart of something without ever once seeming boorish or rude. The way Philip Bliss had lived his life with such intention. Never wasting a moment. Or an opportunity. He'd lived a life that was now living beyond his own.

The kind of life, Sy realized, he himself wanted to live.

He pulled the pages from the envelope and unfolded them, the top page a piece of stationery from Gospel Hymns and Sacred Songs Publisher. Sy's gaze dropped to the handwritten script.

Dear Mr. Rutledge,

It was Mr. Philip Bliss's request that we send you a copy of the sheet music of his most recent hymn upon its publication. Per his wishes, you will find the sheet music enclosed.

It is with deepest sadness that we relay the tragic news of Mr. Bliss's unexpected passing on the twenty-second of October in a train accident in which . . .

Eyes burning, Sy scanned the remainder of the note, then turned the page. He blinked to clear his vision as the sheet music came into focus. His gaze went to the title: "Almost Persuaded." And his chest tightened as he read the words his friend had written, even as he recalled looking up and seeing Bliss standing there that first afternoon on the train.

Almost persuaded, now to believe;
Almost persuaded, Christ to receive;
Seems now some soul to say,
Go, Spirit, go Thy way,
Some more convenient day
On Thee I'll call.
Almost persuaded, come, come today;
Almost persuaded, turn not away;
Jesus invites you here,
Angels are ling'ring near,

Prayers rise from hearts so dear;
O wand'rer, come!
Almost persuaded, harvest is past!
Almost persuaded, doom comes at last!
Almost cannot avail;
Almost is but to fail!
Sad, sad, that bitter wail—
Almost, but lost!

Sy turned the pages over in his hand, hoping for a note from Philip, wishing for one more conversation with him.

With a deep breath, he read the words of the hymn a second time, then slid the pages back into the envelope. Such sobering lyrics. He thought back to what Philip had asked him on the train that day. "Are you a God-fearing man, Mr. Rutledge?"

A sad smile touched his mouth. Not a question a man got asked every day. But a question a man should ask of himself. And often.

"Yes," he whispered to the shadows and silence in the hotel room. "I am, Philip."

Sy deliberately lifted his eyes heavenward. "But I also want to be a man of God. Better than I have been in the past." He clenched his jaw tight. "Thank you, friend, for showing me more of what that means."

⌒⌢⌒

Alexandra stared out the window of the train, cornfield after cornfield bulleting past, each minute taking her closer home. But would she get there in time? *Lord, please let me see him again. One last time.*

She couldn't bear the thought of leaving things between them as they were. Surely her father, so close to stepping into eternity, would accept her now. Would want to mend their differences.

She pulled in a breath, part of her heart still back with Ella and the others. Yet the greater part of it—she paused, realizing that wasn't the right word—the *whole* of her heart rested in another person. He carried it with him everywhere he went, and yet she wondered if he knew that.

The train whistle blew, announcing the coming stop.

Mr. White said he'd booked her the fastest possible route back to Nashville: two stops, but she didn't have to change trains. As the train pulled into the Knoxville station, she looked down at the empty flask cradled in the palm of her hand. Then looking up, she peered through the window, and her gaze went immediately to a black duster and dark leather boots.

And meeting Sy's gaze, she felt almost home.

Alexandra paused outside her parents' bedroom door and reached for Sy's hand.

"Are you certain you want me to go in with you?"

She nodded. "I don't know how he's going to respond."

He brought her hand to his lips. "You already know what you want to say. And I know you'll say it with all the love you have for him. So however he responds is up to him." He brushed the curl at her temple.

She looked up at him one last time, then knocked on the door before gently opening it. Her mother rose from her seat by the bed and met them halfway across the room.

"Oh, my dear . . ." She pulled Alexandra to her, and Alexandra held her tight, relishing the feel of her mother's arms. "You made it. I'm so glad."

"How is he?"

Her mother's features clouded. "Your father slipped into a deeper sleep yesterday, and hasn't awakened since. But," she added quickly, "Dr. Phillips said that he's seen patients move in and out of this kind of sleep for days. So it's possible that he'll awaken, Alexandra." Her voice softened. "And that you'll have the time you need."

Alexandra nodded, then pulled back slightly. "Mother, may I introduce Mr. Sylas Rutledge. A . . . dear friend of mine. And, Sy, I'd like to present my mother, Mrs. Barrett Broderick Jamison." Alexandra made certain to use the formal title her mother had always preferred.

"Mr. Rutledge." Her mother nodded briefly, then touched his arm. "Thank you, sir, for accompanying my daughter home."

"It's an honor to meet you, Mrs. Jamison, and it was my pleasure."

Alexandra looked toward the bed. The changes in her father were marked. Far thinner, his complexion gray and sickly. Her heart twisted. "Has he been in pain?"

Her mother shook her head. "Dr. Phillips has made certain of that. He's also told me that it could be anytime now. That's it's really up to your father. Hence, he advised me to send for you." Her mother hugged her again. "And I'm so grateful you came. I sent telegrams to your brothers too. They responded that they would try to get home if they could. But I don't think they'll be coming."

Alexandra nodded, not surprised. Then motioned toward the bed. "May I?"

Her mother nodded. "But he's very weak."

Alexandra sat on the edge of the chair and leaned close. "Father?" she whispered. "Can you hear me?" She took hold of his hand.

But he didn't respond. She tried again, to no avail.

Her mother laid a gentle hand on her shoulder. "Why don't you and Mr. Rutledge go down to the kitchen and get something to eat. I'm sure you're tired and hungry. I'll sit with your father for a while."

"I don't mind sitting with him, Mother."

"I don't either, my dear. And I'm cherishing every remaining day."

Chapter
THIRTY-THREE

*A*lexandra." Her mother's voice was soft as she entered the bedroom. "You've not left his side for nearly a week. My dear, I fear that the longer he sleeps, the greater the likelihood he'll not awaken again."

"But I have to try." Alexandra squeezed her father's hand, willing him to open his eyes. "After all, you told me he hadn't said anything about changing his mind about me."

"Your father is a very proud man, Alexandra. He well could have altered his opinion and still have kept it to himself, you know that." Her mother kissed the crown of her head. "He loves you very much. You must remember that. Just as I reminded him of your love, so often. Now . . . your Mr. Rutledge is waiting downstairs."

Alexandra looked up to see her mother smile, which prompted her own. She stood and leaned down, and looked long into her father's face.

"I love you, Papa," she whispered, using the endearing term she hadn't used in years.

She found Sy standing in her father's study, and she thought of the first time she saw him, in that very room. How different a man he was from what she'd imagined at first impression.

Glancing beyond her to the open doorway, he smiled, tipped her chin up, and kissed her softly on the mouth, and Alexandra answered. She moved closer, needing to feel his strength, wanting to feel his arms around her. And he didn't disappoint. After a moment she drew back, a little breathless.

He smiled. "Want to get some lunch in town?"

She nodded. "I need to stop by the post office. I have a letter to mail for Ella."

"Have you heard from her recently?"

"I received a letter just yesterday. She had good news too." Alexandra retrieved the letter from atop the desk and began reading. "'Success is now at hand, my dear Alexandra. And due, at least in part, to a change in our program's usual repertoire. A change Mr. White suggested and that I, along with the other singers, did not favor at first. But at his insistent encouragement—'"

Sy laughed. "'Insistent encouragement' is a nice way of putting it."

Alexandra smiled, then continued to read. "'—we have begun singing some of the slave songs that are most dear to our heritage. And what is so surprising, Alexandra, is that white people want to hear them! Sometimes they ask us to sing a certain song again. Our concerts are so well attended now that many are doomed to stand and many more leave for want of room. In some cities excursion trains are going to run to the places where we sing. The people seem to be perfectly frantic about the Jubilee Singers.'"

Sy nodded. "Those songs are among my favorites that they sing. I'll never forget that night in the hotel dining room when Mr. White called us to gather."

"Nor will I." Alexandra folded the letter. "I'm so grateful people are finally hearing them and realizing how talented they are. There's no telling what God is going to do with that troupe."

"And aren't you glad you said yes to accompanying them?"

She touched his arm. "Thank you . . . for giving me the courage to do that."

"God gave you the courage, Alexandra. I only gave you a nudge." He took her hand in his. "Still nothing from Mr. White about your teacher examination?"

She shook her head. "But he did write briefly and ask me to teach again come January. So I'm taking that as a good sign and have decided not to worry about it. Especially with all else going on here."

Over a meal of fried chicken with helpings of sweet potatoes and green beans at a restaurant in town, conversation came easily.

"I've gone over my notes again and again." Sy pulled his notepad from his pocket and handed it to her. "As much as I've wanted to find something, anything, to exonerate my father . . ." He sighed. "I can't. There's one more person I'm going to talk to. One of the signalmen who worked the shift that day for the outbound train."

She nodded, reading and turning the pages. "So many people."

"And so few answers."

"I'm sorry, Sy."

His smile held a sad quality. "On a brighter note, General Harding's project is officially completed."

"Congratulations. I bet the Belle Meade Depot is lovely."

"I'm not sure 'lovely' is quite what I was aiming for, but General Harding is pleased."

She smiled. "And the other project is going well?"

He gave a nod. "Labor issues in West Virginia are resolved and track is being laid from both directions as we speak. The North Carolina crew is slightly ahead of schedule, and we're only a week or so behind on the West Virginia side. So General Harding and the other investors are pleased. And so far they haven't balked at the recent request for more capital. Which is good."

"That connection with General Harding certainly turned out well, did it not?"

"Better than I could have ever imagined." He looked across the table. "Thank you, Alexandra."

She raised her glass of water in mock salute.

After lunch they headed in the direction of the post office, but when they turned the corner, Alexandra slowed.

Sy looked over. "What is it?"

She gestured to the shop to their right. "They publish the newspaper I was telling you about."

"The one Thomas reads so faithfully. Searching for his mother."

She nodded. "I'll meet you later? At my parents' house?"

He continued on and she stepped inside. A young woman greeted her.

"Welcome to the the *Colored Tennessean*. How may I be of help?"

Alexandra approached the counter. "I saw a friend of mine reading your newspaper recently. And I learned that you place information-wanted ads."

She smiled. "Yes, ma'am. That's very helpful for freedmen who are trying to find and reconnect with family members."

"Do you have copies of all your back issues?"

The woman looked at her. "We do. But that's a lot of newspapers. May I ask . . . Are you searching for someone, ma'am?"

Alexandra nodded, surprised to find herself getting emotional. "I am. Someone very dear to me. A woman by the name of Abigail."

∽

As Sy entered the Nashville train station, he knew he was here on a long shot. But this was the last lead he had, however flimsy. And he owed it to his father to see it through.

"Afternoon, Mr. Rutledge. How are you, sir?"

Sy recognized the young porter but didn't know his name.

"I'm well, thank you. Could you tell me in which office the signalman logs are kept?"

"Yes, sir. Down that hallway, up the stairs, and second door on your right."

Sy headed up. No one was behind the desk, but he heard footsteps. An older gentleman walked from the storage closet, spectacles at half-mast on his nose. "Help you, sir?"

"Yes, please. I'm wanting to find out the last name of a signalman."

"Oh, I know all the signalmen, sir. Who is it you're looking for?"

"Fellow by the name of Hank."

The man's expression sobered. "That'd be Hank Lloyd."

"Do you know where I could find him? I've got a few questions for him."

"I do, sir. But I'm afraid Hank Lloyd won't be answering any questions. Not anymore. He died about seven months back. Got his arm caught in a coupler between two freight cars. Gangrene set in fast. He was gone in less than a month."

Sy briefly bowed his head, disappointment knifing deep. "I'm sorry to hear that."

"Hank was a good man. Good at his job too. Doesn't seem fair, what happened to him. Some days I come in, and I still expect to see him perched up there in that tower."

Sy looked out the window at the wooden signal tower and thought again of what Luther Coggins had told him about the man who'd saved his life. Sy realized he'd come here today hoping the very same man might save his too, in a way.

Sy cleared his throat. "I'm sorry for your loss, sir. Sounds like Hank was a good friend."

"That he was." The older man nudged his glasses up the bridge of his nose. "But when you've lived as long as I have, you learn that most of the time justice doesn't come in this world. Not like it should."

Sy looked out the window again and down the long line of track leading to Dutchman's Curve. "No, sir. It doesn't. But it's sure a comfort at times to know that it comes in the next."

Later that evening, Sy sat with Alexandra in the central parlor of her parents' home, having dreaded telling her that his last lead had led nowhere. "So . . ." He sighed. "All that and I'm right back where I started when I first got here."

"No, you're not." She reached over and took hold of his hand. "Neither of us is where we were when you first got here, Sy."

He leaned forward, forearms resting on his knees. "As long as I live, Alexandra, I don't think I'll ever be able to accept that my father was to blame for that accident. Not the man I knew. Not the engineer he was. And yet I have no way to prove otherwise."

"And you don't have to. At least . . . not to me. The more I've come to know you, Sy, to know the man you are, to hear you speak about the man your father was . . . I know that your father wouldn't have knowingly done anything to cause that crash. And if . . . *if*," she said softly, "his actions did contribute to it in some awful way, it doesn't change your love for him. Or his for you. And it doesn't change how grateful I am that God brought you into my life."

He cradled the side of her face, needing to say the words even while believing his father was faultless. "I'm sorry," he whispered, and tears welled up in her eyes.

He drew her against him, and she slipped her arms around his waist. After a moment she looked up, and her gaze sought his, her desire clear. He kissed her, slow and long, the softness of her lips, the way she pressed closer to him and whispered his name, giving him hope that they had a future. And that someday far from this one, after a lifetime of loving this woman, she would know just how cherished and beloved she was.

The next morning Sy walked downstairs on his way to the hotel dining room for breakfast when the manager waved him down.

"Mr. Rutledge . . . A note was delivered for you, sir, only a moment ago."

Sy opened it. From General Harding. The man requested a meeting with him at ten o'clock that morning—and made a point of stating that all the investors would be in attendance.

Which Sy knew didn't bode well.

Chapter
THIRTY-FOUR

Sy arrived early to the meeting and found General Harding and the rest of the men already present and seated around the table.

General Harding locked eyes with him. "Come in, Mr. Rutledge. And have a seat."

Sy shook the general's hand, then did likewise to the investors, sensing a shift in the partnership and wondering if it was due to his request for more capital. He took a seat, eager to share the most current details of the North Carolina/West Virginia venture and the changes they were making. But he knew General Harding well enough to know the man liked to steer his own meeting.

"Mr. Rutledge," the general began, "it has come to our attention that you have made some decisions that do not necessarily align with the way we do business."

Sy looked at him, then around the table. "Are you referring to the safety measures I'm putting into place in the—"

"This has nothing to do with safety measures, Mr. Rutledge," another of the investors said. "It has to do with decisions that do not reflect our own values."

Again Sy scanned the faces around the table. For a moment, he wondered if this had to do with his father. But General Harding had known all about that and would have certainly shared that with the other men from the outset. "I'm sorry, gentlemen, but I'm not following you. Can you be more specific?"

Mr. Stewart leaned forward, hands clasped tightly in front of him. "Pullman Palace cars, Mr. Rutledge. Is that specific enough for you?"

"Pullman Palace cars?" Sy repeated, seeing the anger registering in their expressions, but truly not understanding what was—

Then it occurred to him. "Are you referring to my loaning one of my Pullman Palace cars to the Jubilee Singers?"

"That's precisely what we're talking about, Mr. Rutledge," Mr. Stewart responded. "Perhaps it was simply a momentary lapse in judgment, sir. But it is one with which we do not agree and will certainly not abide."

Sy leaned forward. "So . . . you want me to take back my lending of the Pullman Palace car to them."

"Precisely," another of the investors said. "And furthermore, you will cease any association with that university and will agree not to condone their efforts in any way."

"Or?" Sy asked quietly, his gut churning.

"Or, Mr. Rutledge . . ." General Harding leaned forward. "We will be forced to withdraw our capital from your venture. Which is something we do not wish to do."

Thoughts spinning, Sy nodded. "And it's something I do not wish for you to do either."

Relief filtered through Harding's expression. "I'm glad to hear that, Mr.—"

"However, sir . . ." Sy included the other men in his gaze. "If that's the cost of keeping your capital, then I must tell you . . . the price is too high."

Stewart stared. "You can't be serious."

"Oh, but I am." Sy rose from his chair, a calm moving over him even as his mind raced. And he knew it wasn't a calm from within himself.

Harding looked up. "But you'll lose everything, Mr. Rutledge."

"We'll make certain you lose everything," Stewart added, and Harding shot the man a dark look.

"I'll wire my attorney immediately, gentlemen, and let him know the change in circumstances."

Sy held out his hand to each of them, but only Harding accepted, standing as he did.

"I'm sorry things are working out this way, Mr. Rutledge. I'd held such hopes for this venture."

Sy nodded. "I did too, sir."

He left the office and stood for a moment outside, letting what had just happened sink in. To his surprise, his pulse wasn't racing, his thoughts were calm. And yet . . .

Where was he going to find investors now? And quickly enough to keep the venture alive? He thought of all the railway workers he'd met with during the labor negotiations. They had families to feed, bills to pay. Yet he didn't regret his decision about the Pullman Palace car. He'd do it all over again if he had to.

He took a deep breath and started walking.

Sometime later, on his way to Alexandra's house, he found himself humming one of the Jubilee Singers' songs. He recalled the perfect blend of their voices, the intensity and conviction with which they sang the words—*you can have all the rest, give me Jesus*—and drew strength from them, even as a possibility came to mind about what to do next.

Chapter
THIRTY-FIVE

Fisk University
December 16, 1871

*A*lexandra sat nestled between Sy and her mother as President Spence read off the name of the next graduate. Amidst the applause, the young man made his way toward the makeshift stage to receive his diploma, to the delighted shouts of his family and friends.

Without a building large enough to host the graduation ceremonies, the event was being held out of doors in the common area among the barracks. It was standing room only, but uncommonly warm temperatures and crystal blue skies made the December morning surprisingly pleasant.

President Spence shook the young graduate's hand, then briefly moved aside as Mr. White stepped forward—the two men sharing the honors of reading the names.

Alexandra turned to Sy. "Perhaps there's still hope for those two gentlemen to get along."

"Could be." Reaching down to pet Duke, he looked over and winked. "But I doubt it."

Alexandra laughed softly, then looked at Mother and at Melba seated beside her. Her mother. Sitting in an integrated audience. In a public place. Something Alexandra never thought she'd see. And judging by the quiet attentiveness on her mother's face, she was taking it all in.

"Miss Virginia Walker Halkin."

Her mother had been right. Father had never awakened. As much as Alexandra had wanted to have that closure between them, she was slowly coming to accept that sometimes that simply wasn't possible. Life wasn't all neat and tidy. Along with joy and happiness, there were bitter disappointments and heart-rending loose ends. She looked at Thomas Rutling seated in the audience two rows up, thought of his search for his mother, and knew she still had so much for which to be grateful. She prayed that Thomas's search would someday prove successful.

The same as she prayed to find her beloved Abigail. She'd placed an ad in the *Colored Tennessean*, so time would tell.

"Mr. Henry Alvin Slater."

They'd buried her father on a Tuesday, then had reburied Sy's father beside his mother the following day. Sy had placed a small bouquet of flowers on his mother's grave and a single white rose on his father's. Clean, pure, free of any blemish. And Sy was finally at peace.

She was so proud of how he had handled the situation with General Harding and the investors. And no one had been more shocked than she was when Sy told her that he'd contacted George Pullman himself—who'd already read in the newspaper about the Northeast Line providing the Jubilee Singers with one of his Palace cars—and had offered to sell Mr. Pullman his interest in the North Carolina/West Virginia venture. Knowing Sy wasn't in a place to negotiate, Pullman ended up making a very profitable deal, even with the required investment. But so did Sy. His obligations here were fulfilled and his beloved mountains awaited. As did a position as Railroad Safety Inspector for the Colorado Railway Commission.

She looked over at him, marveling again at how God orchestrated all the events of their lives.

"Miss Constance Baker Worth."

"Thank you again, Sy," she whispered, watching the young

woman accept her diploma, "for encouraging me to pursue my degree. I don't know that I would have decided to do it without you. Mr. White told me yesterday when the troupe arrived back into town that he believes I can finish sooner than I originally thought."

Sy smiled. "You'll be done before you know it."

"And now, distinguished guests and faculty members," Mr. White continued, "we have one last graduate whose name isn't listed in the program today."

Alexandra turned back.

"And I will say this of her . . . She came to us late, some might say, but in my opinion she came at just the right time."

Mr. White's gaze scanned the audience, then came to settle on her, and Alexandra felt a rush of uncertainty followed swiftly by one of excitement. And confusion.

"Join me in congratulating a young woman who scored in the top five percent of Fisk graduates on the finishing exams . . . while serving as an instructor in our introductory classes this year. Miss Alexandra Jamison."

Alexandra turned to Sy and found him smiling. "You knew?"

"Congratulations," he whispered. "I'm so proud of you."

Alexandra felt a squeeze on her arm and turned to see her mother and Melba, tears of joy in their eyes. And maybe a little disbelief in her mother's, which Alexandra couldn't begrudge. She was more shocked than all of them.

She made her way to the stage, able to hear Sy's whistle over all the applause. And, if she wasn't mistaken, she even heard Duke getting in on the celebration.

Mr. White leaned close. "Congratulations, my dear."

Alexandra looked down at the diploma. "But I don't understand. How did—"

"It was Miss Norton's idea to administer the finishing exams to you that day."

"The *finishing* exams?"

He smiled. "It was also her idea to keep the results a surprise."

He gestured, and Alexandra turned to see Miss Norton cheering along with several students who had been in her introductory class.

"She was so impressed with your marks, Miss Jamison," Mr. White continued. "As we all were. I suspected early on, as did she, that you were much further along in your education than you gave yourself credit for. But knowing you as I believe I do"—he gave her a thoughtful look—"I feared that telling you beforehand would only make you more nervous."

"And you were so right." Laughing, she accepted the diploma and his hug. "Thank you, Mr. White, for giving me the opportunities you did."

A twinkle lit his eyes. "I suspect, Miss Jamison, that the opportunities for you are only beginning."

As she retraced her steps back down the stairs she spotted Vinson, Lettie, and Brister sitting together and clapping, along with so many others. But it was seeing Ella standing with the other singers, smiling and cheering, that brought tears to her eyes. On her way back to her seat, she stopped and hugged her friend tight.

"You did it!" Ella cried.

"*We* did it." Alexandra drew back and looked into Ella's lovely gray eyes and knew in her heart, as she had for some time now, that God had given her the sister she'd always longed for.

Later that afternoon, during the graduation festivities, Mr. White pulled her aside. "Let's you and I and that man of yours have a discussion this next week before the singers and I resume our tour. We're opening a freedmen's school in Denver, Miss Jamison, and are in need of a head teacher."

Alexandra smiled, then saw Sy looking their way, and she sensed that Mr. White and Sy had already spoken. "As it so happens, Mr. Rutledge and I leave for Denver next week. Right after our wedding. And yes, I'm most definitely interested. But as I've learned so well over these past few months . . . whatever the Lord wills, Mr. White. Whatever the Lord wills."

BELLE MEADE
PLANTATION

Daily Guided Tours

TOUR / SHOP / WINE / DINE

615-356-0501

5025 HARDING PIKE / NASHVILLE, TENNESSEE

WWW.BELLEMEADEPLANTATION.COM

Author's Note

*D*ear Reader,

    Thank you for sharing your valuable time with me—and with Sy and Alexandra and the Jubilee Singers. When I first read about the history of Nashville's Fisk University and learned about the singing group, I knew I wanted to incorporate a portion of their journey of courageous faith and hope into a novel. Finally that opportunity came with *To Wager Her Heart*.

    One of the first questions my editors asked after reading the first draft was, "Is the story of them finding the chains real?" Yes, it is. I took artistic license in how they found them. But it's true that the rusty chains and manacles from an abandoned slave pen of the city came into possession of the school, were then sold, and the money used to purchase Bibles for spelling books.

    It's also true that Fisk University was first housed in Union Army barracks that were swiftly decaying. Also, it was George Pullman himself who—after hearing the Jubilee Singers in concert—offered one of his own Pullman Palace cars to them for their use.

    There really was a "trip preceptress" who accompanied the singers. Hence, the idea for Alexandra to play that role. The real preceptress's name was Mary Wells, principal of an AMA school in Alabama, who brought along her eight-year-old ward, "Little Georgie" Wells.

    The persecution endured by the Jubilee Singers as portrayed in the novel is only a fraction of what the real singers endured. Yet in less than three years of touring, they returned to Fisk University with nearly one hundred thousand dollars. And during that time they had been received by the president of the United States, performed before the Queen of Great Britain, and breakfasted at the table of her prime minister. As J. B. T. Marsh cited in his wonderful book *The Story of the Jubilee Singers* (published in 1881), "Their success was as remarkable as their mission was unique."

And on a sadder note, though Thomas Rutling searched for his mother for the remainder of his life, he never did find her.

Many of you have grown to love Uncle Bob just as I have. He really did marry Ellen Watkins, and they lived in the old Harding cabin and raised seven children there. Uncle Bob's dying wish was to be buried at Belle Meade, which he was in 1906. Unfortunately, the actual placement of his grave and that of his wife, who followed shortly after him in death, have been lost to time.

The train accident in this novel is also, tragically, based on a real accident that occurred in 1918 outside of Nashville on Dutchman's Curve. With few exceptions, the facts presented in the story about that horrific event are consistent with history. It's reported that up to fifty thousand spectators showed up throughout the day to see the disaster for themselves.

The Ashtabula accident is also based on a real event. Philip Paul Bliss was a nineteenth-century songwriter and composer who wrote many beloved hymns, which I grew up singing. He and his wife were killed in that train accident in December 1876. If only he knew what an impact his songs have had on so many through the years. Then again, maybe he does.

If you're one of those readers who appreciates additional information about the real events in a novel, I invite you to visit the *To Wager Her Heart* book page on my website (www.TameraAlexander.com) and click the link entitled "Truth or Fiction?" In addition to sifting the truth from fiction, you'll find pictures of the real Jubilee Singers and other real-life figures from this story, images from the accident at Dutchman's Curve, and much more.

Coming in October is a novella—*Christmas at Carnton*—that launches a brand-new series set at Nashville's own Carnton Plantation. Three novels will follow, and I'm so excited to share these stories with you.

When you're next in Nashville, both Belle Meade Plantation and Fisk University welcome your visit. If you're part of a book club reading one of my books, I'd love to join your meeting via Skype for a twenty- to thirty-minute call. Visit the Bonus Features page on my website and click "For Book Clubs" for more details.

Finally, each month I offer exclusive giveaways to my newsletter friends. So be sure to sign up for that when you're visiting my website. I love staying connected with you!

Until next time,

Discussion Questions

1. Sy and Alexandra come from very different backgrounds. Discuss those differences and how their varied perspectives shaped their personalities.

2. Alexandra always wanted a sister, a confidante. Do you have that in your life? How is your family dynamic similar to or different from Alexandra's?

3. Before reading this novel, had you heard of the Fisk Singers (or Fisk University) before? Do you share an affinity for music? And if so, what kinds of music?

4. Alexandra's mother states (ch. 2) how the world was changing for women. Discuss the changes she referenced and contrast those with today's culture. What advancements have been made? What common battles are still being fought?

5. We often assume things about one other upon first impression just as Mr. White did with Alexandra. Identify his misassumptions and discuss the challenges that come with making broad assumptions, both then and now, especially in regard to race and culture. Share specific examples from your own life.

6. The tragic accident at Dutchman's Curve in Nashville really did occur—on July 9, 1918. Tamera took artistic license in placing the accident in her story (in 1871) in order to include it in the historical fabric of this novel. But the majority of facts presented about the accident are true. The "Great Cornfield Meet" still stands as one of the worst railroad accidents in American

history. Were you aware that there were Freedmen railroad cars? Discuss how social norms and discrimination played a role in that accident.

7. Sy's thoughts during General Harding's prayer (ch. 10) are revealing about his character. Can you relate to where Sy is in his character journey in that part of the story? Contrast his beliefs then with his later growth in the story. Have you visited any of the places he and Selene Harding discuss in that scene (current-day Garden of the Gods)? Share your personal experiences.

8. Alexandra meets Ella Sheppard, the real-life character who was both Mr. White's assistant and the first black teacher at Fisk University. Discuss their awkward first encounter and Alexandra's thoughts and reactions relating to that experience—and how it served as a catalyst to their friendship.

9. Racial discrimination is certainly a core theme of *To Wager Her Heart*, as are cultural differences and the ways they can divide us. Discuss the various prejudices you noted while reading and contrast those to current-day struggles.

10. Mr. White, another true-to-history character, often quoted in real life, "Anyone devoted to his books is on the road to freedom, while anyone ignorant of books is on his way back to slavery." Do you agree with that statement (for both then and now)? How have you experienced the freedom that comes through learning? Give personal examples from your life or the lives of others.

11. Alexandra and Mr. White discuss her lingering fear pending her decision (ch. 22), and Mr. White challenges her on how she's viewing her situation. Read the portion of White's dialogue beginning with "I fear the Enemy has entangled you . . ." and then Romans 8:35–39 and Hebrews 12:11. Discuss how you believe God uses suffering in a believer's life, and how he used it in Alexandra's and Sy's lives.

12. Standing for your principles takes courage and almost always comes at a cost. What price did the various characters in the novel pay for their convictions? Or for the convictions of others? Specifically Alexandra, Sy, Ella, the singers, Barrett and Laura Jamison, etc.
13. Share your favorite character and scene from the novel and the impression they made on you.
14. Be sure to take a picture of you (or of your book club) holding up your book(s) and send Tamera a copy of the photo at TameraAlexander@gmail.com so she can post it on her website (www.TameraAlexander.com).

Acknowledgments

With gratitude to . . .

My family for your tireless love and support—especially on those late, late writing nights.

Daisy Hutton and L.B. Norton, whose expertise and passion made this story so much better than it would have been on my own.

Natasha Kern, my literary agent, for being your wonderful, encouraging, and challenging self.

Deb Raney, my writing critique partner, for all the catches, suggestions, and TorTs (aka Take or Toss comments)!

The staff at Belle Meade Planation for inviting me (and all my readers) into the Harding's beautiful home. I couldn't have written these books without you.

You, my reader . . . The true joy in writing comes when you connect with these characters and their journeys, and then reach out to me. A thousand thank-yous, and I hope to hear from you soon!

The original and ever-inspiring ensemble of the Fisk Jubilee Singers—Ella Sheppard, Isaac Dickerson, Greene Evans, Benjamin Holmes, Jennie Jackson, Maggie Porter, Thomas Rutling, Minnie Tate, Eliza Walker, and Phebe Anderson. And, of course, their memorable leader, George White.

Jesus Christ, who sees each one of us and knows us intimately. I'm so grateful you love us enough to show us what (and who) we'd be without you. Help us to see each other through your eyes and to love as you love—unconditionally and without measure.

Alexandra's Chocol[a]
CHESS PIE

3 eggs
¼ cup milk
1 teaspoon vanilla
1 stick margarine
3 tablespoons powdered cocoa
1½ cups sugar

In a mixing bowl combine eggs, milk, and vanilla and stir well. In a saucepan, melt margarine over low heat, then stir in cocoa and sugar and mix well. Then add the egg mixture (eggs, milk, and vanilla) a little at a time until well combined. Pour into unbaked pie shell and bake at 350 degrees for 45 minutes (or until the center is set).

*A*mid the shadow of war, the fading dream of the Confederacy, and the faith of a child, a former soldier and a destitute woman discover the true meaning of Christmas and a most unanticipated friendship—and love.

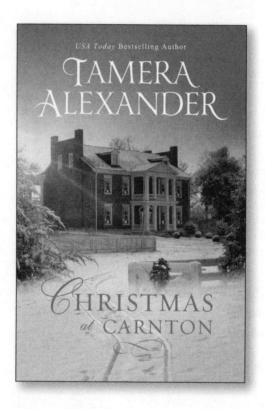

Available in print and e-book October 2017!

An Excerpt from
Christmas at Carnton

by Tamera Alexander

Chapter 1

November 13, 1863
Franklin, Tennessee
21 miles south of Nashville

V ery nice stitching, Mrs. Prescott."

Aletta looked up, not having heard her employer's approach. Focused on her task, she was determined to leave the factory on time that afternoon. It was a special day, after all, and Andrew would be excited. Her son needed this encouragement. They both did. "Thank you, Mr. Bodeen, for your kind words."

"You always do excellent work, Mrs. Prescott. Every stitch so straight and even, perfectly matching the one before."

She smiled her thanks despite perceiving a negative quality in his voice. Not that Mr. Bodeen ever sounded jovial. Unmarried, not much older than she was, he always seemed a sad sort. A discontented, melancholy man. But then, how could any able-bodied, healthy man maintain a sense of self-worth, much less pride, when he'd chosen to stay behind and work in a factory instead of joining the rest of the men who'd left home and loved ones to fight in the war?

Like her beloved Warren had done.

Her throat tightened with emotion. Would it always hurt this much? She swallowed. Nearly one month to the day since she'd received the letter from the War Department, yet she still had trouble believing he was gone. Perhaps if she could see his body one last time, she'd be better able to accept that—

"Would you join me in my office, Mrs. Prescott?"

"In your office, sir?" Aletta paused mid-stitch and looked across the rows of seamstresses to the clock on the factory wall. A quarter past four. Almost another hour before her shift was over. Then she felt the stares.

She looked around only to see the other women quickly bowing their heads and turning curious gazes back to their work. Except for one woman. On the opposite side of the factory. Aletta recognized her. Marian, she thought her name was. They'd begun working at Chilton Textile Mills about the same time. Marian was gathering her coat and reticule—and wiping tears from her eyes.

"Mrs. Prescott." Mr. Bodeen gestured. "My office, please."

Aletta laid aside the garment she'd been sewing, bothered by having to set it aside unfinished, while the greater part of her sensed that unfinished stitches should be the least of her concerns.

She followed him down the aisle, then past rows of coworkers, the click of her heeled boots marking off the seconds as the tension in the room swiftly registered.

Mr. Bodeen's office proved to be considerably more insulated from winter's chill than the factory, and she rubbed her hands together, welcoming the warmth while also trying to control her nerves. Her knuckles were stiff and swollen from long hours of stitching. But she had only to think of what Warren had endured to silence that frivolous complaint.

He'd always been careful not to reveal too many details about the war in his letters. But one night during his furlough home in April—the last time she'd seen him—after he'd banished any doubt she might have had about his continued desire for her, he'd lain beside her in the darkness and talked into the wee hours of morning. He talked all about the battles, life in the encampments, and the countless friends he'd made—and lost—during the war. "Friends as close as any brothers I might've had," he'd whispered, his strong arms tightening around her, his breath warm on her skin. "There's one fellow from right here in Franklin. Emmett Zachary. You'd like him, Lettie. Maybe you and his wife, Kate, could meet up sometime."

She'd never heard him go on like that. So unfettered, as though the weight of his soul had grown too heavy for him to bear alone. His words had painted indelible pictures in her mind. Images she'd have wished to erase, but for Warren's fingerprint on them.

Anything from him was something she wanted to hold on to.

She'd made a point to look up Kate Zachary, and they'd even had tea on two occasions. But the hours in each day seemed to fly, as did the weeks, and she hadn't seen Kate since the afternoon she'd visited her to tell her about the letter she'd received from the War Department. "*. . . slain on the battlefield, having given the ultimate sacrifice for love of home and defense of country*" is how the letter had been worded.

The notice had arrived only two days after she'd received a hastily written letter from Warren telling her he was faring well enough and that he'd penned two more letters to her that he would send shortly. The letters never arrived.

What she wouldn't give to have them now. To have him back.

"Please have a seat, Mrs. Prescott."

Aletta did as Mr. Bodeen asked, her gaze falling to a hand-written list atop his desk. Was it a list of names? She attempted a closer look as she sat. It was hard to read the writing upside down, and yet—

She was fairly certain she saw Marian's name, the coworker

she'd seen crying moments earlier. Aletta swallowed, panic clawing its way up her chest.

"Mrs. Prescott, you know how much we appreciate your work. How you—"

"Please don't take away my job, Mr. Bodeen. Reduce my hours if you need to, but—"

"Mrs. Prescott, I—"

"I'm behind on the mortgage, Mr. Bodeen. And keeping food in the pantry is already a challenge. Mr. Hochstetler at the mercantile has extended my credit as far as he can, and I don't know what I'll—"

"I wish there were something else I could do, ma'am, but—"

"I have a son, sir. Andrew. He's six years old. Today, in fact." She tried to smile and failed. "He's waiting for me even now because we're supposed to—"

"Mrs. Prescott!" His voice was sharp. "Please do not make this more difficult on me than it already is. You are an exceptional worker, and I've written you an outstanding reference. Which is more than I'm doing for the others." He pushed a piece of paper across the desk.

Numb, Aletta could only stare at it, the words on the page blurring in her vision.

"With the war, customers aren't buying clothing like they used to. And there's simply not enough work for the seamstresses we've employed. I'm sorry. You were one of the last women we hired, so it only seemed fitting."

"But you complimented me a moment ago. You said I always do excellent work."

"I know what I said, Mrs. Prescott." He averted his gaze. "I was hoping to . . . soften the blow."

She blinked and moved a hand to her midsection, feeling as though she'd been gut-punched, as Warren might've said. It had taken her weeks to find this job, and that had been almost a year ago—after she'd lost her job at the bakery. The town of Franklin was in far worse shape economically now than then. Up until a couple of months ago, the Federal Army's occupation of the town had made for a tenuous existence for Franklin residents. Especially considering the garrisons of soldiers encamped in and around Fort Granger while thousands of Confederate troops were entrenched only miles away.

But according to recent reports in the newspaper, the Federal Army had moved farther south, leaving only a small garrison behind in the fort. The absence of Federal soldiers in town seemed to substantiate those reports.

Mr. Bodeen rose, so she did likewise, her mind in a fog.

"Mrs. Prescott, today being Friday, you may collect this week's wages from the accounting office as you leave."

She struggled to think of other arguments to offer on her behalf, but none came. And even if they had, she didn't think he would listen. His mind was decided. She retrieved the letter of recommendation, folded it, and stuffed it into her skirt pocket.

Moments later, she exited the factory and walked to the corner, numb, not knowing what to do, where to go. So she started walking. And with each footfall, snatches of the conversation from Mr. Bodeen's office returned on a wave of disbelief. And anger. *"Please do not make this more difficult on me than it already is."*

Difficult on *him*?

She had half a mind to turn around, march right back into his office, and tell him what difficult truly looked like. Yet such a decision would undoubtedly mean she'd forfeit her letter of reference. Which she sorely needed to help distinguish herself from the flood of other women seeking employment.

Already, evergreen wreaths dotted the occasional storefront, some wreaths adorned with various shades of ribbon, others with sprigs of holly, the red berries festive with holiday color. One bold shopkeeper had even hung a bouquet of mistletoe in the entryway. But despite the hints of Christmas, Aletta couldn't bring herself to feel the least bit festive. Not this year.

Approaching the train station, she saw a man seated on the

corner of the street. He was holding a tin cup. Beggars were commonplace these days, and she hated that she didn't have anything to give him. As she grew closer, though, she realized he wasn't seated. He was an amputee. The man had lost both of his legs. He turned and met her gaze, and the haunting quality in his expression wouldn't let her look away.

He was blond with ruddy skin and didn't look like Warren at all. Yet all she could see was her husband. How had Warren died? On the battlefield, yes, but had he suffered? Oh, she prayed he hadn't. She prayed his death had been swift. That he'd been surging forward in one breath and then drinking in the breath of heaven in the next.

She reached into her reticule and withdrew a coin—one of precious few remaining even counting this week's wages—and dropped it in the cup, the *clink* of metal on metal severing the moment.

"God bless you, ma'am."

"And you, sir," she whispered, then continued on even as a familiar sinking feeling pressed down inside her. President Lincoln had recently issued a proclamation to set apart and observe the last Thursday of this month as a day of thanksgiving and praise to the Almighty. But, God forgive her, she didn't feel very grateful right now. And it hurt to even think about celebrating Christmas without Warren.

She hiccupped a breath, the freezing temperature gradually registering as her body cooled from the exertion of walking. She slowed her steps and wrapped her arms around herself as a shiver started deep inside. She tugged her coat tighter around her abdomen, no longer able to fasten the buttons.

Seven months and one week. By her calculations, that's how far along she was.

She knew because that was how long it had been since Warren's furlough. They'd been so careful when they'd been together, or had tried to be. *Oh dear God . . .* How had she let this happen? What was she going to do? She tried not to let her thoughts go to the dark places again, as she thought of them. She was a woman of faith, after all. She believed in God's loving care.

Yet there were times, like this, when her faith seemed far too fragile for the burdens of life. She wished she could hide her thoughts from Him. Wished the Lord couldn't see the doubts she courted even in the midst of struggling to believe. But He saw everything. Heard every unuttered thought. And right now, that truth wasn't the least comforting.

Guilt befriending her worry, she continued down the thoroughfare.

When she reached Baker Street, she turned right. Ten minutes later, she paused at the corner of Fifth and Vine and looked at the house two doors down. Their home. A modest residence Warren had purchased for them four years earlier with the aid of a loan from the Franklin Bank. A loan the bank was threatening to call in.

And now she'd lost her only means of support. And stood to lose all their equity in the home as well if she couldn't convince the bank to give her more time. She'd considered selling, but no one was buying. Yet when—or if—the economy finally improved and houses did start selling again, she couldn't sell if she'd been evicted. She continued past her home and toward her friend's house a short distance away.

She'd waited until late August to write Warren about the baby, wanting to be as certain as she could be—following two miscarriages in the last two years—that the pregnancy was going to be sustained. Yet he hadn't mentioned anything about their coming child in his last letter. Had he even known about the baby before his death? The Federal Army had recently blockaded certain southern ports, seizing all correspondence belonging to the Confederate Postal System. So perhaps he'd never received her letter. Or maybe that explained why his last two letters had gone—

"Mama!"

Nearing MaryNell's house, Aletta looked up to see Andrew

racing toward her from down the street, his thin legs pumping. She hurried to meet him.

"What are you doing outside, honey?" She hugged him tight, his little ears like ice. "And without your coat and scarf?"

"It's okay. I'm not cold. Me and Seth, we're playin' outside while his mother visits with the bank man."

Aletta frowned, aware of Seth watching them from the front yard. MaryNell Goodall knew how susceptible Andrew was to illness and that he needed to bundle up in this bitter weather. Born three weeks early, he'd always been on the smaller side. And despite having a healthy appetite—the boy would eat all day if she could afford to let him—he'd never caught up in size to boys his own age.

What was going to happen to him now that she'd lost her job? How would she provide for him? And, in scarcely two months, the baby?

It occurred to her then that her lack of employment would also affect MaryNell. When MaryNell lost her own job a few months earlier, she'd offered to watch Andrew—and teach him at home like she was already teaching Seth. MaryNell claimed that keeping two boys was easier than keeping one, and Aletta knew there was some truth to that statement. And since dear Mrs. Crawford, the woman who had kept Andrew up until then, had moved to North Carolina to live with one of her children, MaryNell's offer had been a perfectly timed blessing. Only four streets away from theirs, too, and with Seth and Andrew already such good friends.

Aletta insisted on paying MaryNell a small wage each week. Still, she didn't know how the woman made ends meet, having no job and being behind on her mortgage as well. Not to mention not having heard from her husband, Richard, in over three months. His silence didn't bode well. But there was still hope. And MaryNell, as soft-spoken as she was and uncommonly pretty, had never once complained.

Despite the worry settling in her chest, Aletta glimpsed the excitement in Andrew's eyes and attempted a lightness to her voice. "Let's collect your coat so we can go home and start cele-brating your birthday!"

"You're still gonna make my favorite pie?"

"Of course I am." She'd saved for weeks to buy the ingredients for the chocolate cream pie—sugar, vanilla, and cocoa being so expensive and hard to come by. Now all she could think about was how much further she could've stretched that money. But it was Andrew's birthday, and she was determined to make it spe-cial. She climbed the steps to the porch and knocked on the door.

MaryNell answered a moment later, her expression revealing surprise. "Aletta! You're early. But . . . good for you. I'm always saying you work far too hard as it is." Hesitating briefly, she finally stepped to one side. "Come in. I let the boys go outside to play for a bit."

"Yes, I saw them," Aletta said softly, then spotted a man seated on the settee.

He stood as she entered and looked between her and MaryNell, and Aletta got the feeling she'd interrupted something.

"Mr. Cornwall," MaryNell finally said, her voice tight. "Allow me to introduce Mrs. Warren Prescott. Aletta, this is Mr. Cornwall. He's . . . an acquaintance. From Franklin Bank."

Tall and barrel chested, Cornwall was heavy around his mid-dle and a good deal older. He had a commanding air about him, but not one that inspired. And although MaryNell had called him an acquaintance, Aletta found it odd that her friend couldn't seem to look the man in the eye. And since when did *acquaintances* from the bank make house calls?

"Mrs. Prescott." He glanced at her. "Pleasure to meet you, I'm sure."

Aletta nodded, but he'd already looked away. "Likewise, sir."

He turned then, and, whether by intention or not, he angled himself in MaryNell's direction, making it impossible for Aletta to see his face.

"Mrs. Goodall, I appreciate the opportunity to speak with you this afternoon, and I look forward to hearing from you soon."

MaryNell's gaze flitted to his. "Yes. I'll . . . be in touch."

He strode out the door and closed it behind him.

Aletta watched him through the window as he continued past the boys, who were playing cowboys and Indians. As her gaze followed him down the street, a sickening suspicion brewed inside her that she didn't want to imagine, much less acknowledge. But when she looked back at MaryNell and glimpsed the dread and guilt in her friend's expression, she was all but certain her suspicions were true.

The story continues in *Christmas at Carnton* by Tamera Alexander, available October 2017!

Author photo by Mandy Whitley Photography

TAMERA ALEXANDER is a *USA Today* bestselling novelist whose deeply drawn characters, thought-provoking plots, and poignant prose resonate with readers worldwide. She and her husband make their home in Nashville, not far from Belle Meade Plantation.

Tamera invites you to visit her at:

Website: TameraAlexander.com
Twitter: @TameraAlexander
Facebook: Tamera.Alexander
Pinterest: TameraAuthor
Group Blog: InspiredbyLifeandFiction.com

Or if you prefer snail mail, please write her at:

Tamera Alexander
P.O. Box 871
Brentwood, TN 37024

Discussion questions for all of Tamera's novels are available at TameraAlexander.com, as are details about Tamera joining your book club for a virtual visit.